BLITZED

BLITZED

Alexa Martin

JOVE
NEW YORK

A JOVE BOOK
Published by Berkley
An imprint of Penguin Random House LLC
penguinrandomhouse.com

Copyright © 2019 by Alexa Martin

Library of Congress Cataloging-in-Publication Data

Names: Martin, Alexa, author.
Title: Blitzed / Alexa Martin.
Description: First Edition. | New York : Jove, 2019. | Series: The Playbook
Identifiers: LCCN 2019011707 | ISBN 9780451491992 (pbk.) |
ISBN 9780451492005 (ebook)
Subjects: | GSAFD: Love stories.
Classification: LCC PS3613.A77776 B65 2019 | DDC 813/.6—dc23
LC record available at https://lccn.loc.gov/2019011707

First Edition: December 2019

Printed in the United States of America
1   3   5   7   9   10   8   6   4   2

Cover design and illustration by Colleen Reinhart

To my agent, Jessica. Three down, many to go.

ACKNOWLEDGMENTS

Writing the Playbook Series has been one of the greatest experiences of my life and there are so many people to thank for that.

Kristine Swartz, my amazing, badass editor. Thank you for your support and guidance, and for ensuring that my books weren't completely overrun with profanity. I couldn't have done this without you. To the rest of the Berkley team: Jessica Mangicaro, Jessica Brock, Cindy Hwang, Erin Galloway, and Jin Yu, thank you. You all have welcomed me with open arms and changed my entire world. I am forever grateful.

Jess . . . because you deserve two shout-outs for dealing with my craziness. Thank you for scheduling that call and still deciding to take me on after I rambled on and on the entire time. Brynn is for you!

To the wonderful bloggers who never cease to amaze me with their creativeness and thoughtful words. You are the best and thank you for all that you do.

The employees at the Starbucks in Saddle Rock Village, you didn't know it, but your friendly conversation and quiet support got me through some of my biggest slumps. Thank you for remembering my order and only making one Amazon Alexa joke.

Maxym, Tricia, Shannon, Gwynne, and Lindsay. You ladies are so beyond brilliant and I'm so grateful to be able to call you friends. Even though I never show my face, our Zoom calls are always one of the highlights of my month. Thank you for always having my back and being willing to take a stand.

Derrick, thank you for all the date nights and never rolling your eyes when I reach for the cocktail menu to try something new. All the expertise I gained worked perfectly for Brynn.

Of course, my four children. You all are wild and insane and the absolute loves of my life.

And last, but certainly not least, the readers. Thank you, thank you, thank you. For buying this book or checking it out from the library or recommending it to your friends. You all have made this entire experience one I will never forget. Thank you for the emails and messages, and even tagging me on social media. It means more to me than you will ever know.

Prologue

Four years ago
Maxwell

BEAUTIFUL.

I normally hate when the guys drag me out to bars; they just aren't my scene. But Gavin is back in town and I couldn't say no without looking like an asshole, so I gave in.

Then I saw her and my entire outlook changed. I wanted to beeline straight over to her and ask for her name and number, but I couldn't. Talking a little trash on the field I can do, but even just the thought of walking up to a woman and asking for her number makes my palms sweat. So I did the next best thing: I sat at the bar, knowing she'd at least have to take my order.

"Maxwell, right?" Brynn slides my old-fashioned in front of me. She tucks in the piece of hair that fell from the bun on top of her head and smiles.

And that smile? I almost forget how to answer her question.

Her smile is so bright and genuine, it takes her already beautiful face and transforms it to stunning.

"Yeah, and you're Brynn, Gavin has told me all about you." Well, he told me about HERS and how she's been there for Marlee, but he left out the part where she could put any model to shame, even in the sneakers and ripped jeans she's wearing.

"Don't listen to anything he says," she jokes. "Marlee drank that tequila of her own accord, and I had nothing to do with it."

"I haven't heard anything about tequila, but that sounds like a story I need to hear more of," I say and shock myself. I'm not a small talk kind of guy. Usually, I just order whiskey and find a spot in the corner to occupy until I have fulfilled my time. But for some reason, Brynn has me sitting at the bar, wanting to talk until she has to kick me out.

"Oh, I might have to keep you around forever for that." Pink instantly colors her cheeks. "I mean, I won't keep you forever, that'd be creepy and maybe even illegal. I just have a lot of stories to tell. Not that I'm a gossip, I just like to talk." She squeezes her eyes shut, and fuck if she isn't cute on top of being drop-dead gorgeous. How is it even possible for her to get flustered? "Let's just pretend that word vomit didn't happen."

"I'm not sure I could ever forget anything you do." I take a sip of my old-fashioned, holding eye contact with Brynn as I do.

This woman.

I can't put my finger on one thing, but I know in my bones that she's going to turn my world upside down.

One

HOW DID I GET HERE?

I look around my little bar. When I found this building, I had hoped HERS would bring in a moderate crowd and not put me in bankruptcy court. Now it's packed to the brim with reality stars and professional athletes. I never imagined that hiring Marlee would get me here, but holy shit am I glad it did.

"Hey, Brynn," Maxwell Lewis—with his brown eyes that I swear can see to my soul, and full lips that always look so soft and sweet—says, sliding into the barstool across from me. "Wild night."

I smile my brightest lipstickless smile at him and try to not let his overall sexiness cause me to forget how to speak. "Yeah, it's a little crowded."

Understatement of the century.

Tonight is the premiere of *Love the Player*, the newest reality show on TV following the lives of a handful of Denver Mustangs WAGS—wives and girlfriends of sports players, if you've been living under the same rock I was. I assumed the viewing party would be in LA or Miami or someplace super glamorous, but the producers thought since so much of the drama happens at HERS, this was the perfect place to host the party.

Knowing how much publicity I'm going to get from this show sends a thrill up my spine.

Being a "female-centered bar" is a concept not a ton of people understand, but now it won't need to be explained, it will be seen, *nationwide*.

Fucking amazing.

I never thought I'd love Aviana and her flair for the dramatic so much. I've practically been floating in my Vans all day long. When photographers from a major magazine came to take behind-the-scenes photos and started snapping shots of the bar I spent blood, sweat, tears, and my entire life savings on, I almost wept.

And now, as the cherry on top of the already decadent sundae that's becoming my life, I get to talk to Maxwell Lewis, defensive back extraordinaire, whom I've been crushing on since he walked into HERS all those years ago, despite the fact that getting him to talk in a group setting is like pulling teeth.

If you know me, you know I don't do boyfriends and I most certainly do not do crushes.

I'm too old and jaded to act like a twelve-year-old girl anymore. But there's always an exception to the rule. And Maxwell is my four-years-and-counting exception. Plus, I'm always listening to my friends and their stories with entirely too much information. Now I can't look at Maxwell without thinking he probably really knows how to lay down the D. I'm also totally on board for a friends-with-benefits situation, something I assume a professional athlete is very familiar with.

"How'd you get talked into coming to this tonight?" I ask, doing my best flirty eyes and trying to squeeze together my barely there cleavage. "You don't seem like the typical reality show fan."

Ever since our first encounter, whenever he comes to HERS, I try my hardest to get him to flirt with me. And I think maybe, in his quiet Maxwell style, him sitting at the bar *is* him flirting.

He watches me through thick, dark lashes that I know women pay for, and his throaty chuckle, which I've come to the conclusion is so raspy because he never does it, washes over me. "I'm not. But I promised Crosby I'd swing by, he wanted this to be perfect for Aviana and thought a big showing of his teammates would help out."

"That's nice of you." I pull out the lowball glasses I bought just for this event. "Being around the Lady Mustangs without all the extras of tonight can be draining. I feel like Crosby might owe you one." I place an old-fashioned he didn't order in front of him. I know it's not exactly playing it coy, memorizing his drink order and all, but I'm not ashamed to let him know I see him and I'm interested.

"Well, if I get to spend the night talking to you, I think I'll owe him," he says, his light brown eyes never leaving mine.

My stomach does backflips like I climbed onto a roller coaster and just went spiraling toward the ground.

In a room filled with women who have literally been cover girls, Maxwell's attention is on me. And even more than that, he's not the kind of guy who says things he doesn't mean. In all the years I've known him, he's never been this forward. I don't know what changed, but I'm not mad at it.

Maybe a friends-with-benefits situation is actually in the cards. My stomach muscles tense in anticipation.

"So I obviously have to see this through tonight, but maybe—" I start, but the shrill sound of his phone cuts me off.

He cringes. "Shit, I meant to put this on silent. Sorry," he apologizes.

He grabs his phone from his pocket, hitting Answer before even looking at the screen.

"Hello?" he greets, a goofy smile aimed my way.

Then it's gone and the happy-go-lucky, painfully shy man I've come to know disappears right along with it. His shoulders square like he's preparing for a fight, and shutters fall across his kind eyes.

"What?" he growls, his grip so tight on his phone that his knuckles go white. "No," he says after a long pause.

His eyes glaze over as he stares right through me. I know I should walk away, let him have this moment without a witness, but my feet are frozen in place as a ripple of unease flows through my veins. Even my eyes are glued to him, focusing on the twitching of his jaw and grinding of his teeth.

"Don't you fucking dare." He whispers it into his phone so quietly that if I wasn't staring at his mouth so intently, I would've never known what he said.

Then, without any warning, he leaps out of his seat, his phone flying through the air so close to my head that it blows the strand of hair in my face out of my eyes. The glass screen explodes in time with the top-shelf tequila it hit. Then, before I can react, his whiskey in my brand-new glass sails past me, hitting my shelves with the power of a bowling ball and—unfortunately for me—getting a strike. Bottles shatter around me, the bar that I prided myself on for so many years crumbling to the floor in a mess of dangerous shards doused in amber and clear liquids.

Blood roars between my ears. Shock prevents me from lashing out the way I always assumed I would if something so unbelievable happened in my beloved HERS.

I turn wide eyes to Max, hoping that at least a look of remorse would be written across his face, but when I see him, there's nothing except the blind rage of a man who only moments prior I was preparing to ask to go home with me.

I open my mouth to say something or maybe just emit the blood-curdling scream that's trapped in my throat, but before I can get there, TK is yanking Maxwell out of his seat and dragging him out of HERS.

Through the red veil that has fallen over my vision, I see my friends rushing toward me. But I can't. I can't take their calming words or worried glances.

Not right now.

So I move as fast as my long legs will take me until I'm in the quiet comfort of my office, slamming the door shut and locking it behind me.

And then, only then, do I let the tears fall and my hand-muffled scream escape.

Two

SOME PEOPLE CALL ME A WORKAHOLIC.

And they're right.

But considering I own a bar, it's the best kind of "holic" I could be. Plus, my job consists of listening to other people's dramas and hanging out with my girls damn near every day.

"Oh my god! Brynn!" Vonnie's eyes scrunch and her entire face twists into an abstract painting. "Did you put anything besides vodka in there?"

"Gin." I wink and write the latest failed martini recipe down in my notebook.

"Why are we taste testing again?" Charli asks as she leans across the bar and grabs the martini from Vonnie. Vonnie narrows her eyes, probably ready to scold her for her table manners . . . but when Charli gives it a sniff, takes a deep sip, shrugs, and then finishes it, Vonnie's eyes grow wide and her jaw drops.

"Damn, Charli!" I don't know if I'm impressed or disturbed. "I didn't know you had that in you!"

"Don't worry." Poppy snatches the glass away from Charli and walks it around the bar like she still works here even though she quit months ago to go to school and better herself like a selfish jerk. "Shawn's on standby. Final roster cuts come in tomorrow and he's been bracing Charli for bad news . . ." She leans in closer as she passes behind me. "Something she's clearly not handling well."

Reason 8,634 why I could never date a football player.

Basketball? Maybe. At least their contracts are guaranteed and they're gone so often I'd barely have to see them. Baseball? Possibly. I do love sitting outside and eating pretzels and drinking beer. Hockey? Nope, it's basically football on skates—with more broken noses and less teeth.

Luckily for all these athletes I'd have to let down ever so gently, none of them know who I am.

"Your crazy ass better drink some water," Vonnie, always the mom of the group, tells her. "Besides, I think Aviana is coming, and who knows if she's still filming."

"Oh, fucking fuck me," Charli moans. "That damn show is going to be the death of me and I'm not even on it."

I can see Charli is clearly in a fragile state of mind, but I'd be lying if I said I didn't love everything about *Love the Player*. I kinda feel like, even though I'm not a cast member, I manifested the shit out of that show. I mean, the concept for HERS came to life as I was sitting on a shitty-ass date, watching a shitty-ass game, sipping shitty beer. All I wanted was to be out with my girls, drinking a fantastic specialty cocktail, and watching the latest Bravo reality show with a roomful of strangers.

And now, not only do we watch reality shows, HERS is a regular fucking setting for one. It just started to air, but the increase in customers is already noticeable. And people tried to tell me my love of trash television was a waste of my time. To that I say, HA!

"Speaking of the show, that's what we're doing here." I push a much lighter and brighter (hot-pink) cocktail down to Jacqueline, who, even though she's always with us, is still the quietest person I know, and I'm pretty sure she thinks we're all in need of serious therapy . . . which might be accurate. How Aviana talked her into starring in *Love the Player* is still a mystery. "I want to have a few cocktails named after the show ready."

"Great, now the show gives me alcohol poisoning too." Charli lays her head on the bar.

"You're giving yourself alcohol poisoning." Poppy pushes a glass of water to her and starts mixing up a drink of her own. "I know you and Shawn are smart with your money. If he gets cut, it won't be the worst thing in the world. TK loves not playing anymore."

I watch Jacqueline take a small sip of the drink, and almost do a happy dance when her eyes widen. She looks at the drink as if the recipe's written in the cocktail, and takes another sip.

"Success, Jac?" I ask, even though I already know her answer.

"So good, Brynn," she says in her usual, muted voice.

"Yeah it is!" We do an air high five. "I'm naming that one Peter's Angel. Wait . . . no!" I shout like she's not right in front of me. "Fuck Peter. This is your drink. Model Behavior!"

"Oh my god." Poppy jumps up and down, almost spilling her creation all over my potion recipes. "Do you remember that movie? You guys have to come over later and we'll watch a young Justin Timberlake be bamboozled by an artsy high school student!"

"If there were a game show that revolved around random shit, you'd be the fucking queen," Vonnie says to Poppy, tossing a couple of cherries into her Shirley Temple.

"Do you not remember Marlee? She's a trivia freak. The two of them together could rule the world." If world domination were dependent on Disney original movies and pointless trivia.

"Please warn me if they are getting together. I'm not sure I could handle that." Vonnie laughs, but I can see it in her eyes that she means it. "Anyway, the bar looks great. You can't even tell anything happened."

And there it is.

The thing I wanted to avoid for the rest of my life.

"It really does," Poppy pipes in, admiring the handiwork my dad and Mr. Harper spent all night doing.

"Thanks. I'm lucky my dad lives around the corner and that Marlee's will do anything to get an inside scoop."

"What even happened?" Charli sits up, miraculously cured from her earlier bout of drunkenness and gloom. "Max is legit the nicest person I've ever met, and I'm including you bitches and Shawn in that statement. Something had to have happened."

"I don't know and I don't care." I put my nose in the air. Hoity-toity is my go-to attitude for things that make me uncomfortable. "There was a check under the door the next morning and I cashed it before he could change his mind. Plus, because I had free labor, I now have enough to take a trip to the Container Store."

And I don't feel the littlest bit guilty about not giving him the leftover funds. I mean, I had to open late while everything was being finished, so I'm calling it even.

I still don't understand what happened. I thought we were finally getting to the place I'd been fantasizing about for years, and then, *bam!* A glass whizzed past my head.

Whiplash and rage don't go well together.

"The Container Store? I'm coming!" Poppy invites herself. "Ace and TK have started collecting football and baseball cards, and if I come home to my dining room table covered in them again, I'm going to scream. Plus, I saw some blogger organize her pantry and I want to try."

"Look at you, Holly Homemaker, being all domestic and shit," I tease, and duck to avoid the piece of ice she throws at my face. "What? It's cute."

"I can't stand you. I don't know why I still come here." Her eyes narrow. Someone who doesn't know her as well as I do might be intimidated, but Poppy is all bark and no bite.

I open my arms wide and make my way toward her retreating, giggling form when synchronized gasps pull my attention. I look at my terrible taste testers to see them all staring at the door with their jaws on the floor. I follow their eyes and when I see what they see, my vision swims in front of me and my fingers go numb.

"Speak of the devil and he shall appear." Vonnie breaks the silence first. "You have to give it to him, that's a brave-ass man."

I won't give Maxwell Lewis shit.

Brave? My ass. A jerk? That's closer. A thoughtless psychopath? Spot on.

All these years, I thought he was sweet and shy. While all along, he was probably just hiding his asshole tendencies.

I don't have to do anything to secure the scowl on my face, just the thought of him makes it appear. Seeing him has my blood boiling and fists clenched. I thought I never wanted to see him again, but maybe what I really needed was a satisfying face-to-face. I brace and start to mentally prepare my most vicious tongue-lashing yet, but then, in true Maxwell fashion, he doesn't say anything. Instead he makes eye contact and quickly moves to occupy one of the few empty tables I have left in the very back.

What. The. Actual. Fuck?

"What the fuck?" I say to the confused and possibly relieved (Jacqueline is just pure relief) faces staring back at me. "What just happened?"

Charli opens her mouth to talk, but before the words come out, the front door crashes open and Aviana glides through in her five-inch pumps, a small camera crew trailing behind her.

"I'm here, bitches!" She pulls her glasses off in a way I thought was only possible due to movie magic and flips her long, glossy, advertised-on-Instagram hair over her shoulder, finally taking in the expressions of her "bitches." "Oh shit. What did I miss?"

Nobody says a word, but four fingers point to the table in the back occupied by one stupid, but still hot, jerkface.

"Oh shit," Aviana breathes, then turns to the camera crew. "Start rolling, this could get good."

Fucking Lady Mustangs.

Three

STALKER.

Merriam-Webster defines the verb "stalk" as "to pursue quarry or prey stealthily."

I wonder if the behavior of the mopey, annoying, but still-hot guy ruining the entire vibe of my bar for the last week fits under that definition.

"Are you going to say anything to him today?" Paisley whispers into my ear as she passes behind me.

Paisley has worked at HERS since it opened. She said she applied because she was in desperate need of a job, and she stayed so she could watch *Real Housewives* on big screens at work. Now she works here because the football player drama is better than Jersey season one and New York season nine combined.

She thinks I'm next.

She's wrong.

"Nope." I don't look up and it's not because my stupid, traitorous eyes will find Maxwell Lewis no matter how hard I try to avoid him. I'm just really focused on putting the limes in the cute new acrylic bins I bought at the Container Store.

I mean, it's not like I have some secret love for him or anything. Not at all.

I hold a mean grudge; it's gonna be a while before he's off my shit list.

But even my hatred can't change the fact that he's smokin' fucking hot. And him showing up and rubbing his biceps and really nice ass in my face at work is just another thing for me to hold against him. As if trashing my bar wasn't enough for him.

I don't have kids, and as long as my trusty IUD stays where it's supposed to, that won't ever change. But I'd imagine mothers love their kids almost as much as I love my bar. I mean, it's my baby! I conceived it. I labored it. I birthed it. Plus side, HERS doesn't pee on me and I don't have to worry about sending it to therapy in twenty years.

Just financial ruin.

But, you know, can't win everything.

"Well . . ." Paisley's voice is closer and way too peppy for me to ignore her. "I hope you've worked on your silent treatment, because he's coming over now."

She claps once before shoving her hands into her pockets and skipping—yes, skipping—away from me.

Unlike my head that's snapping back and forth between Paisley's retreating form and Maxwell's incoming hard body encased in perfect-fitting jeans and a black tee that might be too tight—but nobody is complaining—my feet are rooted to the tile beneath me.

Fuck.

"You can go back to brooding in the corner." I keep my eyes focused on the task at hand, afraid that direct eye contact will cause a lust-colored haze to fog my wits.

"I'm not brooding." Maxwell almost whispers the words. And since I still heard them, I take that to mean he got closer instead of retreating to the back of the bar like I'd hoped.

The limes are inside their new acrylic home, and Paisley—curse her helpfulness—wiped the bar down with such precision that it's damn near sparkling. All of that is to say I have nothing to keep me from putting my focus on the man in front of me. I contemplate the "stop, drop, and roll" technique to escape, but I know that will blow my "play it cool" act. So on a deep sigh and a very dramatic neck roll, I look at Maxwell.

And fuck me.

Why does he have to be so freaking hot?

"You do brood. You sit in the corner looking all sad and depressed. I don't know if you're here to annoy me or to try to see how many women you can get to approach you every night." He's up to six tonight . . . not that I pay attention or anything.

"I just . . ." He shoves his hands in his pockets and glances around like someone will save him even though he's the one who approached me. "I want to apologize."

Flutters.

NO! Stop it, butterflies. We do not get warm and squishy over a long-overdue apology.

"Cool." I reach for a glass and start making his old-fashioned. Once I'm finished, I push it across to Maxwell. "No need. You paid for the repairs. We're square."

"But—" he starts but is almost instantly interrupted by a brunette in cutoff shorts and a plaid button-up. I had no idea it was *Dukes of Hazzard* night.

"Aren't you Maxwell Lewis?" She giggles even though literally nothing she said was funny.

I fight—and lose—the battle not to roll my eyes, and turn to leave. Even though I think I hate her, I make a note for Paisley to give Daisy Duke her next drink on the house for providing me with my out.

I try my hardest to keep my steps slow and steady, but once the door to my office is close enough, I do a little skip-hop and push the door open. And I swear, I only look back because of . . . whatever, never mind. I look back to see Maxwell. When I do, his focus directed at me and only me is enough to cause me to jump and trip into my office.

Smooth.

"You okay?" Paisley grabs my hand and pulls me off the ground.

"I mean . . . I just ate shit because a guy was looking at me, so I've been better." My cheeks are on fire and I have no doubt I look like a tomato right about now.

"Oh shit."

"Basically." I wipe imaginary dirt off of my pants. "I'm probably going to spend the rest of the night hiding in my office of shame, but when you go out there, the girl flirting with Maxwell gets a drink on the house."

Laughter dances in Paisley's eyes and she bites her lip, no doubt trying to fight back the statement that could put her job in jeopardy. Luckily for me, because I hate interviews and hiring new people, she contains herself.

"Do you want me to pass her an origami-folded note with the drink?"

Never mind. She *almost* contains herself.

"I hate you."

"You love me." She shrugs and pushes the door open, blowing me a kiss before the door shuts behind her.

"Bitch," I say to nobody, but feel better getting it out.

I take a moment and look around my office. My desk is littered with papers, pens, and personalized stationery I might not need but that I don't regret spending too much on. There are too many coffee cups from Fresh in my trash can, and there may or may not be two opened bags of chocolate in my drawer.

But there are also pictures of me standing next to Marlee in my blush, floor-length bridesmaid dress and of me hugging Ace tight while he's clutching the trophy from the soccer tournament he won.

HERS started as a business, but it became my family.

The door opens and startles me, causing me to almost lose my balance . . . again. I guess, unlike my friends, athletic coordination hasn't been passed on to me by osmosis.

"What the hell, Pais?" I yell, blaming her for my inability to stay upright.

"It's not origami, but it's still a note!" she screams, bouncing from foot to foot.

I feel faint and queasy. "You did not give him a note."

"I didn't." She waves the folded napkin in front of my face. "He gave you one after he paid his bill."

I grab the note from her hand and toss it onto the pile of papers I have yet to get to.

Her jaw falls to the floor. "You're not gonna read it?" she asks, her eyes never leaving the note.

"Maybe later." I ignore the crestfallen look on her face and walk back into my Maxwell-free bar.

Now, if only he would get the fuck out of my head.

Four

SOON.

That's it. The entire note. One fucking word.

What the hell?

That one word tainted my mind so hard, I messed up three drinks and two food orders before I tapped out.

But instead of hopping in my SUV—yes, I know I'm single and they are bad for the environment, but I'm a Denver native and when ski season comes around, it's where I spend all my free time—I start the short walk to my dad's house.

I didn't tell him I was coming, but when I round the corner, the porch light is on. I would say it's because he's super thoughtful, which I guess is part of it, but mainly it's because I'm a grown toddler and most nights I crash in my childhood bedroom instead of the condo across town I just had to have.

My dad is like the polar opposite of me.

I'm five foot eleven. My dad is five foot seven. I was taller than him in seventh grade. I have blond hair, my dad has brown . . . well, gray now, but you get the picture. I'm loud and in your face and speak before thinking. He's quiet and kind and contemplates his every word before it leaves his mouth. Even though, when it comes to me, he's still a dad and is quick to call me on my bullshit. Which is probably why even though I'm grown as fuck, I still get scolded for how often I say "fuck."

My dad is a saint, and to keep the metaphor going, my mom is definitely a sinner.

Mom also took off when I was fifteen, not a critical time in a girl's life or anything, because she needed some "excitement" and decided to find that by chasing after every dickhead in the Denver metro area before taking her act cross-country.

So you might see why I find it so shitty that every time I look into the mirror, I see my mom's face. Now, my mom has not held a job in seventeen years because of her looks, so I'd sound like an asshole not to be grateful to inherit them, but when you hate the person whom you are almost a carbon copy of, it causes some serious issues and a lot of time spent in a therapist's office.

I grab the Tiffany keychain I got for my sixteenth birthday and find the same purple, sparkly key I never took off.

"Daddy-o!" I yell, pushing the door open. "Where you at?"

"In the kitchen," he answers unnecessarily. The house smells so good there's really only one possibility.

I toe off my tennis shoes and drop my purse onto the floor—a habit I'm not sure I'll ever kick—and damn near skate across the hardwood floors he must've had polished in the last twenty-four hours. If I fall again, I'm gonna be so pissed.

Luckily for my dad and my backside, I manage to stay on my feet. It seems my coordination only takes flight when I have the attention of attractive men.

Well, one attractive asshole.

All thoughts of scolding my dad for what feels like a slippery setup flee when I get to the kitchen and he's plating his world-famous Maryland crab cakes.

"That smells amazing." I close my eyes and inhale as deep as I can without passing out. "Why so fancy?"

"No reason," he says into the oven, pulling out a cookie sheet with two giant baked potatoes with his oven-mitt-covered hand.

"Umm . . ." I look at the set table and the amount of food he has prepared, and my stomach knots up. "Am I interrupting something?"

Don't get me wrong, I want my dad to date. I have for years now, but he's always blown off my requests. Either he's happy doing his own thing and not having to share his time or space, which is relatable, or my selfish mother ruined him for life—also relatable.

"No." He rolls his eyes like I'm crazy for assuming the single man cooking for two might have a date. "I just had a feeling you might need some comfort food tonight."

"You 'had a feeling'?" I don't doubt my dad's super-dad powers often, but this seems a little far-fetched . . . even for him.

"Dad instinct is a thing, Brynn. If you ever have kids, you'll understand." He cuts open the potatoes and plops a very generous slab of butter on one—mine—and a modest, my-daughter-will-rant-about-my-cholesterol amount on the other.

"Dad," I deadpan with my hands on my hips that make me look more fourteen-year-old boy than thirty-two-year-old slayer of cocktails.

"Fine." He narrows his eyes at me behind his glasses. "Paisley texted me that you were having a night at work and I should expect you."

Snake.

I don't know how I befriended so many well-meaning snakes.

"So he showed up again?"

"Who?" I pull the tongs out of the drawer they've been in since I started sneaking them to serve my Play-Doh spaghetti, and put the bare minimum amount of salad on my plate.

"Brynn."

Ughhh. I hate when he says my name like that, like he found out I was failing a class or got caught in the library kissing Blane Jensen . . . not like that ever happened or anything . . .

"What? I don't know who you're talking about." I avoid looking at him and spoon his homemade rémoulade onto my crab cake.

"You don't?" he says in a way I know means he's going to make me regret walking over here. "So your memory has miraculously erased the man you gave heart eyes to for months until he crushed your dreams by shattering the shelves at your bar? The name Maxwell Lewis no longer rings any bells in that head of yours? You complaining about him sitting in HERS for the last week is no longer on your mind . . . at all?"

Yup.

Totally regretting coming over.

"Okay, fine." I pull the paper towel from the roll with a little more force than necessary, fighting the urge to throw a tantrum when only the top corner rips off. "Yes, Maxwell came in again today. But this time he talked to me and it didn't go well."

A smug smile that doesn't look right on my dad's kind face pulls at the corner of his thin lips. "So, tell me what happened."

I sit down at the table like a sullen teenager . . . or a brooding Maxwell . . . and take a bite of the crab cake that, despite my current mood, still tastes like heaven on earth. "Not much, honestly. He said he wanted to apologize, I told him we were square, then I fell on my face."

His mouth opens at the same time the spoon he's holding falls from his fingers and rémoulade splatters all over the marble countertops. "You . . . fell?"

"I mean, 'tripped' is probably more accurate, but I ended up on my butt." I take another bite of my crab cake, trying to push my embarrassment down with crabby goodness. "And then Maxwell gave Paisley a note to give to me, and now I don't even get to pretend he's not coming back."

"Why don't you just call the guy and get it over with?"

"We never exchanged numbers, for one. And even if I did have it, I don't care enough to call the guy. He paid for the damage he did to my bar and that's that. It should be the end of the story, I'm really just fucking annoyed—"

"Mouth."

I roll my eyes. "I'm just *flipping* annoyed that he won't let it die. At this point, he's just being a selfish ass . . . sorry, jerk, a selfish jerk. Anyways"—I use my perfected diversionary tactic to deflect the conversation away from me—"Poppy wants to know if you'll look over the plans they had drawn up for the apartment they're building above the garage."

My dad is a retired architect, but his love for his profession never went away. Poppy asked about the plans a few days ago, but I've been holding this card in my pocket for this exact moment.

"Of course!" His eyes light up, but I'm not sure if it's because of the architecture help or the fact that if Poppy wasn't a grown woman, he'd try to adopt her. And, since he's convinced (accurately so) that I'll never have kids, Ace is his unofficial grandkid, and he spoils him accordingly. "Tell her to bring them over and if she wants any changes, we can look through all of my *Architectural Digest*s for ideas."

"I'll let her know. She said Ace might tag along, if you don't mind." I told Poppy he wouldn't care, but she still forced me to ask. I think she's finally starting to come to terms with the fact that we will never be sick of her or her cute-as-fuck family.

"I never mind! Plus, I found a Messi jersey the other day for him—this way I can give it to him."

See? Pseudo-Grandpa.

And just like that, all conversations about Maxwell Lewis are long forgotten and instead, my dad fills me in on his plans to camp out at a soccer field for Ace's tournament this weekend.

Something I barely hear, because my mind is still stuck on the note, and my stomach flips at the thought that Maxwell will be back . . . and soon.

Five

THE WINDOWS ON MY LAND ROVER ARE DOWN, THE WEATHER TOO
perfect to even think about using my air-conditioning. The crisp
air is tinted with just the barest hint of marijuana from the strip
of dispensaries I just drove by. My old *NSYNC CD is blasting
from my speakers, blessing those I pass with the vocals of a young
JC Chasez, who was really the star of the band. Don't @ me. I've
already been honked at a few times because I accidentally swerved
into another lane when the urge to do the "Bye Bye Bye" dance
moves was too strong to resist.

I make a left onto a one-way street, navigating my way through
the grid of downtown Denver to the local brewery I'm planning
on ordering next month's beer for HERS from. It's barely even
noon as I pass the Pedal Hopper full of people pedaling and chug-
ging beers. I still can't decide if I want to do that or not—I feel like
it might be too much work for me. I'd definitely place myself in
the "lazy drinker" category.

It's still so crazy for me to think that I went out of state for
college when there's so much to do here now.

I thought Colorado was "too slow." I wanted excitement and something new, so I applied only to out-of-state colleges. I ended up at the University of Texas.

I lasted a year.

It was too hot. There weren't enough seasons. I decided I hated barbecue and Tex-Mex.

My sophomore year I attended the University of Colorado.

Now, besides the very rare vacation, I don't ever want to leave again. I'm a firm believer that there is no place better than Denver, and any native will agree.

I circle the block for longer than socially acceptable seeking out a metered parking spot, but after the car in front of me snags a spot, sending me to the brink of insanity, I accept defeat and park in the expensive-ass lot around the corner from Barley Remix. After I pay the astronomical fee to let my car sit unattended for a couple hours on cracked pavement, I reach for my phone and send a text to Charli letting her know I'm here. After the stress of final cuts, Charli couldn't say yes to day drinking fast enough.

My best friend, Naia, moved to New York for college and unlike me, she never came back. I was so focused on work and not becoming my mom that my lack of a social life never bothered me. Naia and I talk when we have a free second to chat, and whenever she visits, we have the best time, but it wasn't until Marlee showed up in my bar that I realized how lonely I'd been. Then Marlee moved and I came to terms with all of my friends leaving me for the Big Apple. But then Poppy came, and along with her, she brought me an entire crew.

I talk shit about the Lady Mustangs, but the truth is, I adore most of those women.

I push through the heavy iron-and-glass door of Barley Remix, and after a quick glance tells me I beat Charli, I take a seat at the bar.

The bartender, a redheaded hipster with a beard I know Poppy would appreciate, greets me, sizing me up behind his thick, black-rimmed glasses before he reaches me. "Hey, can I help you? Or are you waiting for a boyfriend?"

This is why all of my employees are women.

I fight the urge to roll my eyes. Not because he's picking me up. He's not. He just doesn't think a woman would ever go to a brewery on her own. It's not the first time I've dealt with this. For some reason, people seem to think women don't drink beer and we don't know how to order anything that doesn't come with an umbrella or sugar-coated rim. It's a common misconception. I've found working at HERS that women love beer just as much as men do, but we have better taste. We like good beer and won't chug pee juice out of a can for shits and giggles.

"Yeah, I'm Brynn Sterling. I set up a tasting with Darren so I can place an order for my bar."

His glasses act as a magnifier as his eyes triple in size. "You're Brynn? Not sure why, but I thought you'd be a dude."

"Misogyny." I shrug.

"I—wha—ummm," he stutters, color rising in his face, his skin nearly matching his red beard. "Sorry."

I ignore the apology, even though I do take an immense amount of pleasure at his discomfort. "A friend is joining me, so I'll need two sets of the tasting flights, thanks." I dismiss him and grab my phone when a text lights up the screen.

> I'm so sorry to bail so late, I have a migraine from hell.
> But I sent someone to meet you. Don't hate me.
> Love you!

You've got to be fucking kidding me!
I know a setup when I see one.

And not only because I've been the mastermind of more than one. But because I'm friends with a bunch of sneaky snakes who are dead set on setting me up with a Mustangs player so I can officially be a Lady Mustang . . . something I've never, ever wanted to be. I text Charli back, resisting the urge to fill the screen with middle finger emojis.

You are all on my shit list for the foreseeable future.

So when a gust of warm air hits me as the door opens behind me and Misogynist Mike's eyes glaze over with the childlike joy only a professional athlete can bring forth in grown men, I know who is sliding into the seat next to me before he gets there.

The hairs on the back of neck stand, and goose bumps pepper my arms with recognition. My brain might not be his biggest fan, but my body is clearly not in accord.

I school my face to my most uninterested look as he fills my peripheral vision.

"Brynn." His rich timbre caresses my name in a way where I swear I can feel his tongue wrapping around every letter.

"Maxwell." I turn and glare, but despite my effort to loathe him, a giddy thrill still shoots through me when my eyes land on his fine self.

If he were fug, this would be so much easier. But instead, the guy is sex on a stick. Flawless deep brown skin that looks like it feels like silk. His eyes are a whiskey brown (what? I'm a bartender! I compare anything I can to booze), and his eyelashes are so thick and dark it makes the color pop even more. His short hair always looks as if he just left the barber, the edges cut almost as sharp as his jaw and cheekbones. His barely there beard is perfectly trimmed to frame his full lips.

He raises his hands in the air, you know, the way you'd approach a rabid dog about to attack. "I'd just like to say that this was not my idea," he tells me, as if that makes this situation any better.

"So they forced you at gunpoint to come here?" I ask, clutching annoyance and anger so that I don't accidentally fall onto his mouth. "Don't you have work or something?"

"We get out early on Fridays, and you know your girls. They all showed up at the facility and wouldn't let me into my car until I promised to come here instead of my house."

Fucking Lady Mustangs! They must not understand my superior grudge-holding abilities.

"Well, you showed, you can leave now." I turn to the still-starstruck bartender and wave him over.

He comes over, but all of his attention is directed at Maxwell. "Holy shit. Maxwell Lewis! I'm a huge fan."

Oh for fuck's sake.

"Focus, Mike," I snap. "I only need tasting for one, Mr. Lewis is on his way out."

His eyebrows furrow and he looks at me. "Umm . . . my name is Jake."

"Yeah, sure, Mike. My beers, please?"

Maxwell starts to laugh beside me. I pretend the sound doesn't warm my insides and make my heart grow like the Grinch's.

"And I'll have mine as well, thanks," Maxwell tells Mike, even though I want him gone . . . like five minutes ago. At least I can switch our beer flights because I'm not positive Mike isn't going to add something extra to mine.

"No problem, Mr. Lewis." Mike damn near salutes before scurrying away either to (a) escape the crazy woman who keeps calling him Mike or (b) hurry and fulfill the request of the football god sitting at his bar.

Maybe it's because Gavin and TK are practically my brothers now, but I just do not understand the whole athlete worship thing.

Even though, before Maxwell went full Hulk on me and I was just going off my football pants rating, I wouldn't have minded worshipping a certain part of him.

I shake my head, trying to clear the mental picture of a naked Maxwell in my bed . . . or even in my office at HERS. What? I just wanted a night of fun, not to marry the guy. And desk sex always seems like such a fantastic idea.

A loud phone chimes and even though my ringer is always off, I still check my phone. Not surprisingly, there's nothing there. Maxwell, however, grabs his and swipes open his screen. His eyes narrow a smidge at whatever he sees. Probably Vonnie telling him to stay away after they all forced him to come.

He shakes his head, putting his phone on the counter without replying. "So what's up with the beer tasting?" Maxwell asks, his foot relentlessly tapping on the barstool.

"I try to switch up the beer HERS has on tap every few months with local breweries," I explain. My irritation with his presence starts to fade as I slide into one of my favorite topics: work. "HERS has had a pretty solid customer base for a while now and I know how hard it is to be successful in this industry, so I do what I can to help other small businesses. And people love a good beer, so it's important to me that we offer quality instead of some junk big brand."

"So you're kind of like a beer connoisseur?" he asks, a smile in his voice.

My temper flares. I'm so over being laughed at or doubted because I'm a woman. I look to Maxwell, prepared to tell him off. But when we make eye contact, I don't see humor, I see awe. Like me knowing about beer is somehow the most glorious and magical quality a person could possess.

"I—uhhh—" I stutter a bit, not prepared to say anything other than what a jerk he is. "I wouldn't say that. I just know what I like and I have an idea of what most of my customers enjoy. I can never identify the different notes or anything like that. I just pick four or five different beers to give a decent selection, dark, light, fruity, that kind of thing."

"No wonder HERS is thriving." His gentle tone and kind words shift my insides. "You really didn't forget any details in creating it."

"Thanks." I laugh, trying to downplay his compliment. "You should have been there when I had to pick out the chairs. I never knew there were that many choices. Picking out the chairs was insane."

"Chairs?" Maxwell asks.

"Chairs," I confirm, then let the silence take over.

I turn my head like I'm looking for Mike, but I'm really just trying to hide the furious blush that has my face burning. I mean chairs? Really?

I half expect Maxwell to ask another question to fill the silence, but I'm not surprised when he doesn't. I peek out of the corner of my eye to see him lean back in his metal and wood barstool, his hands folded together on the bar top.

It's the thing that first drew me to Maxwell . . . I mean, after his ass, tatted arms, and smoldering eyes. He's quiet. And I'm sure that doesn't sound impressive or like a turn-on at all. But after spending the last however many years surrounded by NFL players, I learned they all have one thing in common: a massive fucking ego.

Then I started noticing Maxwell when I'd go to Ace's soccer games or to a barbecue at Poppy's house. And when he wasn't talking to me, he seemed like he was this quiet and shy and unassuming guy. He was almost passive to a fault, always offering to pick up the bill, smiling for pictures when he very obviously wanted a night of not being bothered, never jabbing back and forth after TK put him in the center of his comedy routine. He never once mentioned the game he just played in, even the time where he had a record-setting six interceptions and three pick-sixes (an interception that's run back for a touchdown). He actually seems embarrassed when people bring up his career.

It was intriguing and I became a little obsessive about watching him interact with other people and comparing that person to who he was when he got stuck being around just me. I knew there was something I was missing.

Turned out, the surprise was his crazy-ass temper.

"You know, I really am sorry, Brynn." The words are so quiet that I almost don't hear him. "That phone call . . . it was bad. It was like I blacked out. I didn't even realize what had happened until TK dragged me outside."

The self-loathing in his words is familiar on a level that I have to pretend I don't relate to. The rasp that's usually not apparent in his smooth-as-chocolate voice pulls on my heartstrings. Lord knows I've made many a rash decision in my day.

I don't say anything, but I do turn my attention to him.

He drops his gaze to the floor, like he's undeserving of eye contact. "It's not an excuse. I fucked up and my behavior was unacceptable."

"What happened?" I ask before I can stop myself. Something really bad must've happened to cause a reaction like that in a person like Maxwell.

He just shakes his head and I shove the hurt that he won't confide in me back down. I mean, it's not like I've been the most understanding person in the world, I can't necessarily blame him for not wanting to share his secrets with me.

"I don't know if you knew this, but I'm just not a talkative person," he says, and I have to fight back my sarcastic retort. "Something about you though, it just makes it easy for me to talk to you.

You're smart and funny and just a really good time to be around. That party was a nightmare for me, but I was excited to see you again. Even though it meant TK riding me again about you. And then that phone call . . . it was a surprise." He lifts his chin and squares his shoulders, looking me in the eyes. "I just need you to know that will never happen again. I don't want you afraid of me."

All of my air leaves me in a whoosh.

Nobody has ever looked at me like that before. Nobody has ever spoken to me like that either. It's like his entire being depends on my believing him. Like he needs my trust more than he needs his next breath.

I nod my head, my anger and grudge dissipating in record time. "I believe you."

His eyes fall shut as he draws in a breath so deep, it's a miracle there's any air left for the rest of us. But when he opens his eyes, the floor falls from beneath me. Because, hand to god, I've never seen anything like it. His full lips tip up at the corners, his smile mischievous and fucking lush, his eyes dancing with a glimmer that I've never seen before. In five seconds, it's like he became a new person.

"Your beer." Mike interrupts the moment, forcing my eyes away from Maxwell and to his stupid glasses that I'd bet my life are not prescription. "A blond ale, barley wine, milk stout, blackberry saison, and our session porter." His hand hovers over each beer as he tells us the names, and I see a decent bartender for the first time. "Let me know if you have any questions or need anything," he says, meeting my eyes and not Maxwell's.

"Thanks, Jake." I use his real name this time. I guess Maxwell's apology turned me into a big old softy.

Jake's chin jerks and a blush rises from beneath his beard as a genuine smile appears. He turns on a skip and hurries away, probably afraid my nice mood is fleeting.

Maxwell's deep chuckle pulls my attention, his white teeth on full display against his dark skin. "Do you instill fear into the hearts of all the local breweries you try out?"

"Only the ones who staff Misogynistic Mikes behind the bar." I lift the barley wine to my lips because . . . well . . . it's barley wine, and why wouldn't I?

"Misogynistic Mike?" he repeats before his eyes crinkle at the corners, his smile widens, and he throws his head back laughing.

This time, I don't ignore the warmth that floods my system as I take pleasure in knowing that I gave him that laughter.

And while I will never become a Lady Mustang, having a friend like Maxwell could never be a bad thing.

Six

"YOU SERIOUSLY CANNOT STILL BE MAD AT US," CHARLI SHOUTS over the rumble of the packed bar.

The Mustangs game is playing on all of the TVs. Women around the bar are either sports fanatics who are relieved to find a place to watch football without the mansplaining or just here to get a sneak peek of the players' better halves. A few have no idea what's going on and just came for a cocktail.

"Seems like you may have underestimated me." I shove a glass of the barley wine into her hands.

I'm not actually mad. In what I'd consider one of the biggest surprises of the year, I was able to get over my grudge-holding abilities and had the best time with Maxwell. We'd never actually spent time alone together, but it was everything I always imagined . . . not that I imagined it often or anything . . .

At Barley Remix, he just reinforced that I was right with my initial assumptions about him. On top of being the most attractive guy I've ever seen in real life, he's hysterical and so freaking smart

I developed a complex. I learned more about him in two—fine, four, whatever—hours than I had in the time I've known him.

I learned that he went to Princeton and majored in mechanical and aerospace engineering. He also has his own foundation where he works with inner-city children and helps foster a love of STEM and sends a group of kids on a fully paid trip to space camp. He got all shy telling me, but eventually I was able to pry it out of him that when he retires, he wants to go back to school. He wants to work for NASA one day.

A professional football player and literal rocket scientist.

I called him a slacker.

He said he was trying to match my passion one day.

Now I know he's a shit liar.

And I haven't shared a morsel of it with my girls. I keep telling myself it's because I'm holding my pretend grudge. But really, I feel special knowing this about him. I mean, yes, you could probably find all of this in a simple Google search, but still. Maxwell opened up and shared with me . . . and after being around Maxwell, I know that anything from him is a big deal.

So I've held it close and ignored what that might say about me.

"Bitch. Stop. Max came over to give Jagger a signed glove for show-and-tell yesterday before he went to the facility. I asked him how beers with you was, and you know his fine chocolate self was quiet and didn't say a word, but he didn't have to. As soon as I said your name, I swear his ass blushed and those perfect teeth went on full display before he shook his head and walked away." Vonnie arches an eyebrow at me, sipping her signature French martini with a splash of champagne. "That smile coming from that man? It said it all."

"I have nothing to do with these crazy-ass WAGS." Sadie, Poppy's best friend and club waitress extraordinaire, waves a rhinestone-covered nail at me and purses her glitter-covered lips my way. "I want to know everything. The few times Max came to the club, I swear he inspected his shoes the entire time. But that shy man shit does not trick me. I bet he's freaky as fuck."

The thought of what Maxwell is like in bed causes me to miss the shot glass I'm aiming the vodka in.

"I like Max," Jacqueline says. I still startle a little every time she speaks, it took her so long to get comfortable with us.

"I don't want to slash his tires and egg his house anymore, if that's what you want to know."

Jacqueline's eyes grow to the size of quarters. "You were going to slash his tires and egg his house?"

And suddenly, the mystery of why it took Jacqueline so long to warm up to us becomes crystal clear.

"Probably not." I place her Model Behavior on the bar, her cheeks flushing when she sees her namesake cocktail. "I mean, he lives in a gated community and I bet he parks his car in the garage. The logistics were all over the place."

The flush drains from her cheeks and she goes white. "Remind me not to get on your bad side," she whispers into her drink.

"You'll never be on my bad side." I wink, turning to Poppy, who is unusually quiet.

"Yo!" I snap in front of her face, startling her out of whatever daydream she's lost in. "Earth to Poppy! Are you all right? Is this a tequila night?"

"Ummm . . ." Her eyes shift around the room and she doesn't meet my eyes. "I'm not feeling great, I think I'll stick with Sprite tonight."

I narrow my eyes.

Poppy doesn't drink soda.

She said Ace and TK were encouraging too many bad eating habits and soda was the easiest thing to kick. And when Poppy decides on something, she sticks with it.

The gears in my head start kicking into overdrive, and my eyes widen.

I shove the martini glass I was preparing to fill back on the bar and yell for Tanya, the newest HERS family member, to cover me.

"You." I point at Poppy. "Office. Now."

Four sets of eyes turn to us, and four asses rise from their seats to follow us. Poppy turns panicked eyes to me and I can almost see her pulse throbbing in her neck.

"You guys stay," I tell them before they lose their seats. "Save Poppy's seat, and if you could keep an eye out for Tanya, I'd really appreciate it."

Tanya doesn't need help. She's new here, but her family owns the oldest, most amazing Indian restaurant in Denver. The Khatri family is like royalty when it comes to local restaurateurs. The only reason she's working here is because she wants to start her own bar one day, but didn't want to ride her family's coattails to the top.

And since I tell these women everything (except about Maxwell), they are well aware of this fact and all of them, sans Jacqueline, glare at me with pursed lips.

"I hope you know you just bought one night of us barging into your house unannounced," Vonnie, never one to be left out, tells Poppy.

Poppy rolls her eyes. "You guys do that every week."

She speaks the truth. We aren't a group who respects boundaries.

I follow her into my office and lock the door behind me.

"What's going on?" I don't waste any time because if we're gone for too long, those bitches will bust this door down.

"Nothing." She turns away from me and studies the pictures on my wall that she's seen a million times like they are the most interesting things in the universe.

"You're the worst liar in the world," I say, stating the obvious. "Is Ace okay? Did TK do something? You know I have access to a remote plot of land in the mountains and an excavator if you need me to hide a body."

"You know saying shit like that is why Jacqueline was afraid to be alone with us for months, right?" A smile tugs on the corner of her mouth, but the worried look is still haunting her eyes.

"Yeah, I'm figuring that out." I walk over to her, all joking forgotten. "Seriously though, are you all right? I can almost hear your heartbeat from here."

She chews on her bottom lip and clasps her hands together, but even that doesn't stop them from fidgeting. "I'm pregnant."

"I knew it!" I scream, damn near doing a toe touch. My feet move of their own accord and before I know what I'm doing, my arms are locked tight around her as I force us to jump around in circles.

"Brynn!" She pushes me away, her ashen skin green. She runs to my trash can and dry heaves.

I gather her long curls and hold them behind her head.

After what feels like an eternity, but in reality is probably only two minutes, she collapses onto the rug hiding the concrete floors.

"Are you all right?" I ask, and want to slap myself. She's lying on the floor next to my trash can. Of course she's not all right.

She throws an arm across her face. "I'm freaking the fuck out."

"What did TK say?"

"I haven't told him yet," she whispers.

"Poppy." I lower myself to the floor beside her. "Why not? He's going to be so fucking excited."

I don't say that to comfort her. Poppy and Ace are TK's entire world. I mean, the guy walked away from millions of dollars to be with them. Thanks to his crazy-ass mom, he missed out on Ace's early life. It's something he doesn't talk about much, but on the happenstance it's brought up, he can't mask the hurt and regret that he wasn't there from the beginning.

"It's stupid." She sits up, tracing the pattern on the rug with her fingers. "I keep thinking about my pregnancy with Ace and how hurt I was when he wasn't happy about it."

I consider my words carefully; I don't want to upset her more than she already is. "You know that wasn't TK though."

"I know. But I'm in school. We're supposed to be getting married in seven months, and now I'm going to be a freaking whale—you have no idea what pregnancy does to my hips. TK is just getting adjusted to his non-football-playing days and I'm throwing this at him." She brings her hands to her face and I think she's crying until a giggle breaks through.

What the fuck?

"I'm sorry." She snorts. "These hormones have turned me into a maniac."

"You are not."

She is, but I'm smart enough to not agree.

"Liar." She laughs, wiping the tears away from her eyes, and I don't even think to ask if they are from laughing or crying.

"TK had to know that sex means a baby is a possibility, so this can't come as a huge surprise."

"I had an IUD," she tells me. "We thought we were covered."

"Wait." Now I think the color has probably drained from my face. "What do you mean?"

She cocks an eyebrow, staring at me like I'm an idiot. "I had an IUD. When I went to my doctor after my positive pregnancy test, they removed it after confirming I was pregnant."

"Okay, but why didn't it work? Was yours inserted wrong?"

"Brynn, you do know that no birth control is one hundred percent effective, right?"

"Well, yes, but the IUD is supposed to work!" I stand up, pacing the room, fully hysterical now. "I depend on that little fucker!

If the condom malfunctions, I'm still supposed be covered! You mean to tell me it might turn on me?"

"Yeah." She laughs, and I guess I should at least be happy that my internal crisis has lightened her mood. "But you still have to have sex, and I've never even heard you talk about a guy."

That's because I'm on a strict one-night-stand regimen. No relationships. Hell, I don't even like getting their numbers most of the time.

Dammit.

Looks like I have to make better choices.

This sucks.

"I mean, IUDs are still pretty effective. I'm sure you'll be fine."

She's right. I've been living my best, slightly skanky (but I'm grown and I have needs too) life for a long time and I've never gotten pregnant. I take a deep breath, turn my attention back to her.

"I'm back," I say. Her eyes are dancing with laughter, but also questions, and I know I'm going to have to share my exploits with her soon. "How far along are you?"

"Ten weeks. But!" She holds up her hands and hurries on. "I just found out on Wednesday. I thought it was just stress from school and construction."

"Wait here." I know it's a crapshoot on whether or not she'll listen. I unlock the office door and run to the bar, grabbing her purse from Vonnie's lap, and sprint back to Poppy before anybody can question me. "Go home and tell TK," I say when I return.

"But—"

"Nope." I cut her off before she can think of an excuse. "You did your last pregnancy on your own, and as much as I don't mind holding your hair while you dry heave into my overpriced Crate and Barrel trash can, TK is going to spoil the shit out of you, and you deserve that." I shove her purse into her arms, grab my keys from my desk, and pull her out the back door. "Let's go."

"Dammit." She sighs, knowing she has been defeated. "You're a bossy bitch."

"I'm the boss, bitch." I unlock the doors to my SUV. "Now let me take your pregnant ass home."

Seven

THE CITY OF DENVER IS BUILDING A NEW REC CENTER DOWN THE street from HERS. It's a huge project. They've been working on it for almost a year already and aren't even remotely close to finished. Every day before going to HERS, I drive or walk by the construction site to see what progress they've made over the last twenty-four hours.

Every day since they broke ground, that has been my routine.

And the only consequence has been frustration because of how freaking slow they move.

Until today.

I guess when my dad told me I should avoid construction sites because nails and all sorts of shit (my word, not his) get tossed around, I should've listened.

Because it's nearing midnight and I'm stuck on the side of I-25 with a flat tire thanks to a giant nail. And, because I'm apparently still a fourteen-year-old who lives to defy her father, I never replaced the spare tire in my trunk and I canceled my roadside assistance program to help save money for the two-thousand-dollar pair of sneakers I've been dying for.

So if you're keeping score, my life is basically an accumulation of shit decisions.

My dad is the first SOS call I put out, but when he doesn't answer, I don't even attempt to call again. Although he will never admit it, Frank Sterling has a sleep disorder. Once he falls asleep, he is dead to the world. He will not, I repeat, will not wake up until he has had a full eight hours of sleep.

Since it's a Monday, Paisley and Tanya are alone at HERS until close. It's slow, but not slow enough to only have one person. Plus, safety in numbers and all that jazz. I don't like any of my girls being alone. So they're out too.

I shoot Marlee a text. She lives in New York, but I feel like being stuck on the side of a highway means I could meet my doom and she should have one last text to remember me by.

> If I die tonight, know that I love you. And also if you'd kept your ass in Colorado, you could have prevented my untimely death. PS Kiss those babies for me.

I attach a selfie of me standing on the hill opposite of the guardrail, my bottom lip sticking out with my Land Rover sitting sadly behind me.

She doesn't respond. Probably because it's the middle of the night and she has two psycho children who suck all the energy out of her on a daily basis.

I scroll down my contacts until I hit TK. He'll save me.

"Brynny Bear!" he booms into the phone, too chipper to have been asleep. This bodes well for my future. "What it do?"

"I'm stuck on—"

"Oh shit. Poppy just ran for the bathroom again. That's the fourth time tonight. Is this normal? I don't think this is normal. We're calling the doctor tomorrow." He rambles on, talking more to himself than me. "Here," I hear him say. "Talk to Brynn for a second."

"Wait." I try and yell into the receiver to get his attention. "Just call me back!" I shout, but it's too late. I hear the phone drop on what I'm assuming is their pillow-covered couch.

School started a month or two ago, so I doubt Ace would still be up at this hour, but with Poppy out of commission, who knows what shenanigans TK is up to.

"Brynn?" Maxwell's deep, quiet voice comes over the line. "Everything okay?"

"I . . . I've been better." I try to focus on all those clip shows where people get hit by cars on the shoulder of the highway and not fall into a Maxwell-induced trance.

"What's wrong?" His voice takes on an edge that I haven't heard before. There's an urgency that cuts through his calm and laid-back composure now.

"Ummm . . ." I stall, thrown by his reaction.

"Brynn," he barks into the phone. "Where are you?"

I want to whisper, feeling super ashamed of how irresponsible I am all of a sudden. But a semi passes by, tons of metal roaring yanking away the silence and any sense of safety I pretended the small guardrail could provide. Its power causes the ground to shake and the pieces of trash littered around me to take flight. "On the side of I-25, right after University," I scream, my heart in my throat.

"I'll be right there," he says, disconnecting before I can argue.

Not that I was going to.

I want to get the fuck out of here. Thoughts of countless self-centered, drunk assholes too stubborn to call a cab cause my fear to ratchet up a few more notches. It may be a Monday, but I know no day of the week is safe from drunk drivers.

I settle in, knowing TK and Poppy live a solid fifteen minutes away. *Fifteen minutes. That's not too long. You're fine.*

Today was a gorgeous fall day. A perfect seventy-eight degrees. So of course, not counting on being stuck on the side of the highway in the middle of the night, I didn't bring a jacket. The slight breeze is multiplied by the cars speeding by and my teeth are starting to chatter, but I'm way too chickenshit to go sit in my car. I feel like my hazard lights might be the car accident equivalent of a bull and a red flag.

I open up the Internet browser on my phone, noting that it's time for me to order a new phone case. I click the bookmarked Louboutin page and caress the beaded, crystal-encrusted, embroidered shoes through the screen. "Goodbye, gorgeous." I delete the bookmark and go to AAA, saving their number into my phone to call and get coverage as soon as I get home. I know I could just call an emergency tow company, but I've heard some horror stories.

Fuck being an adult, man.

I close the browser, my finger hovering over my social media folder, when a car door slams shut. My phone slips through my hands and lands facedown, of course, in the overgrown grass the city of Denver really needs to deal with.

I look up, hoping it's not some serial killer who picks up stranded women off the side of the road and locks them in their basement, where we are all placed in separate corners, drawing strength from one another but never speaking another word again.

It's Maxwell.

Holy shit. How fast did he drive?

Also, no more Lifetime movies for me.

"Are you all right?" he asks, his voice falling over me, calming my nerves as effectively as if he pulled me into his arms.

"I dropped my phone," I say, dropping to my hands and knees, feeling for it between the weeds and dirt. "Found it!" I pop up, holding it above my head with the enthusiasm of an Olympian carrying the torch.

I make my way back to the danger-infested road, only tripping twice on two different beer bottles. What kind of monsters?!

"You got here so fast," I tell him as I climb over the guardrail, thrilled with my choice of leggings I picked that morning—full flexibility, bitches.

He shrugs, offering me a hand, I'm assuming because he doesn't trust my coordination, which would make sense considering how often I find myself on my ass around him. "I might've pushed past the speed limit in a few places."

I glance at the time on my phone; it's only been ten minutes since we hung up. "In a few places or you floored it?"

"'Floored it' could be another way to describe it." He turns to hide his expression, but thanks to the headlights of the passing cars, I can see the embarrassment written all over his face.

God.

He's so fucking hot. Between the bright lights and the harsh shadows, all of his features seem that much more defined. The strong bridge of his nose, the fullness of his lips and deep cut of his cupid's bow, his cheekbones that look like they were carved from stone. I've invested hundreds of dollars in makeup to contour angles on my face that he was just born with.

So unfair.

"What do you want to do about your car?" he asks, pulling my attention from his full lips.

"Um . . . I . . . uhh . . . would you judge me if I just left it for the night and came back tomorrow?" If it doesn't have to do with HERS, I am the master of procrastination and I just do not have it in me to deal with this shit right now. I need wine and sleep . . . and maybe a good orgasm before I handle my car. Two of those are super manageable.

"No." He opens his passenger door for me, turning on his heel and moving to my pathetic Land Rover. He leans into my passenger side, moving stuff around before coming back to me and placing my purse and some papers in my lap. "Here's all the insurance information I was able to find in your glove compartment. Your registration is expired, by the way." He smirks at me and I take this as a good sign that my carefree—what some people may consider irresponsible—life won't drive him crazy. "Do you need anything else out of there?"

"I don't think so," I say, even though I'm not sure if it's the truth. My trunk is basically shoved full of shit that I bring between my house and my dad's. But I'll be fine for one night without it . . . I think. "Thank you for doing this."

His white teeth flash. "Not a problem." He shuts the door and circles around to his side, pausing as a yellow Mustang zooms by. What is it with yellow cars? He pulls open his door and slides onto the cream leather seat. "Can I see your phone really fast?"

"Umm . . . sure." I hand it to him and watch as he pushes numbers and hits Call. The music suddenly stops and my number appears on the screen in his car.

"Now you have my number in case you ever need anything." He hands me back my phone and puts on his seatbelt. "So where to?"

"Um, DTC area, get off on . . ." Shit. I suck at directions all the time, but I'm really bad at them after Maxwell Lewis gives me his number. I can never remember street names, and I don't know if telling him the exit before the mall will be helpful. "Dry Creek!" I damn near scream, thrilled that I don't have to look like any more of an idiot tonight.

"Dry Creek," he repeats, but before he can put his car into gear and drive, his phone lights up like the Fourth of July. "Sorry." He cringes a bit before pulling his phone out of the cup holder.

Reality is kind of a bitch. He's a professional athlete who is smart, nice, and so handsome it should be a crime. Of course he's getting some late-night texts.

I try to keep my attention focused out the front window, but let's be honest, I'm nosy AF. I look at him out of the corner of my eye and see his jaw twitching under the soft glow of the dashboard light. His fingers fly across the screen before it goes black and he puts the phone back in the cup holder.

"Sorry about that," he says even quieter than normal, before shifting his car into drive and merging onto the highway.

"No problem, can't text and drive, am I right?" I'm not jealous, why would I be jealous? Shit. *Don't be weird, Brynn!* "Sick car." I'm trying to move the subject away from booty texts, but his car is fantastic. I'm not usually impressed with cars. They aren't my thing. But this? It's like being inside a fucking spaceship. My Land Rover is an older version and super reliable (well, when I don't drive through construction sites, that is) but there's still a cassette player in my stereo. Maxwell's stereo controls/navigation looks like they've installed a computer screen into his dash. Streetlights flash above us and I look up to see the sunroof, but there isn't one. It's a freaking glass roof. I try to make out the emblem on his steering wheel, but my eyes can't focus with the lights flashing in and out of the car. "What is it?"

"It's a Tesla," he says. He keeps his eyes on the road, but gestures to the radio. "You can turn on what you want."

I'm not sure I actually know how to work this radio. As a millennial, I'm a low-key failure. Technology is not my friend. Getting online at HERS was a freaking nightmare. Tech support and I are on a first-name basis.

"This is fine," I say. He has on some station playing nineties R & B, and who can argue with that? A song I can't remember ends and the unmistakable notes of Ginuwine's "Pony" float through the air. Without thinking, a smile breaks free on my face and I bust out my best Tom Haverford impersonation. "Girl don't even know who Ginuwine is."

I bounce around in my seat, my fingers dancing across the touchscreen trying to find volume control. All of my chill thrown out the window.

However, instead of the music blaring from his high-tech speakers, the volume is turned down to where I can't hear anything. "Hey!" I turn hard eyes to Maxwell. "What the hell?"

"'Girl don't even know who Ginuwine is'?" he asks, laughter thick in his voice. "What are you talking about?"

Now it's my turn to look at him like *he's* the alien. "Oh no-no list?" I ask, continuing on when he shakes his head no. "*Parks and Recreation*?"

"For the city of Denver?" His eyebrows scrunch together, total confusion taking over his face before he glances over his shoulder, changing lanes.

Oh my god. Is he serious?

"Are you fucking with me?" I turn sideways in my seat, studying him closely. He has to be messing with me, right? Everyone loves *Parks and Rec*!

"No," he deadpans. "I have no idea what you're rambling about right now."

"Amy Poehler? Nick Offerman?" I keep going, sure he's just blanking but actually knows what I'm talking about.

He cocks one eyebrow à la the Rock and shakes his head.

"Aziz Ansari? Chris Pratt? Retta?" I feel my eyes bulge when there's still a look of zero recognition on his face. "How have you never watched *Parks and Recreation* before?"

Now I'm yelling. But what the fuck?

"Oh!" He starts to laugh, his solid chest shaking and trying to distract me from the conversation at hand. "It's a show?"

"Not just *a* show, it's the best show ever," I tell him, feeling unbelievably offended on behalf of the entire cast and crew.

"I don't really watch TV. Just ESPN and the news." He looks

at me for a second before moving to the exit lane. And my stomach drops a bit knowing my time with him is almost up.

"What are you? Sixty-three?" I poke him in the shoulder. "My dad isn't even on the sports and CNN regimen yet."

He shrugs, embarrassment flitting across his gorgeous face.

And in that moment, staring at his strong profile, dread gripping my stomach at going up to my small condo and being alone . . . like always, I don't think, I just let the words run from my mouth. "You're coming inside."

His back straightens and he looks at me out of the corner of his eye, his fingers drumming a beat against his steering wheel. "For what?"

"You are watching *Parks and Recreation* with me." I leave no room for negotiation in my tone.

"Which way do I turn?" he asks, getting off the highway, ignoring my invitation to keep the party going.

"Left at this light, then right at the second light, and then the first left after the roundabout," I tell him, the directions not including street names flowing off the tip of my tongue without a second thought. "There are always a few open spots in front of my building for you to park."

His shoulders relax and he looks at me as we come to a stop at the red light off the highway. "One episode."

I roll my eyes, knowing once he watches one, he'll be stuck for at least six.

I don't let him know that.

"Yes, Grandpa," I joke.

He laughs, but he does it with a glint in his eyes that wasn't there a second before.

And I laugh with him, just with knots in my stomach and excitement flowing through my veins.

Eight

"HOME SWEET HOME."

I push open my door, trying to discreetly kick the pile of shoes I'm too lazy to move to my bedroom closet that's not far at all considering my condo is just over nine hundred square feet.

Maxwell walks in, his thoughtful gaze lingering on my empty brick wall and exposed metal ductwork. "Nice place."

"Thanks," I mumble.

He's full of shit.

It's a cool condo . . . for probably anybody else.

The issue with my place is that where I poured my heart and soul into HERS—even my office—my condo is a total afterthought. My couch, though comfy as sin, is my dad's old one he gave me because he was sick and tired of having to sit on a beanbag when he came over. Luckily for me, my dad has good taste. Not my taste, but not bad. There are no personal touches anywhere, even the one frame I have on my side table still has the stock photo inside. I don't really know why I bought this place. My dad was fine with me living at home. It just felt like the adult thing to do, I guess. Though, I did buy it before real estate prices skyrocketed, so no matter what, it was a good investment.

And I love the security I've created for myself knowing I'll never have to jump from man to man to have a roof over my head. Even if that man happens to be my dad. Ugh. How lame.

"Do you want something to drink?" I ask, hoping he says no because, thinking about it, I'm pretty sure all I have is water.

"I'm good, thanks."

Oh, thank god.

"Cool. Well." I motion to my butt-indented couch. "Get comfy and I'll turn it on." I feel awkward all of a sudden. It's not like I haven't had guys over before, but when I have, they aren't looking at anything except my ass, and I don't have to worry about conversation.

I open the drawer to my coffee table (also my dad's) and pull out the TV and Roku remote, pushing buttons until the NBC peacock flashes on the screen and Leslie Knope makes her glorious debut.

I plop onto the couch, toeing off my Keds, thankful I put on matching socks for once, and laugh at the drunk guy stuck in a slide like I haven't already watched this episode umpteen times. But unlike the other times I've watched this show, I'm more focused on the man next to me. Is he laughing too? I feel like I need to laugh harder to prove how funny this show is. There's actually a lot of pressure sharing your favorite show with another person. I'm not sure I could be friends with someone who doesn't love Leslie.

Sometimes people need politics and religion in common. I need shared sitcoms.

The tension I didn't realize I was carrying ebbs out of my body when Maxwell lets out a surprised bark of laughter. In my peripheral vision, I watch as he leans over, untying the laces to his spotless white sneakers, his gray joggers riding up just so and his biceps flexing under his official Mustangs apparel tee.

Even in casual wear he looks so well put together.

Though, not to brag or anything, I too have mastered the art of slouchy chic. It's kinda my thing.

He leans back, slumping into my couch, rubbing a hand over his nearly bald head, laughing again at whatever's happening on the TV. I laugh belatedly, turning my head back to the screen so I don't get caught staring like a fucking creeper. And soon, I forget that it's Maxwell on my couch. We both laugh at the same spots, me harder than him most of the time, and as soon as the credits hit the screen, we make eye contact and Maxwell says, "One more?"

"Ha!" I clap once. "I knew you'd get hooked."

"Yeah, yeah," he grumbles, but doesn't even attempt to mask the smile playing on his lips. "Just hit Play . . ." He pauses, mischief dancing in his brown eyes. "Brynny Bear."

I can't stand TK. I hate that nickname and I've told him at least a million times.

I growl. Actually, audibly freaking growl. Maxwell's eyes grow a fraction before they snap closed and he throws his head back laughing. Out of reflex, I grab the pillow next to me and launch it at his head, but somehow, he snatches it out of the air like a toddler tossed it to him.

"What the?" I ask just before the pillow smacks me in the face.

I grab the pillow by the corners and swing it over my head, going to maximum force, but I'm laughing so hard, it feels like it's stuffed with rocks instead of soft, fluffy, and light cotton.

"How did you even do that?" I ask through the laughter. "Your eyes were closed!"

"Oh, that?" He tips up the corner of his mouth, raising his hands in front of his chest. "I get paid to do this."

My jaw falls to the floor. Who is this guy? I've never heard anything even remotely cocky come from him and then he says that? What?

But before I can think of a comeback, another pillow hits the side of my head, shifting my topknot bun to the side.

"Shhhh." He puts one finger in front of his mouth while another points to the TV. "I need to see what happens with Leslie's park project."

I sit back down, but not in surrender—I start to quietly plot my revenge.

Then Maxwell starts laughing. And not just a quick chuckle or an abrupt bark of laughter. No, it's body-shaking, eye-wiping, hysterical laughter.

And I forget about the pillow fight.

Well, not really.

But I do remember how long it's been since I had a friend over and laughed so hard.

A really long time.

Don't get me wrong, I love my girls. But they are all married and most of them have kids. They aren't coming over in the middle of the night to binge on a show that's older than some of their children.

Any doubts that I had lingering about Maxwell fade away with his laugh. Who doesn't want a friend whom they can laugh with and who'd speed to rescue them from getting smashed like *Frogger*?

A friend.

A really, really good-looking friend.

That's all.

Nine

I TRUDGE DOWN THE STAIRS TO THE FRONT OF MY BUILDING, holding the strap of my cross-body purse and letting it thump against each step as I go. My hair is a mess, and the oversized sunglasses I grabbed from Target last week are barely hiding the dark circles beneath my eyes. My jeans are ripped at the knee and I'm wearing my "Sorry I'm late, I didn't want to come" T-shirt.

You know, just keeping it super fucking classy.

Maxwell's sparkling blue Tesla is double-parked right where he told me it was in the text he sent me. I pull open the door, glaring at his smiling face from beneath my dark lenses even though he's doing me a favor.

I toss my poor, battered purse onto the floor and tug at the seat belt with some of my pent-up aggression causing it to lock up. "Dammit," I growl. I let it go and try again with gentle hands. This time, it glides across my body successfully and I jam it into the buckle before it decides to act up again. When I look up, Maxwell's eyes are on me, crinkled at the corners like I'm the most amusing person he's ever come across. "Why do you look so happy?"

"What's there not to be happy about?"

Ugh. He's a morning person.

I mark it down in the flaws column.

"You're annoying."

"Here." He shoves a warm cup into my hands, and the first hint of a smile graces my face since my phone rang before the sun came up this morning. "You need caffeine."

I take it, super grateful since I was out of coffee. Just another reason I never come home. Grocery shopping freaking blows.

"7-Eleven?" I take a deep gulp, the nectar of the gods blessing my tongue. It's not as sweet as I usually go for (creamer is my weakness) but beggars cannot be choosers. "I've never had their coffee before, but it's good."

"Better than Starbucks and a fraction of the cost."

"You make a bazillion dollars and drive a Tesla." I remind him of something I'm sure he knows better than I do. "You're not allowed to complain about a five-dollar cup of coffee."

"It's a waste," he says, taking a sip out of his reusable coffee mug. "Why spend five dollars when I can spend one? That's how people go broke, and coffee is not how I'm going down."

"But Starbucks has really good pastries," I shoot back, grumpy enough to debate the merits of Starbucks versus convenience store coffee. "You can't get pumpkin bread or chocolate croissants from 7-Eleven."

I don't even know why I care. I don't go to Starbucks either. I'm committed to local coffee shops. Fresh is my jam.

"And Starbucks doesn't have taquitos."

Well, damn. I guess I lost this round.

"That's true." I look around the car in search of a little paper bag filled with crispy goodness. "Please tell me you got some."

His eyes crinkle at the corners and he bites his bottom lip, which is not a very discreet way to hide his desire to laugh at me.

I do, however, appreciate his restraint.

"I didn't." He keeps his eyes on the road. "I didn't know if you were a Monterey Jack chicken person or more of the jalapeño cream cheese type."

He knows the taquitos.

A man after my own heart.

"Monterey Jack taquitos, Coke Slurpee, and if I'm feeling really freaky, Reese's peanut butter cups." I take another sip of my coffee, deciding to take a trip to 7-Eleven for a Slurpee and a taquito (or three) for lunch today.

Maxwell lifts a hand from the steering wheel and raises a fist over the center console.

"That's what I'm talkin' about," he says as I bump his fist with mine.

Then he makes his fist explode while saying, "Lalalalala."

I pull my sunglasses off my face and turn wide eyes to him. "What in the entire fuck was that?"

He takes his eyes off the road for a second to look at me, his smile so bright I almost squint. "I was watching *Big Hero 6* with Ace last night before he went to bed," he says. "Baymax is the shit."

"I . . . I . . . I don't even know what to do with you right now." I trip over my words.

"What?" he asks. "It's an animated movie where they become superheroes using STEM. I rented out a theater and took the school I sponsor to see it when it came out." His voice drops to a whisper. "And don't tell anyone, but I tear up every time Tadashi runs into that burning building."

"You know what?" I blink hard and put my sunglasses back on, dropping my gaze to his computer car, and finally find the volume control. "It's too early to deal with you." I lean in and turn up the radio until I can't hear Maxwell's laugh anymore.

At Maxwell's insistence, I called a tow truck company last

night before he went home. So instead of having to drop me off on the side of the highway, something I'm pretty sure he wouldn't have done anyways, he takes me to the auto shop near HERS.

We pull up and he parks in one of the open spots. Half-built cars dot the oil-stained lot. The caffeine has settled in my system and I'm finally feeling more human than zombie.

"Thank you again for the ride." I grab my crap from the floor and my empty coffee cup. "Next time you're at HERS, it's on the house."

"You don't owe me for being a decent friend," he says. I try to object, but he talks over me. "But if you really want to do something, we can have another night of *Parks and Rec*."

"Deal." I almost go to shake on it, but then I remember the whole fist bump thing and decide against it. "Where are you off to?"

I don't know how I didn't ask him this before. I guess I can add "self-centered" to my before-coffee attributes.

"To the facility. I'm gonna get in a workout and watch some film."

"Why?" It's Tuesday and thanks to my constant circle of WAGS falling off the face of the earth, I know this is their one day off. Plus, I know he didn't get home until at least three in the morning, probably later, and he was at my place at seven. His ass has to be tired.

He shrugs. "It's my job. You saw what happened to TK last year. I don't know how long I have doing this, so I give it my all while I can. It's a big game this weekend, I want to feel prepared."

Again with the modesty.

Maxwell is the top defensive back in the league. I admit that I haven't always been a follower of the sport and at the beginning I only watched my friends' guys. But I know that ever since I started paying attention, Maxwell has been voted onto the Pro Bowl team.

I guess now I know how he does it.

"I hope some of your work ethic rubs off on me," I toss over my shoulder, climbing out of the car.

He leans over the console, looking up at me through the open door. "You live at HERS. And I know that as a fact after seeing your office and your house."

That is sad, but accurate.

"You're right." I throw a fist into the air and shout, "Workaholics unite!"

Okay . . . so maybe the large 7-Eleven coffee overcaffeinated me.

Maxwell falls back into his seat, laughing so hard that he's shaking his car.

He rubs his hands beneath his eyes. "You're a nut, Brynny Bear."

"Tadashi," I counter, sticking my tongue out at him like the respectable business owner I am.

"Shit," he mutters, but does a terrible job of hiding his smile. "Truce?"

"Never."

"Well, since we both need to reduce our workaholic tendencies, you want to grab lunch today?"

Holy. Shit. Is Maxwell asking me out on a date?

"Yeah, sure, yeah." *Smooth, Brynn.*

"Ma'am?" a grizzly voice calls from behind me, saving me from further embarrassment. "Are you here for the Land Rover?"

I swing around and my metal-embellished purse slams into Maxwell's sparkling, battery-powered car that costs more than my home. I feel my eyes try to escape from my head at the same time I hear the coverall-wearing mechanic let out a hiss of air, saying, "Oh shit, girl."

I don't want to, but my feet move of their own accord to see the damage. When I see the small rows of scratches, I don't know if I want to cry or throw up.

"Oh my god." I look from the damage to Maxwell and back again. "I am so sorry! I swear, I'll pay to have it fixed. I promise, just tell me how much!"

The guy goes out of his way to help me and I ruin his beautiful car! My stomach is in knots and now I'm so thankful he didn't bring taquitos, because they'd be all over the ground. Or, with my luck, the side of his car.

"Damn." Maxwell's voice is somber, like I just punched his baby. "Looks like you owe me season two now." He winks, a wide grin appearing on his face. "It's a car, Brynn, it's not a big deal."

All of the air leaves my lungs in a whoosh and my shoulders fall.

"Are you sure?" My hands are shaking so hard that I nearly drop my cup.

"Positive." He points to the man behind me. "Now go get your car. I'll get you at twelve thirty."

He lifts a hand and gives a short wave before looking behind him (even though he has a rearview camera embedded in his computer car) and pulling out.

"Shit," the man behind me says. "Was that Maxwell Lewis?"

Yes.

Yes, it was.

"No." I move past him to the glass door they clearly don't clean. "That was just a friend of mine. I guess I can kinda see the resemblance though."

Ten

I'VE BEEN STARING AT THE DOOR OF HERS SINCE I WALKED IN . . . three hours ago.

Of course, when Paisley asked why I was, I denied it until I was blue in the face. But now she's onto me and she's been staring at the door for the last hour as well.

I don't actually know what this is. I haven't been on a proper date in . . . well . . . ever. My high school boyfriend didn't have a car, so his mom always chauffeured us wherever we wanted to go. And as a commitment-phobic adult, I've diligently avoided anything that could be misconstrued as a date. In college, when a guy would ask me to the movies, I'd always show up to the theater thirty minutes early and buy my own ticket so they didn't get any ideas.

But lunch with Maxwell? I don't know what it means.

I glance at the clock and see that it is finally ten till twelve thirty.

"I'm going to go to lunch," I tell Paisley and Tanya. "Do you guys want me to bring you anything?"

"Nope," Tanya answers for both of them. "My mom is testing

new recipes and I volunteered us to taste test for her. You sure you don't want to stay?"

Dammit. Taste testing for Tanya's mom is my favorite thing to do. Now they are going to know something is up.

"Well, now I'm not sure, you know your mom's cooking is my favorite. But I'm going to try out a new brewery and I can't cancel," I lie . . . then immediately feel shitty for lying.

"More for us!" Paisley raises a hand in the air for Tanya to high-five.

We are all such dorks.

"Jerks." I stick out my tongue. "I'll see you in an hour. Call if—"

"If we need you." Paisley finishes my sentence. "Yes, we know. You go, we can handle ourselves for a little."

"I'm gone then."

I go to my office to grab my purse and sneak out the back door, running to the front of the building to intercept Maxwell before he blows my cover.

Luckily for me, I get there long enough before him that I'm not out of breath from running by the time he pulls up and I stop him far enough back that there's no way Paisley or Tanya will see me hop in his sleek-ass car.

"Tadashi." I dip my chin. "How's it going?"

"She's got jokes today," he says as he opens the center console. "I got us a super-healthy lunch."

He reaches inside and when his hand comes out, it's holding a small bag that I recognize on sight.

"You did not!" I snatch the bag out of his hand and look inside. "Five taquitos? Who can eat that many?"

He shrugs his shoulders. "I figured better safe than sorry. I didn't want you to still be hungry." He points at the cup holders that are both filled with Big Gulp Slurpees. "They're both Coke, so it doesn't matter which one you take."

Just like we talked about this morning. Would my standards be too low if I fell in love with him over this?

I grab the Slurpee with the pink straw—because I'm really a toddler at heart—and take a gulp so deep I get an immediate brain freeze.

"Ouch!" I squeeze my eyes shut and press on the pressure points at my temple. "Brain freeze!"

"Are you four?" Maxwell says through laughter . . . and if my brain wasn't freezing, I'd have punched him. "Don't drink it so fast."

I wait until the brain freeze fades before I respond.

"You have to drink them fast. If you don't, then it melts and you're just stuck with a flat Coke, and nobody wants that mess."

"Whatever you say." He doesn't bother to fight the smile that lights up his face. He flicks on his turn signal before slowing the car and pulling into a parking lot outside of the Denver Art Museum.

"The art museum?"

"I like that this is the part that is confusing you, not that I'd invite you to lunch and then hand you a bag of taquitos." He parks the car and grabs another bag of taquitos out of the center console.

My brows furrow together. "I told you that I love them, why would I question you bringing me my favorite food?"

"I remember you telling me how many chair options there were when you were creating HERS, and the museum is having an exhibit on contemporary chairs." He takes a sip of his Slurpee. "I thought it would be more fun than sitting in a restaurant, since that's what you do all day long."

Okay.

So we agreed that falling in love over a convenience store lunch was too low of standards, but taking me to an art exhibit based on a passing comment I barely remember making is totally acceptable, right? Right?

"Is that okay?" he asks, and I realize I'm staring at him and not saying anything.

"No." I shake my head. "I mean, yeah, this is okay. It's great actually."

"Good, I'm glad." He focuses on his food, and I swear I can almost see a blush creeping up his cheeks.

Lunch and a museum with Maxwell!

Shit!

This is totally a date! And I'm totally okay with that.

I'LL ADMIT THAT when Maxwell said we were going to see an art exhibit on chairs, I was a little skeptical. I mean, chairs. How exciting can they be, am I right?

Wrong.

This is the coolest thing I've ever seen. There are only eight chairs in the exhibit, but they are all vastly different and they reveal the different methods and tools each designer uses in making their masterpiece.

I've never even thought of chairs as art before. Look at Maxwell, getting me all cultured and shit.

"I think this one's my favorite." I point to the copper chair in front of me.

"You've said that about every chair we've seen."

"Yeah, because I really like them all." Duh. "But I think this is my new favorite. And it was made from a 3-D printer. I feel like I could make a chair now."

Lie. I can barely sign onto the Internet, and it took me a solid week to get the regular printer I have at HERS to work.

Maxwell lets out a deep, throaty laugh. "I think it might be harder than you're thinking."

"Nonsense." I wave him off. "You just—"

His ringing phone cuts me off . . . again.

Since we've come into the museum, his phone has rung no less than five times. He turned off the ringer, but I can still hear the buzzing of the vibrate mode each time someone calls.

"Sorry about that." He pulls his phone out of his back pocket . . . again . . . and declines the call . . . again.

"Who is it?" I ask, my nosiness superseding all thoughts of being polite.

He shows me the screen as he says, "No caller ID."

"That's annoying." And odd. Who gets back-to-back no-caller-ID calls? Sketch. "Why don't you just answer? They obviously want to talk to you. Then maybe they'll stop calling."

"Maybe." His shoulders tense up and the smile on his face dims. "Hey, what do you think about this chair?"

He points to the *Meltdown Chair*, which looks as dangerous as it does cool, but he's also very clearly trying to move the subject away from his phone.

"Did they melt poles together?" I lean in closer, still afraid to get too close and set off alarms. "I feel like this is from a cut scene in *Final Destination*. I think I'm too clumsy for this one to be a favorite."

"Then it will be my new favorite, I don't want it to feel left out," he says and I almost laugh.

Almost.

Because the phone goes off again.

"Maxwell, I swear to God, if you don't answer the phone, I will throw this chair at your head."

A little too violent? Possibly. But I can't deal with this shit anymore.

"Fine, I'll be right back." His jaw locks and his hands fidget for a moment before he swipes to answer the phone. "Hello?" I hear him say, but that's all I hear before he hurries out of earshot.

The optimistic side of me thought it was probably just a relentless telemarketer, but I've never met anyone who wants privacy talking to one. So the realist side of me knows two things. Not only is the person on the other end of the line not selling something, Maxwell knew exactly who he'd be talking to the moment that phone rang.

And now I feel awkward AF standing in the museum staring at chairs during my lunch break. I check my phone and startle when I see the time. Almost two o'clock. My hour lunch break has turned into two. There's no way I'm going to avoid questions. I need to head back.

I look longingly at the remaining three chairs, one of which is so shiny, it calls to the very core of who I am as a person, and go to track down Maxwell.

When I find him, his back is to me as he looks over the railing to the bottom floor.

"Saturday night I'll be at the hotel with the team, I'll text you the address and you can meet me there." His hushed tone perks up my ears. "I gotta go. Bye."

The taquitos I scarfed down in a very unladylike manner suddenly feel like bricks. The vibrant art scattered strategically all around me seems dull and colorless as what he said processes in my mind. No wonder he didn't want to answer the phone in front of me—nothing kills the mood like the other women you're talking to. And I want to get mad. I want to stomp away and tell him to go screw himself, but I have no reason to. He owes me nothing. We are friends and he's never hinted at wanting more. Me getting ahead of myself and letting his full lips and beautiful eyes get my hopes up is on nobody except me. I've just never met anyone who is as thoughtful and attentive as he is, and I guess I read more into things than I should have.

This was not a date. This was lunch with a friend.

A friend I really wanted to kiss.

He slides his phone back into his pants without turning around.

"There you are!" I say way too loud, and garner dirty looks from a guy in a very official headset. "I just realized what time it is, and I really need to head back if you don't mind."

"Oh." He looks disappointed for a second. But then his eyes turn up at the corners and he smiles. It's a smile that, even though I'm mad disappointed, I still can't deny will probably make people come over and stare, thinking he is a thing of art. "I guess I can't keep you to myself all day. Let's get you back to HERS."

If only he knew how much I wouldn't mind if he kept me to himself.

Eleven

IF THERE IS ONE THING THAT CAN TAKE MY MIND OFF THE crushing disappoint of my non-date with Maxwell yesterday, it's Wednesday meetings.

Once a month, every month during the football season, I close HERS to the public and open it up to the Lady Mustangs to have their Wednesday meeting.

The first Wednesday meeting we unofficially hosted was a sneak attack to basically piss off Marlee while she was working here.

It was a shit storm that ended up becoming a viral video that has since been remixed and turned into quite the catchy tune. It was insane and I ended up passed-out drunk in my childhood home that night. However, the bill was large enough for me to offer up a space for them to hold future meetings.

I just got smarter and closed them to the public.

I love hearing the ridiculousness that occurs and not feeling left out of the drama. Plus, these women drink like fish, especially considering that their meetings take place in the middle of the afternoon.

"So, is everything in place for the auction next week?" Vonnie, who happens to be the new president of the Lady Mustangs, asks me.

"Pretty much." I tell her what she already knows, since we talked on the phone for at least an hour last night. "I just need the final okay on the menu and three names for the specialty cocktails we'll be having. I'll close up after the lunch rush and you guys can come and set up."

The Mustangs Player Auction is the first big event that HERS will be hosting, and I'm freaking out. When the Lady Mustangs came up with the idea of a player auction to raise money and wanted to use HERS as the venue, I tried my hardest not to get my hopes up. Sure, they have their meetings here, but as much as I love it, I know there are bigger and fancier venues for them to use. And also, I had no idea if the Mustangs organization would go for an auction.

The whole thing sounded doubtful.

So when Jane Hart, the Lady Mustangs liaison, came to me with an offer of ten thousand dollars to hold the inaugural Mustangs auction, I damn near passed out.

Instead, remembering how women don't ask for enough money and knowing that the first offer is always the lowest, I countered for fourteen thousand.

Jane agreed.

Then she told me they would've gone to seventeen.

I would've done it for four.

So clearly, I was the winner here.

And then the panic set in.

I've been going over every detail with Vonnie for the last four months. We've done everything from meeting with event coordinators, to bringing in a new chef to help spruce up my existing menu and come up with new things just for this event, to even taking a few bartending classes to help spark some cocktail creativity.

Because if I want the Mustangs organization to see HERS out-side of being a gossipy point of interest on a reality show, I have to nail this event.

"Good, then me and a few of the girls"—that's code for Aviana, Charli, Jacqueline, and Poppy, even though she's not technically part of the group anymore—"will hang around after and hammer those final details out. Five more days, ladies, and it's here." Vonnie does a great job of keeping her voice steady, concealing the nerves she's fighting so hard not to let anyone see. "I'm so thankful for all of your hard work, and I know this is going to go off without a hitch. Northern Harbor is going to be able to help so many women and children, so know that your dedication means something."

Northern Harbor is a local women's shelter in Denver. They have a huge location with living spaces for women and their chil-dren who have left abusive relationships. With the money we will hopefully raise at the auction, they will be able to staff full-time caregivers for children so the women can go on job interviews and not have to worry about day care once they are employed. It will also go to paying the rent for women when the shelter is full.

Vonnie also had an idea for a clothing drive and collected a lit-eral truckload of women's and children's clothing for the shelter.

So not only is this a huge opportunity for HERS, I get to feel really good about the work we're doing.

"Any other questions, comments, or concerns?" Vonnie asks the room. When she's met with silence, she lifts the glitter gavel that still makes me laugh and hits it against the table. "Fantastic, meeting adjourned." Then, almost as an afterthought, she shouts, "And don't forget to tip your server!"

That's my girl.

Paisley, Tanya, and I scurry around the room, collecting checks from some and delivering fresh drinks to others. Poppy still likes to feel involved but is having a hard time with standing for long periods of time, so I stuck a stool behind the bar and she's been helping with the cocktails.

We do this for another hour until the final two Lady Mustangs finish their last drink and leave a tip so big, Tanya almost cries.

"That was a good meeting," I say to Vonnie without a hint of sarcasm in my voice.

She lifts her chin. "It was, wasn't it?"

"Yes," Aviana answers, even though I think it might have been a rhetorical question. "Now that Dixie left and you took over, I don't actually dread them. And it feels like we're accomplishing something and not just listening to her talk about herself."

"I ordered us T-shirts," Jacqueline says. "I got a new jersey from the Jersey Lady, and she said she'd give me a discount if I ordered a bulk amount of shirts, so I did. I was hoping they'd be here by now, but I won't get them until the next meeting since it was such a huge order." She flushes scarlet and looks at Vonnie. "Yours says 'Boss Lady' on the back."

We all stare at her, our mouths agape.

I looked at the Jersey Lady's website for shits and giggles once. To send in your jersey and have her cut, sew, and bedazzle it into a new creation was five hundred dollars . . . for the most basic style.

Jacqueline had to be out at least three grand for this.

But I guess crushing the Victoria's Secret runway, making men all over the world want you in *Sports Illustrated*, and becoming the darling of *Love the Player* gives you spending freedom.

Damn. Come to think of it, Jacqueline's fucking killing it right now.

"Dammit, Jac," I say once my brain kicks into gear again. "I was going to order shirts too! You stole my idea."

Her face falls and three heads swing my direction.

"Except I was going to go to the little booth in the Aurora mall and get some white tees airbrushed. I was thinking a giant Mustang riding out of a cloud would be really fitting."

A cherry from Poppy's Shirley Temple hits me on the cheek. "You're an idiot." Poppy laughs, quickly adding another two cherries to her glass.

"I can't stand your ass." Vonnie laughs before turning back to Jacqueline, who looks relieved, but also like she may be reconsidering how much time she spends around me. "Thank you, that's seriously the nicest thing you could've done. I love that you guys are actually proud to be Lady Mustangs now." She looks to the ground, her voice thicker than usual. "It means a lot to me."

"Are you crying?" Charli yells out. "Group hug, people!"

Charli jumps onto Vonnie's back as we all rush around and join in before Vonnie turns on us all. I normally hate hugs, but since the purpose of this one is to irritate Vonnie, I decide to join in.

"'We love Vonnie' on three," Charli instructs with a goofy grin on her face. "One. Two. Three!"

"We love Vonnie!" we all yell in sync, laughing our asses off, clinging on as tight as we can as Vonnie tries to escape.

"Oh! I love Vonnie too!" Paisley cries out, running out of the back office, jumping in on the action.

"And I love hugs!" Tanya runs and piles on.

"What the fuck?" a deep voice calls from across the room. "Careful! You're probably squishing my baby!"

TK rushes over, extracting Poppy from the lovefest and giving Vonnie her out.

"They can't squish the baby, killjoy." Poppy rolls her eyes, but even that can't detract from the hearts in them every time TK is near.

Love. Gross. Bah humbug.

"Better safe than sorry." He wraps a huge arm around her tiny body and then turns his attention to me. "How's the car? Sorry about the other night."

"Not a problem. It's good now, thanks." I walk around the bar and grab a rag to clean the tables.

"Wait," Poppy says. "What happened to your car?"

Oh. Shit.

You know that moment where you see something bad coming and you know it's going to hit you, but you're too close to do anything to avoid being hit? This is that moment.

"Flat tire, it wasn't a big deal." I try and downplay it, but when I see the evil smirk under TK's beard, I know I'm fucked.

"She was stuck on the side of I-25 in the middle of the night." TK gives them unnecessary details. I wonder how angry Poppy will be if I kick her fiancé hard enough that this will be their last baby.

"What?" all five say together.

"Why didn't you call me?" Charli asks. "I would've gotten you!"

"And me," Aviana chimes in.

"Me three," Jacqueline says quietly.

"Bitch, you know I would've been there in a second." Vonnie wags a pointy nail in my face. "What did you do?"

"It was fine, I'm here, aren't I?" I say at the same time TK's big-ass mouth says, "Maxwell picked her up."

My friends even fell in love with snakes!

"WHAT?" Poppy shouts. "That's why he left without saying bye? And you didn't tell me?" She glares at TK, and I use all my self-control not to blow a raspberry his way and say "nanny-nanny boo-boo."

His eyes go wide and he holds his hands in front of his chest. "She's your friend, I thought she'd fill you in."

She turns to me, her pregnancy hormones making her a really scary, angry person. "Why didn't you fill us in?"

I swear, her eyes are two seconds away from glowing red.

"Because there was nothing to fill in. He took me home and that's it."

"Is it, Brynn?" TK asks, his lips pursed together but laughter in his eyes. "Is that really it?"

"I hate you," I snarl.

TK is officially the newest member occupying my shit list.

"What else happened?" Jacqueline grabs my shoulders, shocking me so much that I accidentally tell them everything.

"He picked me up, we went back to my place and watched a few episodes of *Parks and Recreation* because, can you believe that he's never seen it? I mean, Leslie Knope is a freaking icon and I couldn't let him go through life without knowing—"

"I swear to God, if you ramble one more word about that old-ass sitcom, I'm going to end you," Vonnie says, cutting me off.

"Geez." I look at her with big eyes, but she's not having any of it. Dammit. "Then he went home and picked me up yesterday morning to take me to the mechanic."

This is why I was like a secret agent going out yesterday. "No witnesses" might have to be my new life mantra.

"That's it?" Charli narrows her eyes like she's some kind of human lie detector.

"Yes, crazy lady!" I lie, and throw the rag at her. "Now will you leave me alone?"

"Does anyone believe her?" Aviana asks.

"No." Poppy looks greener now than she did a minute ago, but even near vomiting, she has no problem calling me on my shit.

This is why I was fine having one friend who lives almost two thousand miles away.

"You were all up in my business with TK. If you think I'm letting you out of this easy, you are so wrong." Poppy rushes through the last words before spinning on a flip-flop and sprinting to the bathroom.

She has a point, and as bad of a friend as it might make me, I'm so thankful she has to throw up or she'd probably see the guilt written all over my face.

"And you." I point an unpolished, in-desperate-need-of-a-manicure finger at TK. "You need a hobby. Or a job. Go get a job."

He throws a large hand over his chest. "You wound me, Brynny Bear."

"Boy, you better take your fine ass to go check on Poppy." Vonnie points to the bathroom door. "That's your job."

"Aye, aye, Captain." TK salutes like he wasn't itching to run after Poppy already.

I was right, obviously.

As soon as Poppy told TK she was pregnant, he turned into her dutiful servant. When I swung by her house Monday morning to bring her a muffin from HERS, TK had a pile of pregnancy books covering their coffee table.

Poppy told me that he also bought Ace and the baby matching shirts and Jordans.

"That man." Vonnie clucks after him, color tingeing her cheeks. "He just does something to me."

"I'm more of a Maxwell admirer myself," Aviana says, her eyes glued to me for a reaction.

I roll my eyes. "He's just a friend."

"Suuuure." Aviana nods, tossing her glamorous locks over her shoulder.

I shake my head, pushing past them and ignoring the cackling so I can wipe down the tables like I've been attempting to do for the last fifteen minutes.

Twelve

"ARE YOU OUT OF HERE?" PAISLEY ASKS FROM BEHIND THE BAR.

"I am, but call me if you need anything. I'll just be at my dad's so I can come back fast if anything happens."

My dad stopped by after the Wednesday meeting had finally cleared out, and made promises of my favorite seafood spaghetti and his homemade breadsticks if I committed to dinner at his house tonight.

Obviously I said yes.

I still haven't gone to the grocery store and I'm not sure how much longer I can live on protein bars and spoonfuls of peanut butter.

"I think I can handle it." She waves me off. "Tell your dad I said hi."

"Will do, see you tomorrow." I push through the heavy all-glass door I had installed over the summer, holding it open for a group of five women, all dressed to the nines, as they file in.

Friday nights are always busy, but on a night like tonight, when the stars are out, the weather is beautiful, and the Colorado air is so crisp you just want to bottle it up, it's extra hectic. HERS has had a steady flow of customers all day long, and when I hit the sidewalk, I see we are not alone. Fresh has started staying open later, offering Friday night poetry readings, and people of all different colors, shapes, and sizes are packed inside. The window is full of plaid, denim, and cutoff tees.

Backspin Bistro, the restaurant with Ping-Pong tables covering half of their space, has a line out the door of people waiting to either play tennis or eat. Men in beanies, even though it still has to be at least seventy degrees out, chat with women who are determined to rock their short shorts until winter tells them not to.

It's weird to me. That all of us can come to the same places, laugh, smile, and for a moment, our lives are in sync. But then we leave and those bonds we had so casually made are severed. The women you laughed with as you both fixed your lipstick in the bathroom are forgotten. We are so intertwined, yet at the same time, so distant that no cocktail or Ping-Pong game can ever bridge the gap. But for a moment, these places change that. For a small window in our lives, differences are forgotten and the only thing that matters is being happy with whoever surrounds you.

The chiming of the bells and rumble beneath my feet alert me to the approaching light-rail train. Even though it's across the street, I still move closer to the building. It's like that fear that the garbage disposal will magically turn on when I stick my hand in the drain to clear whatever utensil weaseled its way down there. I don't know why, but the train freaks me out.

"Brynn!" someone from somewhere shouts, causing me to bump into the brick wall I'm damn near hugging.

I turn around, ignoring the stinging radiating up my arm from the brick-inflicted scratches, to see who called me.

It doesn't take me long. Even though the sidewalks are crowded, it's almost as if Maxwell wanders the streets with an angel hovering above him, shining perfect lighting onto his perfect face. I haven't talked to him since he dropped me off at HERS on Tuesday, and it's like he somehow managed to get better looking in these last few days.

"What are you doing here?" I ask, only realizing how rude that sounded after the words floated into the air. "I mean, hey, how are you? And also, what are you doing here?"

TK and Poppy are the only people who live around here, and they take Ace out for Friday fun every week. So there's really no reason for Maxwell to be out and about this way.

"I went into HERS and Paisley told me I just missed you, but that you'd probably be close by." He fails to explain why he's here. "You're usually there so late."

"Oh yeah." My forehead scrunches in unattractive confusion. "I'm going to my dad's for dinner tonight. He lured me over with the promise of carbs on carbs on carbs."

Under the lighting of heaven, I watch as his smile falls half a centimeter.

"That sounds fun." The excitement in his voice sounds forced. "I was just seeing if you wanted to watch some more *Parks and Rec* when you got off. Sorry, I should've called first."

It takes a few seconds for my brain to recognize what's happening here, but when it does, a weird warmth filters through my veins and causes the butterflies in my stomach to flutter. Maxwell drove clear across town, during rush hour—which has gotten indescribably unbearable over the past few years with the influx of Denver transplants—to see if I, Brynn Sterling, wanted to watch an old sitcom with him.

"You want to come to dinner?" I ignore the warning sirens blaring in my head.

"I couldn't impose on your night with your dad, we can do it another night that works for you." He aims a weak smile—that, even weak, causes my knees to tremble—at me and pulls his keys from his back pocket.

"No!" I snatch his keys from his hand. Heat floods my face, but I manage to hold eye contact even through my cringing. "Seriously, come. My dad loves company and he makes enough spaghetti to feed an army. Trust me, TK randomly shows up to talk about construction or whatever other crazy scheme he's coming up with, and my dad can feed him and still have leftovers waiting for me."

"Are you sure?" His almond eyes crinkle at the corners, but because he's a flawless demigod, of course there are no lines.

"Positive." I nod, tucking his keys into my purse so he has no choice but to listen. "Then before the food coma sets in, we can catch up with Leslie."

"Then you lead the way."

"WOW." MAXWELL PLACES his cloth napkin on the table next to his empty plate. "That was the best thing I've ever eaten."

Pride pools my stomach like I did anything other than bring the perfect wine to accompany the meal.

"Thank you," my dad says. "It's Brynn's favorite, and I perfected this by the time she was twelve."

My dad's seafood spaghetti isn't anything you'll find in a restaurant. He doesn't just stop with mussels and shrimp, and even though I've tried to re-create the sauce damn near a hundred times since I moved out, I still cannot figure it out. And he refuses to tell me. He told me he typed it up and put it in his will, but that is the only time I can have it, otherwise he won't be able to use it to get me over to his house.

It's nice of him.

I'm over here so much, I'm surprised he didn't give me the recipe two years ago and tell me to leave him alone.

"Were you a chef?" Maxwell asks.

My dad is a HERS regular. He helps out when needed and will drop in occasionally to test the new beers I have on tap or just to chat it up with whoever is around. Because of this, my friends oftentimes tell me things about my dad that not even I know, and I just assumed Maxwell was among them.

"No, I was an architect. My wife couldn't cook and I enjoyed it, so it became a hobby of mine." My dad takes a deep swig of wine, his shoulders visibly tensing as he mentions my mom.

Thankfully, Maxwell is as observant as he is smart and talented, so he notices the sudden change in my dad's disposition as well.

"I'm not a great cook," he admits. "Nancy, the chef at the Mustangs facility, always puts together a to-go box for me at the end of the day so I can have dinner that's not from a drive-thru window or the freezer section of the grocery store."

"So there *is* something you can't do." I smirk. "I was beginning to think you were a bot or something."

"Good to know you thought I was perfect." He brings his glass to his lips, winking at me before he takes a sip.

My eyes bug out of my head and my cheeks flame . . . again. Never in my life have I blushed more than I have when Maxwell is nearby.

"I did not say that."

"You didn't have to," Maxwell says. "Reading between the lines is one of my other talents."

My dad clears his throat, dropping his fork onto his plate with a loud clatter. "Well then"—he pushes his chair out from the table—"I think I'm going to call it a night. Poppy's coming over in the morning to go over the new addition again, and I don't want to be too tired. The older I get, the more important eight solid hours of sleep has become."

When my dad is put in an awkward situation of any kind, he rambles the most unnecessary details.

Maxwell stands and rounds the table, extending a hand to my dad. "It was very nice to meet you, sir."

Dammit.

He's all chivalrous and shit.

"It was nice to meet you too." Color tints my dad's white-stubble-covered cheeks. "Hopefully I'll see you around soon."

Even my dad looks like he's at risk of developing a crush.

Like daughter, like father I guess.

"Most definitely." Maxwell glances over my dad's shoulder and makes quick eye contact with me.

Or does he?

Between the wine, food, and his eyes, I might be hallucinating.

"You staying the night, Brynn?" my dad turns and asks.

I blink hard, trying to anchor myself to the here and now and not the fantasyland where Maxwell looks at me every chance he gets.

"You know it, Daddy-o." I put my plate on top of Maxwell's, starting to clear the table. "Driving on a stomach this full is a ticketable offense."

"All righty then," he says, and I struggle not to laugh at what a nerd he is. "I'll see you in the morning."

"See ya." I snap my finger into a finger gun while simultaneously clicking my tongue and winking. Then I grab the plates and try not to run to the kitchen, mortification that I'm a bigger nerd than my dad ever was weighing down my legs.

I don't even have the water turned on when Maxwell is at my back.

He pulls the plate out of my hand, his fingers brushing lightly again mine. "I'll do the dishes, you go get *Parks and Rec* ready?"

He's close, so close that I can feel his warm breath against my ear. Goose bumps cause the hair on my arms to stand on end, and the chills down my spine make me shake. And thank goodness I forgot to put on my Apple Watch; I'm pretty sure the heart monitor on it would alert me to seek medical treatment.

"Uh, I could, um . . . I mean . . ." *Holy shit, Brynn! Pull your shit together! Remember the phone call!* I bite my lip to prevent any more bumbling words to escape. "I can do the dishes. The remote is on the coffee table, you can go turn something on until I'm finished."

"Does your dad have some dish-washing routine that I'm not aware of?" he asks, still not handing me the dish back.

My eyebrows knit together. My dad is a single man. Half the time he doesn't even rinse plates before he shoves them into the dishwasher with such disarray that I cringe just thinking about it. "Uh . . . no."

"Then I'm doing the dishes."

He steps back, allowing just enough room for me to pass him, but not enough that I can do it without our arms brushing against one another.

I'm almost out of reach, my heart rate starting to make its return to normal, when his hand reaches out, snaking into mine.

"Thank you for inviting me over." He squeezes my hand once before releasing it and turning his full attention to the sink. "I love spending time with you."

I don't say anything. I couldn't even if I knew how to respond to that.

I walk in a Maxwell-clouded haze to the living room, grabbing the remote from the spot on the table my dad would probably label if it wasn't just him living here, and fall onto the couch.

I turn on the TV, switching modes so whatever streaming device my dad is trying out this month is on, and click my way to the *Parks and Rec* home screen.

I put the remote back in its spot, barely registering the sound of running water still coming from the kitchen. Instead, all of my attention goes to the picture hanging on the wall. The picture I've told my dad to take down at least a million times over the years.

The ornate frame with intricate carving and notching accentuated with gold leaf doesn't match the new comfy, modern decor. But it's not just about the frame. It's the picture inside. A picture of my dad, my mom, and an awkward fourteen-year-old me. Whenever I come over, I avoid that picture, my eyes trained to look anywhere but at the eyesore anchored to the wall.

Resentment and anger that I try to hide, resentment and anger that feels so natural that even the therapist I went to for years thought I had divested of it, rises from where it's always lingering just below the surface. The naivete of the bright-eyed girl who wore the same outfit as her mom. We are standing in front of my dad, our matching smiles both overtaking our faces, our heads thrown back in laughter, our fingers intertwined while my dad looks down at us, his warm eyes shining with pride and love.

A few months after that picture was taken, I came home to my dad, his face tearstained, sitting on our old couch, the framed picture over his head like some fucked-up joke taunting us as my dad told me Mom had left. That she had met somebody else and had to choose what made her happy.

And that it wasn't us.

That it wasn't me.

How blind was I that I didn't realize she was already cheating on my dad . . . cheating on us? The hours-long trips to the grocery store that would yield only a gallon of milk—I ignored all the signs. All the phone conversations she'd abruptly end when I'd walk in the room. *Phone calls like Maxwell had?*

I wonder if what I'm feeling with Maxwell is how she felt. If she ignored all the hints that something wasn't meant to be, or if she let the excitement cloud her judgment until she had none left.

I feel a warmth flow through me as if my veins are pumping with hot chocolate and my heart squeezes in my chest at just the thought of him. Electricity shoots up my spine at the barest bit of contact. And I feel like for the first time in my life that I'm finally living and if he were to suddenly disappear, nothing in the world would ever sparkle the way it does when he's around.

Are these the same feelings that made my mom throw her family and life in the trash with such careless abandon that she couldn't even tell me she was leaving? The reason she didn't even reach out to me for an entire year, and when she did, it was because the luster of Heath had finally faded and she was left with nothing?

Of course my dad gave her money. Every month, still to this day, my dad sends my mom a check she doesn't deserve. Whether it's from kindness or pity, or to keep us clear of her toxic energy, I'll never know.

But that picture?

It's a reminder of why I limit my life to friends and flings.

People let the temporary adrenaline distract from the permanent consequences that follow. And I might be a carbon copy of my mom, but I will not repeat her mistakes. I won't repeat *my* mistakes and ignore signs that are staring me right in the face.

No matter how tempting it might be . . . how tempting *he* might be.

As if on cue, the water turns off and Maxwell walks into the living room.

"All right." He claps, his solid muscles straining under his smooth skin. "Let's go."

I reach for the remote, but before I get there, Maxwell grabs it.

"Real fast," he says, tossing the remote from one hand to another. "I was wondering if you wanted to come to the game this weekend? I know game day is a busy one for HERS, but it's a big game and it might be fun."

If I hadn't made a bad habit of watching Maxwell and studying his every expression over the last few months, I might not have noticed the way his jaw clenches twice after he asks or the way he looks everywhere but at me until after he's finished talking. But I did, so I'm well aware of the nerves he's trying not to show.

"Sure, I'd love to," I blurt, like I wasn't just sitting here lecturing myself about rash, sexy-man-based decisions.

"Cool." He sits on the opposite side of the couch, tossing the remote back to me. "Now I want to see what crazy shit Leslie's up to."

Crap.

So much for not giving in to the sexy man haze.

Thirteen

I'VE NEVER ACTUALLY BEEN TO A MUSTANGS GAME BEFORE.

Of course Marlee and Poppy and the rest of my merry crew tried to talk me into going over the years, but HERS was just getting started and I never wanted to feel like a pity date. So when I mentioned that I might be going to the game, I almost had to physically pick jaws up from the floor.

Maxwell offered me his tickets, but when I told Vonnie that I was going and she told me I could sit in the suite with her, I was all over it.

Poppy and Marlee had some weird thing about sitting in the stands and not wanting a suite.

It's one thing we do not have in common.

Free food and drinks in a temperature-controlled room is much more my idea of a good time. And who knows when I'll ever come to another game? I want the VIP treatment while I can have it.

Let me tell you, I am very content with this decision.

"This is fucking amazing." I spin around the suite in awe. It's actually nicer than my house. The counters are a beautiful white granite, the floors are those tiles that look like wood planks, the seating is plush with buttery soft leather, and there are three flat-screen TVs scattered around the room. Hell, even the bathroom has nicer fixtures than mine.

"It better be for how much we pay for it." Vonnie pulls out a glass, pouring a healthy amount of rosé in it. "But with these monsters?" She waves a hand in the general direction of her kids as they pick through a bowl of gummy bears. "I couldn't do it any other way."

She hands me the filled-to-the-rim wineglass and I take it from her diamond-covered hands, feeling a little underdressed.

Witnessing the extravagance that comes with Wednesday meet-ings, I should have been prepared for this. But Vonnie is decked out in a way I'm not sure I could've prepared for. I thought maybe she'd be in a crystal-covered jersey and some heels.

So. Wrong.

She's not wearing a jersey at all. Instead, she's donning a black blazer that has "Mrs. Lamar" spelled out on the back, Justin's number—94—on each sleeve, and the Mustangs logo over her right breast . . . all in crystals. But that's not the end. The tight tank she's wearing underneath also has a blinged-out 94 on it. Her Louboutins are covered in ombré crystals fading from navy blue to orange, and she has a Chanel bag that's also been defaced.

Taking in her clothing and accessories that already cost an arm and a leg before sending them off to be covered in thousands of crystals, I decide it's the level of rich I aspire to be. To be so rich I can just recklessly decorate items I can now barely afford to window-shop for.

I'm wearing a Mustangs hoodie and my navy glittered Keds that were on sale over the summer.

"So . . ." I take a much larger sip of my drink than anticipated. "Who are we playing again?"

"New England. We lost to them last year, it should be a good game." She walks to the table in the middle of the room and pulls out two chairs. "No more gummy bears or I'm taking you to the day care," Vonnie yells at her kids, who look like wide-eyed chipmunks with their mouths almost overflowing with candy. "'Have kids!' they said. 'It will be fun!' they told me."

I struggle to keep a straight face. "But they're so cute." Vonnie's boys are like a mini fraternity chapter. They are insane, but I wasn't lying, they are three of the most handsome kids I've ever seen.

"They're lucky they are too. That's the only reason I keep them some days." She narrows her eyes at Jax, who is trying to sneak his way back to the gummies. He sees that his mission has been compromised, but instead of shriveling up from the fierceness of Vonnie's glare, he starts giggling and runs out the door to our exclusive set of stadium seats, where his older brothers are waiting. They don't look back, but I have no doubt they sent their brother on the suicide mission so they could claim plausible deniability.

"Is this suite yours?" I don't know how any of this works and I find the logistics super interesting.

I rode with Vonnie because . . . well . . . because she offered and she gets free parking. We came in through a side entrance reserved for family and friends of Mustangs players and coaches only. Then, inside, we didn't go into the main corridor at all. I followed the boys in their "That's my dad!" jerseys as they skipped down the carpeted hallway lined with pictures of the Mustangs dating back to the midsixties until we reached an elevator. At the elevator, we were met by attendants on both the outside and inside, like our delicate fingers couldn't handle the burden of pushing a button.

When we got off on our level, we followed the boys again as

they raced and tackled each other in the hallway. "This is why we get here early," Vonnie said as her boys dog piled on top of Jax.

But the box seats twenty people and there are only five of us.

"We share with the Kranzes. We could probably fit another group in here, but we like the extra space."

I try to put a face to the name, but I cannot picture anyone with the name Kranz for the life of me. "Kranz? I don't think I've met her."

"You haven't," Vonnie says very matter-of-factly. "She's part of the Lady Mustangs because her husband is a Mustang, but she's never been to a meeting and only volunteers if I beg her."

"I didn't know that was an option."

"It's not like we go to everyone's houses and hold them at gun-point." She laughs. "It's not a requirement to participate, and some of us just like it more than others. Lucy is more of a . . . well, you'll see. She hates attention, so the idea of doing a fashion show or auction causes her to go faint."

"Mom!" Jett bursts through the door and grabs Vonnie's hand, pulling her to the outside seats. "They're starting to come out!"

"I swear." Vonnie looks over her shoulder to me, gracefully gliding across the tiles like she's not being dragged by a mini human while wearing five-inch heels. "Every game, it's like they've never seen this before." She doesn't sound annoyed. She sounds grateful. Grateful that her kids get this experience and that her husband is still out there living his dream.

I thought I understood loud considering I live ninety percent of my life around drunk women. I now know that HERS doesn't even begin to scratch the surface of loud. The ground beneath my feet rattles as the screams begin to crescendo. Cheerleaders and horses file out of the tunnel before fireworks shoot out from the top of the stadium.

I wonder how much a pyrotechnics guy would charge to get some fire at HERS.

Eh. Never mind.

I'll just buy some sparklers.

A deep voice rumbles from the speakers. "Mustangs fans, get on your feet and make some noise for YOUR DENVER MUSTANGS!"

I get that it's his job, but considering everyone is already on their feet and I could barely hear him over the noise, his instructions felt a bit redundant and unnecessary.

"Look for Daddy," Vonnie tells Jagger, Jett, and Jax as the players filter out of the tunnel, jumping around and pointing to the fans engulfing them.

While they do that, I look for Maxwell.

I thought it would be easier.

Whenever the game is on at the bar, my friends can find their men like they are holding neon signs above their heads. I know Maxwell is number 29, but everyone matches and my eyes aren't what they used to be.

"Did you tell Maxwell you were sitting with us?" Vonnie asks curiously.

"No, I didn't have time to talk to him, why?"

She points to a Mustangs player standing by the bench, looking into the crowd. "Because he's staring at his empty seats like someone kicked his puppy."

"Oh shit." I tug my bottom lip between my teeth. "I didn't even think about that."

"Damn, girl. Are you trying to chew a hole through your lip?" She turns away from me and starts waving her arms above her head, matching the frantic motions of her kids.

I follow her line of sight until I see Justin turning our way. I'm not really sure why they're waving. If Maxwell can find his two seats in a crowd of what? Seventy thousand? Then I'm pretty sure Justin can locate his box without their help. Holding his helmet with one hand, he waves up to his family with the other.

"No!" Vonnie yells like there's a chance in hell that he could even remotely hear her. "Tell Maxwell . . ." She points wildly at Maxwell. "That Brynn . . ." She grabs my hand and starts waving it with her. "Is sitting with us!"

Holy shit.

And I thought the cheers were loud. My ears are going to be ringing for a month.

"Vonnie." I plug and unplug my ears. "He can't hear you and now I can't hear anything."

"Look." She points to the field.

I watch in shock as Justin jogs over to the sideline, taps Maxwell on the shoulder, and then points to us.

My jaw falls to the floor and I wave like an idiot to Maxwell, who, now that I know it's him, I don't know if I'm going to be able to look away from. "Do you guys have ESP or something? That was impressive."

"Once you've been with someone as long as we've been to-gether, it's more of a surprise *not* knowing what the other person is thinking." She sits down, unfolding the cushy seat and putting her glass on the built-in table in front of us. "It's a blessing and a curse. Sometimes I want no part in the craziness going on in that man's head."

"We're here!" a frazzled woman with a topknot bun and a baby strapped onto her chest shouts. "And we didn't miss kickoff! Suck it, Ethan!"

I follow her pointing finger to a huge . . . and I mean huge . . . man in a 96 jersey with shaggy red hair falling around his face aiming his helmet toward our seats, his broad smile apparent even from here.

"Oh, shoot." She brushes a loose piece of hair out of her eye before extending a hand to me. "Sorry about that. I'm Lucy, you must be Brynn."

"I am, nice to meet you." I shake her hand, slightly taken aback.

I know that Vonnie told me she wasn't big on attention and wasn't a card-carrying member of the Lady Mustangs, but I still *ass*umed she'd be decked out with hair, makeup, heels, and crystals.

Instead, Lucy is wearing a pair of brown riding boots that have the scuffs of being well-loved, black leggings, and a plaid tunic I'd kill for. There is not one speck of makeup on her gorgeous, caramel complexion, and her tight curls are trying their hardest to escape from the elastic band holding them on top of her head.

"What was with the entrance?" Vonnie asks, not bothering to stand up.

"Ethan bet me five nights of midnight feedings that I wouldn't make it to the game before kickoff." She wiggles her hips, holding the tiny little head against her chest. "Never underestimate the determination of a sleep-deprived mother."

"Sounds like a good deal to me," I say.

One of the many reasons I don't think I'm mom material is my dire need of sleep. When I don't have it, I fear that I will end up being an episode of *Dateline* called "Why She Snapped." It will show a close-up of me in a padded room, rocking back and forth chanting, "Sleep. Sleep. Sleep."

"Eh. Olly doesn't really take a bottle, so I don't think it's going to actually happen, but it doesn't mean I can't hope." Lucy shrugs the enormous diaper bag off of her shoulder and tosses it carelessly onto the seat next to her. "Ruth and Clara, no candy before you eat some real food," she yells back without looking.

I turn around just in time to see two little redheaded girls' shoulders slump as they put the gummy bears back in the bowl.

I'm really starting to believe that moms do actually have another set of eyes in the back of their heads. "How do you guys do that?" I ask like a little kid at a magic show.

"Do what?" Vonnie asks.

"Know what your kids are doing without looking," I clarify.

Lucy smiles and I swear her eyes sparkle. "Kids are creatures of habit. Everywhere we go, every single time, they do the same thing and I repeat myself a million times. I'm always talking, but I only say the same ten phrases."

"Mommy, can you help me and Clara?" the taller of the redheaded girls asks from the doorway. She's painfully adorable with loose, messy curls framing her round face. She has a sprinkling of freckles across her nose, and her green eyes pop against her tan skin. She's in a polka-dot dress paired with striped tights and sparkling ruby-red Mary Janes. I might not want kids, but my ovaries ache looking at her.

"Of course, darling," Lucy says, rising from her seat. "Do you want anything while I'm in there?" she asks me and Vonnie.

"No, thank you," I say.

Vonnie points to the half-full glass in front of her. "I have everything I need right here."

I turn my attention back to the field as the crowd who had settled down for a few moments rumbles back to life. The Mustangs players are taking their places on the field. The crowd—impressively so—slow claps in rhythm, speeding up with each step the kicker takes, bursting into maniacal applause as the ball takes flight and sails past the end zone.

"You ready for this?" Vonnie asks.

This question catches me off guard and I tear my eyes away from Maxwell's ass as he jogs to the far side of the field to stare at her. "It's a football game that I'm not playing in, how ready do I need to be?"

She purses her lips and aims a wicked side-eye my way. "Just you wait," she mutters forebodingly. "Charli, Poppy, even Aviana, their guys play offense—there's a whole other level of stress for defense."

I kind of feel like an idiot, but I have no idea what she's talking about. "I'm not following."

"Don't worry." She lifts her glass to her lips. "You will soon."

Fourteen

"DEAR GOD." I LOOK AT MY PHONE, WHICH HAS ZERO RECEPTION. "How long can it possibly take for them to get dressed? I'm about to hop on a train and head to HERS. I feel like I need a pitcher of tequila to calm my nerves."

I'm leaning against a white cinder-block wall, with two large orange-and-blue-painted stripes along them, as if that somehow makes them look less like a prison wall—not that I've ever actually been inside a prison, but I have watched movies with them. I'm shoulder to shoulder with Vonnie and Charli, and by the way they're staring at me with amused eyes, they can feel the anxiety coursing through my system.

My rubber-soled tennis shoe hasn't stopped bouncing since the first pass attempt to Maxwell's side of the field. And even though the Mustangs won 21–17, the knots in my stomach haven't dissipated.

It took me approximately a minute and thirty-two seconds to realize what Vonnie was talking about. Whenever the girls watched the game at HERS, I only really noticed the cheering and happy-go-lucky nature that came with a great catch or a decent run.

I never really paid attention to the other side.

And the other side sucked.

Because you can be the best defensive back in the league, which—according to me—Maxwell is, but you cannot defend a perfectly thrown ball. It didn't matter how much film Maxwell had poured himself into this past week, he couldn't intercept every ball thrown his direction. And even though I knew this logically, it didn't prevent my stomach from dropping or my nails from cutting into my palms every time the New England quarterback looked Maxwell's way.

"You seem awfully worked up for someone who is 'just a friend,'" Charli says.

Vonnie snorts. "This is nothing. You should've seen her during the game. Best case, she was going to have a bald spot. Worst case, I was going to have to call nine-one-one while Lucy did CPR."

"I'm right here!" Heat rushes my cheeks when all eyes turn to me.

"Hmmm . . ." Charli taps her chin. "A little testy too."

"I'd say so," Vonnie agrees, her teeth bright against her red lips.

"Really, you two." I roll my eyes, but my heart's not in it. "Give me a break. That was a nerve-racking game and it was my first time actually attending a game."

"Oh my god! This was my first game, too!" pipes up a very peppy blonde standing on the other side of Vonnie.

She's a little taller than me, but without the heels she's wearing, I bet we'd be the same height. Her long, blond hair made blonder with highlights has waves that rival a mermaid's. She's tan without being orange, and her makeup is executed so well, I wouldn't be surprised if she had it professionally done.

Actually, she reminds me of myself . . . if I actually tried. And had breasts.

"Cool," I say, my nerves making it impossible to even attempt to mimic her excitement.

"I'm Eloise Withington." She stretches her hand across Vonnie without acknowledging her whatsoever.

"Um." I put my hand in hers and she shakes it with the strength of a three-hundred-pound man. "Brynn Sterling," I say hesitantly, trying not to cringe.

"Brynn Sterling? The owner of HERS?" she asks.

My eyes flicker between Eloise and Vonnie. Then, when I see the expression on Vonnie's face, I decide to focus all my attention on Eloise.

"One and the same." I give her a tight smile that doesn't show my teeth.

"How fun is this?" She giggles, her laugh reminiscent of Minnie Mouse. "I work for Pearson, Withington, and Thomas." She looks to the ceiling and juts out a hip. "I'm a lawyer."

Is that supposed to mean something to me?

"That's . . . nice?"

She opens her mouth to speak, but Vonnie beats her to it.

"Wow. You work for your dad?" Vonnie gives her an appraising once-over. "That must've been a tough interview."

The smile never falls off Eloise's face, but her eyes do narrow a fraction.

"My father's firm is one of the top law firms in the nation. I wouldn't work there if I weren't qualified." She looks away from Vonnie as if she isn't deserving of any more of her attention.

She must not know Vonnie.

"Yes"—Vonnie straightens her back—"I know all about PWT. I turned them down to work for Clark Simpson, of Simpson and Associates, you know, *the* top firm in the nation."

I ignore the way Charli's hand clasps my elbow as she doesn't even try to laugh quietly.

Eloise doesn't respond, but then again, I'm not sure there is a response to getting your ass handed to you in a cold hallway full of nosy Nellies who will—without a doubt—be relaying this story to their significant others before they even make it to the parking lot.

"Our firm is one of the sponsors for the auction tomorrow night, so I'll see you there," Eloise says to me.

But, because Vonnie holds a meaner grudge than I do and instead of the silent treatment, Vonnie makes it her mission in life to let you know where you stand with her, Vonnie responds. "I know, girl!" Vonnie aims a bright, fake smile at Eloise, and rests her hand on her shoulder like they are old friends. "You know Tom . . . wait, sorry, do you call him Mr. Pearson? Well, Tom is still trying to get me to come work there, so I told him I'd consider it if he'd sponsor the event."

A warm, calloused hand grabs ahold of mine, tearing my attention away from the entertainment that is Vonnie Lamar.

"Hey." Maxwell's quiet voice and timid smile silence the world around me. "Can I take you home or did you drive?"

"I rode with Vonnie, so that'd be great."

"What if I wanted some more Brynn time, Max?" Vonnie asks, no longer worried about Eloise Withington in the least. "You might be sexy as hell, but that doesn't mean you can just walk around stealing my friend."

Under the harsh florescent lights, I swear I see Maxwell's cheeks turn red. "She's my friend too."

"Friend," Charli repeats. "The only people you two are tricking with this friends nonsense is you two."

"You guys are ridiculous." I look to Eloise, who is damn near openmouthed gawking at Maxwell. "Nice to meet you, Eloise. I guess I'll see you tomorrow."

"Close your mouth, girl." Vonnie nudges Eloise with her shoulder. "I know Max is standing here looking like a chocolate-covered snack, but you're gonna catch flies. Pull it together."

Vonnie is not wrong.

Maxwell is undeniably attractive on any given day. But right now? Wearing a suit?

Holy shit.

I know he has a tailor, that much is evident from his slim-cut navy pants. But it's more than just the fit. It's his style that he usually hides behind jeans, T-shirts, and Mustangs gear. His pants are cropped so his oxblood and navy patterned socks are visible in the small gap between the hem and his chestnut wing-tip oxfords. He's wearing a plain white button-up shirt paired with a gray wool tie and has on—again with the perfect tailoring—an oxblood peacoat.

He looks amazing.

Eloise shakes her head, glaring at an unfazed Vonnie, before she aims a weak wave my direction. "Nice to meet you too."

"Bye, ladies," Maxwell says before walking away at a pace that seems a few steps faster than his normal speed. Thankfully, I'm wearing sneakers and I can match his pace with only a small amount of struggle.

As soon as Maxwell pushes the button, the elevator doors slide open—something that always makes me feel like the heavens are smiling down on me. The elevator attendant must have packed up and headed home, because we are forced to find the correct level and fill the silence all on our own.

Luckily for us, rambling is kind of my thing.

"That was a really good game. I feel like my heart rate still hasn't returned to normal. I don't know how you stay so composed out there. I was just sitting down and I was a nervous wreck. And what was with some of those calls the ref made? I don't even know football that well, and I knew the call at the end of the second quarter was complete bull—" The elevator doors sliding open and the rush of bass-filled voices calling out Maxwell's name like preteens at a Backstreet Boys concert cuts me off.

Men draped in Mustangs jerseys wave team merchandise they either hoard in their basements or sell for an unreasonably high amount on eBay over the barricade set up to keep them from rushing the players.

Sorry about this, Maxwell mouths before grabbing a Sharpie from the older gentleman in a blue vest and walking over to sign autographs.

I don't want to get too close, but considering there's only about ten feet between the rows of yelling fans, I don't really have much of a choice.

His hand flies across the items shoved in his face as he makes his way down the line, nodding and smiling as he goes. He does stop, lowering himself on a suited knee to take special care and time to talk to a small girl in a pink Mustangs Jersey. Her dad stands behind her, and even from where I am, I see his eyes glaze over.

Friend, Brynn. He is just a friend.

It takes about ten minutes before we reach the street and Maxwell is able to pull himself away from the still-unsatisfied fans.

"Gotta go, you guys," Maxwell says ruefully. "I'll stay longer next week."

He reaches me in three long strides and places his hand on the small of my back, guiding me to the players' lot that is being manned by four uniformed police officers.

"Great game out there today," one of the officers says to Maxwell.

"A little too close for my liking, but I appreciate that."

We navigate our way through the maze of luxury cars and

SUVS until we reach Maxwell's Tesla, which is sandwiched between a BMW and an Aston Martin.

"Damn," I say over the roof of the Tesla. "You guys are serious about your cars."

"Them more so than me, so try not to throw your purse at any of these ones." He winks before folding himself into the driver's door.

"Smart-ass." I punch him in the shoulder once I'm in the seat. "You know I still feel so bad about that."

"I'm just messing with you." He smirks, throwing the Tesla into drive—and then reverse and then drive again—maneuvering around the cars that are packed in tight. "I looked for it and could barely notice it."

"You're a shit liar, but I appreciate the effort."

We reach the entrance of the players' lot and one of the officers jumps onto his motorcycle, turns on his lights, and proceeds to give us an escort.

I stare wide-eyed at the scene in front of us as lingering fans disperse and cars that have probably been stuck forever in the postgame traffic struggle to get out of the way. "I can honestly say this was one perk I was not anticipating."

I feel like this might be a misuse of authority, but I'm not sure I care. Traffic is the bane of my existence.

"It's nice, but I'm always afraid I'm going to accidentally rear-end them or something," he says.

I start to laugh until I look at him and see how tight his grip is on his steering wheel and how tense his shoulders are. "Wait . . . you're serious?"

"Yes, so don't distract me."

Not laughing at him is no easy feat.

The officer escorts us all the way to the highway entrance. Maxwell rolls down his window, giving the officer a slight salute before releasing one hand from his steering wheel and relaxing back into his seat.

"You're a psycho," I say.

"I've managed to stay out of the headlines my entire career, the last thing I need is to get there for taking out a police officer." He laughs, but there's a bitter undertone to it that I decide to ignore.

I change the topic. "Are we going to my place? Season two has been calling my name."

"Have you gone grocery shopping yet?"

I bite my bottom lip and look at him out of the corners of my eyes. "Uh . . . no."

"Then we're going to my place. I need food." I start to protest, but he talks over me. "And no, those nasty-ass protein bars you keep pushing on me don't count."

"They aren't gross!" I protest, even though he's right and the only reason I still have them is because I can't manage to convince myself to eat them. "Anyways, I thought you wanted to be an astronaut, shouldn't you start getting used to nasty dry food?"

"I want to work at NASA, I don't want to be an astronaut."

"NASA, astronaut? Potato, potahto."

"I can't do this with you." He reaches for his computer screen and pushes a few buttons, swipes the screen once, pushes another button, then turns up the volume.

The unmistakable "dun da dun da dundun" right before Leslie Odom Jr. sings the opening lines to "Alexander Hamilton."

"Oh my god!" I slap Maxwell's thigh with more enthusiasm than I had meant to. "You got the *Hamilton* soundtrack? Don't you love it? Isn't it the best?!"

All rhetorical questions since I turn up the volume even louder and sing along with the cast, only slightly butchering the lyrics.

After the awkward ending at the art museum, I avoided any meaningful conversation by rambling about my current obsession with the musical *Hamilton*. It's not something most people know about me, but I am a huge theater freak. In high school, I always helped design sets for our musicals, and now I sneak off to the Denver Center for the Performing Arts whenever I get the opportunity. I actually love to sing, but I have a massive case of stage fright. It's why HERS will never have karaoke. The thought of someone putting a mic in my hands and shoving me onto a stage makes me literally sick to my stomach.

I bounce and dance to the informative lyrics Lin-Manuel Miranda skillfully crafted to the catchy hip-hop beats, song to song flowing with such ease that I never want the car ride to end.

However, when we turn into a neighborhood with a guarded gate that—unlike most gated neighborhoods these days—is manned with an actual, living guard, my interest in the music fades a bit.

The houses are enormous.

And I don't mean like the mini mansions that are sprinkled all over the city now.

No, I mean actual mansions with lots to match. Each house is located on what has to easily be at least an acre. Not one house is like another, and even the driveways are different. Some are short, some are long and paved with cobblestones, others loop into a circle complete with fountains. It's an extravagance I only thought possible in HGTV specials.

"Home sweet home." Maxwell repeats the words I said to him when he came to my house as he turns into the drive of one of the more modest homes in the neighborhood. It's a ranch-style home, with different textures of wood, stucco, and stone framing the huge windows covered in fabric that conceals the inside of the house. The deceptively long driveway, shaped like a reverse C, curves uphill to a two-car garage with the nicest doors I've ever seen. Dark wood with frosted glass windows, they look more like an artistic feature than a functional one.

"Wow." I climb out of the car. Even the garage is impressive. Built-in cabinets and cubbies line the walls, a hanging storage rack lingers over our heads, and the floor isn't oil-stained concrete like most garages, no, his floors are granite. I could barely afford it on my tiny kitchen counters and he used it as his *floor*. I've never felt more out of place, and we haven't even entered his living space. "Your car's room is nicer than my bedroom."

Maxwell chuckles. "It came like this. Trust me, I had nothing to do with the design."

That makes me feel marginally better . . . by like half a centimeter.

I follow him to the door leading into his house, fighting the urge to ask him to take me home.

Then all thoughts are forgotten as I stand, staring in wonder at the nicest house I have ever stepped foot in.

Sure, Vonnie's house is freaking gorgeous, but she also has three small children who have taken crayons to the walls and have suctioned Nerf gun bullets to unreachable parts of the ceiling where they are waiting for their inevitable fall back to the ground.

Maxwell's house is all the lavishness without any of the mess.

"Holy shit." I freeze, taking in the beauty around me as Maxwell moves deeper into the house. "I might never leave."

Though I am an admitted fan of things that shine and are pretty girly—hence my bar—that doesn't mean I can't admire the more masculine design of Maxwell's house.

Gray paint covers all the walls that aren't already decorated in shiplap or intricate stonework. The nearly black wide-plank floors sparkle so much they have to be waxed on a regular basis. But it's the back wall that truly takes my breath away. A wall of glass with a door seamlessly worked in leads to a deck that mimics the nature around it. There are no houses to be seen, only an iron fence about a hundred yards back and a perfect view of Pikes Peak.

"That's why I bought this house." He hands me a cold glass, following my gaze out of his back window. I take it from him, grateful to have something to keep my hands occupied.

"I can't say I blame you, I've lived here my entire life and sometimes the sight of the mountains still takes my breath away." I take a sip of whatever he gave me, not bothering to ask what it is. My attention flies to him as the sweet and bitter notes of the blackberry saison from Barley Remix register.

He shrugs, a shy smile on his face. "I asked them to send some to me. This house came with a beer tap in the kitchen and I never used it." He nudges me with his hip. "You inspired me to fill it, I guess."

Warmth flows through me knowing Maxwell made any decisions in his home while thinking of me. "So." I turn to his U-shaped couch, hoping he doesn't see my flushed face. "You ready for some Leslie?"

"And Tom. That guy is a trip." He follows me to his couch, unlatching the top of his coffee table, revealing a surprisingly messy interior of loose papers, *Sports Illustrated* magazines, and about five remotes. "I'm still waiting for this Ginuwine thing you were talking about."

"Oh, just you wait, Mr. Lewis, the oh no-no list is worth the wait."

"I'll have to take your word for it, but since you were right about the beer, the *Hamilton* soundtrack, and Leslie, I believe you." He turns on his TV, switching screens and devices until he's made it to the right episode.

Holding my glass tight in my hand, not wanting to ruin his couch like I did his car, I struggle to get comfortable, which is impressive since his couch is the most comfortable thing that has ever graced my backside. My stiffness doesn't go unnoticed by Maxwell. Before I can register what's happening, he tugs the glass out of my hand and puts it on his coffee table without a coaster—which gives me minor anxiety.

But the soon-to-be-water-stained table flees from my brain the second he reaches for my ankles, flicking off my sneakers, tossing them behind the couch, and draping my legs over the tops of his thighs.

His eyes are focused on the massive flat-screen mounted above his mantel, and a laugh rips from his throat when Leslie says something to someone that I don't see or hear because all of my attention is focused on his hands massaging my feet like it's the most natural thing in the world.

His strong hands kneading at the arches of my feet feels so good, I struggle to keep my eyes open. The only thing going through my mind is how thankful I am that I decided not to wear my stinky, old Converses to the game.

"You were right, Retta is the shit," he says through laughter, catching me staring at his hands on my feet.

"Told you so," I say, pretending he didn't catch me staring.

One of his hands pulls away and I suppress the urge to groan in disappointment and beg him to keep going. But then, he leans over, his finger gently grazing the side of my face as he tucks a stray piece of hair behind my ear. All of the air inside my lungs evaporates and my chest burns with the need to breathe, but I can't. My body has suddenly forgotten how to do anything except stare at this gorgeous man and accept any attention he's willing to show me.

We hold eye contact for a moment—or an eternity, who really knows, because it's a proven fact that time ceases to exist in the monumental moments in life. The air around us thickens and my hands begin to tingle with the need to reach for him. My lips part, preparing for his mouth, and my eyes flutter shut as the space between us slowly becomes smaller and smaller.

"Maxwell!" booms a familiar voice before the doorbell starts chiming and a fist connects with his door. "I brought pizza and wings, and if you don't let us in soon, Poppy's going to decorate your rosebushes from being stuck in the car with the food."

"Hurry!" Ace's small voice calls out. "You gotta see how green she turns!"

Ace's voice lacks any indication that he is concerned for his mother. Instead, the glee in his tone holds the fascination that is possible only in a tween boy when it comes to bodily fluids.

"Fuck," Maxwell mutters, rubbing a frustrated hand over his short hair. "Here I come." He jogs to the front door and makes quick work of the locks.

"I'm so sorry," Poppy says, pushing past him and taking off down the hallway, the bathroom door slamming behind her, but her gagging and retching still notable from my spot on the couch.

If I ever wondered before, I now know for sure that the sound of your friend vomiting is an extremely effective mood killer.

"Crap, Ace, cover your eyes!" TK runs in front of Ace when he sees me. "Did we interrupt something here?" He wiggles his eyebrows, and Ace starts giggling uncontrollably behind him.

And your friend's obnoxious husband can ruin what was left of it.

Fifteen

I FUCKING HATE HIGH HEELS.

I have fancy tennis shoes.

But when I told Vonnie that, she threatened to find me and beat the term out of me.

I told her that I'm working the auction, not actually participating in it, and I needed to be comfortable.

She told me if I showed up in bedazzled tennis shoes, she'd pull all business from HERS.

So here I am, looking like a newborn giraffe, tripping all over my restaurant and spilling copious amounts of alcohol all because of the torture devices some masochist decided to call fashion that are strapped to my feet.

And the event hasn't even started yet.

"Damn, maybe you should've worn the tennis shoes," Vonnie says, eyeing me with both concern and embarrassment.

"I know where you live and I will hurt you while you sleep, Lavonne Lamar."

"Touchy, touchy." She tsks.

I'd go after her with my bare hands right now, but there's no way I could catch her.

The crashing and subsequent sound of shattering glass gives Vonnie the distraction she needs to escape my wrath.

"Shit, sorry!" Vince yells, swiping his unruly hair underneath his baseball cap and lifting up the now-ineffective stage light.

I close my eyes and count to ten. Despite all of my planning for this night, I conveniently forgot this would be filmed for *Love the Player.* I've gotten to know the crew over the past few months they've been in and out for filming. I love them, and most of the time they don't have mountains of equipment, but for an event like tonight's, they brought enough to film a Hollywood movie. And these lights are going to give me a heatstroke.

"Fuck it," I mutter beneath my breath, yanking off my heels and marching to my office, where I have a pair of UGG slippers tucked away. "Okay, what do you need me to do?" I ask when I return.

"Oh hell no," Vonnie yells, eyes laser focused on my sheepskin-covered feet. "I forbid you to wear those monstrosities!"

"It's my bar! You can't forbid me to do anything in here. I can't wear the heels during setup, I'm fucking useless. When we're done, I'll change." I swing a broom at her to prevent her from physically removing the slippers from my feet. "Now go do whatever you were doing and let me sweep up the glass before one of the players comes in, slices their feet, is out for the season, and you're blacklisted."

She narrows her false-lash-adorned eyes at me. "I don't trust you," she says, turning back to the step and repeat she's been perfecting.

Eh. I can deal with that.

"All right, Vinny-boy. Let's get this glass cleaned up before you get us all sued."

IF I WASN'T part of the setup, I'm not sure I'd be convinced I was still in HERS.

My usually laid-back and welcoming bar is being manned by giant security guards the Mustangs organization provided. There is a booth with five young men in khakis and crisp white polos providing valet parking for the throngs of luxury cars starting to arrive.

The entryway looks as if the outside has been brought inside. The wall is covered in greenery with the Mustangs logo made out of orange flowers Vonnie had shipped in from California. A group of about ten photographers chat while snapping pictures of guests as they begin to filter in.

The ceiling can barely be seen behind the white lanterns strung over our heads and the twinkling lights dancing like stars. The TVs are running a slideshow with the names of all of the sponsors who helped make tonight possible. Everything turned out better than I could've imagined, which is saying a lot considering it's all I've thought about since I signed the contract.

"Are you going to put these drinks on the menu, or is this a onetime thing?" Aviana drains the last drops of her Dreamsicle— an orange Creamsicle-inspired cocktail—from the bottom of her Mustangs-etched martini glass. "Because I've been trying really hard not to get drunk on camera, but I'll make an exception if I have to stock up on these."

Not getting drunk on camera is a second-season rule she came up with. During the first season, they took a trip to Miami to watch an away game. Aviana got so drunk and caused so much drama, they stretched it into two episodes. I thought it was brilliant. Aviana was understandably mortified.

I push a glass of water her way. "You know drunk Aviana thoroughly entertains me, but I can make this for you anytime."

"Oh good, because being embarrassed on camera is one thing, but Crosby might not be thrilled if I show my ass at a charity event hosted by his job." Considering the champagne-sequined dress she's wearing has no back, I'm not sure if she means that literally or metaphorically. "When is everyone else going to get here?"

It's still early in the night. Aviana usually makes a fashionably late entrance, but Crosby is part of the auction and wanted to get here early to make sure he knew where to go and what was going to happen. In their relationship, Aviana is definitely the one who flourishes under the spotlight, and Crosby is all too happy to take a back seat to his gorgeous wife. Right now, a few of the rookie players are lingering around the bar, soaking in the attention they are getting without the veterans around, and Vonnie is in the back with her makeup artist getting ready.

"They should be here soon." I glance at my phone, which is conveniently tucked away underneath my bar. "The event is officially starting in eight minutes."

"Ugh. This is why I'm always late, I hate waiting." She rolls her eyes and throws her head back, dramatic responses coming as naturally as breathing to Aviana. "I guess I'll just have to have another cocktail."

I can't help but laugh at her. "Oh, the hardship."

She sticks her tongue out at me, but she has somehow managed to even make that look like it should be made into a Snapchat filter.

I give Aviana her Dreamsicle and then walk down the bar, greeting people as they arrive and making sure the bartenders I brought in for the night are doing okay.

"This is why I fucking love working here." Paisley grabs my arm so hard I'm sure her fingerprints will be there tomorrow.

She's practically radiating with joy, bouncing in heels that don't seem to bother her.

Because I was able to hire other bartenders for the night, I gave Paisley and Tanya the night off and two tickets each for tonight.

"It looks freaking amazing!" Tanya says, looking up at the lanterns, her hand intertwined with her girlfriend's. "Too bad you have to give this back."

"Tell me about it." I've already considered asking to buy the lanterns and lights from the company who set them up, but I'm trying not to blow all the money I made from the event before the night even begins.

Something that will be a struggle when Maxwell's fine self steps foot on that stage.

Dammit.

Maxwell.

I've been doing so well at not thinking about him and our almost kiss from last night. Any lingering effects of lust were zapped up the second Ace and TK plopped down on either side of me on the couch and turned on ESPN. Maxwell and I kept accidentally catching each other's eyes throughout the night, but there was never any heat behind his gaze, and after a while, I started to wonder if I had imagined the entire encounter. Even when I left with TK and Poppy, Maxwell didn't even give me the hug he gave Poppy. Instead he lifted his hand in the air for a high five.

A fucking high five.

WHAT?

I lay in my bed until I started hearing the birds chirp outside of my windows, trying to dissect everything before I decided I had to shut it down until after the auction. Something I had succeeded at until this moment.

"Hello?" Fingers snap in front of my face. "Earth to Brynn, are you in there?"

I blink hard, shaking my head. "Shit, sorry!"

"Damn," Charli says, laughter thick in her voice. "Where'd you go?"

"I didn't get much sleep last night. Now that everything is set up, the adrenaline is fading and I'm tired," I half lie. "But holy shit, look at you! You look freaking amazing!"

And that is not a diversionary tactic—well, not totally. Charli is pretty. She has big doe eyes and naturally rosy cheeks. She's petite and somehow manages to have curves, but also a dancer's body even though she couldn't keep a beat to save her life—her words, not mine. Her style ranges from preppy to bohemian. But tonight? Tonight she pulled out all the stops and she looks hot as hell. Her hair, which she recently dyed black, is down in loose waves that just graze her shoulders. The contrast between her hair and pale skin is already striking enough, but add her scarlet lipstick and emerald beaded dress, it's hard to pull my eyes away from her.

"How did you manage to get Shawn to not lock you in the bedroom?" I ask.

"You should see how hot he looks," she retorts. "I had to pull out all the stops to keep his ego in check. He can't look all hot and have random people bid to spend time with him without getting a little reminder of who the good-looking one in this relationship really is."

"Well, mission fucking accomplished."

One of the controversial rules to this auction was that the wives and girlfriends are not allowed to bid. Vonnie actually had to duck from flying french fries when she announced it. It wasn't her idea, and after all the calls I've had with her while planning this, I know she might be the most pissed-off of all of them. But Mustangs management decided it wouldn't be a good look to sell tickets to the public for an auction only to have them all lose out to WAGS.

I kinda agree.

Even though I never said that to Vonnie.

What can I say? I like living.

The other plus side of this is the next Wednesday meeting is going to be fucking amazing. I can't wait to listen to them air their grievances about who won their husbands—which is a sentence I never thought I'd say.

"Thank you," Charli says. "And look at you! Are you wearing heels?"

My feet hurt so bad that I almost snarl. "Don't remind me. Vonnie forced me."

Even though, seeing everyone around me, I might be a little bit thankful. This really isn't a tennis-shoe-appropriate event.

"Damn right I did," Vonnie semi-yells, making her grand entrance. And hell, if it's not the grandest damn entrance ever, I don't know what is.

Where everyone else is in a cocktail-length dress, Vonnie's is floor length . . . and bright yellow. It has cape-style sleeves and a slit up the middle of her skirt, and with every step, it moves as if she has a fan blowing directly on her. The deep V cut and cinched waist hug her body perfectly and make my angular body ache for curves . . . any curves at all.

"Yassss, queen!" Aviana slow claps and motions Vonnie to do a spin. "You. Better. Work." She snaps between each word. "You know the executives of *Love the Player* are going to lose their minds until you agree to sign on, right?"

"I hope they have a good psychiatrist then, because there's not a chance in hell I'd ever sign up for that nonsense."

Most people would be offended by someone turning their nose up at their job like they're too good for it.

Not Aviana. It's why she's so great on reality TV. She loves herself enough for everyone in the entire world.

"We'll see." Aviana pulls out her lipstick, reapplying the vampire-red shade without a mirror like some kind of witch. "You should see the pay raise we got for this season."

"Lawyer," Vonnie says. "I'm a lawyer. I cannot go on your ratchet-ass show and get my spot back at the firm I want."

"The Bachelorette was a lawyer and she's still working." Aviana is always ready with a reality show rebuttal.

"You know what?" Vonnie lifts her French martini to her lips, still not changing her drink even though she helped me pick out the specialty drinks for the night. "I'm not letting you get me worked up tonight. I have to talk in front of people. I should be meditating, not dealing with your crazy asses."

"You made me wear torture devices, you are stuck with us or I will heckle you," I threaten her, and she knows I mean it.

"You're evil."

I point to my feet that might be bleeding at this point. "Heels!"

"Oooh! Those are cute!" Poppy, my puking, mood-ruining friend, says. "I didn't think you owned heels."

"I don't," I say. "I came in my fancy jeans and my HERS T-shirt. Vonnie provided this entire outfit."

Vonnie lifts a single appraising eyebrow. "She says things like 'fancy jeans.' I knew to come prepared or she'd be sticking out like a sore thumb in dark denim and scuffed sneakers. Even the bartenders and waitstaff you hired are in black skirts and white button-up shirts."

She has a point, but again, I ignore it. "My shoes were not scuffed."

"And that's exactly why I dressed you. Maxwell is going to be here and someone is going to bid on him." Vonnie reminds me of something I do not want to think about. "You want him to walk out of here looking at all the women who will be, without a doubt, throwing themselves at him while you're in the back wearing fancy jeans and sneakers?"

"We're just—" I start, but Vonnie does the zip-it motion in front of my face . . . so I zip it.

"That was a rhetorical question," she says. And even with the music playing on the speakers and the growing crowd chatting around us, the laughter of my friends still rises above the noise. "And knock it off with the 'just friends' crap. We all saw you two together after the game last night. I thought you guys were gonna rip each other's clothes off in the hallway."

"Oh, you are so full of shit." I roll my eyes.

"Girl." Vonnie tilts her head to the side, pursing her lips like she can't believe she has to have this conversation with me. "Are you really trying to stand there and tell me you weren't staring at Max looking fine as hell in that suit for a solid two minutes before your mouth remembered how to form words?"

"I did not!"

"You should have seen them both when we showed up at Max's with dinner last night," Poppy, the traitor, chimes in. "He must've forgotten that we made plans. Even though I was midstride to his bathroom when he opened the door, I still didn't miss the crestfallen look on his face, and I swear I could hear Brynn's heavy breathing from across the room."

"Fine!" I throw my hands up. "Yes, I think he is extremely handsome. I mean, I do have eyes. But," I rush out before the squeals of my crew rupture my eardrums. "Whenever we are together, he's always dodging texts or taking calls out of the room. We are friends, but I don't think he's in the position to commit to one person. And I'm not really a relationship person anyways."

There. Now maybe they'll leave me alone.

"Bullshit!" Charli does a terrible job of masking the word in a fake sneeze.

Okay, maybe they won't.

"You know." I glare at the group of laughing faces circling me, noticing that Jacqueline snuck into our huddle at some point. "I don't know why I'm friends with any of you."

I turn to leave, trying my hand at an exit as dramatic as Vonnie's entrance, but I only make it three steps before someone steps in front of me. Thanks to my numb feet, I can't stop in time, and topple into a hard, suited body.

Maxwell's hard, suited body to be exact.

His hands wrap around my waist, preventing me from going down, and with my luck, starting a domino effect with my affluent guests.

"You all right?" he asks, staring into my eyes, making my insides melt and my cheeks blush. I hope he didn't overhear my crush declaration!

"Yeah. Sorry. Heels," I say, suddenly unable to form complete sentences.

"Like I said, bullshit," Charli says behind me, followed by a gaggle of giggles.

Ugh.

Fucking Lady Mustangs.

Sixteen

I REMEMBER WHEN—ALL THOSE HOURS AGO—I THOUGHT Maxwell looked as good as he was ever going to look.

It's such a shame, because I thought I was prepared to see him tonight.

Update: I was not prepared.

Yesterday he was professionally dapper.

Tonight? Well, tonight he's "I want to be the hottest player on the stage and bring in the most money" hot. And let me tell you, it's a level of hot I've never encountered in real life.

I think he must have gone to the barber again, a barber who used facial hair as a contouring tool, because his cheekbones and jaw—while always notable—are striking . . . like cut-from-granite, what-mythological-gods-are-modeled-after *striking*. His full lips look fuller, and I'm not sure if that is from another contouring trick, the lighting, or my imagination replaying our time on his couch. And he's in a red suit.

Quiet and shy Maxwell in a red suit.

A red suit that fits so well, it might as well be his second skin.

And that's saying something. While Maxwell isn't a lineman, he's still an athlete and his legs are thick, solid muscle. Wearing a slim-cut suit like it's the only thing you were made to wear is impressive as fuck.

It would probably be a good thing if I had enough shame to at least pretend I'm not ogling him, but I don't and I'm taking my time adhering this image to my brain so I can think back on it in bed . . . I mean at some random time in the future. Then my gaze reaches his feet and I gasp.

"Oh my god." I grab his shoulders, personal space obliterated because of a fantastic fucking shoe. "Please tell me those are not the Louboutin loafers."

"Um . . ." He glances down at his spike-embellished black loafers. "They are."

I struggle not to fall to the ground to inspect them closer. "Holy shit, they are even more beautiful in person."

"I've never seen a woman get so excited over men's shoes," he says.

I manage to tear my eyes away from his feet. "I usually don't. But I'm strapped and locked into shoes that make me feel as if a new bone in my foot is breaking with every step I take." I point to the deceptively beautiful metallic stilettos I'm wearing. "And I've been lusting over a pair of Louboutin slip-on sneakers for months, and after my car debacle, I'm pretty sure this is going to be the closest I get to them."

"Aren't all of your girls wearing Louboutins right now?" he asks, looking around at all the women congregated in circles throughout the space.

"Yes, but theirs are high heels, which, while gorgeous, are my archenemy. I can't properly admire them because all I can do is think about how much they hurt, and make a mental list of all the reasons I would never wear them. I want the comfort *and* the extraness."

Maxwell's face screws up in confusion and, somehow, still manages to look ridiculously handsome. "Is 'extraness' a real word?"

"I mean, we both just said it, so I'm gonna go with yes." I shrug, fighting back memories of the evil eye my English teachers always directed my way.

He shakes his head, his smile stretching across his face like he doesn't know whether or not he wants to gift me with a dictionary or appreciate my quirks.

But before I can find out, a hand with long, thin fingers and short nails painted a predictable red that nearly matches Maxwell's suit wraps around his Apple Watch–covered wrist.

"Maxwell," Eloise cries like he's her long-lost lover. "How lovely to see you again!"

Maxwell's mouth snaps shut, and I watch as the man I was just laughing and joking with slides away and a polite, professional version of him takes over. His smile dims, shutters slam over his eyes, and his back straightens.

"Yes," he says. Even that one word sounds stiff and forced. "Nice to see you again, as well."

Eloise clearly came prepared for tonight, considering last night she couldn't even close her mouth.

"Hey, Eloise." I wave carefully so I don't lose my balance. "Love that dress."

I don't, in fact, love the dress.

But mainly because she looks fucking hot in it and still has her hand on Maxwell.

Hi, Jealous, party of one. Thanks.

"Brynn!" she yells with the fake, sugary sweetness that makes my teeth ache. "This place looks fantastic!"

Suddenly, I feel like I've been zapped from HERS and straight into a scene from *Mean Girls*. I'm sure that as soon as I turn my back, Eloise is going to tell everyone that this is the ugliest fucking bar she's ever seen.

She doesn't even wait for me to respond before her attention—and other hand—is back on Maxwell. "So, Maxwell—" she starts, getting so close I'm afraid she might start dry humping him.

"Please," Maxwell cuts her off, his white teeth on full display. "Call me Max."

Her eyes sparkle at the invitation, and my eyebrows furrow together.

I think of all of my friends . . . all of *his* friends . . . and how I'm the only one who calls him Maxwell. He's never, not once, asked me to call him by his nickname, and it's such a mind fuck that I don't even notice that Maxwell—or Max—has excused himself until Eloise has invaded my personal space.

"God, he is such a dish." She fans herself as he disappears into the crowd. "Sorry I interrupted you guys. You two, aren't, like, a thing, are you?"

She doesn't sound sorry at all.

"No, not at all. We're just friends." Or at least I thought we were.

No.

We are.

We binge-watch a show together, he had dinner with my dad, he saved me from getting smushed on the highway. I am not going to let a stupid nickname and a woman who makes me want to get my eyebrows threaded doubt myself.

"Oh good, because I'd hate to have to step on any toes." She winks. "But I'd still do it."

Eww.

I think I hate her.

"Anyways, I'm off to mingle, toodles." She smiles, showing off her too-perfect veneers and wiggling her fingers so close to my face that her fingernail grazes my nose.

Okay.

Now I know I hate her.

"What the hell was that?" Poppy, my only stone-cold-sober friend, asks.

I stare at Eloise's shiny, highlighted hair as she makes her way to somebody I've never seen before. "I honestly have no fucking idea."

"Can I help behind the bar or anything?" she asks, but hurries on when I open my mouth to tell her to enjoy the party. "Not because I think you need help. I feel so awkward being here. I left TK because I hate this sport so much and no doubt a lot of people here know that. The only reason I'm here is because I promised Vonnie I'd support her first big event. And the only reason I promised her I'd support her first big event is because I thought I'd be able to get drunk enough to forget the night in its entirety. So I really need you to let me make some cocktails since I can't drink any."

Poppy is rambling, and Poppy rarely rambles. She's actually the exact opposite of me in that regard. It's like silence is a comfort to her whereas I—and most people I know—would rather make an ass of myself than let my thoughts simmer in my brain.

"If you want to, you're more than welcome to join me. The list of specialty cocktails and their instructions are taped behind the bar." I wasn't going to be behind the bar tonight, but it's pretty clear to me that I'm going to need something to occupy my mind and my hands. Some people knit or paint to calm themselves. I make cocktails.

"Thank you." She practically leaps into my arms.

It takes a solid twenty minutes for us to work our way through the dense crowd, Poppy greeting girlfriends and wives, me saying hello to the men and women in smart suits who wanted information on how they too could rent out the space for their next big event. When we finally slide behind the bar, both of our shoulders slouch in relief to have a barrier from the mobs of people.

But before I can relax too much, Vonnie's voice booms through the speakers, and her gorgeous face appears on all of the TVs scattered around.

It's in that moment that I decide I have to convince her to do *Love the Player*. Nobody who looks that good on multiple high-def plasma screens should be hidden in a courtroom. The world should not be deprived of seeing her stunning face in the comfort of their own homes.

"Hello, ladies and gentlemen!" she calls out, already working the stage like the queen she is. "Thank you all for coming out tonight to join us for this wonderful cause. I'm Lavonne Lamar, president of the Lady Mustangs, and on behalf of all the Lady Mustangs who worked so diligently over the last few months to make sure we not only have a wonderful night, but raise a lot—and I mean a lot—of money." She winks, pointing into the crowd, and I know just by the cloud of smoke (even though there are laws against smoking inside buildings) that she is talking to the Mustangs owner. "Yes, I'm talking to you, Mr. Mahler," she says, and the crowd bursts into laughter. "We want to thank you for coming."

"She's freaking killing it," Poppy says. Her eyes are glued to the stage because, like the rest of us, she is hypnotized by Vonnie's charm, beauty, and wit.

"I know, right? How is she not a superstar?"

Vonnie continues her welcome, keeping the audience enraptured. She has everyone laughing when she jokes, draws a heady silence over the loud—and intoxicated—crowd as she discusses Northern Harbor and the crucial work they provide, and then ends her speech to an applause so loud, it rivals what I heard at the stadium yesterday. She walks off the stage, handing her microphone to Jeremy Yepsen, the local radio host who's emceeing the auction, and in front of me, a man in a boring blue suit with thick-rimmed glasses leans over to a woman with beautiful hair and a professional yet stylish dress, whom I recognize as the news anchor from channel seven, and says, "She's brilliant. Looks like Denver is going to have a new host for a morning talk show."

It takes everything in me not to jump up and down and run to Vonnie, proclaiming that she is going to be the next Oprah and I'm calling dibs on being Gayle.

Poppy starts hitting me repeatedly on the arm and pointing to the man in front of us, trying to be discreet but failing miserably.

I know! I mouth, my eyes feeling as though they might pop out of my face.

"She's going to be Oprah!" she whisper yells, grabbing my hands and bouncing up and down.

"I was going to say the same thing!" I yell, figuring Mr. Blue Suit won't know what we're talking about, but also adhering to the friendship rule that you must get overly excited when you and a friend are thinking the same thing at the same time.

It's how I know Poppy is going to be my friend until I'm old and gray. When you build a friendship on a mutual love of alcohol and Oprah, you have a foundation that can last through anything.

While setting up the auction, Vonnie decided the best lineup would be reminiscent of a music festival, with the lesser-known names acting as a warm-up for the main event. Most guys seemed to check their ego at the door . . . well, not the whole ego, but part of it, and not make a big deal about their placement in the lineup. I'm not sure if it's because of appreciation and respect for Vonnie and the charity they are supporting, or fear of the wrath of Mr. Mahler if they cause a scene.

The first twenty or so guys fly by. Jeremy moves through the auction like a pro, starting the bids at an impressive one thousand dollars and proving that people came to play tonight. Even the few players that I've never heard of go for over three thousand dollars.

Then the bigger names start coming, and shit gets wild.

Justin, Vonnie's husband, goes for a solid ten thousand dollars. He practically charges off the stage, running straight to the older man who placed the winning bid and then picking him up, spinning in circles.

"You better get that money, baby!" Vonnie yells over the cheers and laughter.

Crosby brings in eight thousand. Poor guy was so nervous, his shoulders damn near hit the floor in relief as he walks off the stage. Cameras inch closer to Aviana's face as she blows him a kiss before boldly declaring she'd go for at least double.

"And coming to the stage next, you might know this guy. He makes quarterbacks shake in their cleats and wide receivers cry," Jeremy says, bouncing up and down in anticipation, eyes laser focused to the curtain starting to part behind the stage. "Seven-time all-pro cornerback, Maxwell Lewis!"

The crowd roars to life as Maxwell runs through the curtain, his game face plastered on. He jogs to center stage, his teeth sparkling beneath the spotlight as he points to the crowd, and bursts into the dance move I always see Ace trying to do.

The cocktail I was making is long forgotten. Trying to focus on anything other than this outgoing version of Maxwell is pointless, something Poppy must notice because she grabs the ice-filled shaker in front of me and picks up where I left off.

"What should I start the bidding at?" Jeremy asks the crowd.

"Hey, you better not do me dirty," Maxwell says, and I swear I can almost hear bras unsnapping as his deep voice comes through the speakers. "I have to be worth more than Lamar."

I let out a startled, very unattractive snort. Maxwell is always funny, but in a smart, quiet way. This Maxwell in front of me is different. This is Mustang Maxwell. Competitive and outgoing and not intimidated by the thought of charming a crowd filled with some of Colorado's most powerful people.

And as much as I try to ignore it, I can't deny the way my heart stutters in my chest.

"Me?" Jeremy covers his mouth in much astonishment. "I would never."

"Hey!" Aviana and her camera crew are suddenly in front of me. "Can I have one more of those orange drinks?" she asks, clearly over her not-getting-drunk rule.

"Sure." I smile, but only for the camera. If I could throttle her right now, I would, but I already signed the papers allowing the producers to put me on the show, and looking like a bitch would probably be the one time they decided not to edit me out.

I grab a shaker, tossing in ice and measuring the vodka, all while trying to ignore the quickly increasing numbers Jeremy is shouting out.

"Eight thousand! Can anybody give me eighty-five hundred? Eighty-five hundred!"

I reach for the orange juice, trying to think happy thoughts.

"Eleven thousand!" I hear. I chance a quick peek at the stage and regret it immediately. Maxwell is jumping up and down, pumping his arms in the air, hyping up the crowd to keep bidding, his biceps straining against his suit jacket with every move he makes.

I turn around and reach into one of the mini fridges tucked into the back of the bar, singing the ABC's in my head, anything to distract me from the spectacle happening on the stage.

I pour the half-and-half and put the lid on the shaker, shaking it with a lot more force than necessary.

"Thirteen thousand!" Jeremy yells. "This is amazing! Can we get it any higher?"

I keep shaking, only stopping when I notice Rich—the camera-man who is always willing to be a guinea pig for new concoctions I've created—leaning around his camera and staring at me with an open mouth. I pick up the sugar-rimmed custom martini glass and start straining the frosty orange drink into it.

"Twenty-five thousand dollars!" A shrill, familiar voice rises above all others.

The glass falls from my hand and shatters on the ground, sugar-coated shards scattering around my cocktail-covered feet. My head snaps up and my gaze follows everybody else's to Eloise Withington standing on top of a table with a hand in the air.

"SOLD!" Jeremy screams like he's not holding a microphone.

The crowd snaps out of its momentary shock and thunders back to life. I even spot Mrs. Mahler with her cigarette holder, who stands up from her seat and cheers.

"That bitch," I growl, my eyes glued to the back of Eloise's stupid dress as the crowd parts for her and she makes her way onto the stage to hug Maxwell. "I fucking hate her."

"Oh my god!" Aviana squeals, pulling my attention away from the stage. "I never saw this as a potential story line, but I fucking love it." She grins and it looks fucking diabolical. She turns to one of the cameramen and asks, "Did you catch it?"

My eyes widen for a second, taking in the shocked faces of Rich, Vince, and Poppy. Then I squeeze them shut as tight as possible, hoping a hopeless hope that somehow this is all a terrible nightmare.

I crack one eye open, but much to my dismay, not only is Vince still standing there with his camera, so are Maxwell and a giddy Eloise.

"So," she squawks. "What'd we miss?"

Fucking, fucking Lady Mustangs!

Seventeen

"DAD." I TRY TO INFUSE AS MUCH FEELING AS POSSIBLE INTO THAT one little word. "I just do not want to talk about it anymore."

It's been five days and the damn auction is still all anybody can talk about.

After the game on Sunday, I'd managed to convince myself that I misheard his conversation at the museum. Or that maybe he was trying to end things with whoever was on the line. Maxwell's a stand-up dude, he wouldn't break up with someone on the phone. But ever since I saw Eloise plastered to his side, the doubts have been creeping back in. And luckily for me, I'm not sure anyone is going to let it drop anytime soon. No matter how many times I ask.

"But they even talked about it on the news today," my dad says. "They said the Mustangs wouldn't even tell them how much money they made, only that it was historically high. And the news anchor was there too. She said it was the best event she'd ever attended and that HERS is her new go-to spot. You should be thrilled."

I stand up straight and stare at my dad. "I am thrilled." I point to the fake smile on my face. "See?"

"I just don't understand why you aren't over the moon right now."

Obviously, I did not tell my dad all of the details of the auction.

I'm still trying to pretend like I didn't unintentionally become a story line for the next season of a reality show and that said story line isn't outing me to the world for an unrequited crush I developed on a guy so far out of my league that somebody spent twenty-five thousand dollars to hang out with him.

Although, to be fair, it wasn't a dating auction and there were very clear guidelines set forth about what would be allowed to happen and what wouldn't. And Eloise attended to represent her father's firm and was given "carte blanche"—her words, not mine—to both give back to charity and have a player spend the day at their firm.

I guess when it comes to spending someone else's money, Eloise is as charitable as they come.

"I am!" I snap, throwing the rag I've been using to scrub a speck of dirt off the bar, only to realize it's a nick in the counter.

"Ooh," Tanya says, snapping her gum as she passes. "You must've mentioned the thing we aren't mentioning that happened here on Monday night with people from that team we also aren't mentioning."

I glare and my dad laughs.

"I can fire you."

To that threat, she blows a bubble and winks.

I throw my hands in the air. "Does nobody here respect my authority?"

"I know you still aren't trippin' over that spoiled brat bidding on Max." Vonnie slides onto the barstool next to my dad.

Why? What did I ever do to deserve this?

"Oh." My dad's eyes widen behind his glasses and he nods his head slowly. "This is about Max. That makes sense."

"What? Why?" I trip over my words. "Why does that make sense?" I ask, then point at Vonnie. "You stay out of this or I'm banning you from HERS."

She turns her head to the side for the sole purpose of giving me a wicked side-eye. "Suuure."

Clearly, I've been living in a land of delusion thinking anybody in my circle takes me seriously.

"I mean it!" I shout, startling customers around us.

"Okay, girl," Vonnie says, even though it's obvious to everyone that she's just humoring me. "You want to come to the game tomorrow? Lucy already called me asking if you would come to this game too."

Aww.

Hearing that Lucy wants me there is almost enough to shake some of the foul mood I've been in since Monday. "That's sweet of her," I say. "But I don—"

"She'll be there."

"What? No, I can't," I say at the same time Vonnie claps her hands and says, "Fabulous! I'll text Lucy right now."

"Vonnie, I really can't miss two consecutive Sundays. They've turned into one of our craziest days for business."

"Nonsense." My dad sounds exactly like he did when I was seven. "I'll cover for you. You need to get out of this bar more often. And who says no to a suite at the Mustangs game?"

"I already texted her. You can't back out now." Vonnie tosses her crystal-encrusted phone case into her oversized Louis Vuitton bag. "She said Clara and Ruth have been asking about you all week."

Sorcery.

She knows how obsessed I was with those curly-headed balls of cuteness.

"That was sneaky." I glare at her, my resolve weakening. "I still can't go."

Tanya slides a French martini that Vonnie no longer needs to verbally order in front of her. "Thanks, girl!" Vonnie says.

"Anytime!" Tanya leans over me and adds a splash of champagne to Vonnie's drink.

"So." She lifts her martini to her lips. "What time am I picking you up tomorrow?"

"Same time as last week," I mumble. I grab my phone from beneath the bar and start to walk away, calling out, "I hope you're proud of being a bully," as I go.

"I'm not fucking ashamed," she says, and I refuse to turn around even when I hear all of their laughter following me out.

Eighteen

DON'T CHECK YOUR PHONE. DON'T CHECK YOUR PHONE. DON'T check your freaking-ass phone.

I check my phone.

And it's still depressingly blank.

"Are you okay, Miss Brynn?" Clara asks, sitting on my lap.

I flip my phone over and slide it onto the table in front of me. "I'm perfect." I tug on one of the red curls in her wild pigtails. "Are you excited to watch your daddy play football?"

"Not really. Football is long and boring, but Mommy said I can play on my tablet if I don't sneak candy." She sounds more fifteen than four. "I thought sitting with you would make it easier to pretend there isn't candy in there." She jabs a finger at the glass door leading into the suite.

"Is it working?"

A shy smile pulls at her lips, and she shoots a quick glance to Lucy, who's nursing a fussy baby Oliver a couple of rows in front of us. "Not really."

"Mile High City!" The deep voice from last week is back just in time to distract Clara and me. "Get on your feet for your Denver Mustangs!"

And like the well-oiled machine they are, fireworks shoot out from the top of the stadium, and the blue-and-orange flood breaks free from the tunnel.

I wish I could say that after seeing it once, it wasn't as impressive, but I'd be lying. I'm not sure the grandeur of this ever fades, and I suddenly understand the people who camp out for tickets and spend more than some people make in a year on season tickets. The energy, the excitement, it's like a drug, and it's addictive as fuck.

My blood crackles through my veins as I watch player after player run onto the field. Clara's weight on my thighs is the only thing anchoring me to my seat. Even though I try to play it cool, I only last a few seconds of my eyes straining for Maxwell before I crack. "Is Maxwell not playing today?" I ask Vonnie or Lucy . . . hell, even Clara and Ruth probably know more than me.

If he's not, that could be one explanation for him not texting me back when I wished him good luck earlier.

"He's playing." Vonnie doesn't bother to hide her smug smile. "They're introducing the starting defense today, so he'll come out when they call him."

"Oh, yay! I love when they call Daddy!" Clara claps, her bony butt bouncing on my lap. "Ruthie, Daddy's gonna get the fireworks!"

"Yay!" Ruthie pushes Clara's legs to the side and climbs on my free leg. "I'm so glad Mommy didn't make us miss it!"

"Everyone's a critic on the one day they actually put on their shoes the first time I ask." Lucy angles her entire body so she can aim a mock glare at her girls, but her eyes widen when she sees them testing my chair-like qualities. "Girls! Look at all of these empty seats, get off of Miss Brynn!" she yells, startling a nodding-off Oliver so much that he pops right off her boob.

"Mommy's boob!" Clara points and giggles, causing Lucy's cheeks to turn hot pink.

"Shoot!" She struggles to snap her bra back into place. "Sorry about that."

"I might not have kids, but I do have boobs," I say. "You don't need to apologize."

"And they're still great boobs," Vonnie says. "Mine did not look like that with Jax."

I expect Lucy to get flustered again, but instead she says, "That's because they're still slightly engorged. This is the porn-star-boob phase. Once he's done, they're gonna be deflated and hanging to my belly button."

I let out a horrified gasp. "Oh my god. I'm never having kids."

"Sure." Vonnie rolls her eyes. "Whatever you say."

Clara looks at Lucy and asks, "What's a porn star?"

And proving there really is a god, it's at that exact moment the announcer's rumbling voice through the speakers cuts off my comeback. "Number ninety-six, Ethan Kranz!" he says.

"Oh, thank the heavens," Lucy mumbles and the laughter I've been holding tumbles out.

Both girls hop off my lap faster than the Flash, skipping steps to the bottom of the box. "Go, Daddy!" they cheer, their light-up, bedazzled sneakers struggling to keep up with how fast they are jumping.

Ethan runs onto the field, quickly transitioning to a side shuf-fle and aiming his helmet up to the suite.

The fans below us look up, letting out a collective "awwww" at the sight of Clara and Ruth.

"God. That man." Lucy stands, bouncing Oliver and somehow

managing to wave down to the field and not drop the baby. "He's so sexy."

Okay.

Lucy and Ethan are officially the cutest.

The announcer calls out another player who I'm not super familiar with, other than the fact that he brought in about ten thousand at the auction, before Justin's picture pops on the JumboTron.

All the times I've been around Justin, I've never seen him without a big grin plastered on his face. He's probably one of the nicest, happiest guys on the planet, but then again, he snagged Vonnie, so he should be. But the picture on the screen is one of him looking serious, his eyes narrowed in his most intimidating expression. I can't help it, I start to laugh.

"I know," Vonnie says without even asking what I'm laughing at. "He's a big teddy bear. His tough-guy look is ridiculous."

"Number ninety-four, Justin Lamar!" the announcer yells, but I almost can't hear him because the Lamar boys are losing their ever-loving minds.

"Yeah, Dad!" Jagger pounds a fist against his chest so hard that I cringe.

"Go, Dad! Beat those losers!" Jett turns wide, apologetic eyes to Vonnie. "Sorry, Mom," he says before she's even able to scold him.

"Yay, Daddy!" Jax, the youngest of the wild bunch, sounds all sweet and innocent.

They cheer for a few more seconds before Jett accidentally trips into Jagger and Jagger pushes Jett into Jax and Jax starts crying as Jett punches Jagger.

Seriously, in like two point six seconds, it went from a cute father-son scene to WrestleMania.

But it isn't just the boys, because as soon as Jett falls down and

Jax jumps on him, Clara and Ruth yell out, "Dog pile!" and join right in.

Never. Having. Kids.

"Clara! Ruth!" Lucy yells, shoving Oliver into my arms. "Get off of them right now or you lose technology privileges for a week."

"Jett, Jagger, Jax!" Vonnie magically climbs over the table and into the seat in front of us in a single motion like she's not wearing five-inch heels. "Didn't I warn you before we picked up Brynn that you better not act out and embarrass me in front of all the nosy people looking in here? You couldn't even wait until the game started?"

I know both Lucy and Vonnie are low-key mortified right now, so I bite the inside of my cheeks to keep from laughing at them.

While they are busy disassembling the pile of limbs and screaming kids, I lean back into my seat, looking down at Oliver and reconsidering my never-having-kids stance as he does a baby stretch and yawns, shifting the noise-canceling baby headphones that are smashing his chubby little cheeks together.

Oh my god. My uterus.

Of course, because my luck is only the bad kind, when I look up, it's Maxwell's picture staring back at me. And while Justin's made me laugh, Maxwell's makes me melt because, damn, that man knows how to do a smolder.

I stand, clinging on to sweet little Oliver—knowing I don't have the multitasking skills that are only granted to those who have held a baby for more than two minutes—trying to get a good look at Maxwell as he makes his grand entrance.

Fire shoots out of the end of the tunnel, probably a welcome blast of heat compared to the cold Colorado air that has finally arrived, something we are thankfully immune to in our glass box. Maxwell jogs onto the field, pointing to the crowd before breaking into a sprint and jumping up into the air doing an impressive chest bump with Justin.

It's like Cinderella at the ball.

Except, instead of a woman in glass slippers, it's a man in spandex and cleats.

He stands at the front of the group of players, bouncing back and forth to an imaginary beat and chest bumping with the final players that the announcer calls to the field.

"Sorry about that." Lucy shakes her head and tucks the pieces of hair that fell out of her ponytail behind her ears. "You'd think I'd actually have some upper-body strength considering how often I have to pick up deadweight children, but I'm still as flabby and weak as ever. Thanks for holding Olly, I can take him back now."

"I'm fine." I look down at Oliver, who has somehow managed to fall back asleep despite the chaos raging around us. "Go have a drink and something to eat."

"Are you sure?" she asks.

"Positive."

"Oh my god, thank you!" Her shoulders sag in relief. "I dropped my eggs all over his head trying to eat breakfast this morning and I'm starving."

Before I can say anything, she's up through the door and scooping food onto her plate.

"Look at you." Vonnie scoots past me, back to her seat. "You're a natural."

"It's easy because I can give him back if he cries," I joke.

After the hubbub dies down and both teams make their way to their benches, I don't even have to try to find Maxwell this time. He's standing next to the bench, bouncing up and down as the captains stand on the field for the coin toss. He turns, but instead of looking to his seats, his gaze cuts straight to the box.

And I swear, even from hundreds of feet away, I can feel his eyes on me.

I carefully extract one hand from beneath Oliver and offer a lame wave, but when Maxwell waves back, it doesn't feel lame anymore. It feels like I've won the jackpot. Seventy thousand people around us, cheering and dying to be acknowledged by him, and he finds me.

After the auction, I was inundated with phone calls, emails, and meetings.

Maxwell came by Tuesday night to see if I wanted to watch some *Parks and Rec*, but I was so busy, I didn't even leave my office until well after close. When I made it to my dad's house, I couldn't even climb the stairs to my bed and passed out on the couch.

We texted each other a few times, but it always ended with me thinking I sent a text, but actually getting interrupted and not sending the text until hours later.

Add on the producers of *Love the Player* blowing up my phone and showing up uninvited to my office trying to convince me to sign on as an official cast member, and I was an overwhelmed disaster.

When I was climbing into Vonnie's industrial-sized Escalade to come to the game this afternoon, she was busy sending a text to Justin.

"I always send him a good luck text before the game so he can get it in the locker room before he takes the field," she said.

I thought it sounded like a good idea, like a good morning text, except sportier. So I sent one to Maxwell as well. But when Justin texted her back thirty minutes later and I never heard from Maxwell, I began to think he might be annoyed with me for blowing him off.

But now, with his attention focused on me right before he goes into battle, my worries evaporate into thin air and electric excitement fills me instead.

Maxwell lifts his helmet off his head so I can get an unob-
structed view of his smile as he mimics my baby-holding position.
I shrug, carefully pointing to Ethan, who is standing nearby. His
smile grows a notch and he gives me a glove-covered thumbs-up
before putting his helmet back on and jogging to a coach with a
clipboard in his hand.

"Damn, girl. It took Justin and me a few seasons to do the
silent conversations you and Maxwell just had." Vonnie looks at
me from over her sunglasses, even though we are still technically
inside. "Still going with the 'just friends' story?"

"It's not a story." I roll my eyes, trying to hide the smile threatening to break free and the way my stomach is being overrun with
oversized wings fluttering all around. "He's my friend."

I nearly break down and tell her about the art museum, but
I hold it in. It's hard, because I love having him as a friend,
but I know there is chemistry between us and a part of me really—
and I mean *really*—wants to explore it. However, Maxwell is a
literal genius, he's smart enough to know that ruining things with
me could cause mass damage, and I think we're both treading
with extra caution.

Also, he might have a million other girls hooked, but we're not
going to talk about that.

"Whatever you say." Vonnie turns back to the field, her crystal
jersey blinking under the fluorescent lighting of the box.

Special teams take the field, and the Mustangs kicker moves to
the center of the lineup, fiddling with the ball until it is in just the
right position to kick.

Just like last week, the crowd gets on their feet and starts their
slow clap as the kicker walks backward, raising his hand in the
air and signaling for all eleven Mustangs players to take off in a
sprint. The crowd cheers in a perfect crescendo to the arching ball

as it takes flight over the field and into the end zone, where a player in red catches it and drops to his knee.

Half of the crowd stays on their feet, while the others unfold their seats and sit down. The easygoing vibe that had been floating around the box disappears as Ethan, Justin, and Maxwell all take their places on the field. The thought of any of these guys getting injured and going through what Poppy went through last year is terrifying, but even more than that, I know how hard Maxwell works and I want him to perform well.

The quarterback yells something indecipherable from where we are, and the center snaps the ball through his leg and right into the quarterback's hands. The wide receivers take off down the field, and Maxwell backpedals for a few steps before turning and sprinting alongside him. The offensive line does a good job of holding Ethan back, but before the quarterback can find the open player he's looking for, Justin breaks through the line, charging at him.

"Yes, baby!" Vonnie leaps out of her seat, holding on to the edge of the table. "Get him!"

The Lamar boys jump out of their seats, repeating after their mom.

Justin reaches out, snagging the quarterback's jersey, but before he can pull him down, the quarterback spins and breaks free of his grip. He takes two steps to his right, looking down the field to the receiver running next to Maxwell with his hand in the air before pulling his arm back and launching the ball down the sideline.

I stand up, eyes glued to the ball and at the red player pulling slightly in front of Maxwell. Knots form in my stomach, making me feel like I ate rocks before I came here, and my breath gets caught in my throat thinking that the other player has Maxwell beat.

I really should have more faith in him.

The receiver turns with his hands in the air, ready to catch the ball, but just before he can reach for it, Maxwell jumps in front of him, securing the ball against his chest and taking off in the other direction.

The crowd goes insane. Everyone is screaming and jumping up and down as Maxwell runs past offensive players who are now on the defense. He breaks past one tackle, spins around another one, and easily stiff-arms the quarterback, who is his last obstacle.

"Go, go, GO!" I scream, making up for my inability to clap since my hands are full of baby.

He looks over his shoulder, sees he's all alone, and jogs into the end zone, tossing the football to the ref as if he didn't just make the *SportsCenter* highlight reel the very first play of the game. The rest of his teammates catch up to him, jumping up into chest bumps that he meets with equal enthusiasm while others just hit his helmet as he runs by.

I'm still jumping—well, not really. I'm bouncing very gently, screaming like a maniac with everyone else in our box as Oliver sleeps soundly in my arms thanks to his headphones.

But then the world around me freezes when Maxwell takes off his helmet and points to me just as the cameraman zooms into his face, showing a close-up of the way he winks up at me.

My knees go weak and Oliver and I slide back into our seat, my heart pounding against his fuzzy little head.

"Mmm-hmmm," Vonnie mutters. "Friends my ass."

Nineteen

THE GAME WAS A BLOWOUT.

Like so bad that Clara fell asleep before she ever got her tablet and Lucy packed them up at the end of the third quarter. Maxwell ended up with two more interceptions before the coach pulled him out to give the second-string guys some playing time.

"That wasn't even fun," Charli complains from her barstool, taking a deep sip of her beer. "I like a little competition, otherwise what's even the point?"

"Being able to sit back and not be a nervous wreck?" Vonnie says. "These are the only games I enjoy."

"Whatever, win's a win, I guess." Charli shrugs, ready to move on. "Are Aviana and Jac coming tonight?"

"No, thank god," I say. "I can't deal with the *Love the Player* people anymore. I begged them to stay away for a bit and maybe start some drama that would make the producers forget about me."

"You think that's actually going to work?" Vonnie asks.

"No," Charli says at the same time I say, "Yes."

I roll my eyes, wishing I had something to throw at them. Ever since Poppy and TK worked things out, I've been their single-lady project. I need to find them a distraction.

"Welcome to HERS," I call out when the front door opens, letting a rush of cold air into the room.

"Welcome to HERS," I hear Tanya repeat after me from the hostess table. "Would you like to sit at the bar or a table?"

"The bar is perfect, I'm just waiting for someone." I hear the familiar voice that vaguely reminds me of nails on a chalkboard.

My eyes shoot away from my girls sitting in front of me to Eloise Withington looking her polished, flawless self in an emerald pea-coat, a Breton shirt the Fug girls would love, skinny jeans in the perfect dark wash, and ankle boots that are so cute that even though they have a heel, I'd still wear them. "You've got to be fucking kid-ding me," I say under my breath, but still loud enough that Vonnie's and Charli's heads both snap back to see what I'm looking at.

"Oh hell no," Charli says. "What the fuck is she doing here?"

"Hey, girls!" Eloise waves as she makes her way over to us, peeling off her coat as if she's walking a runway.

Charli and Vonnie both turn back to face the bar without ac-knowledging her. It's the kind of loyal, bitchy behavior I love them for. Her steps falter a little at the blatant disregard, but she pow-ers on and takes the open seat next to Charli.

"Hey." I plaster a fake smile across my face. "Fancy seeing you here."

Fancy seeing you here? What the fuck, Brynn? Are you a bar-tender in the Wild Wild West?

She glances at Charli and Vonnie, who still aren't acknowledging her, before smirking at me. Alarms blare in my head as I have seen this smirk multiple times during Lady Mustangs meetings right be-fore someone says something that is liable to bring a person to tears.

"I know, I'm not really a bar girl, I like places that are a little more . . . upscale. But Maxwell thought this would be a good place to meet up since it's where we met." A dreamy look drifts over her face. "He's just so sweet. He even insisted that I sit in his seats at the game tonight."

This garners Vonnie and Charli's attention.

And thank the lord, because they distract her enough that she misses the just-been-punched look that is no doubt written all over my face.

"You do know you didn't pay for a date, right?" Vonnie asks. "It was charity, not prostitution."

"Of course, silly." Eloise pokes Vonnie's shoulder, gambling her life. "The auction wasn't for me personally, I was just the mouth-piece for PWT."

"I'm sure you're great at that," Charli says without looking at her.

"Anyways." Eloise's smile grows scary and she turns her attention back to me. "We got to talking at the event and just really hit it off, so here I am."

So here she is. Looking every bit the part of the athlete's girlfriend. A role, I remind myself, I never wanted. Anybody's girlfriend, actually, but definitely not an athlete's. Vonnie gave up being a lawyer. Marlee moved to another state. Charli had to switch schools to follow Shawn. And I'm not willing to give up anything for a man, no matter how rich or hot he is.

"I'm so happy for you guys," I say so earnestly that all three women in front of me stare at me like I might be on drugs. "You two make a really hot couple."

"Um, thanks," Eloise stutters. It's hard to keep your composure when you're ready for a fight that isn't going to happen.

And with the comical timing that is my life, the door to HERS opens again and Maxwell steps inside, making me question my dedication to staying single.

"Hey, Max!" Tanya raises up a fist and does the fist bump that's become the customary greeting between them both.

"Tan-tan." He says her nickname, and it's so sweet I almost forget he's here to take another woman on a date.

Damn.

The man is a fucking charmer.

"Ladies." He smiles when he reaches the bar, not even a little fazed by the glare Vonnie is aiming at him.

"Nope," Vonnie says. "I'm going to have words with you, but not here." She aims a pointed stare at Eloise. "Not in mixed company."

His eyebrows knit in confusion and he looks to me like I can help him out. I wasn't going to explain, but even if I was, I wouldn't have had enough time.

"Hey! Great game today." Eloise jumps up and wraps her arms around Maxwell. "You ready to go? I'm starving." She grabs her jacket from the back of the barstool and puts it on.

"Yeah, sure," Maxwell says, still looking confused.

"Great." Eloise wraps her hand around his and waves with her free one. "Bye, girls!"

"Bye." I try my hardest not to stare at the way Eloise loops her arm around his and force a smile that I'm afraid might pop some blood vessels in my face.

Max opens his mouth like he might say something else, but at the last minute decides against it and offers a lame wave instead.

I don't watch them leave. I turn to the back of the bar, re-arranging the bottles that I just fixed last night.

I know it's what I need. To have this temptation ripped away from me. But I still don't want to see it happening.

I feel the blast of cold air from the door opening just as Charli says, "What in the entire fuck just happened?"

"Justin might have to hold me back again," Vonnie says. "I never thought Max would be on my shit list."

I turn and look at her with wide eyes. "He destroyed my bar!" I shout.

She rolls her eyes. "He threw a glass and broke some shelves. And he felt so bad about it that he gave you double what you needed to fix it before you could even think to ask."

"Still." I look at my new containers I was able to buy with the leftover money he gave me. "I think that was a little worse than going on a date."

"It just doesn't make sense." Charli ignores me completely. "They don't even work together. Max is so nice and laid back. I barely even know Eloise, and I'm positive she's the polar opposite."

"I agree. Max is too thoughtful to meet a date right in front of Brynn," Vonnie says like I'm not standing here.

"Yeah, he would never." Charli takes a sip of her beer. "Something isn't adding up here."

"Okay," I interject. "I'm going to my office to catch up on paperwork since you guys don't seem to need me anymore."

"Bye," they say in unison before diving back into conspiracy theories as I leave.

"I'LL SEE YOU tomorrow, Tanya."

"Later, Brynn!" she calls out before the door shuts behind her.

HERS is empty.

Charli and Vonnie left a few hours ago. Sundays stay busy during the day, but the evenings clear out faster than most nights. I guess some people are responsible when addressing the upcoming workweek. Just another reason why owning a bar was what I was destined for.

I glance at my watch. We stay open until midnight, but it's already quarter to twelve, so I make the executive decision to lock up early.

I trudge across the floors, the voices of the Real Housewives of

Atlanta yelling at one another and my sneakers squeaking against the tile creating my favorite HERS soundtrack.

Just as I'm about to reach the door, a large figure appears, pushing the heavy glass door open as if it's a feather.

I jump back, his unexpected presence shaking my nerves a bit.

"Hi," I say on a squeal. "I was just about to lock up."

"Sorry." The man holds his hands out. Now that some of my surprise has ebbed, I note that he's very attractive. "I didn't mean to startle you."

"No." I wave off his apology. "You're fine."

And he is. He's tall, well over six feet tall, and muscular. His mocha completion is highlighted beneath his white T-shirt, though he's not wearing a jacket, which makes me question his sanity. And there's something so familiar about him, I just can't seem to put my finger on it.

"I was just seeing if someone was here, but I see that you're empty."

"Oh, yeah. Sundays get quiet quickly here." I look behind me at the empty tables and scattered chairs. "Who were you looking for? Lots of women come in and out of here."

I don't know why I asked that.

Sure, he's good looking, but he could still be crazy, and I'd never give information on one of my customers to a stranger.

"I'm not actually looking for a woman." The corners of his mouth quirk. "I heard about the event here the other day, so I thought I'd see if Maxwell Lewis was here."

Oh. A fan. Which might make this even creepier.

"Oh yeah, that event was a onetime thing, he doesn't come in here usually," I lie.

"Really? That's not what I heard." His tipped lips now grow into a full-blown smile.

"Who'd you hear that from?" I ask, the beginnings of unease starting to race through my system.

"My dad." He cringes a bit. "I forgot to introduce myself." He extends his hand to shake mine. "I'm Theo Lewis, Maxwell's brother."

Twenty

"MAXWELL HAS A BROTHER?" POPPY ATTEMPTS—AND FAILS—TO whisper. "How has he never mentioned him before?"

"Who knows?" Considering I didn't know either, I am clearly not the authority on all things Maxwell Lewis. "Theo said they are half brothers, same dad, but Theo mainly lived with his mom growing up."

"Who cares about that?" Charli leans in, succeeding where Poppy failed and keeping her voice down. "Is he hot? I mean, have we been out here living our lives not knowing there is Maxwell hotness multiplied?"

Three sets of eyes focus in, waiting for my answer like I'm about to give them the key to world peace and climate change. "I mean, he's attractive, and once he told me he was his brother, I was able to see some of Maxwell in him." I think Maxwell is better looking, but no way am I putting that out there. "Theo is bigger—taller. He's a police officer, so he keeps in shape, just not professional athlete shape."

"Oh lawd." Vonnie falls back into her seat, fanning herself. Not that she's dramatic or anything. "The other Lewis brother also wears a uniform and carries handcuffs? Somebody needs to write that book."

"Nope." I pull their drinks away from them—well, not Poppy's. She's been craving Shirley Temples, and I'm afraid I'd lose my arm if I touched hers. "I am not dealing with you today."

"Paisley," Vonnie calls across the room. "Come get your girl."

"I'll be right there!" Paisley yells back as she leads two women to their table.

"I'm the boss!"

Ugh. Why do I even bother?

"Anyways . . ." Charli reaches for her drink, also not fazed by my threats. "The guys are going to be here soon. We demanded a date night since tomorrow they have to spend the day with whoever won the auction. We're gonna go next door to play Ping-Pong, if you wanna come."

I look around HERS, and the crowd is decent, but not overwhelming. "I should be able to sneak out for a bit."

"Good." Poppy pops a cherry in her mouth. "Because we told Max you were coming and I'm pretty sure it's the only reason he agreed."

"He's seeing Eloise." Her name tastes bitter in my mouth. "I don't think he's worried about me."

I wonder if, when they were together, he dedicated all of his attention to her or if he was checking his phone like he does with me? Is she the one he's willing to give that all up for? I mean, I wouldn't blame him if she was. She's a lawyer who probably doesn't make up words and definitely dresses like an adult woman. I'm kind of—FINE! Totally—a disaster. Yes, HERS is thriving, but every other aspect of my life is like a reality show gone wrong.

"He is not seeing her." Vonnie drains the remainder of her martini. "Justin asked him and Max said they just talked about the details for tomorrow."

"Oh yeah, I'm so sure that's why he took her to dinner and gave her football tickets." I narrow my eyes and purse my lips. These girls are more worried about our relationship than I am.

Charli opens her mouth to say something, but—luckily for me—her phone lights up in front of her. "Wrap it up, ladies." She shoves her phone into her Louis bag. "The guys are next door."

I wave them away. "I'm gonna take care of a few things and then I'll meet you over there."

"If you try and bail, we'll come over and drag you next door," Poppy threatens. "So save yourself the embarrassment."

Geez. I thought pregnancy was supposed to make you all loving and one with the earth. I'm beginning to think she's carrying the spawn of Satan or something.

"Okay." I lift my hands up in surrender. "But only because you scare me."

She stands, tossing her purse over her shoulder and pulling her long curls from beneath the strap. "As long as you come, I'm okay with that."

They snake their way through the tables, Vonnie stopping to talk to a couple of customers who recognize her from the interviews she did leading up to the auction, and then they're gone and the volume at HERS seems as if it has decreased by about ten decibels.

"You good back here? I'm going to head to my office," I ask Abby, the other bartender working tonight.

"Yup," she says as she pours beer out of the tap. "I'll holler if I need you."

I push into my office and take a deep breath. I know most people get stressed when they walk into a cluttered office with a desk covered in loose papers that are trying to escape to the floor, but not me. Because I remember when I opened HERS and didn't know if I would last a year and was praying for the kind of chaos swirling around my life now.

I do probably need to do some filing though.

I spin my desk chair with the flourish of a six-year-old and throw my body onto it, squeezing my eyes shut and hoping that I don't land on the floor.

"Eeee!" I throw my hands in the air and bring my knees to my chest, riding out my victory.

"What are you doing?" a deep voice says.

I immediately slam my feet to the floor and my hands to my desk like that somehow saves face.

"Gotta make work interesting, am I right?" All the blood from my body has relocated to my face, whether from spinning or the mortification of Maxwell Lewis catching me acting like a toddler, we will never know.

"You're a nut." He shakes his head, his smile unwavering as he moves farther into my office.

"This is not a new development." I watch as he lowers his black-denim-clad legs into my Barbie-sized, armless acrylic chair. His body is much too big for it, but it doesn't seem to bother him as he leans back, shoulders relaxed, his long legs sprawled out. "Would you like to know what is a new development?"

"That you're better at Ping-Pong than you are at dominoes?"

"Hey!" I push out of my chair, pointing an unpolished nail at him. "That's not fair. I'd never played before, and I'm pretty sure that TK was sabotaging me!"

Last summer, TK had a barbecue, and some might say I was a bit of a sore loser when he tried to teach me to play dominoes. I'm not proud of it, but it happened.

"Whoa there, killer." He raises his hands in surrender.

"Sorry." I sit back down. "I'm a little competitive."

"You don't say." His voice—and body—shakes with laughter.

"Whatever." I roll my eyes and look to the computer that I still haven't turned on. I click my mouse and type "Aceisthegreatest" into the password field. Ace obviously was here the day my new computer was delivered, and I couldn't say no to him. I did however draw the line at "#Wheresthelie." It was just too long, and who uses hashtags anymore? "What I was going to say"—I glance at him as the files open on my screen—"was that you have a brother you never told me about!" There's a little too much pep in my voice and my smile feels too large.

In fact, I'm working so hard at looking unbothered that I nearly miss the instant change in Maxwell. His back shoots straight up and his hands ball into fists on his thighs.

"Did you google me?" he asks, trying—and failing—to joke.

"Um, no." I choose my words carefully. "He came in last night right before I closed."

"You're talking about Theo, right?" he asks.

"Yeah, tall, matching eyes, police officer?" I tick off, leaving out that he's not quite as good looking as the Lewis brother who's in front of me, practically vibrating with something I'm not sure I understand.

"Did he say where he's staying?"

I shake my head. "No, he just said he'd come back soon if he didn't hear from you."

"Fuck." Maxwell scrubs his hand over his face. "Listen, if he comes back, call me."

"Okay . . ." I drag out the word.

"No, Brynn." He stands and walks around the desk until he's standing over me. "I mean it. Do not talk to him. Do not engage. If you see him, call me and get away from him."

My eyebrows furrow, and fear snakes down my spine. "You're freaking me out."

He places his hands on my armrests. "I don't trust my brother, so being freaked isn't a bad thing."

"I mean, he's a cop though," I say, mainly trying to make myself feel better. "He can't be that bad, Max."

"That little bit of power makes it easier for him to be the worst kind of person. And, Brynn." He's so close that I see his jaw twitch and every emotion fighting for dominance across his flawless face. "You call me Maxwell."

And then I don't see what emotion wins because his lips are on mine and my eyes close as the world around me explodes.

I have kissed a lot of guys—and I mean a lot of guys—but I have never, not ever, had a kiss like this.

Admittedly, most of the kissing I have done in my life was me rushing them to get to the meat of the event or sloppy and in a bar as I bid farewell to my acquaintance of the night.

So I'm not one hundred percent sure whether my mind is being blown to smithereens because I'm kissing a man whom I actually care about—I have heard that actually liking the person you're kissing can make a difference—or because of his skillful, full, soft lips.

Maybe both.

Because holy shit. His mouth is perfection. The way he gradually increases pressure, not trying to thrust his tongue into my mouth. How he tugs my bottom lip with his teeth, then lets go and closes his mouth over mine again. I'm not in charge of my body anymore. My hands move to the back of his head of their own accord, pulling him closer to me, wanting everything he's willing to give me. His hands trace the outline of my body, gliding over the small curve of my waist, one hand slipping beneath my

T-shirt, his rough, calloused hands a stark contrast to the silky pillows that are his lips.

I open my mouth, sliding my tongue into his mouth, but that's as far as I get before he takes over, setting the tempo, the rhythm of this sensual dance.

My skin is supercharged, sensitive enough that even the slight breeze from the heater sets my skin on fire, the loose strands of hair against my neck cause shivers to race down my spine, and the feel of Maxwell's hands against my back makes me wonder if it's physically possible to orgasm from kissing and gentle caressing alone.

The way my stomach tightens and my thighs clench together leads me to believe that not only is it possible, it's probable.

"Poppy texted me to come take over and—oh! Sorry!" My dad bursts into my office, effectively extinguishing any and all embers of lust floating around the room. "I . . . um . . . hey, Max." He nods to Maxwell, *not* leaving like I assume most normal people would do in this situation.

"Mr. Sterling." Maxwell straightens, tucking his hands into his pockets. "Um, sorry about that."

Sorry!

"Don't be sorry." My dad waves him off. "You two are adults, don't mind me."

"It's hard not to mind you when you're still standing here, Dad." I push to my feet, grabbing Maxwell's arm and tugging him past my cock-blocking dad. "We're going to play Ping-Pong now."

I don't wave to Abby or Paisley or anybody as I stomp to the front door, yanking Maxwell along with me.

Screw Ping-Pong. I'd much rather try my hand at tonsil hockey.

Twenty-one

DEATH.

I feel like death has come for me. I am going to die all alone in my empty apartment with pictures of strangers still in my frames.

Ping-Pong was—begrudgingly—a really good time. I had a bad attitude at the beginning but once we split into women versus the men and made full-on brackets, my competitive side couldn't help but be all the way in.

We ordered a disgusting amount of food. I drank drinks with far too much sugar content, and I laughed as the professional athletes got their asses so handed to them that Shawn actually threw a tantrum and left.

When it was all over, I almost gave in and went to my dad's, but after the earlier events of the night, I didn't want to deal with his questions.

If only I had the emotional maturity of an actual adult woman, I would've dealt with the minor discomfort of discussing my love life with my dad and moved on. Then I wouldn't be in my apartment, facing death all alone.

I was a little queasy on the drive home, but I figured anybody would be after shoveling the amount of crap I did into my mouth. I'd go home, drink some water, and sleep it off.

Wrong.

I slept for maybe an hour before the churning in my stomach startled me out of my sleep. I rolled out of bed, and even that motion made my stomach hurt so bad, I had to lie with my body half on and half off my bed before I was convinced I wouldn't decorate my beige carpet with the nachos and chocolate cheesecake from earlier.

I crawled—literally crawled—through my bedroom and into my bathroom.

I didn't even bother to turn on the lights as my hands and knees dredged along the cold tiles to the bathtub. I turned the knob, hearing the rush of water and keeping my hand under the faucet just until I felt it heat, then I collapsed to the floor, resting my head on the floor mat, thankful that I splurged on the memory foam one.

When the bathwater was high enough, I damn near dove into it, hopeful that warm water would do the trick and help bring some relief.

Wrong again.

Did you know you could get seasick from a bath?

Neither did I.

I tried to ignore the telltale sign of sweat beading on my forehead, blaming it on the water being too warm. I rolled over, letting my cheek rest against the cool, porcelain ledge of the tub, thinking that if I immersed my stomach beneath the water, I'd magically feel better. Instead, it made everything worse. The water gently lapping around me caused my body to float slightly among the ripples. My vision swam, dizziness propelling the nausea when, suddenly, I was jumping out of the tub, racing to the toilet as fast as the vomit raced up my throat.

I just made it and spent what might have been hours emptying the contents of my stomach. Then maybe hours more choking on the taste of bile and retching because there was nothing left to come up. I yanked the decorative towels off the towel bar, using them as makeshift blankets to cover my shivering body, and fell asleep in front of the toilet like I did that one time in college.

Ringing wakes me up.

I don't know what time it is. All I know is the sun is shining into my bedroom. I try to make a mental note to order new curtains because the ones I have clearly don't do shit.

I pull myself up using the counter as leverage and as soon as I catch a glimpse of myself in the mirror, I want to throw up again.

And I do.

But more from the motion of standing up than my face.

My dad always makes fun of me because I "don't know how to throw up." I strain my face. I fight a losing battle and then when it comes, I try to force the contents out. And after I've been sick, I'm a splotchy mess because I have, quite literally, burst the blood vessels in my face.

I don't know what I'm throwing up. Maybe the lining in my stomach? Maybe I'll throw up my organs and that's what's going to kill me. At least I'll have some cool postmortem special on TLC.

To try and postpone my death for as long as possible, I grab my bathroom trash can and make the trek to my living room. I grab my phone, about to send Paisley a text that I need her to open HERS today, only to see multiple texts from her asking where I am and that she opened. I text her back, hoping I reach her before she sends some poor, unassuming police officer to my apartment of doom for a wellness check.

Stomach flu.

I was going to send more, but even the tapping of the letters and the flashing on my screen cause my nausea to roll back in.

I squeeze my eyes shut—wishing I paid more attention in first Communion classes and remembered any of the prayers they taught me—and wait for the nausea to pass enough that I can grab a glass and some crackers from the kitchen.

Even though my throat is so parched that I'm sure if vomiting up my intestines doesn't kill me, dehydration will, I still don't get water. I remember when I was sick as a kid, my mom lying in bed with me, holding a bucket in one hand and a glass of ice in the other. She'd said water was too heavy and would make my stomach hurt worse, so she'd lie with me for hours, giving me a spoonful of ice whenever I asked, running her slender fingers through my hair when she wasn't spoon-feeding me. It's one of the few positive memories I have left of her and so I choose not to question it.

I move at a sloth's pace back to my couch, hoping my slow and even steps will ward off any more bile trying to escape my stomach. I lower myself onto my couch at a speed that challenges the most demanding exercise instructor's squats, closing my eyes and releasing a moan that holds more pleasure than any one-night stand I've ever had.

My phone lights up and chimes beside me.

Paisley: Oh no! Do you need me to bring you anything?

I love that she asked. I'm proud of HERS for so many reasons, but I think number one on that list is creating a community of strong women who support and care about each other. Women get such a bad rap, but there's nothing more powerful than a group of women. And every day in my bar, I'm surrounded by women who spend their nights laughing with new and old friends and handing out genuine compliments like it's the most natural thing in the world—which I'm pretty sure it is.

Still, I love Paisley too much to ever expose her to the state of my apartment . . . and my face. My fingers dance over the screen.

> Stay away. It's a straight horror movie over here. Vomit.
> Everywhere.

The bubbles pop up on my screen immediately.

Paisley: You don't have to tell me twice. But if you want me to drop soup outside your door, don't hesitate to ask! Don't worry about rushing back in, we have it under control. Take care of yourself.

I send back a random string of emojis that make no sense put together, but I know that Paisley will love it. She's basically a human emoji.

I lean over to grab the remote from my coffee table, and my nonexistent abs groan in protest. I mean, the stomach flu isn't the most ideal workout routine, but if it causes an ab or two to pop out, I'll take it. Rainbow to every storm and all that jazz.

I turn on the TV and Amy Poehler's smiling face greets me. I almost click, but my favorite part of *Parks and Rec* has turned into watching it with Maxwell. What's the point of Tom Haverford without hearing Maxwell's deep chuckle?

Maxwell.

Shit.

We kissed.

It was amazing and long and did I say amazing?

Fuck.

We kissed and now I'm like a scene straight out of *The Exorcist*. I have to warn him. Nothing says "please kiss me again" like telling a guy you may have given him the stomach flu.

I scroll down to Maxwell's name.

> Hey. Just warning you that I ended up with some wicked stomach bug last night. I hope I didn't give it to you.

I hit Send and stare at my phone, waiting for the bubbles to pop up, but they never do. Then I remember that it's Tuesday and Maxwell is with Eloise at Pearson, Withington, and Thomas.

I never even asked what was going on with him and Eloise. They could be dating. I could've kissed a guy with a girlfriend. And Eloise. Oh lord. The thought of Eloise's hands all over Maxwell makes me sick.

Literally.

I grab the trash can and stick my head inside, trying to empty my already empty stomach. By the time I'm finished, I fall back onto my couch, peeking at my TV through tired eyes, and suddenly feel like Amy's smiling face is now mocking me.

"Fuck off," I mutter.

I hit the Power button with a little too much force and fall asleep on my couch without even cleaning out my trash can, and discover a new rock bottom.

Twenty-two

THE DEEP BANG OF THUNDER WAKES ME UP. THERE AREN'T MANY thunderstorms this time of the year, but in Colorado, you learn to expect the unexpected.

Sweat is pouring off of me, but my teeth are still somehow chattering. I don't know whether to cling to my blanket or toss it across the room.

"Brynn!" a deep, familiar voice calls at the same time I realize that it wasn't thunder, but someone knocking on my door, that woke me up.

Now, pride is not something I possess in spades, but Maxwell seeing me like this is something I'm pretty sure I could go my entire life without experiencing.

"Brynn!" he shouts out again. "If you don't let me know you're alive, I'm calling the police . . . or your dad."

"Hold on." I try to yell, but my throat is raw from throwing up.

I toss my blanket to the side, but when I look down and see that my white T-shirt is now transparent thanks to sweat, I wrap myself up like a burrito and make my way to the door as fast as my stomach allows.

I crack the door open and peer into the hallway at Maxwell, who is holding plastic and paper bags. "I'm alive," I croak. "You do not want to come in here." I cast a quick glance back at my couch and I swear, the vomit-filled trash can is mocking me. "Trust me."

"I thought you said stomach bug, why does it sound like you have strep?"

"I think it hurts from how much I've been throwing up," I say. "But, with my luck, I probably managed to simultaneously catch strep and the flu."

"Go lie down," he demands, pushing the door open and ignoring my warning. "I brought Gatorade, crackers, and soup. I'll call my doctor, she makes house calls."

I want to stay and fight him on all of this, but as his foot hits my entryway, I gather all of my strength and run to the couch, grabbing the little trash can and rushing to the bathroom to rinse and empty it. I might not be able to avoid letting him see me, but I can do my damnedest not to let him see that grossness.

Only one problem.

I don't have any strength left to gather.

The ice I was going to eat is melted in the glass on my coffee table. Plus, on top of throwing up everything from last night, I still haven't eaten today.

So even though I make it to the bathroom, the room starts to spin around me the second my feet hit the tile. That combined with the odor from my trash can do me in. So instead of Maxwell being free from my trash can, he gets a front row seat to the next show.

Fuck. My. Life.

I fall to the floor—my knees hitting the ground with such force, I know they'll be black and blue tomorrow—and heave into the toilet. I curse what I said about abs, each wave feels like a round in a ring of getting punched in my stomach. My throat feels as though I drank lighter fluid and swallowed a lit match. The sounds of my retching mix with my sobs as tears stream down my face and I pray for this to be over.

Suddenly, my heavy hair stuck to my neck is gathered to the top of my head and a hand is gently rubbing circles on my back. "You're all right, Brynn," Maxwell whispers, his voice the only piece of calm in the shit storm swirling around me. "Get it out, you're okay."

At last, the heaving fades and I fall to the side of the toilet, landing without any dignity or grace on the floor.

"Fuck," Maxwell hisses, and I'm sure if I had the energy to open my eyes, I'd see a face filled with regret that he didn't heed my advice to get the fuck outta Dodge. "I'll be right back."

"I'll be waiting," I mumble, my words beginning to slur.

I'm not sure if I fall asleep or pass out, but when my eyes open, the shower is running and Maxwell is lifting me to my feet.

"Take a sip," he says, and I'm suddenly aware of the straw pressed to my lips.

I part my mouth slightly, which is harder than I imagined considering my mouth is usually one thing I never shut.

I take a small, hesitant sip. As thirsty as I am, I'm even more nervous to throw up again. But when the fruity flavor hits my tongue, I damn near groan in ecstasy. I let go of my death grip on Maxwell's arm and cling to the glass, gulping down whatever this is.

Then Maxwell pulls it away.

"Hey!" I whine, desperate to have more.

"If you drink it too fast, you're going to get sick again." He raises the straw to my mouth, but doesn't let me hold the glass. "Small, frequent sips."

"Whatever." I want to argue, but my stomach is already start-ing to swirl and groan.

He lets me have a few more sips before he takes the glass and sets it on my bathroom counter. "I called my doctor, she'll be here in an hour." He points to the shower, its glass door starting to fog up from the steam. "I thought you might want a shower. I'm go-ing to sit in your room while you're in there. Leave the bathroom door open, and if you start to feel dizzy or you need me, just yell and I'll be there."

I nod, but words don't come out as something other than bile warms my stomach. Besides my dad, no man has ever gone out of his way for me. Which, to be fair, is partly by my design. It's not something I've ever wanted. But standing in my bathroom, smell-ing like a zoo exhibit and looking like the zombie apocalypse has begun, Maxwell is still staring at me like I'm a fucking treasure.

I would never ask him for help, but it's nice to have the offer.

"Is that okay?" he asks, misconstruing my silence for objec-tion. "Of course you can close the door if you want and I can go sit on the couch if that makes you more comfortable."

"No," I say adamantly. "You can stay in my room. Thank you."

He nods, pulling his full lips between his teeth. A shy look that doesn't seem to belong crosses his perfect face before he turns on his heel and leaves the room.

I do my best to avoid the mirror as I strip out of my disgusting sweat- and vomit-stained clothes. Not only is Maxwell the nicest guy ever for coming to check on me, he's a fucking saint for get-ting so close—the stench coming from my body is downright offensive.

I step under the warm stream of water, and all else is forgot-ten. I scrub my body, wash my hair, and brush my teeth, and by the time I get out, I feel human again. It's amazing what a good shower can do for a person.

I step into my room, forgetting that Maxwell is there until I see his legs dangling off of my freshly made bed.

"You made my bed?" I don't even make my bed.

"Oh, yeah." He scissors up and off of it. "It felt weird just sitting here, I figured I could help out a little bit. I hope you don't mind that I went through your stuff."

"Uh . . . no. Not at all." I grab on to my towel, afraid that despite being sick, I'll toss it off and jump him. "I actually really appreciate it."

The corners of his mouth tip up slightly and he opens his mouth to say something but is cut off by his phone's ringtone cutting through the awkward tension. He grabs his phone off of my bed, glancing at the screen before swiping and putting it to his ear.

"Hello," he says in the deep, professional voice I heard when he was signing autographs and doing interviews. "Yes, that's the building. I'll come down and get you." He hangs up the phone and tucks it into his back pocket, making me aware for the first time of the jeans he's wearing and how freaking well they fit him. "That was Dr. Bowen, I'm going to grab her from the parking lot and then we'll be back up. Are you okay for me to leave?"

"I think I'll be able to survive five minutes on my own." Not even the stomach flu can beat back my sarcasm.

"Smart-ass." He smiles and crosses the small space between us. "But I'm glad to hear you joking a bit, you had me worried."

Then he leans in and drops a chaste kiss on my cheek and goes to let in the doctor.

I watch him until the front door shuts behind him, my hand absentmindedly moving to my face, the spot where his lips touched me still tingling.

Twenty-three

"SO YOU GUYS ARE TOGETHER NOW," VONNIE SAYS, CRACKING open one of the Gatorades Maxwell dropped off this morning for herself.

"No." I tuck my feet beneath my butt, thankful that I'm finally able to hold food down, not thankful that the forty-eight hours of vomiting seems to have zapped away any extra cushion my ass had to offer. "We haven't talked about that at all, he's just been a really good friend."

A good friend who still found every opportunity to hold my hand, rub my back, and give me quick kisses whenever he could.

"Girl." Vonnie aims her renowned side-eye at me. "The man braved your nasty-ass apartment, chanced getting the stomach flu, and took care of you. He's your man. No man does that for someone they don't want to be with. Hell, I don't even help Justin when he's sick. I only risk my health for my kids."

"What about Eloise?" I voice the question that's been running on a loop through my head for the last four days.

"What about it?" she asks. "If you're still not convinced that man is into you after he risked the ire of an entire sports fandom to take care of you, then ask him. Life is too damn short to let all of these hypothetical situations run rampant in your mind. Don't twist a really good thing into something bad. I don't think he's the kind of person to drag you along when he's not interested."

When Maxwell and Dr. Bowen walked into my apartment, she took one look at me and deemed me severely dehydrated. She pulled out a banana bag, stuck a needle in my vein, and made me rest while pushing fluids back into my body. Maxwell turned on *Parks and Rec* and sat next to me, explaining the merits of the show to a very skeptical doctor. When the bag was empty and all was said and done, she prescribed me fluids, rest, and no actual drugs.

What's the point of a doctor if they don't give you medicine?

I figured Maxwell would head out with her, but instead he camped out on my couch for the rest of the night, making sure I drank enough and even holding my hair back when the second wave of nausea came over me in the middle of the night. Besides when he has to be at work, he hasn't left me since. Even if that means watching film on the couch next to me on his computer as I binge on the latest season of *Vanderpump Rules*.

"Okay, I'm going to tell you something, but you have to promise not to make a big deal over it." I brace myself, knowing this conversation could go in two very different directions.

"You know, after that opening, I can't make that promise, but you're going to tell me anyway."

Crap. I knew that was going to happen.

"Fine, but remember that I'm in a fragile state right now and—"

"Girl!" she interrupts me. "Just talk!"

"Fine." I take a deep breath, knowing I'm never going to hear the end of it after I fess up. "So remember that time I got a flat on the highway and Maxwell came to get me?"

"Yes . . ."

"Well, the next day when he dropped me off at the mechanic, he asked me to lunch."

Vonnie jumps up, her Gatorade splashing out of the bottle and onto my couch. "I knew there was more to that story!"

"Yeah, well, when he picked me up for lunch, he had Slurpees and taquitos in his car." I smile thinking of the supersweet details of the day, but when I look at Vonnie, her eyebrows are drawn in a deep V, not at all impressed with the 7-Eleven delicacies. "That morning I told him how much I loved Slurpees and taquitos, so he brought me tons of them and took me to the art museum.

"When you all had him ambush me at the beer tasting, I mentioned that picking the chairs for HERS was crazy difficult. He remembered that and took me to the new exhibit at the art museum about contemporary chairs." Even knowing how the date ended, my heart still flutters at how thoughtful and attentive he can be.

"Oh, shoot. That's cute as fuck." Even Vonnie has hearts in her eyes now. "Justin has never taken me to the art museum for a surprise date."

"Right? I thought so too!" I lean back into my couch, hating the next part of the story. "So we're looking at the chairs and his phone keeps going off and he keeps sending them to voicemail. Finally, I told him to just answer so whoever it was would stop calling."

"Uh-oh." Vonnie bites her lip.

"Yup," I agree. "So he excuses himself and answers the phone, and when I find him, I hear him telling the person to meet him at the team hotel and that he'd text them the address later." The disappointment that weighs me down feels as heavy as it did the day it happened. Maybe even heavier now that we've kissed and he's been so sweet.

"Is that it?" Vonnie asks, the deep-V eyebrows back.

"What do you mean is that it? He invited another girl back to the hotel while he was out with me!" If I thought it wouldn't cause me to throw up, I'd strangle her. "I thought we were on a date, and he was making other plans . . . at a hotel! Nothing innocent can happen at a hotel!"

"All right, Brynn." Vonnie puts the lid on her Gatorade and repositions her body so I can't escape her eye contact. She's like the human version of those creepy Renaissance paintings. "You are new to this football thing, so I'm going to enlighten you. When these guys go to the hotel, they are on a strict schedule with the tightest security you can imagine. Justin's rookie year, he told me to come to the hotel with him, and not only did I get kicked out before I even made it to the elevator, Justin was fined ten grand. Maxwell is a longtime veteran, he knows this. Whoever he was talking to, and you don't even know if it was a woman, he invited them there because he knew he'd have a controlled environment and wouldn't be able to talk for long. Nothing happened and I'd put money on it."

"Wait . . ." I try and comprehend everything she just said. "Are you serious?"

"Dead." She shakes her head and I'm pretty sure I know how her kids feel when she's disappointed in them. "You've been looking so hard for a reason not to try with him that you've ignored how into you he obviously is."

"Okay, so what if he is into me?" Even the thought of it causes my stomach to flutter. "Then what? I mess it up somehow? I am my mother's daughter. What if after all of this, we start seeing each other and I pull a Holly Sterling and become disinterested and leave him in the dust? Would I lose you guys? I can't chance that."

"I don't know your mother, something I think I'm very grateful for, but I know that you are not her." Vonnie wraps her hand around mine. "A lot of us have shit parents, it's the most overpopulated club there is. But the best part about it is that we have a road map on exactly what not to do in life. I had to go to school and find a strong, dependable man. You just have to not be a horrible person and you're killing it. Don't let your demons ruin something that could be really good."

I need to find friends who aren't so smart and wise.

"Why do you push me to become a better person?" I throw my head back onto the couch like I'm auditioning for a role in a soap opera. "Fine, you're right. I'll talk to him when he comes over."

"That's my girl," Vonnie says, yanking the remote out of my lap. "Now turn this shit on. I have to pick up my kids in two hours, I need to see what Jo and Chip think I should do with my living room next."

"I BROUGHT PANERA!" Maxwell holds up two massive bags as he makes his grand entrance.

"Did you invite someone else?" I look at the empty doorway behind him.

"No, I just brought options. Three different soups, a few different sandwiches, two pastas, and salad, but I figured lettuce can be hard on your stomach, so I only got one of those."

And that's the moment I fell in love.

Kidding.

Kinda.

My stomach starts to growl. I've been living on saltines, juice, and ice for the last four days. I'm pretty sure I now have a legitimate fear of throwing up, and I've been too nervous to eat anything. But the smell of Panera wafting through my apartment is one way to guarantee that I at least try to eat.

"Oh my god." I close my eyes, breathing in the fresh-baked goodness as Maxwell starts pulling out all the containers of food and lining them up on my countertop. "You are my favorite person in the entire world." My eyes fly open. "I mean . . . you know what I mean. I'm hungry and this smells amazing."

"If I knew sandwiches were the key to your heart, I would've hit Panera up instead of groveling for so long." He winks. "Now, come make your plate."

I want to shovel everything in my mouth, but the memory of using the toilet seat as a pillow forces some self-control—just not a ton of it. I nab the chicken noodle soup and almost squeal when I see my favorite sandwich. "This is the best!" I grab half of it from the unfolded paper wrapper.

"Yeah, your dad told me." He hands me the yellow Gatorade from the fridge. "I just wasn't sure if you'd want to branch out or if it would still sound good, hence all of the options."

My eyes go wide and I stop walking. "You called my dad?"

"Was that not okay?" he asks, suddenly looking nervous. "I would've called you, but if you were sleeping, I didn't want to wake you up. I figured your dad would know what you like."

"No, I don't mind." I stare at him, my conversation with Vonnie from earlier running through my mind. "You didn't have to do any of this, I just really appreciate it."

"Of course I had to." His eyebrows furrow together and he takes a step toward me. "Brynn, I don't know where you are, but I really care about you."

"What about Eloise?"

His head jerks back. "Eloise?" One of his hands moves to the base of his neck like he's trying to work out a knot that's just appeared. "What about her?"

"I mean . . . I thought . . . Are you seeing each other?" My grip on my plate is so tight, I'm worried I might snap it in half, but I can't seem to loosen it.

"Eloise Withington? No . . . no. Not at all," he says with steel in his voice. "Where'd you get that from?"

"From her." My eyes dart around the kitchen, trying to find anything to look at other than Maxwell's gorgeous, confused face. "She said you gave her your tickets to the game and then you guys went out after."

"Brynn." He touches his hand to my cheek. "Will you please look at me, I need you to see me when I tell you this."

I pull my lips between my teeth and nod, staring deep into his light brown eyes. Nausea rolls in my stomach, but for the first time in days, I think it's from nerves and not the need to actually throw up. Or at least, I hope so. I'm pretty sure throwing up all over his shoes could ruin the moment.

"There is nothing going on between me and Eloise," he says. "She paid a lot of money to have me at her father's firm. You know me, the idea that she could spend that kind of money and I wouldn't deliver made me a nervous wreck. I offered my tickets because it felt like the least I could do, and then we had dinner and talked about what I could expect when I went into PWT." He moves his hand to the back of my neck and squeezes gently, never dropping eye contact. "That's all we talked about. She seems very smart and nice, but the only person I have feelings for is you."

Thank god I don't have silverware on my plate, it'd be rattling like crazy with how much my hands are shaking.

"You are the most interesting, insanely beautiful woman I have ever met." He inches closer, eating up the small space that

separates us. "I haven't pushed anything because I just love having you in my life, in whatever capacity you wanted. You make
me forget about football and remind me of who I am outside of it
and that sometimes, the best part of life is sitting on the couch
and laughing with your best friend."

I don't know when I stopped chewing on my lips, but now I'm
staring at him with my mouth hanging open. "Wow."

Wow?

I never stop talking, and in the moment where I really need to
say something beautiful and poignant, all I can say is "Wow."

FML.

"It's not that . . . I mean—I . . ." I stop and take a deep breath,
trying to find an ounce of composure inside. "I care about you,
too. It's just, I've never done the relationship thing before, and
after seeing what being attached to an athlete has done to my
friends, I'd be lying if I said that didn't make me nervous."

There.

I said it. Like a fucking adult woman who knows how to com-
municate.

"I'd have to be intentionally obtuse not to see that a relationship
was not on your to-do list." He pulls my plate from my shaking hands
and rests it on the counter, wrapping my hands in his. "You are the
most fiercely independent woman I've ever known. It's both intimidating as fuck and the biggest turn-on. I've been around for those
relationships as well, and I've watched and learned from them the
same way you have. If you give us a chance, I'll never make you
choose. I would never test your independence or dedication to your
career."

He keeps causing my mind to go blank. How do you respond
to that? Nothing I can say can measure up to the words this
man—who honestly might moonlight as a poet—says to me.

So with my mind blank and without overthinking it, I don't say anything. I roll onto my toes and touch my lips to his.

"I want to give us a chance," I tell him before I pull my hands from his and wrap them behind his head. I kiss him deeper this time, hoping I'm not contagious anymore, but not caring that much because for the first time in my life, I have a boyfriend.

Twenty-four

"YOU LOOK LIKE THE HEART-EYES EMOJI," CHARLI SAYS.

I do.

"I do not!" I shout anyways. Gotta keep my street cred and all that.

"You kind of do," Jacqueline pipes in quietly. "But it looks good on you."

"Whatever," I mumble. I'm physically unable to yell at Jacqueline the way I do the rest of the girls, she's just too sweet and I'm already afraid we're going to break her.

"I'd look like the heart-eye emoji too if I had Max in my bed," Vonnie says.

I look at Vonnie, my eyes wide in horror that she would say that in my bar packed to the brim with strangers just waiting to hear the newest bit of gossip to take home and bring to the *Love the Player* blogs and chat rooms . . . if chat rooms are even a thing anymore. "Jesus, would you like a megaphone so you can announce my business to the entire world?" The only saving grace is that the film crew isn't set to get here for another hour, so at least it won't end up on TV.

"I don't know why you haven't," Vonnie yells. "Maxwell Lewis is *your* man. I'd be shouting that shit from the rooftops."

"Is he as sweet in bed as he is out of it?" Aviana asks, clearly ignoring my wishes not to discuss this in public. Not that I'm surprised it's coming from her. The girl has absolutely no boundaries, it's why she's reality TV gold.

"I don't know," I whisper yell. "We haven't . . ." I look around to see if the group next to us is paying attention. "We haven't had sex yet."

All four women in front of me fall back into their chairs with their jaws in their laps, staring at me in silence until I start to fidget.

"What? Why are you looking at me like that?"

"You . . . ," Charli starts but just shakes her head, not finishing her sentence.

"You mean to tell me"—Vonnie leans forward, finally whispering—"that you've spent the last . . . what? All this time together and you haven't slept together?"

I learn that's a rhetorical question when I open my mouth to answer but she screams out over me, "What the fuck have you been doing?"

This time when I look at the groups surrounding us, they don't even pretend not to be listening, they are all turned in the seats, eyes focused directly on me.

Rude.

"I told you, we watched Netflix and talked."

"You said you guys Netflix and chilled," Charli says.

"Well, yeah." I shrug, not understanding the disconnect. "We would chill and watch Netflix . . . well, Hulu, but same thing."

"Oh, sweetie. No." Aviana shakes her head. "'Netflix and

chill' means you turn on a movie you don't actually care about and fuck."

"What?" My eyes bulge out of my head and my cheeks heat. "Why would it mean that?"

Dear god. I'm the most celibate I've been in my entire adult life and I've been telling people the polar opposite. Now I know how my dad felt when I used to judge him for not understanding what I was talking about.

Aviana shrugs, her long beach-waved hair bouncing along her shoulders. "I didn't come up with the term, I just know what it means because I'm not eighty-five."

I flip her off. "Shut up."

The most professional decision I've ever made? No. The most satisfying? Pretty close.

"Whatever, that's not even the important topic of this discussion," Aviana says, not fazed by my irritation. "You're seriously telling us that you and Max are officially a couple and you haven't even had any nookie? How'd you manage that?"

"For real," Vonnie chimes in. "If I was alone with that man, I'd be all over him."

"Okay, first of all, Vonnie, you talk a big game, but I don't believe you'd do any of the shit you say," I say.

"Hmph." Vonnie rolls her eyes. "You want a character witness, you can call Justin. I did not tiptoe around wanting him, hence our three boys and this rock on my finger."

I don't respond to her. Vonnie chose being a lawyer for a reason—I know I'm not likely to win any debates with her.

"We were friends." I feel like a broken record with how often I've said that phrase. "We hung out and talked and laughed. You don't actually have to have sex before you enter in a relationship, it's not like we got married."

"I thought only the Amish did that anymore." Aviana's beautiful face crumples like she smells something putrid.

A lot of blogs think that Aviana is putting on an act for the cameras, but I can say with one hundred percent certainty that she is not. She's just as over the top and ridiculous in her everyday life.

She also has a makeup artist on call.

She's glam goals.

Plus, Crosby adores her and they have one of the healthiest relationships I've ever been around. Granted, I did miss their rather messy beginning.

"I literally cannot with you right now." I shake my head to keep from laughing. "I'm going to go walk around, but if you need anything, Abby's been informed of all of your drink preferences."

The Mustangs are playing in Seattle today so the game is starting a little later than when they have a home game, but the early risers and enthusiastic drinkers are already here. While home games are still full here, it's the away games that bring the huge crowds to HERS. And now that the film crew will be here, everyone who wants the chance to be seen on TV signs a release form before they're seated. I have select tables away from where filming usually takes place so they don't need to worry, but today every person who has stepped foot inside has signed a release.

I'm making my rounds around HERS, catching up with old customers, introducing myself to new ones, when a large hand squeezes my hip.

One thing to know about me, I hate being touched, like loathe it. I've had to train my friends that I'm not an enthusiastic hugger and to try and avoid it at all costs. So I know two things about the hand on me right away. One, it belongs to a man, and two, he is not a friend.

My hackles instantly rise and my bitch face slides into place as I turn while removing the hand from my body. Then my bitch face slips just a bit when the person staring back at me is none other than Theo Lewis.

"Theo! Um, hi!" I take a step back, Maxwell's warning to stay away from him bouncing around in my head. "How are you?"

"I'm good." He—thankfully—stays in place and doesn't try to close the space I just created. "I heard this is the spot to come to on game day, figured I'd come early to get a seat to cheer on my baby bro, but it looks like I underestimated the female fan base's dedication."

"Most people usually do." And luckily for me because I was able to tap into an underserved market. "There are some open tables further in the back, but I just added more TVs so you don't have to worry about missing the game."

"But what if I'm more worried about missing you?" His gaze slides down my body in a move I'm sure has turned on more than one woman, but leaves me feeling the opposite.

I let out a laugh that sounds as awkward and uncomfortable as I feel. "Well, you're SOL on that one. Game days leave me swamped, but my waitresses are the best."

"But are they—" He starts what is sure to be another lame pickup line but is cut off by the shrill voice I never thought I'd be happy to hear.

"Brynn!" Eloise yells out before wrapping her arms around me, making me go stiff.

Ugh. What is it with people's lack of respect for personal space today? This is why I like being behind the bar, it's an automatic barrier.

"Hey, Eloise." I pat her back once and pull out of her arms. "What are you doing here?"

"HERS is the official place to watch Mustangs games and have good drinks, isn't it?"

"Unofficially official, I guess," I say warily, eyeing the woman in front of me who has mastered casual glam.

"That's what I thought." She smiles, and it's a real, warm smile, and loops her arm through my elbow, leaning into my ear. "I texted Max last night seeing if he wanted to get together this week and he told me that you two are seeing each other. I made some bad jokes while I was drinking, but I'm really happy for you both. I just want you to know I'm not that person who'd try and step on another woman, especially for a man. A hot man, but a man. Plus, I really love HERS, so I don't want you to ban me."

She talks a lot, but even so, when she's done, I can't manage anything besides an openmouthed stare. This has been a weird week, but this is probably the thing I least expected to happen.

When I don't say anything, her ruby lips spread wider and she turns her attention to Theo. "Brynn, I think since you got my last love interest, you should introduce me to my newest."

Damn.

I think I might actually really like Eloise.

"Oh." I pause, contemplating if I should introduce them or not. I know firsthand how messy family shit can be and just how much grudges can take on a life of their own. "This is Theo Lewis, Maxwell's brother."

"Oh." Eloise lets go of my arm. "I guess it's only fair that if you get Max, I get to meet his insanely attractive brother."

Theo's eyes widen just a fraction at that. "So you're who has my brother so distracted," he says, not waiting for an answer before he turns his attention and hand over to Eloise.

Eloise places her manicured hand in his, her pale skin against his dark a flawless combination.

"And he's a cop," I whisper in her ear, forgetting all about what Maxwell said and getting lost in Eloise's fun, flirtatious attitude.

"Well then." Eloise's chest pokes out a little further than it was moments ago. "Where are we sitting, Theo?"

I take that as my signal to leave. When I turn around, my gaggle of nosy bitches—said in the most loving way—are staring at me with jaws to the floor . . . again. Vonnie comes out of her stupor first, lifting a single finger in the air and crooking it my way.

And like the obedient friend I am, I curve through the tables, making sure to not forget a single detail along the way. Besides, what good is owning a bar if part of your day doesn't revolve around gossiping with your girls?

Twenty-five

I'VE NEVER BEEN THE GIRL TO STAND AROUND, WAITING FOR MY boyfriend to come home.

Partly because I resented the idea of my world revolving around a man and also because I've never had a boyfriend.

But when Maxwell called me after the game—they won—and asked if I'd wait for him at his house, I damn near ran people off the road to get over here.

He gave me the code to unlock his door and turn off the alarm system and told me to make myself at home.

I'm not sure what exactly he meant by "make yourself at home," but I do that by arranging the swanky bar cart he must've forgotten to get around to. Bar carts are as close to interior design as I'll ever come. Anyways, it's almost criminal the way Maxwell has tucked away his ridiculously priced scotch collection in the back of his pantry.

Once finished, I consider starting a blog with how freaking fantastic the bar cart looks, but what to do next is a bit of a struggle. By nature, I'm what some people might call a snoop. I mean, I do host the Lady Mustangs just to hear the dirt firsthand. I like to say I'm adorably curious. I kind of want to go check out his medicine cabinets and bedside drawers . . . that's what they always check in the movies. But, I don't know . . . this thing with Maxwell, I feel like it could go somewhere. I feel like there is a future, and I've *never* felt that before. I wouldn't want my quizzical nature to change that. Plus, jumping to conclusions before is what held up our relationship.

So I make the very adult decision to sit my stomach-flu-depleted ass on his heaven-lined couch and push buttons until the TV comes on. Then I push more buttons until the serious news anchors disappear and screaming housewives flood his speakers.

If I have learned anything during my time at HERS, it's that nothing can make you feel less in need of a therapist than a well-produced reality show. Sure, I'll never have enough money to carry around a new iPhone without a case, but I will also never flip a table on national TV. That, my friends, is called balance.

I lose myself in the opulence of Beverly Hills—sitting in Maxwell's house, I'm basically a member of the cast—when the gentle thrum of an opening garage door snaps all of my nerves back into place. Heat washes over me, my skin feels damp to the touch, and my stomach is filled with brick-winged butterflies. I should've gone home and showered . . . or at least used the spare deodorant in my glove compartment.

Should I stand and go greet him with a kiss? Do I pretend that I didn't hear him and act surprised to see him in his own house? Why isn't there a pamphlet about this? It would come in handy much more than the ones in my ob-gyn's office now.

Before I can make up my mind, the door to the garage opens.

"Brynn?" Maxwell's deep voice fills the house, drowning out

the high-quality vocals of Erika Jayne as the door rattles shut behind him. Not seconds later, his large, solid, *suited* body fills the opening to the living room.

I didn't need to worry about what to do, because as soon as I see him, my brain shuts off and my body moves on its own. He drops his suitcase on the floor and watches, his eyes glued to mine, as I quickly shorten the distance separating us.

"Hey," I whisper, my voice thick with wanting—my fingers itching to touch him.

And for the first time, I don't stop myself.

I move into him until my toes bump against his loafers. Instead of wrapping my arms around his neck and pulling him in for a kiss, I let my hands travel up his strong arms, feeling them underneath the navy-blue jacket that hugs his biceps like the perfectly wrapped gift that they are. I take my time, feeling his muscles tense beneath my soft touch, marveling at the way his breathing has deepened and my core has tightened . . . before we've even kissed.

"I'm glad you decided to come over." His words sound forced, like he's trying to hold a conversation during the last mile of a marathon.

"Me too," I say without looking at him.

My fingers fall down his chest. Even through the thick material of his button-up, I can trace the ridges of his abs with my fingertips. I have to bite back my moan at the thought of retracing this route with my tongue.

Unable to wait any longer, I reach for his jacket, pulling it off and tossing it haphazardly onto the floor by his suitcase. I don't hesitate before I start undoing his buttons, and Maxwell's hands come unfrozen from his sides to viciously rip off his tie before diving into my hair and pulling my mouth to his.

Every time we kiss, I have to struggle to stay in the moment. I have to fight not to fall under his spell so I can remember the way his full lips cushion mine, distracting me from the slight ache in my scalp. The way he sucks my bottom lips into his mouth, as if my lips are a treasure he needs to explore every inch of.

My shaky hands make quick work of his buttons. I let my hands glide over his smooth skin, my sightless senses savoring every inch of him. The heat of him, the feel of goose bumps as they cover his skin when the moan I can't hold back any longer escapes my throat.

I swallow his deep growl as I slip my tongue into his mouth, wanting more than I'm sure I can even handle. I wrap my arms around his neck, melding my body to his, nearly dissolving into a puddle when I feel the bulge in his pants push against me.

"Fuck." Maxwell drops his mouth to my throat, nipping his way to my collarbone. "You have no idea how long I've been waiting for this."

"Yes, I do," I say through moans. I throw my head back, giving him as much room to explore as he wants, chills shooting up my spine with his every touch. I let one hand fall from his head and slip it between our bodies, rubbing against his erection. He lets out a groan so deep, it reverberates between my thighs.

"Fuck, Brynn." He nips my ear, his tongue tracing away the sting, before his hands drop to my ass and lift me up like I weigh no more than a feather. "Can I take you to my room?"

I press my mouth to his. All of my nerve endings are short-circuiting and my brain can't keep up with my body. Maxwell kisses me back, our mouths tasting and exploring, saying things we can't express, but he still doesn't move.

"Brynn." He pulls back, his light brown eyes now completely black. "I need to hear the words. Is this what you want?"

"Yes." I wiggle my ass in his hands, trying to rub against the tented crotch of his trousers. "I want this."

"Thank fucking god," he growls, but then I lose sight of him because his mouth is on mine again and he's moving.

And holy fucking hell.

I'm not sure I'll last until we get to his bedroom.

My legs are wrapped tight around his waist, leaving me spread and merciless against the feel of him as each step causes me to bounce and rub against him. One of his hands kneads my ass cheek while the other one drops between my thighs, drawing wicked circles against the seam of my jeans.

"I can feel you through your pants," his gravelly voice whispers.

Sweat starts to form on my neck, my entire body tensing, fighting against the onslaught of sensations. I don't want this to end, but I'm not sure I can prevent it for much longer. My thighs are shaking and I've long forgotten kissing Maxwell back. My arms are locked so tight around his neck, I can only pray that I'm not choking him, because there's no chance in hell I can loosen my grip. My eyes are clenched shut and everything within me is wound so tight that I know that when I come, I'm going to explode. I'm going to be ripped at my seams, and when I'm put back together, Maxwell will be sewn into the very fabric of my being.

"Stop fighting it." His voice is distant over the roaring of blood rushing between my ears. "Let me feel you come wrapped around me. Then, after you come, I'm going to strip you down, spread you over my bed, and watch you come again. This is just the beginning, Brynn. I promise, I will take care of you," he says.

I've imagined sex with Maxwell more than I'd like to admit. And I've imagined Maxwell being fucking fantastic in everything. But what I never imagined and never could've even guessed was that Maxwell would talk dirty and do it fucking well.

And it's that.

It's knowing that, somehow, he's better than in my fucking

dreams that causes every bit of pressure coursing down my body to settle directly in my core before exploding into a million tiny pieces. I let out a scream so loud, I'm sure his neighbors hear me. I both cling to him and push him away, barely registering the soft mattress beneath me as he stops to kick off his shoes and pull off his pants.

"Jesus, Brynn," he whispers into his dark room. "How the fuck did I get this lucky?"

My skin is already on fire, and lava is lapping through my veins, but even so, his words somehow manage to warm my stomach and cause my cheeks to heat even more. There's no way he could see the blush rising in my cheeks, but that doesn't stop me from hiding my face behind my hands.

He climbs up the bed, his bare legs straddling my torso, and pulls my hands from my face. "Fuck, you're cute. The most beautiful woman I've ever seen and you still get shy hearing it." I can hear the smile in his voice, then I feel it against my throat. His hands run down my arms until his fingers link with mine. "Stand up for me."

I've heard my friends tell stories about their sex lives. My gorgeous, curvy friends with breasts and asses that I would kill for, letting the most ridiculous hang-ups about their stunning shapes detract from the times they should be enjoying. And while I know that Maxwell has probably been with women who would make me feel like I have the sex appeal of a prepubescent boy, I don't let it get to me. This is me and I'm fucking proud of it. Who cares if I have a few dimples on my thighs or stretch marks on my hips? Not I and, clearly, not Maxwell.

So I don't hesitate when he asks me to stand, and I don't balk when seconds later the room is covered in soft lighting.

And who's to say? Maybe I would've thought twice about it if

Maxwell wasn't standing in front of me in nothing but boxer briefs, his heated eyes memorizing everything about me.

But I doubt it.

He doesn't move for what feels like eternity. His gaze is so intense that even feet away from me, my thighs involuntarily push together. Something Maxwell doesn't miss.

The thin layer of sweat makes his smooth, dark skin sparkle. His abs look as good as they felt under my fingers, and the cut in his hips, the arrow pointing to the tent in his briefs, makes my insides quiver. His quadriceps flexing thick and strong with each step he makes. He doesn't rush his movements. He knows I'm enjoying the show and exactly like the man of my dreams, he lets me revel in the moment, adhering this image to the backs of my eyelids.

"I love looking at you." The words slip out of my lips before I can even think to hold them in. Something, I'm realizing, that is happening more and more in his presence. "You're perfect."

This spurs him into action.

Before I can blink, he's on me. His mouth is hot and wet on mine, and one hand is in my hair, the other gripping my hip so tight I pray that there'll be fingerprint bruises there tomorrow—any kind of physical proof to tether me to this exact moment.

He pulls back. His hands grab the hem of my shirt and yank it off of me before I can even process what's happening. His fingers dance up my spine, shivers chasing his touch, until they undo the clasp of my bra and it joins my shirt on the floor somewhere.

He steps in. His eyes are on mine even as the cool air swirling around us causes my nipples to harden. His lips touch my throat. "So . . . ," he says, then they move to my shoulder. "Fucking . . ." Then both of his hands cover my breasts and he's looking at me from beneath his thick lashes. "Lucky," he finishes before his mouth closes over my nipple and he's mimicking the motion of his mouth with his hand on my free breast.

He goes back and forth, lavishing my chest with attention it's never before received. I struggle to keep up with him, relaxing into his touch and then tensing away, not wanting to come again with my pants still on.

"Please," I hear myself beg, my voice unrecognizable to my own ears.

Maxwell doesn't answer.

Not with words at least.

He falls to his knees in front of me, biting my thighs through the thick fabric of my jeans as his fingers deftly undo the button fly of my jeans that I always loved until this exact moment in time. His fingers loop into my thong, pulling it down with my pants. Maxwell's fingers wrap around each of my ankles, sliding my feet out of the bottoms, leaving me completely naked in front of a kneeling Maxwell.

My entire body is trembling. My knees feel weak and my core is pulsating. I reach out for Maxwell, but before I get to him, he pulls back and sits on his heels.

"Just give me a second," he says, his voice thick with want as his eyes travel up my naked body.

A second is all I can give him. I can feel the moisture gathering between my legs, and my breasts are heavy with desire. "Maxwell"—my hand drops between my thighs—"I need you."

He doesn't make me ask again. He springs up from the ground, tackling me to the bed like it's his job . . . which I guess it sort of is.

He puts my hand back between my thighs, letting out a groan that causes the bed to vibrate beneath me. "Don't stop, Boss," he says. His eyes don't move from the show I'm putting on for him even as he stands up and walks to the bedside table, pulling out a foil-wrapped condom. He walks back to the foot of his bed, placing the condom wrapper on the mattress before his hands go to his briefs and he finally—*finally!*—pulls them off.

Oh.

My.

God.

I mean, I assumed.

It was making itself known all night.

But I still had no idea.

I mean . . . can a penis be pretty? Is that a thing? Because this . . . Maxwell . . . what he's working with . . . it's fucking fantastic. It's thick and long and honestly maybe a little scary.

But hell, if there's one fear I'm willing to overcome, this sure as hell is it.

"Boss," Maxwell says, amusement cutting through the need. "You're staring."

"I know," I say . . . still staring. "Will it fit?"

"You already got me where you want me, you don't need to keep buttering me up," he jokes, his hand rolling on the condom. And I change my mind. This . . . this is the moment I want burned behind my eyelids.

"You're right," I say, my voice quavering. "You might need to butter me up."

"I think . . ." He climbs onto the bed and over my body, dropping a finger between my thighs and pushing it inside of me. "You already are."

Listen.

I'm no virgin.

Not even close.

So I don't expect a single finger to send me sailing to another planet, but it does. And I know, without an inkling of doubt, that Maxwell is the only person on this earth who could do it to me.

It's everything about him. The way his gaze travels over my body like I'm the most beautiful woman who has ever graced his presence. The rough touch of his calloused hands that are so contradictory to the gentle way they caress my body. It's how outside of these walls, he's shy and sweet, and right now he's letting me—only me—get a taste of the wonderfully wicked way his mind works.

His hard to my soft, the dark to my light, everything about him causes something inside of me to unravel. He shoves me outside of myself and makes it impossible for me to keep hiding . . . to hold back.

He nips at my ear, whispering words I can't hear, finding a spot with his finger that draws out every last bit of my orgasm, and as soon as I start to come down, his hand is gone and he is inside of me. Filling me so completely that I forget how to breathe.

"Oh my god," I gasp, my back damn near hovering off the bed.

My body moves of its own accord, my legs and arms wrapping around him, pulling him in closer . . . and deeper. He doesn't move. He peppers my face with kisses, his soft lips offering a distraction while my body gets used to his size.

It's like a switch is flipped inside of me.

One second I'm not sure I was ready, the next I don't think I ever want him to stop.

My arms and legs loosen around him and it's all the encouragement he needs.

"Are you okay?" he asks, his movements slow and measured. His arms are shaking, and beads of sweat are starting to fall from his hairline.

"Yeah," I try to say, but it comes out as more of a moan than anything else. "Move, Maxwell, I need you to move."

I knew he was holding back, but not until I whisper those words do I know how much.

He grabs my legs from around his waist and pulls them to-gether, holding them with one hand while his free hand grabs onto my hip for leverage as he thrusts inside of me, keeping a steady pace of fast and hard.

Never in my life have I appreciated the body of an athlete more.

Each time he slams back inside of me, the coils of my core bunch tighter and tighter. "Please don't stop!" I cry out between thrusts. I'm clinging to his arms so tightly, I'm sure my nails are going to draw blood.

"Never going to stop," he says, like it's an impossible promise only he can fulfill.

Every part of my body tenses up, from my fingers to my toes. His movements slow just a bit, but I know it's not because he's tired. "Come for me." He drops a hand to where our bodies are joined.

The one added sensation on top of a mountain of sensations causes an avalanche. I let out a silent scream, my hands gripping the sheets and tethering me to the ground. I come so hard that even though the room is lit, my world goes black.

I'm holding on for dear life and tremors are rocking my system when Maxwell lets out a deep groan and his body stills before his weight falls on top of me.

Neither of us makes a move or says a word. We lie there, our sweat-covered bodies melded together for what could be hours . . . but is likely only moments.

"Holy shit." I break the silence as flashbacks from our night start to filter through my mind, each moment hotter than the next. "That was . . . it was—" I start, but I can't come up with a word that does justice to what we experienced.

"It was the best," Maxwell finishes for me.

It's such a simple description, but it's right. What we did was the best and just like I knew he would, Maxwell has left me completely and utterly ruined.

I can't go back to average after him.

I can't be satisfied by anything other than the best.

Twenty-six

"MAX GAVE YOU THAT D," VONNIE ANNOUNCES TO ANYONE within a three-mile radius as soon as she sits on her barstool.

I feel my face heat as my jaw falls to the ground and I try to remember if I had "Fucked by Maxwell Lewis" stamped on my forehead the last time I looked in the mirror.

I didn't.

So how Vonnie makes such a confident declaration is a mystery I don't even want to attempt to solve.

"What are you talking about?" I try to get a grasp on those acting classes Naomi, an ex-Mustangs wife, gave me a few years ago.

Vonnie actually repositions herself so she can give me the side-eye. "He did," she says casually. "You have a glow that one only gets from a night of no sleep and great sex."

"He didn't!" I screech. Which I realize, after the high-pitched sound leaves my mouth, makes me look even more guilty. "Dammit, come here," I mutter, heading to my office without checking that she's following.

I know she is.

When your friend has hot sex with a hot guy, you are required to get all of the details. It's a real rule. I know this because it's been written on more than one sticky note stuck to the bathroom walls.

Plus, Vonnie is married. And yes, they're happy and blah blah blah. That doesn't mean you don't want to hear the exciting beginnings of a new relationship. That's when all the fun stuff happens.

Or actually? Maybe not. Vonnie and Charli tell me some wild-ass stories about their sex lives. I think that, maybe, there are things you are only comfortable requesting from somebody who is legally bound to you.

"Spill," Vonnie says before the door to my office can even shut. Her arms are crossed, her hip is out, and her lips are pursed. I know that no amount of acting lessons could get me out of this conversation.

Oh well, it'd be a crime against humanity not to share.

"We consummated our relationship and it was . . ." I look to the ceiling, searching for the right word to describe it. "It was like a religious experience. Like, I know there has to be a god and there's a good chance Maxwell might be a direct descendant."

"Ah hell." Vonnie eyes the door like she's contemplating her exit. And I realize that brutal honesty might actually be my ticket out of this conversation. "Now I have to go to church and pray for listening to your sacrilegious ass."

"Do you even go to church?" I'm not even being a smart-ass, I genuinely have no idea.

"I go to Bible study every week." She scrunches her nose. "Well, almost every week."

I roll my eyes, but decide not to make a snarky comment considering that's still way more than what I do. "Well, do you want me to tell you or not?"

She doesn't answer right away. Instead she locks my office door and plops down on the couch like she's prepping for a session with her therapist.

"Okay"—she adjusts my martini-print throw pillow behind her head—"now I'm ready. Tea, please."

And to think I ever complained of loneliness before.

"I lost count of how many times I came. And one of those times, swear to god, was from him kissing me."

Vonnie's eyes widen and the carefully positioned pillow is long forgotten as she shoots off the couch. "I knew it!" she yells. "I knew his shy, fine ass was hiding all sorts of treats below the surface."

"So many treats." My eyelids feel heavy just thinking about all the activities from last night . . . and this morning. "I honestly don't know how he doesn't have a bevy of brokenhearted, sex-with-everyone-else-is-ruined-forever women following him around."

I'm sure if I googled hard enough, I'd find a fan club or something. I add it to the running to-do list floating around my mind.

"I need more," Vonnie demands. "How many condoms did you go through? Did you use condoms? Did his kisses travel south? How well endowed is he?"

"Oh my god." My hands fly to my eyes as my skin burns from a head-to-toe blush.

This.

This is why I didn't want to talk about it. My friends might have boundaries, but if they do, I haven't found them yet.

"Oh no." Vonnie is suddenly in front of me, peeling my hands from my eyes. "*You* don't get to wuss out of this. You are the ringleader of getting all the details out of us, and if you don't start to spill, I'm calling in reinforcements."

Dammit. I guess I should discover boundaries as well. I curse my adorably curious nature.

"Ugh, fine!" I throw my hands up in the air before sitting on the now-empty couch. "But if you mutter a single word to Justin about this, I will hunt you down and hurt you."

Her head jerks back and her lips curl in disgust. "Obviously. We barely discuss our sex life, we are definitely not discussing yours."

"Fine." I narrow my eyes, but inside I'm bouncing with glee to brag about the literal best sex of my life. Maybe the best sex in the world. "We went through four condoms. His mouth moved south. He did it so well and so often that my lady bits are still quivering." At this Vonnie's smile grows so big, I'm concerned it's going to damage her facial muscles. "And let's just say that angels rejoiced when he was created because he is blessed between the legs."

"Big?" Vonnie asks, clearly in need of more details.

I nod, my eyebrows reaching my hairline. "In every sense of the word."

"Damn." She falls onto the couch beside me. "Now the next time he passes me in those tight-ass pants he wears so well, I'm not going to be able to look at anything else."

"Me either," I say. Even though this is definitely not a new problem.

The shrill ringing of my office phone breaks up the heavy silence in the room.

I jump off the couch and lunge for the pink rotary phone I paid a stupid amount for. If possible, I don't like it to ring more than three times, and since I'm sitting by it, I want to get it before the second.

"Thank you for calling HERS, Brynn speaking." I rattle off my customary greeting.

"Hey, Boss." Maxwell's deep voice flows through the phone, causing goose bumps to cover my arms.

"Hey," I say. A goofy-ass grin spreads across my face, and I see Vonnie's face brighten out of the corner of my eyes.

"I know it's late notice, but I wanted to see if you could get off early tonight and I could take you out?"

It takes every single ounce of discipline in my body not to crack a joke about getting off with him, but thankfully, I manage. "I'm sure I could figure something out. What time were you thinking?"

"I was hoping to get you at around six. Does that work?"

I wish I could say I'm being a responsible business owner and thinking about all of the emails I have yet to send or promotions I have yet to make before agreeing, but I don't. Instead, the opportunity to go on a date with Maxwell—my orgasm-inducing *boyfriend*—eclipses all of my responsibilities. "Yes," I damn near shout into the phone. I flip off Vonnie as she dissolves into a fit of laughter across the room. "Six is perfect. From my place or HERS?"

"Dress code for tonight is no jeans," he says. "So I'm thinking your place?"

"My place," I agree, looking down at my denim-covered legs.

"Thought so." I can hear the laughter in his voice, but it doesn't bother me. Instead, my heart warms at how well he knows me already.

"Then I'll see you—" I start my farewell, but Maxwell cuts me off.

"Just so you know, there should be a delivery for you soon. So keep an eye out."

"Really?" My smile widens and I start to bounce on my toes, childlike excitement taking over. "I love deliveries!"

I may have never been in a serious relationship before, but tons of my friends have. So when they started talking love languages and all that crap, I didn't want to feel left out and took the quiz too. Gifts are *so* my love language. Next is quality time, then physical touch . . . a checklist Maxwell is thoroughly marking off.

His laughter flows through the phone. "You don't even know what it is."

"Doesn't matter. The UPS man is my fave—er . . . second fa-vorite man. I mean, you know what I mean." *Smooth, Brynn. Real fucking smooth.* I squeeze my eyes closed, cringing at the way only I could turn this conversation unbearably awkward.

"I know what you mean," he says. But I'm ninety-nine percent sure he's just saying it because he's nice and doesn't want me to feel like a complete idiot.

"Okay, then I'm going to hang up before I make a bigger ass out of myself. I'll see you tonight."

"Tonight," he promises with a smile in his voice.

I put the phone back on the receiver, not trusting myself to say anything else.

"Girl," Vonnie says, wiping away her tears of laughter. "You have no fucking game."

"I hate you," I say.

"You fucking love me and it's a good thing, because I'm going to call the girls in so we can give you a crash course in game. It's really a sin that you are as gorgeous as you are and you have no idea how to talk to men."

"I can talk to men!" Panic starts to course its way through my veins as I envision the Lady Mustangs gathering in my living room with glitter gavels and a PowerPoint on how to flirt. "I've just never been in an actual relationship before."

It's out of my mouth before I can stop it.

"Never?" she asks, and to my pure and utter mortification, whips out her phone, no doubt assembling an emergency meeting of minds on what to do with me. "How is that possible?"

I open my mouth to answer, but before I can, there's a knock on my office door.

If I wasn't so busy sprinting to the door, I would have sagged to the floor in relief for the distraction.

I turn the lock and pull it open.

"Sorry," Paisley says. Her eyes narrow on the maniacal smile that is no doubt on my face. "But there's a delivery for you and they need your signature."

"Not a problem, thanks!" I cringe at the amount of pep in my voice as I push past her.

I'm expecting to see a handsome man in a brown-and-yellow uniform waiting for me, so I'm a little taken aback by the gorgeous woman in a pencil skirt and sky-high pumps holding a silver box with a large silver bow.

"You must be Brynn." She smiles and holds out a hand with a tablet. "If you could just sign here, please."

I use my finger to scribble my illegible signature on the screen. When I finish, she tucks it into the killer tote hanging on her shoulder and extends the box that I can now see has a Neiman Marcus tag hanging from the ribbon.

"I hope you love it," she says, genuine excitement in her voice. "Mr. Lewis spent some time making sure he found something you would enjoy."

I already knew this was from Maxwell, but hearing her say it makes it even more exciting for some reason. I don't even know what's in the box, but I already feel like Julia Roberts in *Pretty Woman* . . . minus the prostitution.

I keep my eyes on the box, afraid that if I blink, somehow this fantasy will disappear. "Thank you."

I have to bite my lips to try and hide the smile threatening to overtake my entire face. My hands are shaking so hard that I nearly drop the box when she hands it over. She doesn't say anything else . . . or maybe she does? I don't actually know. As soon as it's in my hands, I turn on my heel and dart back into my office without so much as a goodbye.

"Neiman's?" Vonnie claps her hands together as soon as she sees the box.

Clearly, she's much more well versed in the gift packaging designs of upscale department stores than I am.

"Yeah." I put the package on my desk, wanting to both tear the box open and leave it as it is.

"What the fuck are you waiting for?" Vonnie's bouncing on her toes, and her hands are curled into fists at her sides, like she can't trust herself not to open the box for me. Part of me wants to end her misery and open it. The other, evil part of me wants to revel in the one time I have ever seen Vonnie lose her cool exterior.

But my curiosity and love of gifts beat my sadistic alter ego.

My fingers glide over the silk bow, committing the feel to memory before pulling it loose and tucking it into my desk drawer. I lift open the lid and unfold the crisp tissue paper inside, the sound of the crinkling paper barely noticeable over the sound of my heartbeat roaring between my ears. My lungs stop working and all of the oxygen becomes trapped in my chest as a brown box with "Christian Louboutin" written in white script appears beneath my fingertips.

"Holy shit." I breathe deeply as the monster butterflies knock my lungs back into commission.

"Damn," Vonnie whispers, completely out of character. "Max is playing no games."

She is not lying.

Any hesitation I was feeling disappears and excitement replaces it. Adrenaline pumps through my body as I rip off the lid and throw the little red bag I've been dreaming of to the side. I can only see the embroidered, jewel-encrusted sneakers I had to delete from my phone for a few seconds before my vision completely blurs out and I turn into a blubbering pile of tears and collapse into my desk chair.

"They're . . . the . . . shoooes!" I hiccup between my sobs.

"What?" Vonnie asks at the same time as Paisley pushes into my office and yells, "Oh my god! Are you okay?"

I swipe uselessly at my face as the tears fall, trying to gather some composure, but probably just irritating the skin on my face even more. "He bought me my shoes," I say once I've caught my breath. But, hearing the words outside of my head brings forth a fresh wave of tears, and I bury my face in my hands as they pour down my cheeks.

"Is she happy or upset?" I hear Paisley ask Vonnie.

"I mean, they might be tennis shoes—which seems a little pointless because how do you even see the red bottoms?" Vonnie says, the irritation that her friend wants tennis shoes instead of pumps evident. "But they're still red bottoms, and it's against the law to get upset over getting a pair. Trust me, I'm a lawyer."

"I didn't know you were a lawyer," Paisley says.

Their conversation turns my sobs into snorts. When my vision clears, they are both staring at me like I'm crazy—which, let's be honest, I very well may be, but even if I am, I'm not the only one.

"Do you need anything?" Paisley eyes me carefully, like I'm liable to crack at any moment.

"Yeah, like a Xanax?" Vonnie adds.

"Oh, whatever." I attempt to roll my eyes, but they are too sore from crying and I have to abandon ship midroll.

"So no meds? What about a shot of tequila?" Vonnie asks.

I contemplate this.

Whatever the question, I'm a firm believer that tequila can always work as the solution.

Then I remember that I need to go shopping to find an outfit worthy of these shoes for my date with Maxwell tonight.

Then I almost start to cry again when I realize that this is my actual life and not some cruel *Black Mirror* version of my life.

"If you start to cry again, I'm out," Vonnie says.

"Fuck." I squeeze my eyes shut and use my hands as fans to blow back the tears. "You can't leave." I know as I'm saying this that I will come to regret this in a matter of hours, but that doesn't stop me. "I need to go shopping. I need a date outfit to go with these shoes."

Vonnie's entire face lights up. "Thank you, Bible study," she says. "My prayers have been answered!"

All right.

Hours was a generous estimate.

I already regret this.

Twenty-seven

SHOPPING WITH VONNIE IS A STRANGE MIX OF TORTURE AND pleasure . . . kind of like nipple clamps.

On one hand, I might need to put my condo up for sale. On the other hand, I look fucking phenomenal.

Vonnie didn't stop at the knit royal-blue pencil skirt or the black-and-white-polka-dot blouse. No, that would've been quitting, and Vonnie is no fucking quitter. Which may be why she still didn't stop after the faux leather jacket I just "had to have" or the matching bra and panties or the tote she swore she saw Meghan Markle carry. It might also explain the new red lipstick I'm wearing even though I already have three shades of red that I've never worn.

"Hold still!" She scolds me like I'm the daughter she never had.

"I'm trying!" I yell back, my patience waning. "Am I even going to have hair when you're finished?"

My bathroom looks like a beauty salon exploded.

There are two different straighteners, three curling irons, one set of curlers, five hairsprays, and more eye shadows than I can count.

"Your lighting sucks." Aviana aims an appraising look my way. "More highlighter for sure. And what do you think, V? Matte red lips or should I swipe some gloss on top?"

Vonnie releases her death grip on my hair and walks around to examine my face. "Hmm . . ." She taps her chin with her manicured nail. "I like the matte with the cat eye, I think it's more of an authentic retro look."

"Agreed," Aviana says. "But something is missing, don't you think?"

Even though I don't wear makeup often, I still love it. I've never left a Sephora empty-handed and I watch beauty videos on YouTube like someone is paying me. So if these two ruin makeup for me, I will hurt them.

"You guys, it's Maxwell," I say for the thousandth time since they commandeered my condo. "He's not going to care if my lips are glossed or if my hair is wavy or in an updo."

This, apparently, is not the right thing to say.

I know this when both of the women in front of me assume the sass action of hands on hips and narrow their own perfectly lined eyes at me.

"Is this not your first official date?" Aviana asks.

"Well, yeah—"

Vonnie interrupts me. "And did he not just make you see stars last night when he put it down?"

"Yeah, but I—" I start, but Aviana cuts me off this time.

"Did he or didn't he send a pair of two-thousand-dollar shoes to your job? Which, by the way, I don't even understand the point of Louboutin sneakers. How do you even see the red bottom without the sexy arch of the heel?"

"That's what I'm saying!" Vonnie yells before I get the chance to answer, even though I'm starting to get the impression that these are all rhetorical questions.

"But he doesn't—" UGH! Foiled again!

"He does. He dicked you down and bought you shoes that turned you into a sobbing mess for a solid thirty minutes." Vonnie returns to her position behind me and jams another bobby pin into my hair.

"Ouch!" I jerk my head out of her reach and turn to face her. "It was not thirty—"

"Zzzzip!" Her eyes go scary wide and she does the zipper motion in front of her lips. I open my mouth again, and she pinches— yes! Pinches!—my lips shut. "No talking!"

I normally wouldn't listen, but she's scaring me, so I stay quiet.

"Just give me this." She lets go of my lips and looks at me with puppy dog eyes. "Let me bask in the wooing and newness of this with you. Let us get you over-the-top, make-other-girls-go-home-and-cry beautiful. We know Max would think you're the most beautiful woman in the world in your pajamas, but I want to see him speechless. Pleeeeease!"

Vonnie doesn't beg.

Vonnie gets what she wants without even asking for it.

It might be fun being the first person to tell her no.

Kidding. I give in right away.

"Fine, but can you at least try not to stab me in the head with another bobby pin?" I glare, but my heart's not in it. Now that she mentioned it, I kinda want to see a speechless Maxwell too.

"Ew. So many demands." Aviana rolls her eyes, a dimple appearing on her cheek even as she tries to fight back her smile. "What a diva. Are you sure you don't want to join *Love the Player*?"

"Positive," I say at the same time Vonnie says, "She's sure!"

"Well, I never." Aviana brings a hand up to her always exposed chest, doing her damnedest to act offended.

"Girl, bye." Vonnie laughs while putting my head back in position. "Apply that highlighter."

I HAVE ONE of my new shoes on when there's a knock at the door.

"Okay, you." Vonnie points to Aviana. "You go let Max in. And you"—she points to me—"stop acting like those shoes are going to dissolve. They aren't. And if it takes you another five minutes to put on the left shoe, I'm going to throw them out the window."

"Bossy much?" I roll my eyes and smile a little bit, but I also hurry the eff up because Vonnie doesn't do empty threats.

Once they're on my feet, she continues on like I didn't speak. "I'm going to go sit down on the couch and pretend like I'm on Twitter or something, but really, I'm going to film his reaction to seeing you. So make sure you don't fuck up my angle."

"Max!" we hear Aviana yell from the other room. "What a surprise! You look so handsome."

Seriously? These are the two I picked for this covert mission? They are the least discreet people I know. I should've called Jacqueline. Max wouldn't have even known she was here and she probably has a world-famous hairstylist who wouldn't have made my scalp bleed.

Oh well, live and learn, I guess.

"After I leave, count to thirty so I can get my camera all set up, got it?" Vonnie does a final once-over, giving me a nod of approval at her and Avi's handiwork. "He's. Going. To. Die!" she whisper shrieks, complete with air claps.

Now I remember why I invited Vonnie . . . or why I didn't fight when she invited herself. Because giddy Vonnie is the best Vonnie. It's one thing to have a friend. It's another thing completely to have a friend who gets more excited for the good things happening in your own life than you do. That's what these women do. In our group, we celebrate joys and mourn losses, and we do it together and authentically.

And right now, my joy includes hot freaking shoes and a— nearly impossibly—hotter man.

Vonnie closes her eyes and uses the deep breathing techniques Charli is always pushing on us to school her features into a mask of perfectly crafted disinterest.

"Oh, hey, Max," she says right before my bedroom door closes behind her.

I don't bother counting to thirty. Not because I'm ignoring Vonnie's instructions, but because I'm so nervous that I lose count after seven. Instead I move to the mirror, in need of an Issa-style pep talk, but when I look in the mirror, I forget that too.

I barely recognize myself. My hair that is usually pulled into either a ponytail or a bun is falling in long waves down my back with pieces pulled into a braided ropelike crown. Aviana killed the cat eye and lined my lips to perfection. The body-hugging pencil skirt paired with the billowing blouse with maybe one too many buttons undone gives my curveless body the appearance of Jessica Rabbit—well, maybe not quite, but a girl can dream! And then my shoes. Some girls think a crown goes on their head, but my crowning glory is on my feet. I squeeze my eyes tight and turn on a red sole to the door. I may have lost track of time, but not enough to forget that Vonnie is liable to barge in and drag me out by my ear at any second.

"What even is a hashtag? Back when I was a kid that was a pound sign . . . or a tic-tac-toe board," I hear Vonnie say on the other side of the door.

I pull open my door. "Oh my god. We are not old enough to talk about the good old days, do not age us like that."

Vonnie's shenanigans—does saying "shenanigans" age me?—distract me from the task at hand so much that I don't even look at Maxwell right away. Not until I hear his sharp intake of breath and the air around me becomes supercharged.

"Jesus, Brynn. You look . . . I mean, you're always beautiful, but wow." He stumbles over his words, and somehow the stumbling makes everything he's saying even more meaningful. "How'd I get this lucky?"

And with that, my abused head, glued and ripped eyelashes, and my underwire-tortured breasts are all worth it. Not to mention, he looks fucking phenomenal too.

"Well, you kids have fun tonight." Aviana moves behind me, pushing me into Maxwell, then pushing us both out of *my* door. "Be safe! Wear your seat belts and condoms!"

"Especially the condoms." Vonnie hands me my purse. "I'm done having kids and I don't need some mini Maxwells convincing me to open the baby shop back up."

My jaw drops to the ground as heat fills my face. I don't know why they wasted their time on blush when they planned on doing this the entire time.

Fucking Lady Mustangs.

Twenty-eight

WE WALK DOWN THE STAIRS OF MY CONDO COMPLEX IN SILENCE.

I'm not sure if it's because negative five seconds into the date Maxwell is already regretting it, or if he's just waiting until my face returns to its regularly scheduled hue.

When we reach his car, he opens the door for me like the old-fashioned gentleman he is before moving to the driver's side door.

"I'm so sorry about that," I blurt as he reverses out of the parking spot. "Vonnie was there when the shoes were delivered and I couldn't ditch her after that. I know they love me, but I think they get some sick pleasure out of embarrassing me."

"You don't need to apologize." His gaze stays focused on the road in front of him, but his hand drops from the steering wheel and finds its way to my knee. "Vonnie has put me on the spot many times. You've never come to training camp, but I swear she goes out of her way to say something humiliating right in front of the press." His chest starts to shake with laughter. "The training camp when Poppy started seeing TK, she dragged TK next to me and asked Poppy if she was sure she liked white chocolate or if she was getting a craving for dark."

My eyes damn near fall out of my head. I wish I could say I didn't believe it, but I do. I so do. "What did Poppy do?"

"She stuttered and stared for a solid five minutes. TK started to think she was having a stroke and picked her up and carried her off the field." Poor Poppy. "Then as I was signing autographs, I lost count of how many women told me they craved dark chocolate all the time and slipped me their numbers."

"Oh shit!" I choke, trying to hold back my laughter.

I'm only successful for a few seconds. Tears fall down my face, testing the adhesive power of the false lashes Aviana spent almost an hour applying. "I'm sorry," I say, wiping the tears off of my face. "I shouldn't laugh."

His fingers tighten around my leg. "There's not a single sight more beautiful than you laughing." All the humor in his voice has fled.

Ho. Lee. Shit.

"I . . . I . . ." My mouth opens and closes like a fish out of water trying to come up with something to say. "Thank you?"

Maxwell smirks and glances at me from the corner of his eye. "You're very welcome." Then, praise baby Jesus, he turns into a parking garage and gives me the perfect topic change.

"You never told me what we're doing tonight." I stare out the window. I know it's just a parking garage, but something about *this* parking garage is super familiar, I just can't quite put a finger on why.

"We're almost there. Why spoil the surprise now?"

"Because surprises are the worst." I poke my bottom lip out, a move Ace helped me perfect.

"Really? Because Angela told me you seemed very happy signing for your shoes." He raises a single eyebrow.

Dammit, Angela. What kind of traitor—

I look down to my beaded, bedazzled, embroidered feet, and my bravado fades. That lovely woman brought me my shoes. She's an angel on earth.

"Shoes don't count. So unless this is a fancy sneaker warehouse, I'll like this better if you tell me in advance."

He glances at his phone before pulling into a reserved parking spot. "I guess that's a risk I'm going to have to take."

Ugh.

Men.

He grabs my purse from the ground of the back seat for me and gets out of the car. He hands it to me and links our hands together when I meet him behind the car. The parking spot he took is right next to a door, and before we even reach it, a man in a navy suit is opening the door.

"Mr. Lewis, Miss Sterling." He holds out his hand to shake ours as we pass him and enter the building. "We're so excited to have you in our audience tonight," the man says.

As he talks and I look around, things start clicking into place and my heart rate picks up considerably.

"The cast is thrilled to meet you. It's not often we get an all-pro football player in the theater."

"Oh my god." I stop walking. The room is spinning and I'm pretty sure my system is overflowing with adrenaline and pure, unadulterated fucking joy. "You didn't." I shove Maxwell. "Please tell me you didn't!" I squeal, my feet bouncing as fast as my heart. "No! Tell me you did! If you didn't, then I'm going to cry because my hopes are all the way the fuck up!"

I throw my hands over my mouth. I don't want my filthy mouth to get us kicked out of the theater.

"I don't know what you're talking about," Maxwell, the smug jerk, says. "I thought you were hoping for a warehouse of shoes?"

I'm about to answer—or fall to my knees, begging him to tell me where we are—when the door at the end of the hallway opens and three women dressed in silk taffeta dresses à la the Revolutionary period file into the hallway.

"The Schuyler sisters!" I screech. It's so high-pitched as it leaves my mouth that I wouldn't be surprised if a flock of dogs rushed to us. I should probably be embarrassed or apologetic . . . or both, but I'm too fucking happy to even consider it. "No! Oh my god!" I jump into Maxwell's arms, peppering his face with kisses and wrapping my arms so tight around his neck that he has to loosen my grip. "*Hamilton*? How did you even do this? It's been sold out for months!"

"I have my ways." He touches his lips to mine, his eyes boring into mine. I can't tell you what passes between us in that moment; all I know is that it's big.

Battle of Yorktown huge.

"ARE YOU STILL crying?" Maxwell asks, and I'm stuck in the hard place of trying to decide whether or not to punch him or wipe my tears.

But when the snot threatens to fall with my salty tears, I decide to wipe my face.

"How are you not crying? When Eliza was hovered over Philip's body and then after Hamilton died and she was all alone, just ensuring his legacy and starting an orphanage? How did you not cry?" I narrow my puffy, cat-eyeliner-smeared eyes at him. "Are you a witch?"

It would make sense. There has to be some wicked flaw as to why he's still single. I wonder if his dick is his wand?

"What are you looking at?" he asks, which makes me acutely aware that I'm staring at the bulge in his pants.

I snap my head forward and focus on the taillights of the car in front of us. "So where are we off to next?"

His bed?

Dammit!

I never used to be such a creep. He for sure put some kind of spell on me.

Thankfully, he lets my change of topic slide. "Do you like Mexican food?"

"What kind of question is that? Do you even know me?" I don't think you can be a Denver native and not love Mexican food. And besides Mexico, Colorado makes it best. I could live a long and happy life on a diet consisting of nothing more than green chili. Do you know what it was like for me to move to Texas and not have green chili? Torture! If I dedicated half the time I spent calling restaurants and asking if they had it on the menu to my studies, I would've graduated in a year. But you know . . . priorities.

He smirks and it warms my heart that he seems to find my slight dramatics endearing. "That's what I thought. I made a dinner reservation at La Loma."

I almost lean over and start kissing him right then. La Loma is hands down my favorite restaurant in the entire world. "You know, some might worry that you are peaking way too early."

The "some" in that statement would be me.

Shoes, *Hamilton*, and green chili in one day? There has to be a catch.

"Then they would be underestimating me, and I love proving people wrong."

The timbre of his voice makes my toes curl because I'm pretty sure that he means me and he's going to prove me wrong in bed.

And I am not mad at it.

I squeeze my thighs together and bump the number of margaritas I'll be drinking tonight to two. "Well, okay then."

La Loma recently moved from their longtime location in the Highlands to prime real estate in the heart of Downtown Denver right across the street from the Brown Palace. It's a boss move I can only dream about making. This new location also comes with valet parking instead of the pothole-ridden parking lot you'd have to navigate because their food was worth the risk of ruining your tires.

The valet attendant climbs into the driver's side without acknowledging what a sick car the Tesla is or who's driving it. It's probably the most professional shit I've seen in a long time, and now I'm equally as impressed with the curbside and table-side service.

Even though I'm about as fancy as I'll ever get, we fit right in with the eclectic Monday night crowd. Maxwell places his hand on the small of my back as we walk in. Normally, this is just the kind of possessive he-man move that would turn me all the way off. But like everything to do with Maxwell, this feels different. With him, it's not possessiveness, it's desire—like he can't handle being close to me and not touching me. A feeling I completely understand because I feel the exact same way, and it takes everything in me not to completely melt into his touch.

"Killer shoes," the hostess says to me as we approach. Her lustful eyes are directed at my shoes and not the fine man beside me.

"Oh my god, aren't they?" I twist my ankle around, giving her a good look at all angles. Then I realize how rude I sound. "Shit, sorry." Heat rises in my cheeks as I plant my feet firmly on the ground. "I meant to just say thank you."

She waves off my apology. "Girl, don't apologize. If I had those on my feet, I'd be standing on tabletops and carrying around a megaphone so people would look."

Well, shit.

Now I want to poach La Loma's employees because I really want her to work at HERS.

"I'm Brynn." I stretch out my hand, taking her by surprise.

"Romy," she says, shaking my hand back.

She's got a great handshake.

"How's your insurance and do you enjoy reality shows?" I ask before I can think this all the way through.

Her eyebrows furrow together and her face scrunches up in confusion, and Maxwell lets out a deep bark of laughter and speaks before she gets the chance to answer. "We have a reservation under Lewis for two."

"What? Oh! Right." Poor, flustered Romy shakes her head, her long, bouncy curls falling in front of her face, and reaches for two menus. "This way."

She leads us to our table, the faint music and loud conversations distracting from the awkward silence that's fallen between us.

"Here you are." She gestures to the small corner table nestled against the brick wall. "Julia will be your server tonight."

"Sorry for making that awkward," I say as I take my seat, successfully making this interaction more awkward. "What I meant to say is if you ever find yourself at HERS in Five Points, and I'm not there, tell whoever's working that Brynn said your bill is on the house."

Her eyes light up and my shoulders fall by what feels like a solid three inches. "Oh my god. I've been dying to go there! I knew you looked familiar. *Love the Player* is, like, my new favorite show. Me and my girls have watch parties every week. I don't know much about football, but I'm a reality TV expert."

Don't offer her a job again. Don't offer her a job again. Don't—

"Well . . . I'm always looking for new people to join our staff.

And giving genuine compliments and being well versed in reality TV are two of my main requirements, if you're interested in joining our team."

Oh well. I only have so much restraint. Okay. Whatever. I have zero restraint but that's what makes me a motherfuckin' go-getter.

Romy looks over her shoulder like she's afraid her boss is going to appear and ream her out for encouraging me. "Is it true a lot of Mustangs players and their wives come in or is that just for the show?"

I studiously ignore Maxwell, who is watching me with unabashed interest in my answer.

"Lots of wives come in and a few players, but nobody impressive." I watch Maxwell's reaction out of the corner of my eye and am super satisfied when he has to pick up his menu to hide his smile.

Romy shrugs. "I doubt I'd recognize any of the players anyways. Except TK Moore." She closes her eyes as if she's conjuring up a maybe-dressed picture of him in her head. "It's a shame he retired. That hair and that body? He was the only reason I watched." Her eyes fly open and both hands cover her mouth, and I have no doubt her brown skin is warm to the touch. "Oh my god. I am so sorry."

Maxwell is full-out laughing now, and I'm pretty sure I found Vonnie's long-lost sister.

"So you're hired. Seriously, if you want it, stop by and we'll get things sorted." I pull out one of my business cards that I always have stocked in my wallet and hand it to her. "Also, would you happen to be related to Vonnie Lamar?"

"No, I don't think so. Why?"

"Come work at HERS and you'll see," I say. I think adding a little bit of mystery is always a good idea when courting new employees.

"Okay, I will." She looks at the card and then smiles a mega-watt smile. "Enjoy your dinner."

"I'm not used to sitting with a celebrity," Maxwell jokes as Romy hurries back to the empty hostess stand with a growing crowd. "Do you think she'll validate our parking now?"

"It's complimentary valet." I roll my eyes.

He smiles wide, his white teeth bright against his full lips. "For ballers like you, maybe."

"This is true. You really need to step your game up, Lewis."

"Eh." He lays his menu flat on the table and cocks his head to the side. "It's a turn-on being with a powerful woman."

"Hi, I'm Julia." A peppy woman in black slacks and a white button-up appears next to us. "Can I start you folks with something to drink?"

"A margarita on the rocks, and stat, Julia."

"I'll just have water, thanks." Maxwell's heated eyes don't move from me as he orders.

"Got it." Julia tucks her notepad into her apron and turns on her heel.

Maxwell looks at me over the top of his menu. "And to think, this entire night is just the appetizer for when we get back home."

Oh.

My.

God.

"We could always just order to go," I suggest.

At that, he throws his head back and laughs. His entire beautiful face somehow becomes more beautiful, and my insides go liquid knowing that I made it that way. And I know, without a doubt in my mind, that nothing in this world could ruin this night.

"Brynn?" A finger taps me on the shoulder, and I turn to see Eloise. "Oh my god! Hi!"

But she's not alone.

Well, fuck. I guess there is something—or someone—who could ruin this night.

"Hey, Bro," Theo says, something so off about his tone and the glint in his eyes that a chill goes down my spine . . . and not the good kind either. "You're a hard guy to get in touch with."

Twenty-nine

"BRYNN," MAXWELL SAYS. THE CAREFREE MAN WHO WAS JUST IN front of me is long gone, and a version of him that I've never seen is in its place. His eyes are like ice. The tendons in his neck are bulging and his hands are balled up in fists against the tabletop. "Go find Julia and tell her we'll be taking our order to go."

"We can't take margaritas to go," I joke, but Maxwell's eyes slice to me and shut me up.

"You know how much I love your smart mouth, but please, just this one time, please just go."

My eyes flicker between him and his brother. Both of them are still, the only movement is the twitching of their square jaws.

Side by side, they look nothing alike. Though I thought Theo seemed built when we first met, he looks a bit like a slouch with Maxwell in front of him. There are deep lines surrounding Theo's mouth that can only come from frowning, which is a stark contrast to Maxwell's unmarked face.

"Umm . . ." Eloise shifts nervously beside me, looking between the two brothers. "Am I missing something here?"

I jump out of my seat, and the loud squeak of the chair against the distressed wooden floor draws the eyes of diners nearby. "Come with me?" I ask Eloise, but I grab her hand and start pulling her away before she has an opportunity to answer.

"What the hell is that about?" she asks once we're out of ear-shot.

"I have no idea," I tell her honestly. "I knew they weren't close and that Maxwell wasn't Theo's biggest fan, but I think there's more going on than I ever imagined." Not that I actually gave it much thought . . . at least before. Now the adorably inquisitive side of me is dying to get to the bottom of this.

When I find Julia, she's standing behind the bar, grabbing what I can only pray is my margarita. "Excuse me." The pitch of my voice raises a few decibels. "Is there any way we can order our meal to go? Something came up."

"Of course." She eyes the margarita in her hand. "Do you still want this?"

"Is water wet?" I ask before I can check myself.

I should really invest in some kind of class to help me develop a filter.

Luckily for me, she laughs, and even if she didn't find me funny, I'm standing much too close for her to spit in my drink.

"Then here you go. Are you ready to order now, or do you want me to come find you in a few?"

"Um . . ." I know what I want. I'm a creature of habit when it comes to food. But Maxwell and I are too new for me to know what to order for him. "Let me go ask him what he wants and I'll find you." I glance at Eloise, who is on her tippy-toes, craning her neck, trying to get a good look at what's happening at our table. I tap her shoulder and she spins around with the same expression Ace wore when I caught him standing by the freezer, eating ice cream out of the container.

"What? Hi! Sorry, what?"

I bite the inside of my cheek not to laugh at her. "Watch my drink for me?"

"Can I have some?" she counters.

"I knew I always liked you," I say. Even though . . . lies. I totally hated her, but mainly because I was just being a hater. "Of course you can."

"Then yes, I can." She smiles and I'm pretty sure the group of businessmen sitting at the table behind us fall in love.

"Be right back."

I don't make it far. Only four steps to be exact before two angry sets of eyes stop me in my tracks.

"Um, I was just coming to get your order." I bite my lip, hating the hesitation in my voice.

I keep my gaze leveled on Maxwell, but it's hard to focus when Theo's angry one is damn near burning a hole in the side of my face. But even distracted, there's no missing the warring emotions crossing Maxwell's beautiful face. "I'm so sorry to do this, but I have to go," he says.

My head jerks back so fast, the room starts to spin. "What?"

"I don't want him near you," he whispers, his mouth so close that his lips graze my ear as he talks.

But even though my body is a fucking traitor and even that tiny bit of contact sends lightning bolts straight to my core, my mind is sound and my hackles shoot up. "What does that even mean?" I keep my tone hushed, not wanting to draw more attention to our group than the hostile waves rolling off Maxwell and Theo have already garnered. "I'm grown."

He closes his eyes and takes a deep breath. I know he's holding on by a thread and I think on my words. I'm grown enough to put myself in his situation and think about how I would feel if my mom suddenly showed up. The last thing I'd want is for him to witness that.

"Okay," I say before he gets the chance to speak. "Go, I'll take an Uber home."

"No." He reaches into his pocket and pulls out the valet ticket. "Take my car. I'm going to ride with Theo and I'll call you when I'm done."

"I . . . I . . ." Okay, now my mind stops working, and before the circuits repair themselves, he sticks the ticket in my hand and is out the door. "I can't drive your car! I'm a terrible driver!" I yell to the now-closed door.

Fuck.

I really need that margarita, and now I can't have it.

"I'm a fantastic driver." Eloise places the cold margarita glass in my hands. "And you look like you need to get drunk."

I contemplate saying no and heading back to Maxwell's house to wait up for him. But that only lasts for about one point two seconds. Then I realize the best date I've ever been on ended in catastrophe and I won't be getting any tonight. I lift the salt-covered rim to my mouth and down the remainder of the margarita, not even stopping when my brain freezes in my head.

"Let's go to HERS." I put the empty glass on the table and dig out enough cash to cover my drink and give Julia a sizable tip. "I know the owner, we can drink for free."

Thirty

MAXWELL HAD TO COME SEE ME.

Taking the keys to someone's car is a fantastic way to make sure they follow up. Only if they offer, of course. Don't go to jail trying to get a second date. But if the opportunity presents itself, I definitely encourage taking it.

He was properly apologetic, and I was—if I do say so myself—properly understanding. But that was where it ended. I didn't invite him inside and he didn't ask. I think it was a heavy evening for all involved, and a short break was needed.

The problem with this? Our break has now lasted a week. I mean, we text and shit, but I'm not sixteen anymore, and a good-morning text doesn't do what it used to. I understand that the regular season is coming to an end and if they want to keep their playoff hopes alive, he needs to focus. If anyone understands the demands of a job, it's me.

What is pissing me the fuck off though, is he's had this job for years and still managed to multitask.

This is a problem.

Maxwell doesn't like confrontation. He doesn't like getting angry or having people angry at him . . . which is funny when you think about how many crazed football fans hate him. Whereas I don't give a single fuck. If I have a problem, I want it dealt with immediately. I'd rather get in a scream fest than walk on eggshells pretending things are fine when they're clearly not.

"Ew." Charli slides into her reserved, game-day chair across the bar. "Who peed in your Lucky Charms?"

"Gross." My stomach turns. "I don't think that's even the saying, and now you've fucked up marshmallows for me." Which makes me even more irritated because I just ordered some for the seasonal hot cocoa cocktail I'm putting on the menu.

"I know, but when's the last time you bought a cereal that wasn't marketed to children? Have you ever even bought Cheerios?"

"Once, they had a special edition for the Olympics that had marsh—never mind." I grab an olive out of the container and aim it at her forehead when she starts to laugh.

Of course, she's just as athletic as her husband and snatches it out of the air and pops it on her finger. "Give me more, I wanna do E.T. fingers."

"You're so strange," I say . . . but I still fill a cup with olives.

"Oh god." Vonnie sits next to Charli. "You're worse than my fucking kids," she says.

"But you loooove me." Charli wiggles her olive-covered fingertips in Vonnie's face, doing what I think is her version of an alien voice.

"I do." Vonnie stills Charli's hand and eats one of the olives off her finger.

I stare wide-eyed as Charli feeds Vonnie another fingertip. "You guys are fucking disgusting," I say.

When I was a kid and I pictured being an adult, this is not what came to mind. Hell, when I turned thirty this wasn't what I pictured.

"Hmmm," Vonnie says when she's finished chewing. "You still haven't seen Max, have you?"

"Ooooh! That's why she's such a grumpfish!" Charli sounds way too excited about my foul mood and turbulent relationship.

"Why don't you just go over to his house? You have the code to get in, right?" Vonnie asks.

I open my mouth to answer, but Poppy magically appears and beats me to it.

"Max and you are still weird?" Poppy's hair, which is always glorious, is somehow even more wonderful. She's not wearing any makeup, but it looks like someone bronzed her skin, and her lips look like they're swollen from being kissed all morning. Which might be the case, but since she hit the second trimester, they've been like this all the time. Her boobs are fucking huge and her bump is tiny and adorable. I already know that if I ever got pregnant, I'd be covered in acne and probably carry in my ass. Poppy looks like a fucking supermodel.

"No, we're fine." I shrug and start rearranging glasses that don't need to be rearranged.

"Shit," Poppy says. "You only organize when you're really stressed. It must be bad."

Ughhhh!

I close my eyes and start to count to ten, taking deep breaths through my nose. This is the downside to having a great group of friends. They notice things about you that you don't notice about yourself, and it makes it impossible to hide anything from them.

"You know what? You're right," Vonnie says before I get to seven. "When we were getting her ready for her date, Aviana threatened to tape her hands together so she'd stop trying to organize the eye shadows."

"When I was working here, some magazine was doing a

feature on HERS, and she spent the night before it was published alphabetizing the files and writing a new manual that included the direction the toilet paper must face."

"Oh my god! I'm standing right here!" I abandon my deep breathing on my third attempt to count to ten. "First of all, organizing is an extremely healthy way to deal with stress, especially when you have multiple bottles of tequila at your fingertips."

Upon hearing "fingertips," Charli starts to wiggle hers at me again.

"Also, nobody here can tell me that toilet paper shouldn't go over instead of under. That was a perfectly reasonable addition to the manual."

Poppy ignores me. "She also added that if one of us goes to Fresh for a break, we are required to ask everyone on shift if they need a caffeine pickup as well."

Dammit. I don't have an argument for that one. I wrote it and even I know that was batshit crazy. "Fair point."

I don't give in often, so Poppy's face lights up—even more, the glowing bitch—knowing she beat me.

"Okay," Vonnie says, her voice all business and a stark contrast to Charli, who is loading up her fingers with more olives. "So we watch this game, and when it's over, we all meet at Brynn's to come up with a plan on how this should be handled. But no more talking about this here, because there are too many ears and Avi and Jac are going to be here soon and they're filming."

"Sounds like a plan," Charli says.

Poppy nods her head in agreement. "Agreed."

"You guys want my input?" The snark is heavy in my voice.

"Nope," Vonnie says. "We're good."

I throw a handful of cherries in Poppy's Shirley Temple and put it in front of her with a little more force than necessary. "Ugh, Lady Mustangs."

"Bitch, please," Vonnie says. "Enough of that. You're a Lady Mustang too."

"Am not," I say, but I don't even convince myself.

"Oh, you so are," Charli chimes in. "You attend more meetings than me."

The world around me turns silver as everything explodes into a combustion of crystals and glitter.

"Fuck." I rest my head on the bar, which is something else I added to the manual on things that were not allowed. "I am."

"Oh my god! Look at this place! I'm going to have to call a babysitter more often." Lucy shouts over the noise of HERS. I almost don't recognize her without her massive diaper bag over her shoulder and a baby strapped to her chest. She reaches us, pulling out the empty seat next to Poppy. "So, what did I miss?"

"Oh, girl." Vonnie pushes her martini over to Lucy. "If we're gonna play catch-up, you're gonna need one of these."

"Yes!" Lucy punches the air and drains Vonnie's glass. "The only gossip I ever get is which preschooler picked their nose. I came in an Uber and I'm so ready for this."

Well, at least that makes one of us.

Thirty-one

SURPRISING NOBODY AT ALL, THE MEETING OF THE MINDS AT MY apartment solved absolutely nothing.

I did, however, discover that Lucy is so much fucking fun, and if I could, I'd get her drunk every day. The pictures she sent me the next day of her with circles under her eyes and children literally climbing on top of her in bed with the caption "Send help" are being printed out so I can frame them in my office.

HERS doesn't open for another couple of hours, but I got in early to catch up on all the work my sex-addled mind has forgotten about. Even though there are speakers built into the ceiling, I use the wireless speaker I ordered specifically to use while I'm doing paperwork. It's covered in magenta Swarovski crystals. Was it a waste of money? I mean, who can really say? Can you really put a price on joy?

I blast my playlist—aptly named "Get Shit Done," which is filled with gangsta rap and Spice Girls . . . it might sound like an odd combination, but it keeps my mind sharp—and get to work.

I return emails and check the inventory. During the holiday

season, I use these things as my excuse to get out of all Christmas-related activities.

I used to love Christmas. My mom was like Queen Christmas. We hung the lights, decorated the trees (multiple), made the cookies, and did whatever crazy festive thing she deemed was necessary. We started listening to Christmas music at Halloween, and she wouldn't take down the decorations until Valentine's Day.

Then she left.

And every white light and jingle bell reminded me of the gaping hole she blew into my life. I know I hold a mean grudge, but even I feel like this is a little long for poor old Saint Nick.

I'm going over the marketing schedule for the next three months when the doorbell I had installed goes off. People don't often ring it, mainly because we are a bar, and what kind of bar needs a doorbell, but it always makes my day when they do because it rings to the tune of "Turn Down for What." I don't think I have a delivery scheduled for today, but as a member of Amazon Prime and an Etsy enthusiast, I know that anything's possible and make my way to the door.

As soon as my glass doors come into view, my heart soars and my feet falter when I see Maxwell standing on the other side.

It's Tuesday, but since we've been going strong on a steady diet of text messages and avoidance, I didn't have high hopes for seeing him today. And now that he's in front of me, I'm not sure how I feel. I keep my steps even as I approach. No way will he get the satisfaction of seeing me run to him after he's basically ignored me for a week.

When I unlock the door, I fold my arms in front of my chest and keep my mouth closed. My stubbornness beats out my need to jump his bones.

"I'm sorry," he says with no hesitation. "Seeing Theo really fucked with me, and talking to him only made it worse. I haven't seen him in years and it was intentional. We don't like each other, and a lot of really bad shit has gone down between us. I should've handled this better. My mind has been a mess and I didn't want to drag you into the darkness that Theo brings. And to be honest, things are still a fucking mess and I know I should stay away from you, but I can't. I can't make myself leave you alone when you're the only person who can give me back the light."

And call me a softy, tell me I'm a fool for forgetting about how angry and hurt I've been for the last week, but that's all I needed to hear before I'm yanking him into HERS and locking the door behind him. You can also blame it on the fact that I have literally been dreaming about sex with him for days now and I'm so sexually frustrated I could cry.

"My office." I point to the open door, where the distant sound of DMX yelling at me is coming from. "Then take your pants off." You know, 'cause I'm all classy and emotional and shit.

"But first"—Maxwell pulls me into him, our chests pressed against one another—"I need your mouth."

I tilt my chin and he touches his mouth to mine.

"I'm so sorry, Brynn." Another kiss. "I promise I won't do it again." Another kiss. "You can trust me."

"Shut up," I whisper before opening my mouth and deepening the kiss. Because I know I can trust him, implicitly and to my bones. What I don't know is if I can trust myself. I am, after all, my mother's daughter.

We don't pull away as we walk to my office. It's not pretty and I'm sure I'll have multiple bruises on my legs from running into the corners of tables, but what it is is raw. There's no faking what runs between us.

I kick my office door shut behind us, and as much as I want the movie-perfect scene of swiping all the papers off my desk, I have a brand-new Apple computer and it was freaking expensive.

"Pants off." I point at his sweatpants with the tented crotch before I move to my desk and unplug my computer and very carefully relocate it to the empty desk I bought for Ace when Poppy worked here. Then, when I'm sure it's not going to topple over onto the rug-covered ground, I peel off my yoga pants and white tee.

I take my time walking back to my desk. I bask in his attention and add a little swing to my hips. I know I look good naked, and I know Maxwell thinks I look good naked. And holy shit, is there power in that. I reach my desk, bending over slowly, and finally sweep it clear of all paperwork.

Papers fly into the air, taking their time to swoop around before landing on the floor. I prop my ass on the edge of my desk, my legs spread just so, and watch as Maxwell's sexy ass steps over the mess on the floor and makes his way over to me.

It only takes him a few long strides before he's standing in front of me, reaching out to touch me.

"No, no, no." I tsk. "I'm not sure you get to touch yet."

"What?" His eyes are too heavy to widen much, but he does pull his hands back to his side.

"You ignored me this week." I keep my eyes on his, but the same can't be said for him. No, he's laser focused on my hand that's slowly, but surely, drifting up the inside of my thigh. "Do you know how that made me feel?"

"How?" he grinds out between clenched teeth.

I spread my legs open wider and put one hand behind me on the table as I arch my back, pushing my breasts toward him. "It made me feel frustrated and lonely." I slide the hand up my thigh higher and higher until—"Mmmmh"—I moan. My eyes close of their own accord and I pull my bottom lip in between my teeth.

My fingers dancing between my thighs start to move in circles, and I feel Maxwell harden against my thigh. It's not easy, but I manage to pry my eyes open. It's a mistake, because when I see the look on his face and his hand stroking his length, my little game is almost over immediately.

"You like watching, don't you?" I speed up the circles before dipping a finger inside. "Oh my god!" My free hand flies to the edge of the desk and clings to the small ridge as I lie flat on my back.

"Jesus, Brynn." Maxwell's voice is barely recognizable. I faintly hear the tear of a foil wrapper as I switch back to the circles.

I start working my hand faster and harder. A pace that I need . . . that I crave . . . and that is nowhere as good by myself than with the man staring down at me.

Beads of sweat are dripping down his forehead and his chest. His black eyes are watching me so closely, it's like I can feel his hands on me. And as much as I love this, I love what he can do even more.

"I want your mouth on me," I groan, my throaty whisper at least an octave higher than normal.

He drops to his knees and yanks my ankles until my ass is dangling off the table and my ankles are over his shoulder. "Fucking finally."

I've wanted this since our date. I was already primed and ready before the little show I put on. So once his mouth latches onto my center, it's only a matter of seconds before my back arches off the desk and my hands fly to his head, anchoring myself to him. But after I let go of his head, I realize I didn't need to hold him to me because he still doesn't come up for air. He keeps his mouth attached to me even as my body quakes and trembles through at least two, but maybe three orgasms.

"No more," I plead through labored breaths. Every nerve in my body is lit and even the soft kisses he's trailing up my stomach cause my core to clench. "I need you inside of me."

"Why didn't you just say so?" He straightens at the base of the desk, lifting my hips to position himself right at my center. "You're the one in charge here."

He pushes in hard and fast, but my body is so primed and ready to go that it adjusts to him the second he enters me.

He pounds into me over and over again, but it's not enough . . . I don't know if I'll ever get enough of him.

"Wait." I place my palms on his hard, sweat-covered chest.

He pulls out without hesitation, concern coloring his expression. "Are you okay?"

I don't even entertain that question with an answer. Instead I turn around and bend over my desk. "This way."

When I look over my shoulder, his eyes are on my bare ass tilted up, and it only takes a second before his hands are gripping my hips, his fingernails biting into my skin, as he enters me from behind.

I arch my back, needing him deeper, wanting to feel him throughout my entire body. He drops one of his hands from my hip and wraps it in my ponytail, pulling my head back and deepening the curve of my back.

It's exactly what I needed. That dull ache against my skull causes my body to tense and my core to throb around him. He speeds up his thrusts, each one harder and better than the last until my eyes close and my bones turn to jelly as the orgasm rips through my body.

"Oh my god!" I shout over the sounds of our skin slapping together and the moan Maxwell lets out as he comes.

Maxwell lifts me off of my desk and carries me to the couch. My body is still trembling from the intensity of my orgasm, and I know if I were to come again, I'd most likely die. But as soon as he tucks me into his front and I feel him behind me, I'm ready to go again.

I start to wiggle my butt against him, but before he can even respond, the doorbell rings again and I hear Paisley shouting my name.

"Shit!" I scramble off of the couch, searching for underwear and then realizing I def didn't put any on this morning.

Well, crap.

This is going to be a long day . . . and with any luck, a longer night.

Thirty-two

I THOUGHT I HATED THE LADY MUSTANGS BEFORE.

I had no idea.

"It is freezing and I despise you all and how did you trick me into this?" I ask Vonnie, who, even though it is negative one million degrees outside, has somehow managed to still look fabulous and glamorous.

Me? Well, I'm bundled up in all of my skiing gear to the point where my arms can't even rest flat against my body.

Vonnie drew the line at my goggles though.

This is the final regular-season game of the year. I learned upon eavesdropping that the Mustangs always save the food drive until this week. It doesn't make sense to me. I thought they'd do it around Thanksgiving. But they said, when I acted on my eavesdropping and voiced my opinion, it's because people forget to donate after November and they like to give a large donation to start off the New Year. It's nice, I guess. If it were me, I'd do this in September when I couldn't see my own breath.

"It's for a good cause, Brynn," Vonnie throws over her shoulder as she collects another bag of canned goods from some fans. "And if you are so miserable, why are you smiling?"

"This isn't a smile!" I try to fold my glove-covered fingers to point at my face, but they are too thick, so I have to gesture with my whole hand. "My face is frozen like this!"

"I'm so sorry," Vonnie says to the fans. "We love her, but she's a little dramatic."

Me? The dramatic one in this group? Is she serious right now? If glaring didn't take up so much of the energy I'm using to keep warm, I would level her with a nasty one.

"Aren't you from Colorado?" Jacqueline asks. "Shouldn't you be used to this weather?"

"Yes, I am from Colorado, but unless I'm flying down a mountain, adrenaline heating my veins, I seek shelter, take my ass inside, and look at the snow through a window." I know it doesn't make sense because I really am not a fan of the cold, but I really do love skiing.

Jacqueline holds her Burberry-gloved hands up in front of her. "Geez. Sorry. The cold makes you sassy."

I have a solid comeback on the tip of my tongue when a young boy, bundled in a North Face jacket and a Mustangs hat and scarf, walks up to me with a paper grocery bag filled with cans.

"Thank you so much." I crouch into as deep of a squat as my layered legs can go. My voice shifts into my peppy customer service voice. "This is so nice of you. Are you so excited for the game today?"

"Yeah! We're gonna kick Arizona's butt!" he yells, giving me an unsolicited high five that stings some of the feeling back into my numb limbs.

"Heck yes they are! Those other guys aren't even going to

know what to do in this cold weather, buncha warm-weather babies." *Note to self, check prices for Arizona trip.* "Who's your favorite Mustang?"

He unzips his jacket despite his dad's protest and the snow-flakes that are beginning to fall. "Maxwell Lewis!" He bounces up and down on his toes, color rising in his already rosy cheeks. "All the kids in my class all wanna be the quarterback, but not me. Well, my mom and dad will only let me play flag football, but even in flag, I always love defense. I got eight interceptions last season."

Holy cow. I thought Aviana talked fast.

"Eight?" I force my eyes wide like I have any clue what I'm talking about. "That's incredible, dude!" I raise my hand and he gives me another glove-padded high five.

"Thanks! It was the most on my team and—" He starts to tell me more, but his dad steps in.

"All right, bud, I think we better get inside and find some of that cocoa before kickoff, don't you think?"

The kid was starting to pout until he heard "cocoa," and then I was nothing but a long-forgotten memory.

"Yes! Cocoa!" He turns on his boot and speed walks away.

"I wish I could say that was the first time hot chocolate has been more appealing than me, but it's not," I say to Vince, who, even though it's freezing, is still wearing his usual uniform of jeans, a hoodie, and a baseball hat.

He doesn't pull his face away from the camera to respond. "Same, Brynn. Same."

Because *Love the Player* was so successful, they decided to film during the entire season. They aren't allowed inside of the stadium, that's the only hard line the Mustangs drew. All of the footage they use on the show from the games comes from the flip cameras they gave all the cast members—so filming right outside of the doors while the women were all dolled up in their gear and talking with fans is—I assume—the production equivalent of an orgasm.

"See, I knew you'd be great at this," Vonnie chimes in after sliding a twenty-dollar bill into the giant white bucket for cash donations. "You were so focused on the little boy, you didn't even notice the dad drop cash in here while you were talking."

She's right, I didn't see that. But she's also right because I also knew I'd be pretty good at this. Again, I own a bar. Interacting with strangers is literally my livelihood. Being able to give back is just the icing on the cake. I'm not lying about hating the cold though. I really hate the freaking cold.

"I mean, I only agreed because I knew you guys needed me." I gesture to Jacqueline in her (faux) fur-lined earmuffs and navy peacoat, her cable-knit socks sticking out of her boots—a look that only a real-life supermodel could wear and not look ridiculous. "Without me, your approachability level is a negative fifty-two. I even the score."

Just as I say that, two guys with no shirts and a blood alcohol level that has to be nearing deadly levels run straight to Jac. "Can we take a picture with you?" the future pneumonia victim with an orange-painted face asks.

"Please," his equally idiotic friend with the blue face—hopefully from paint and not because he's turning into an icicle—says. "We're your biggest fans."

Ew.

Gross.

I can only imagine the things they have done to Jac's pictures. Suddenly, I feel a little bad for how beautiful she is.

"Did you bring any cans?" She changes in front of my eyes

from the shy, quiet woman I've grown to love into her sexy, runway-ready alter ego.

"No, but . . ." The blue face guy's head moves back and forth between Jac and his friend with a look of sheer panic peeking out behind his drunk eyes.

"There's a bucket for cash donations." She points to the bucket and Vonnie models it like she's on *The Price Is Right*. "If you make a donation, I'll take a picture with you."

She barely manages to finish the sentence before the guys almost bowl me over to throw their money in.

"See," I say to Vonnie once I've regained my balance. "What would you do without me?"

"I'd have to find a side hustle to pay for my martini habit, that's for damn sure." She winks and then plasters on a smile when more fans start to approach with bags and boxes of canned goods.

"Thank you," I say between clenched teeth, grabbing a box that I did not expect to be this heavy. "Holy crap." I grunt and hope that nobody's filming me because I'm pretty sure I just pulled a muscle or two.

"Brynnnnn!" I hear called in the distance and use that as an excuse to give up on this box.

"You've got to be kidding me." Vonnie narrows her eyes at Eloise's incoming form, but she does it without letting her smile falter. I'd be lying if I said it wasn't the tiniest bit terrifying. In that moment, I see her serial killer quality. "I thought she went away."

"I told you I was with her a few weeks ago. Just give her a chance, I think you'll actually really like her." I rush the words out before Eloise makes it to us.

"I'll try."

"I don't think I believe you." I want to say more, but before I can, Eloise is standing in front of me, looking her normal polished and gorgeous self. "Hey! How've you been?"

"I'm good." She smiles, but I can see a hint of concern lingering on her face. Not surprising since the last time we saw each other I was drowning my sorrows in margaritas. "How are you? Are you an official Lady Mustang now?"

"No," I say, but I don't think she can hear it over Jac and Vonnie shouting, "Yes!" in perfect synchronization and scaring the group of drunk twentysomethings in the middle of a rousing rendition of a song that I'm not hip enough to know the name of.

The concern is pushed off her face as her smile grows. "I knew it! I couldn't tell you the night we were together because . . . well, you know. But you guys look so good together and every time you hear his name, your eyes go all soft."

I roll my eyes and shake my head. "They do not."

"They so do!" Eloise's voice rises about three decibels.

"Soft," Jacqueline repeats, like she's testing the word. "That's exactly it."

"What are you guys talking about?" I look between the two gorgeous blondes in front of me. "I look at him the same way I look at you."

"She's right," Vonnie says like it physically pains her. "Your eyes turn to liquid every time you see him."

Eloise nods her head rapidly, her long blond hair bouncy beneath her Mustangs beanie, and holds up an expectant hand toward Vonnie. I can't tell if she's just powering through Vonnie's cold shoulder or if she really just doesn't notice that Vonnie isn't running for president of her fan club anytime soon.

Vonnie doesn't hesitate at all as she slaps her wool glove against Eloise's. "Who'd you come to the game with?" she asks Eloise.

Wait . . . what?

"My dad and Paul." Eloise rolls her eyes and points to the surly old men checking their watches. "I don't think they even like football, I'm pretty sure they just like telling people they have tickets."

"My boys stayed home because of this . . ." Vonnie points to the pile of cans and the money bucket. "So I have plenty of extra room in the box if you want to join us."

Okay? Has hell frozen over along with the Denver metro area?

"Really?" Eloise voices the question I'm thinking.

"Yeah, really." Vonnie shrugs. "Plus, it's been like pulling teeth getting this one"—she points her thumb at me—"to tell us about Max's fine-ass, handcuff-wielding brother. Promise you won't be stingy on the details?"

Something that I can't read crosses Eloise's face and her smile fades. But by the time I blink, it's gone and she's walking away to tell her dad to enjoy the game without her.

"What just happened?" Jac asks before me, and I know that I didn't just imagine everything.

"I like her." Vonnie shrugs her shoulders and turns to greet more fans. "Thank you so much," she says as she adds more cans to the pile/sad attempt of a pyramid we have going.

"Since when?" I ask.

"Would you mind taking a picture with us?" a woman who has to be a solid ten years younger than me with a bun and UGGs asks me.

ME!

"Ummm, I'm sorry." I wave Jacqueline over. "I think you mean her?"

Never in my life did I think I'd get mistaken for a supermodel, especially when my nose is most likely in serious competition with Rudolph for whose nose is brighter—even though I've got the frozen-snot title on lock. I might have complained for the last hour and a half, but now I will go home and write in my diary (that I will buy on the way home) that today is the best day of my entire life. You know, next to sex with Maxwell and opening day at HERS.

"Ummm . . ." my style sister says as Jacqueline approaches. "I mean, we totally love Jacqueline, but you're Brynn Sterling, right?"

My head jerks back in surprise and welcome heat floods my freezing face. "Uh? Yeah. I am."

"Oh my god. I just love you." She leans in and gives me a dreaded hug that suddenly, coming from a random young woman who knows who I am, doesn't seem so dreadful. "I'm a senior at Metro. I'm a brewery operations major and you are my idol. What you have done for women in the Denver bar scene has literally been life changing for me."

"It's true," one of the people in her group says. "You're like her LeBron James."

"Shut up!" she hisses beneath her breath. "I mean, she's not wrong though. I was a nursing major. I hate blood and was probably going to fail, but my parents both convinced me it was the smartest option. But then I read the article on you in *Westword* and you talked about women wanting to have quality beer and a space to go where we were celebrated instead of used. It was my aha moment. I mean, my parents stopped paying for my school, but now I'm studying something I'm passionate about."

"I . . . um . . . I, wow." I try to organize the millions of thoughts colliding in my head. "I don't even know what to say. I mean, thank you."

I opened a bar.

A cute bar that I love. But a bar. Yes, it's given me the family and community I've always wanted, but I never thought of HERS doing anything besides giving women a night out with good drinks and a fun atmosphere. That's it.

Never. Not on a single vision board did I imagine this happening.

"No, thank you," she says.

We both look at her friend aiming a phone in our direction and smile.

"Do you have a pen?" I ask, silently cursing Vonnie for convincing me to leave my purse in her car.

"Ummm . . ." She opens her small purse and starts digging around. "Sorry." She aims an embarrassed smile my way. "I thought a small purse would help, but I still have the same amount of crap I had in my big purse, just shoved inside here. Ah!" She holds up her hand with the kind of dramatic flair that I really appreciate. "I knew I had one."

"Okay." I start to write on the scrap of paper I had crumpled inside of my coat pocket, realizing that we all have smartphones and this entire scene was completely unnecessary. Oh well! Too late to turn back now. "I'm writing down my number and my email. If you need . . . Crap!" I cringe at how ridiculous I sound. "I didn't even get your name!"

"Dani." She makes the face I'm sure I just made. "Well, Danielle, but everyone calls me Dani."

"Well, Dani, if you need a part-time job or internship or anything, please don't hesitate to reach out." I hand her the piece of paper. "There aren't many of us in this industry, so we have to stick together."

Dani eyes the paper like I just handed her a bar of gold. "Thank you." She stares at the paper until one of her friends not so subtly clears their throat. "Oh. Right! Um, my friend wants to know if you are . . . um . . . you know, if—"

"Oh my god. Are you really dating Maxwell Lewis?" Dani's friend asks.

My eyebrows shoot to my hairline. I mean, I know Denver is small and all, but I didn't realize we were already news. But I think the thing that surprises me most is how excited I am to

squeal to the world that Maxwell Lewis is my man. "Yeah, I am."
My lips are so numb from the cold that I don't even notice I'm
biting it until Eloise reappears.

"Soft eyes and a lip bite? She's definitely thinking about Max."

Geez! All this crap from Eloise and she isn't even a freaking
Lady Mustang!

Thirty-three

"ARE YOU EVER GOING TO TELL ME WHERE WE'RE GOING?"
Maxwell asks for the hundredth time.

It's the first round of playoffs this weekend. But because the
Mustangs have Maxwell—and some other quality players, I
guess—they won their division and were granted a bye game dur-
ing the first week. Which is a thing and I totally knew it and
Charli didn't have to explain it to me at all. Because of the bye,
Maxwell has the weekend off, and when I found that out, nothing
could stop me from ditching my responsibilities and dragging
Maxwell out of Denver.

The food drive was a bit of a wakeup call for me, and suddenly, I didn't feel comfortable talking about him behind the bar,
or giving him a quick kiss on the sidewalk. The streets were
watching and I got hit with a bad case of stage fright.

"You know what?" I chance a quick glare at him as we hit the
base of the foothills. "You're worse than Ace. Just sit back and
enjoy the ride." I jab a thumb to the back seat. "It's not a super-
long drive, but I brought snacks in case you get hungry."

He grabs the bag of baby carrots I packed as an afterthought for the hummus I stuck in the cooler and starts eating them . . . without the hummus.

"What are you doing?" I have to beat back the urge to pull to the shoulder of the highway.

His eyebrows scrunch together, the glare off the bright, snow-covered boulders lining the highway blinding him temporarily. "Uh . . . eating a carrot?"

"Yeah, I know." I roll my eyes, but he can't see, because unlike him, I didn't forget my sunglasses. "Put them back."

He starts to fold the top of the bag over, but doesn't look any less confused. "You just told me I could eat the food you packed."

"Not the carrots." I mean, what is he not understanding? "You can't eat carrots in the car on a road trip. Eat the chips or candy. Oh! Or wait, there's a store up a little bit that has fudge, so many different fudges. We can get a sampling of all the flavors. But if you don't want sweets, we can stop at Coney Island and get a hot dog, the food's just okay, but it's shaped like a giant hot dog, so I feel like atmosphere makes up for everything else."

"What are you talking about?" Maxwell interrupts my rambling just as I was starting to find my way back to the topic.

"No carrots, junk only while we're in the car." I really should've printed out a list of rules. "But, I am willing to concede one major road trip law." I pause for dramatic effect and to rev up suspense, but I think all it actually does is make Maxwell reconsider ever getting in the car with me again. "You may take charge of the radio." He doesn't even say thank-you before he's reaching for the aux cord (because yes, my car is too old for you to do it wirelessly) and pulling out his phone. "Wait!" I shout and accidentally honk my horn. "You are in charge under the condition that if you turn on trash, it must be changed."

"So I'm only in charge if I pick music you like?"

He sounds a little confused, which I don't understand. It makes perfect sense to me.

"Exactly." I focus on the road in front of me as snow begins to fall a little faster and the heavy fog that comes with climbing altitudes thickens. Thank goodness I had my snow tires put on yesterday.

"So essentially, you're in charge of the radio still?"

"As long as you don't turn on some podcast about rocket science or heavy metal, I'm sure we'll be fine." I sit up a little straighter. I'm not afraid to drive in the snow. Denver native, here. But I do respect it and its dangers. Also, could you imagine if I got into a car accident with Maxwell Lewis in the car before the playoffs? It would be like Marlee and the ice skating multiplied by a million.

"Well, damn, Boss." He clucks his tongue. "Those were my first two choices."

"Smart-ass," I say through laughter. "Now shut up. I need to focus. Killing us would ruin my entire weekend."

LIKE EVERYTHING WITH Maxwell, his taste in music is perfect. So much so that I'm almost a little disappointed when the mountains part and the valley holding Buena Vista comes into view.

Almost.

"Holy shit," Maxwell breathes. "Now that's a view."

Pleasure flows through me at his words. His excitement is almost tangible in the car, and it makes not flooring it into town a struggle. But Buena is my place, and the last thing I want to do is get a speeding ticket to start our weekend and piss off the police.

Buena Vista—pronounced "Boo-na," not "Bway-na," which always confuses me and has caused me to lose countless hours of productivity wondering why that is—is one of my favorite places in all of Colorado. Most Coloradans wouldn't understand. Hell, my dad doesn't understand; he has a condo in Aspen that he rents out most of the year. But Buena Vista feels like a secret. A tiny little town with one bar and only a few more restaurants, it's not the typical go-to for a relaxing weekend away. Which is exactly why it's the perfect place for me and Maxwell.

I turn into town, driving the three blocks through their downtown until the business turns residential and our Airbnb comes into view.

Now, I don't like to toot my own horn or . . . who am I kidding? I love it! The house that I found for our weekend is the cutest house that I have ever seen. The Blue Tower, as they have it listed, is the house of my childhood dreams, and when I saw it, it didn't matter how much it cost or that it was much too large for only two people, I needed it.

"This looks like a storybook," Maxwell says with his face pushed against the window, and he's not wrong.

See, the Blue Tower is exactly that. A little blue house with a tower. They had pictures from the summer that sold me right away, but as I double-park on the cobblestone street and see the snow-dusted roof and garland-draped front porch, I know I would sell my soul to never have to leave. It's still daytime, so the lights aren't on, but I can still see the Christmas lights framing every window in the house . . . and it has a lot of them. Behind the house, Midland Hill looks so close that I'm sure I'll be able to touch it from the balcony.

Not much is better in reality than in pictures. And this weekend, I get to spend my time with two of them: the Blue Tower and Maxwell Lewis.

"Do you have the key? Or how does this work?" Maxwell snaps me out of my head.

"I'm not sure, hold on." I grab my phone and open up the

email with the instructions. "The key is on top of the light by the front door."

"All right, well, why don't you let us in and I'll grab the bags?" he suggests, and since I overpacked and my suitcase is stupid heavy, I agree.

"Sounds like a plan, Captain." I mock salute, snatching my purse off the floor behind my seat and tossing my phone inside.

As soon as my door is open, the frigid mountain air socks me in the gut. But unlike at the food drive, it's rejuvenating. There's a freshness to the mountain air. A freedom that's impossible to find in the city. It snowed yesterday, but unlike the snow that's plowed by HERS, the small piles against the sidewalk are still white.

I climb up the freshly shoveled and carefully salted stairs to the front porch. The key is exactly where they said it would be. Actually, it's not well hidden at all, and if that's not a testament to how safe this little town is, I don't know what is.

I put the key into the lock, and a sudden bout of nerves causes my stomach to sink. Maxwell and I have spent a lot of time together, but this is the first time we've spent this long together without a break or our friends around us. What if we realize we don't work? What if what is supposed to be a romantic weekend turns out to be the end of us? How long can I even last in a relationship before I feel the need to move on? Maybe once the chase is all the way over, I'll get bored and leave.

"What did you pack?" Maxwell grunts behind me, his presence the pressure I needed to open the door. "We're only staying two nights, right? Or did I not pack enough?"

"I'm a girl," I say as an explanation.

"I'm well aware of that." He drops my duffel bag and small—fine!—average-sized suitcase on the tiled entryway. "But did I get the dates wrong?"

"No." I shrug a shoulder. "I just pack heavy."

I've always done this. It used to drive my dad crazy because I would always pack a minimum of three stuffed backpacks to sleepovers when I was a kid. And because I brought so much stuff, a significant amount of things I didn't even know why I was bringing, it was inevitable that I'd forget something and he'd have to go on a retrieval mission, which usually meant he'd be stuck in my friend's kitchen with their parents for a solid two hours while we "looked" for the lost item. Now, with the help of my well-meaning Lady Mustang friends, it has reached a new level of insanity. I have all of my makeup . . . which I doubt I'll even wear . . . more hair products than I even know what to do with, and so, so many shoes.

"Good, I started to get a little worried. It didn't look like there were many shopping options in town." He leans in and drops a quick kiss onto my mouth, which causes my knees to go a little weak, and I sag into the wall behind me. "I'm gonna grab the rest, I'll be right back."

"'Kay." I push off the wall, closing the door behind him so we don't let too much cold air inside.

I move from the entryway and go deeper into the house. Even though the house is flooded with natural light from the abundance of windows, I still flick on all the lights as I go. Where the outside is flawless, the inside is a little dated. I mean, don't get me wrong, it's still beautiful, but I can't help but slip into a daydream where this is my house and I imagine all the changes I would make. The wood-burning stove would definitely stay, but the floors would be gone. I picture the window treatments I would hang to frame this perfect view and the comfy couch I'd put in the living room. I see me and Maxwell getting our Chip and Jo on as we gutted the kitchen.

"How'd you find this place?" Maxwell walks over to me,

slowly unwrapping his scarf from around his neck. Something this normal is not meant to be sexual at all, but he looks so damn sexy that I have to pinch my arm to force myself to focus.

"I come up here every year and I always see this place. I was pretending I wasn't the boss at work the other day and looking at Airbnb. When I saw it was available, I couldn't pass up my opportunity to stay here."

This story is only half-true.

I was bored and wasting time on the Internet. But I wasn't at work since it was Christmas.

Maxwell spent the day with TK, Poppy, and Ace. I know this not only because I was invited, but also because Ace got an iPhone—something TK now owes Poppy for—and Ace spent the entire day flooding my phone with selfies and videos. It was almost cute enough to thaw my frozen heart.

Almost.

"Thank you for bringing me along." He tosses his scarf and jacket onto the recliner in the corner, and his bare feet pad across the tile until he reaches me. He brings his face in so close that I just know he's going to kiss me again. My eyes flutter shut in anticipation and my lips part. "What are we doing today?" he asks instead of kissing me.

"Ummm . . ." I blink a few times, trying to get myself together and remember the answer, because we really do have an itinerary. What can I say? I love planning vacations. I glance at the clock and realize it's later than I thought. "Shoot! Go get changed! Warm clothes and snow boots."

Hopefully having him dressed in layers will lower my need to jump his bones all the time. But I seriously doubt it.

Thirty-four

"HI! I'M BRYNN, WE'RE HERE!" I SLAM MY DOOR SHUT AND RUN TO the bearded man standing outside a nondescript log cabin that I totally would've missed if not for my handy navigation. "So sorry we're late, the roads were worse than I expected."

And also, Maxwell got carsick from all the twisting and turning up the mountain roads, but I figure that's a detail he'll want to keep between us.

"Not a problem," he says, his gruff voice exactly what I was hoping for from the mountain man. "During this season, we actually put you on the schedule for thirty minutes after the time you booked for that reason." His eyes glance over my shoulder, and his posture changes instantly. "Holy crap! You're Maxwell Lewis!"

Figures.

I had hoped he would go unnoticed in the small mountain town, but the Mustangs are an integral part of Colorado culture.

"I am, but please, call me Max," Maxwell says, his voice a

little weaker than normal as he extends a hand to greet our tour guide. "Nice to meet you . . . Sorry. I didn't catch your name."

"Cary," he says, introducing himself to Maxwell even though I'm the one who set up the freaking tour. "Sorry, man, we've never had a Mustangs player up here before. I'm a little starstruck. But lucky for you guys, the dogs don't watch football." Cary laughs at his own joke.

"Dogs?" Maxwell's eyes widen and he looks at me with a mix of excitement and fear plastered across his perfect face.

"Dogsledding!" I yell, jumping up and down, little bursts of snow exploding beneath my feet. As much as I love surprising people, I suck at keeping secrets. It's why I do most of my shopping last minute, because there's no way I can wait an entire month before giving someone their gift.

"Seriously?" I see apprehension cross his face, and he's probably thinking about how well he didn't handle the car ride and imagining that same thing . . . but with dogs. Even I have to admit that sounds terrible.

"I've never done it before, but I've heard great things." I move closer so I can talk to him without Cary being all the way in our business. "I think the cool air will stop you from feeling sick like in the car, but if you do, I'm sure they'll know how to handle it."

He doesn't look convinced, but he nods his head anyways. "All right, Cary," he says. "Show us these dogs."

"Let's do it." Cary turns on a booted heel and starts power walking up a narrow path that someone did the very minimum to shovel. Not that I can blame them, shoveling is freaking hard.

The sounds of dogs barking are audible long before the sled and team of ten dogs come into view, but when we see them, I think even Maxwell's reservations are forgotten. Ten dogs, all different colors, lose their minds when they see us. Their tails are wagging like crazy, as if we're doing them a favor by letting them pull us around the mountain. The sled behind them is surprisingly small and vaguely reminds me of a shopping cart that's been chopped down with its sides covered in fabric.

"So, Max, I'm going to have you climb in here first, and once you're comfortable, we'll get Brynn right in front of you," Cary instructs, putting his fandom aside to get us all set.

Maxwell grabs the glasses we picked up at a gas station on the way up here and settles them on his face. It's true that everyone looks hotter in sunglasses, but it's *extra* true in Maxwell's case. I spend more time than I'll ever admit trying to find a pair of sunglasses that don't screw up the dimensions of my face, and this jerk just snatches a pair off the rack and looks like a freaking sunglasses model. Aside from famine and war, this might be the most unfair thing in the entire world.

"Are you all good?" Cary asks Maxwell and breaks my sunglasses trance.

"All good." Maxwell pats his thighs. "Climb on in, Boss."

I roll my eyes at the nickname to hide the thrill I get at the thought of sitting in Maxwell's lap for the next hour and a half. But when I sit down and feel him already hardening against my ass, I realize I'm not the only one excited by the thought.

"Sorry." He lifts the edge of my beanie and whispers into my ear. "Your ass looks fucking fantastic in those pants."

I wiggle my butt, giggling at his harsh intake of breath.

"All right, you two." Cary takes his place at the back of the sled. "Ready to go?"

"So ready!" Giddiness creeps into my voice. Maxwell's grip tightens on my hips.

"Then let's go."

The ride starts slower than I anticipated. Which, to be fair, I had no idea what to expect. Besides watching *Balto* as a kid, I have zero knowledge about dogsleds. I did read a few Yelp reviews and made sure Cary treats the dogs well, but that's it.

But I think I love this pace, and it definitely sets Maxwell at ease. I relax back onto his chest as we pass by all the snow-covered pines until they become a little more sparse . . . then a little more . . . and then they're gone and we have an uninterrupted view of mountains around . . . and below us.

"Holy shit." I pull off my sunglasses and look around. Unlike when I get to the top of a ski lift, it's easy to tell that people don't come up here and the ones who do don't do it often. Other than the lines from the sled and Cary's shoes, the snow is undisturbed. It's like the sky dumped glitter around us. I can't stop squinting from the glare of the sun and the bright white snow, but no amount of wrinkles could stop me from looking.

There are some moments you know you'll never have again and this is one of those. And I'll be damned if I don't do my best to commit every single bit of it to memory. The smell of unpolluted air, Maxwell's warm breath against my freezing skin, the sound of the wind cracking against the snow. It's perfect.

"This isn't usually part of the tour, but I figured if Max is really going to represent Colorado, he needs to see exactly what that means," Cary says.

Finally, the perks of dating a Mustangs player start rolling in.

"Point taken, man," Maxwell says, his eyes still roaming over the mountaintop. "This is incredible."

"Hey, Cary." I climb onto my knees and turn around in the sled . . . which is much more difficult than I originally guessed. "Can you turn around for a bit?"

"That I can." He winks.

Normally, this would embarrass me. But not this time. I mean, I can almost guarantee my cheeks are hot pink from the cold.

Also, we're practically on top of the freaking world and it's romantic as fuck. There's no way we're leaving this without a kiss. No way. No how.

"Thank you for bringing me here," Maxwell says before I have the chance to talk.

"Thank you for being someone I can experience this with." I feel my eyes begin to tear up so I lean in to kiss him before they fall. Nothing distracts from crying like Maxwell's mouth on mine.

I pull my head away when the dogs start to grow impatient. Maxwell drops his hands to my ass and squeezes. "Let's get this show on the road, Cary."

"You got it!" Cary does something with the giant leash system anchoring all the dogs together while I turn back around. "And hold on, this is the fun part," he warns us, but takes off before I can prepare.

The dogs start sprinting down the mountain. Snow from their paws whips around our heads, and I let loose a high-pitched scream. It's like being on a roller coaster and not knowing if there are brakes.

Which is basically how I've felt since the moment Maxwell walked into my life.

Thirty-five

I WISH I COULD SAY THINGS GOT REAL SEXY WHEN WE GOT BACK to the Blue Tower after dogsledding. But that would be a lie.

What started out as a perk of Maxwell's fame turned into a downside real fast as what I was told was an hour-and-a-half sled ride turned into a four-hour tour. It was like the mountain version of Gilligan's Island. Add to that the one-hour return trip to our house, and by the time we got back, we both barely made it to the bed before we were asleep.

I roll over and reach for Maxwell, but I'm met with cool, empty sheets.

I sit up too fast. I squeeze my eyes shut, hoping it will stop the windows of the tower from spinning around me. I open them slowly and let out a deep, contented breath. From this spot in the bed, I literally have a panoramic view of the mountains that surround Buena Vista. If it weren't for the sound of a running shower, I'd probably lie back down and never move.

But if there's one view that could beat this, it's of a naked and wet Maxwell Lewis.

I don't have a plan as I inch closer to the open bathroom door, but as soon as I see Maxwell's soap-covered body through the fogged-up glass, one comes to mind.

I slip out of the satin nightie I had enough mind to put on last night—I normally sleep in old T-shirts I've hoarded from high school, but in an overwhelming victory, Vonnie, Poppy, Avi, Jac, and even Paisley forced me to leave my field hockey shirt behind. The steam from the shower has warmed the bathroom as I pad across the tiles and open the shower door.

Maxwell startles but is quickly placated as he takes in my naked body.

"Good morning," I say over the gentle sound of running water.

Maxwell pulls me into him, turning our bodies so I'm positioned beneath the water. "It is now." His hands run up and down my bare back, causing me to shiver despite the warm water. "You could spoil a man. It would be real easy to get used to my days starting this way."

"Is that a bad thing?" I drop my hands between our bodies and stroke his hard, wet length as hot water streams down on my head.

"Fuck no," he hisses out between clenched teeth. He leans in, touching his forehead to mine, and braces both hands on the tile behind me. "Not at all."

As I speed up the pace, he begins to pump into my hands. His eyes are closed, but mine are wide open and taking in the wonder of watching this strong, amazing, beautiful man fall apart in my hands. My hips start to move and my thighs press together. I need him inside of me.

Now.

"I'm on birth control and I'm clean."

He stills in my hands, and his eyes fly open.

"I mean, if you want." I try to backpedal. "I can go grab a

condom real fast." I drop my hands to my sides and try to slide under his arm to leave, but his hand on my arm stops me.

"I'm clean too. We get tested before every season and I've never not used a condom." His eyes bore into me, heating me up more than the steam floating around us. "I'm okay with no condom if you are."

I nod my head and wrap my arms around his neck. "I'm okay with that."

Before I can even try to hide the smile threatening to consume my entire face, his mouth is on mine and his hands are on my thighs. He lifts me up and pushes my back against the cool subway tiles. My legs wrap around him and my ankles lock behind his back just as he thrusts inside of me.

I cling to him for dear life as he pushes in and out of me. His thighs are shaking beneath me, from either strain or need. I don't know and I don't care. All I care about is the tingling in my core that's transforming into full-blown throbs.

I pull his mouth to mine, parting my lips and using my tongue to taste him as desperately as he's pounding into me.

He squats down lower and it changes everything. Every stroke hits the elusive spot that so many men spend a lifetime chasing. Each time he enters me, electricity charges through my veins. I throw my head back against the tile, but I barely even register the headache I'm sure will require Advil later. All of my energy is going into holding on to him even though my limbs are trembling as my need grows more and more.

"Touch yourself," Maxwell's strained voice says over the drumming in my ears. "I won't drop you."

Slowly and carefully, I remove one hand from his neck. I know I don't weigh a ton, but I'm still nervous to let go; I mean, how long can he really hold on? But as I move my hand between my legs, his rhythm doesn't so much as falter.

"That's it," he says as my hand starts moving between my legs. "Jesus. You're so fucking beautiful."

I don't know if it's his words, my hand, his dick, or all of the above, but an explosion goes off inside of me. My core grips onto him and his mouth comes to mine, swallowing my moans, and he slams into me one final time.

"That was . . . I don't even know what that was," I say when my breathing has returned to normal and my body has stopped shaking enough for me to stand without the wall supporting me.

"That was me and you." He grabs the loofah off the floor and pours body wash on it, lathering it up. Once he's satisfied with the bubbles, he turns me around and starts washing my back. The water has cooled significantly, but we take our time cleaning one another.

Maxwell turns off the water and steps out of the shower before me, haphazardly wrapping a towel around his hips. Then he grabs another towel and takes special care in drying me off, paying close attention to my ass and chest as he does. Then I return the favor and slowly dry him off, taking special care of his still-impressive member and tight ass.

He throws on a pair of very small, very amazing boxer briefs while I twist my hair into a towel and dig into my suitcase.

"There's a coffee shop a couple of blocks over." I toss my clothes over my shoulder until I find my fleece-lined leggings and the long-sleeved tee I'm looking for. "Wanna walk and go grab some?"

"Sounds good to me," he says as he shimmies into his jeans. "I'll go turn the coffee machine off downstairs then."

He was going to make me coffee. I bite back my smile. The perk about never having had a serious boyfriend is it makes every single thing Maxwell does for me seem extraordinary, even the little things . . . maybe especially the little things.

I'm running a comb through my hair so it won't turn into a complete rat's nest later, when I hear Maxwell call my name.

"Brynn, your phone is blowing up down here," he says from downstairs.

Crap.

My phone. This is how I know I'm into Maxwell; I never forget about my phone.

"Hold on! Here I come!" I abandon the comb and just twist my wet hair into a bun as I hit the stairs.

"Thanks." I roll onto my toes and kiss Maxwell as I grab my phone.

"Not a problem," he says, but he looks concerned. "Everything okay?"

I look at the screen, and knots form in my stomach. Nearly thirty missed calls and almost as many voicemails in the last hour, all from Poppy and a number I don't know.

"I'm not really sure." I don't look at him as I check my voicemails, but before the latest one begins to play, my phone starts to vibrate in my hand, the same 303 number flashing on the screen.

Dread fills me as I swipe to answer and bring it to my ear. "Hello?"

"Hi, is this Brynn Sterling?" a friendly voice on the other end asks.

She sounds like she could be a telemarketer. She's probably a telemarketer. I try to convince myself despite my heart telling me it's not true. Instinctively, I reach for Maxwell. He doesn't hesitate before gripping my hand.

"This is. May I ask who's speaking?"

"Hi, my name is Deanna. I'm a nurse at Saint Joseph Hospital and I'm calling about your dad."

My stomach falls to my feet and the room swims in front of me. It's my worst fear come to life.

"What . . . how? Is he okay?" I'm staring at Maxwell, but I don't see him. It's like I'm in a bad movie and everything around me is a blur.

"He had a heart attack," she says. I can't read her tone. Is she being so calm to keep me calm because it's actually really bad? Or is she so calm because everything is okay? "Do you know a Poppy Patterson?"

"Yes. Why?" I'm sure one day I'll feel bad about how short I am with her, but that day is not today. I need her to not ask questions and just tell me what is going on.

"She's at the hospital. She was with him when it happened. She did CPR and called nine-one-one. She's also the person who gave us your name and number. So your dad isn't alone, but I think it would be good if you came in and did so quickly. We need to decide the next step."

I try to answer.

My mouth is moving.

But the words don't come. They are being pushed away by an onslaught of tears that I'm refusing to let fall. The harder I try to talk, the louder the gasping becomes. Each breath feels as though I'm inhaling nails. It's like every emotion has wrapped around my throat. I don't even notice when the phone is no longer in my hands and Deanna's voice isn't grating in my ear.

My breathing is coming faster, but not deeper. I bend over, grabbing on to the counter like it's the only thing keeping me on my feet. But even that is failing me. My body is quaking and my grip is slipping and I realize that I don't care. I let go and don't try to stop myself from hitting the ground. Maybe the hurt from anything else will distract from the excruciating pain seeping into every corner of my being.

But the floor doesn't come.

Maxwell's arms wrap around me and he lifts me into him.

I know he's trying to help because he cares about me. And maybe that's what undoes me? Comfort that's not coming from the only man who has always been there for me feels like a betrayal.

"Don't touch me!" I thrash, shoving at his chest.

He doesn't let me go—if anything, he holds me tighter as he walks into the living room. "Everything is going to be okay," he whispers over my weak attempts at deep breaths and then sets me on the couch against the back wall.

Everything is going to be okay? Is he insane? I mean, how fucking *dare* he. I stand up and shove him away from me. "My dad's in the fucking hospital, Maxwell! How could you say that? Everything is so far from being okay that I don't even know . . ." My eyes slam shut and my head falls back. My hands are wet from my hair that I've yanked out of the elastic band I put in five minutes ago when everything in my life made sense. "She said it's—" My voice cracks as it starts to hit . . . really hit. "Oh my god. What if he doesn't make it? What will I do if I don't have my dad?"

My body fails me and I fall into Maxwell. He wraps me tight as sobs rip straight from the depths of my soul, and he holds on tight until I've cried for so long that even though my body is still wailing, my tears have dried up. And then he carries me to my car and straps me into the passenger seat.

"I'll be right back," he says but I don't respond.

I'm numb. Completely numb to this fucked-up world around me where good people—no, the best people—can end up in the hospital and the dregs of the earth will live unharmed until they're a hundred.

I close my eyes and let my head fall back onto the headrest. I don't want to see the house of my dreams. I don't want to see this beautiful, sunny day to remind me that it doesn't matter if my world falls apart or not, the world will go on with or without me.

With or without my dad.

Thirty-six

"BRYNN," SOMEBODY SAYS.

My head is pounding and my mouth is so dry that my tongue is sticking to the roof of my mouth. I don't even know the last time I got this drunk. Years of watching people get sloppy drunk takes away the appeal.

"Brynn," the voice says again. "We're here."

I try to open my eyes but they are so sore that I can't. "Ughhh," I groan, and rub my eyes. "Why do my freaking eyes hurt?"

"Brynn, babe," another, feminine voice says. "You gotta get up."

Then everything hits me. Maxwell. The shower. The phone calls. My dad.

My dad.

I shoot up, but quickly realize I'm still in the car when my seat belt locks up and sends me back into my seat. My hands are shaking so hard that I can't unbuckle myself.

"Here," Maxwell says, and I realize he was the person trying to wake me up at first. "Let me get that."

"Thank you." I exhale deeply, trying my hardest to not fall

apart at the seams again. The seat belt unbuckles, but I'm stuck to my seat. There is this war going on in my head. I know I need to see him. He's my dad and I love him and I want to be there for him and, god forbid the worst happens, I'd never forgive myself if he was alone. But the other part of me—the batshit crazy side—is terrified to see him. All of those *Crossing Over* shows I used to watch run through my mind, and I wonder if he's only hanging on until I get there. What if me staying away is keeping him alive? And I know, medically and logically, that's not possible, but . . . what if it is?

"Come on." A pair of warm, soft hands grab mine. "Let's go see him."

I look over and see Poppy's kind, worried eyes staring back at me. I open my mouth to say something. Ask something. But I don't know what to say, so I close it and square my shoulders instead. The world might be crumbling around me, but if my dad deserves anything, he deserves me to keep myself together and be the best advocate for him that I can.

"I'll text you the room number," Poppy says to Maxwell before looping her arm through mine.

The entire walk to his room is a blur. I watch Poppy push the elevator buttons. I register the vibrations as it lifts us to the floor where he is. I see the words "Intensive Care Unit" above the door. And when I hug Poppy and thank her for being there for my dad when it meant the most, I note her tears as they seep through my shirt. But I don't feel anything.

Not until the nurse pulls back the curtain to my dad's room and I see that he's not alone.

Then I feel something.

But it's not sadness or sorrow or any of the other things I've been preparing for.

No. It's rage.

"What the fuck are you doing here?" I ask my mom.

"Brynn." She unfolds herself from the chair across the room. "The hospital called and told me what happened. I'm listed as next of kin. They asked if I could come, in case any decisions needed to be made."

I almost don't hear her over the blood roaring between my ears.

"What do you mean?" My hands are bunched into fists at my side. I've never been in a real fight and I'd like my first one not to be with my mom, but if she doesn't wipe that faux concerned look off her face, I'm not above doing it for her. "Why would you be next of kin?"

Her eyebrows draw together, and if she hadn't indulged in too much Botox, I know she'd have the same concerned lines on her forehead as me. The last time I saw her, I was a child. Seeing her as an adult is a complete mind fuck. And my mind is already too scrambled to deal with her added bullshit.

"Frank never told you?" There's a glint in her eye that makes my stomach turn. "We're still married."

"You're so full of shit." My lip curls in disgust. I cannot believe I share DNA with this horrid fucking woman. I start to walk toward her and I must look as crazy as I feel, because she takes a step back as I approach. "I don't know what your endgame is here. Dad's going to be fine and you aren't getting a fucking thing."

"I don't know what you're talking about, Brynn," she says. "I was at home when they called. I know how much you love your dad and he's been good to me. I'd never wish harm on him. I know you probably don't believe this, but I love you. I think about you every day."

For a split second, I almost believe her.

Then I think about the picture hanging on my dad's wall. My mom, this woman in front of me, she's a liar and she doesn't care who she takes down in her path.

I pick her designer bag off the floor and fight back a new wave of anger that my dad's been sending her money, and she has a purse that cost more than my monthly mortgage. "You're right, I don't believe a single thing you say." I loop the strap over my shoulder and gesture to the hallway.

The nurse who showed me into my dad's room is typing on one of the computers at the nurses' station. "Excuse me, ma'am." I get her attention. I know she told me her name, and while I'm normally great at remembering them, I have no idea what it is. "This woman is not to be alone with my father."

I don't turn to look at my mom, but I hear her quick inhale of breath and I can imagine what she looks like. The nurse in front of me, however, looks like I've put her in a terribly uncomfortable situation. Well, join the club, lady.

"I'm sorry, Miss Sterling," she says to me, but her eyes flicker between me and my mom. "But Mrs. Sterling is on your father's insurance and listed as his wife. We can't ban her."

If it wasn't for the woman a little bit younger than me with a baby bump and a tearstained face passing us, I might've lost my cool. But I keep it together. Getting kicked out for attacking my mom won't do anyone any good. So instead, I take a deep breath and make a mental note to schedule an emergency session with a therapist.

"It's okay," my mom, forever the actress, says to the nurse. "I'll let my daughter have some alone time with her dad and be back later."

"I'll walk you out then," I say through gritted teeth.

It takes exactly thirty-seven steps to reach the hallway.

"You are unbelievable!" I shout, unable to hold back any longer. "I haven't so much as gotten a Christmas text from you in fifteen years and you want to show up now? *Now* with this bullshit? What is wrong with you?"

"Well what did you suppose I would do when the hospital called me and told me they couldn't get in touch with you? Huh? Do you propose I just let him lie there all alone while you're off doing god knows what?" She steps forward and wraps her bony, manicured finger around her purse strap, pulling it off my shoulder. "Not everything is about you, Brynn. You'd do well to learn that."

"How could it be when literally everything is about you?" I'm still yelling and I know I need to stop, but she's brought forth a lifetime of resentment and anger, and I'm not sure I can push it back down.

"You have no idea what happened all of those years ago, and don't you dare start acting like you do." She snarls, and looking at her face is like looking in a mirror. And for some reason, the resentment I feel is reflecting back at me.

"How could I know? You left and never looked back! I was fifteen and you abandoned me!" I'm only a few inches taller than her, but it might as well be twenty with how I'm towering over her.

Her face turns bright red, and I know I've hit the hot button. "You never loved me like you loved your father," she screams in my face. "You abandoned me first!"

She couldn't have struck me harder if she physically slapped me.

I rake my chewed-down fingernails over my face and cover my mouth with both hands, trying to come up with words . . . any words at all. But only three come to mind. "Are you insane?!"

"No, you—" she starts but is immediately cut off.

"What in the world is going on?" Poppy appears between me and my mom.

Maxwell doesn't have to say anything for me to know he's here. The look on my mom's pathetic face says it all.

"Are you okay? Do you need me to get security up here?" Maxwell whispers into my ear, his strong, confident hands on my hips the exact balm I needed to deal with my mom. "Who is this woman?" he asks when I relax against him.

I spin to face him. "Seriously?" He can't be serious. There's no mistaking Holly Sara Sterling for anybody other than my mom.

"Seriously." He raises a single eyebrow like I'm the confusing one here. "I've never seen this woman before. Am I supposed to know her?"

I step to the side and gesture to my mom, who's still staring at Maxwell with her jaw on the floor. "Maxwell, Poppy, this is Holly Sterling, my mom. Now"—I don't wait for their mouths to close before moving on—"will one of you call Vonnie? I need a lawyer."

"Oh cheese and crackers." Poppy pulls her phone out of her purse. "Of all the times for this to happen, it happens when I can't drink. Selfish," she mutters before lifting her phone to her ear. "Vonnie? Hey, I'm at Saint Joe's—no, I'm fine. It's Mr. Sterling . . . I know. I'll tell you later. Wait, no, that's not why I'm calling. Brynn's mom is here and Brynn needs a lawyer—yeah. Super crazy. Bring Eloise. From the sound of their yelling, she's gonna need a cavalry."

I fucking love the Lady Mustangs. I nearly crack a smile for the first time in hours. But then I remember that my mom is here and that squashes it.

"Why are you still here?" I look down my nose, giving her my iciest glare.

"Lawyers, Brynn? This seems very unnecessary." She adjusts her purse on her shoulder and does her best attempt at sounding bored, but I can still hear the tremble of fear beneath her words.

Good.

"I disagree." I look at my unpolished nails like they're the most interesting thing in the world. "Plus, they're two of the top lawyers in the state, and it seems like a shame to ignore this opportunity to see them in action. Or you could"—I shrug my shoulders—"go back to doing whatever you were doing, wherever you were doing it, and forget about us like you did all those years ago."

Color starts to rise up her porcelain cheeks, and I know I'm getting somewhere. "I was just worried about your father." She purses her lips, and the wrinkles that point to a smoking habit she must've picked up become more pronounced. "Maybe you should spend less time acting like some desperate Mustang groupie and prioritize."

If my mom was someone I had even an ounce of respect for, that might've stung. But considering she knows nothing about me or my life, her attempt at a dig doesn't faze me. The same cannot be said for the people around me however.

Maxwell's fingers flinch against my hip as his entire body tenses behind me, but it's Poppy who really loses it.

"What did you just say?" She turns back to my mom with her phone still at her ear. "Because I know I must've misheard you, right?"

My mom, not a genius that one, doesn't back down. She mistakes Poppy's small size, bubbly smile, and growing baby bump for someone who'd be an easy target. "This is a family matter, honey, why don't you move along."

Poppy keeps her eyes glued to my mom as she talks into her phone. "Maybe bring another lawyer for me." She touches her screen and drops her phone back into her oversized bag that I know for a fact has Tums, Sour Patch Kids, wet wipes, and Chap-Stick. "Here's the thing, Molly."

"Holly," my mom corrects her.

"Like I said, Molly. You don't know me, so you might not understand that I'm not the one. And you might also not understand that despite you being a shit mom and an overall terrible human being, Brynn turned out to be one of the strongest, smartest women I've ever had the pleasure of coming across." She looks my mom up and down, letting her gaze linger. "I know you probably can't recognize the look of a man who is head over heels for you, because you threw it away, but anybody with eyes can see that Maxwell is freaking crazy about her and you're starting a fight you cannot win."

Mom grits her teeth before turning her attention back to me. "You think you're better than me? You're just like me. Always have been and always will be." She takes a menacing step toward me, but before she gets too close, Maxwell steps in front of me.

"I think it's time you leave." His deep voice sounds even deeper and the roughness that doesn't often make an appearance is there.

"You think you're special because you've made some money?" she asks, her voice laced with venom and bitterness that can only come from years of regret. "You aren't. She'll leave you too."

Everything she's said, I could brush off. Everything except that. Like some sideshow at a carnival, she does have some innate ability to single out my biggest insecurity.

I move to the side of Maxwell. "You don't know me," I say with false bravado.

"Tell yourself that all you want." Her lip curls with the sick satisfaction of knowing she landed a direct hit. "You know I'm right. You act like Frank's some victim here, but he knew who I was. He knew I didn't want to be tied down but he still pushed and pushed for a family until I gave in. And you, you're my daughter in every way. I can see it in your eyes, you know I'm right."

Jesus.

I always knew she was a little bit crazy, but now I know she's full-on loony tunes.

"What you see in my eyes isn't me agreeing with you"—I move to her and take her hands in mine—"it's pity. I'm not like you. I know you want that to be the truth, but it's not." I don't even know that I mean it until the words are out of my mouth, but once they're out and this boulder has been lifted off of my shoulders, I know how true it is. "If you were this miserable, leaving was probably the best thing you could've done for me and Dad."

"You—" She tries to cut me off, but I keep going.

"You don't know me anymore and if you did, you'd know I'm not the person you've painted. Look around you. Look at how these two people went to bat for me. Look at how close Dad and I are." I wrap my arms around her, giving her a hug that I know she won't return. "I learned from your mistakes. These relationships are earned, and I'm not going to do anything to jeopardize them." I step away from her and I know in my heart that I will not be seeing her again. "I'm going to see Dad now. Take care of yourself." I shift my attention to Poppy and Maxwell, and if this was any other time, I'd probably take a minute to bask in the glory of the way they are looking at me, but I can't. "Thank you guys for coming. I'll text you with updates."

I hug Poppy once more and give Maxwell a quick kiss before I hurry through the ICU doors.

The lights in my dad's room are on, and a nurse is checking his vitals with a smile on her face when I walk in.

"You're back." My dad's weak voice pulls my attention away from the happy nurse. "Do you know how hard it was to fake being asleep for that long? Thanks for making her leave."

I don't even have a chance to fight back the tears before they're streaming down my face. If I weren't afraid it'd give him another heart attack, I'd totally yell at him. I cross the room as fast as my legs will carry me and try to hug him around all of the wires hooked up to him. "Don't you ever do this to me again," I choke out between hiccups.

"Trust me." His fingers attempt to sift through my knotted hair. "It wasn't too fun for me either."

"Well then." I stand up straight and swipe my arm under my nose very attractively. "I think we have a few things to talk about."

And the student becomes the teacher.

Thirty-seven

THANKFULLY FOR MY DAD, IF YOU ARE GOING TO HAVE A HEART attack, you want to do it near Saint Joseph's.

The doctors, though not quite the Preston Burke or Derek Shepherd I was hoping to ogle throughout my dad's stay in the hospital, are all very accomplished and good at their job—which I guess is equally as important.

After speaking with the doctors, we decide on the coronary artery bypass graft surgery. It sounds gory and horrific, but also like my dad's best chance of not going through this again. In the room, I hold my head up high and keep my shoulders back. I don't stutter as I ask the questions I've never wanted to ask. I don't flinch, and I fight back the tears causing my sinuses to burn as my dad uses my hand as a stress ball. I talk him through his worries and fears and don't throw a temper tantrum when he mentions his will or when he tells me he absolutely wants to be cremated and not put into an overpriced box and stuck in the ground to rot.

I hold on to his hand and give him a giant smile and a bogus thumbs-up that causes me to have such immense and utter hatred for myself. Then, the moment he's out of his room and—hopefully—out of hearing range, I lose my ever-loving mind.

I crumple into the vinyl chair in the corner of his room and stare at his bed, willing, praying, hoping with every fiber of my being that he comes back. And knowing just as much that even though I'm a grown-ass woman, I still need my dad.

Nurses come to check on me, but they don't say anything. They bring new boxes of tissues and put bottles of water beside me—and nudge them closer when I ignore them. I appreciate their gentle concern. I'm sure that working in the ICU, seeing meltdowns like mine are par for the course, but that doesn't make me any less grateful. When your world is detonating around you, the last thing you want is to pretend you're surrounded by fireworks instead of bombs.

It isn't until the sun has set completely—the night sky still bright from falling snow—and the skin around my eyes has been rubbed raw that I decide to venture out of Dad's hospital room. He will come back. He has to come back. And when he does, I'm not going to look like the disaster I know I do. No, I think of all the moments he's been there for me, and I know that this is my moment to pay him back.

I walk in silence out of his room and past the nurses coming in and out of patient rooms until I reach the double doors leading in and out of the ICU. The doors are barely cracked when I hear the echo of familiar voices.

I follow the voices down the empty, fluorescent-lit hallway lined with mass-produced art prints until I see a break in the wall.

I turn the corner and when I see the scene in front of me, I burst into a fresh bout of tears. The room is packed to the brim. Vonnie and Justin. Charli and Shawn. Poppy and TK. Aviana and Crosby. Jacqueline and Peter. Paisley, Tanya, and Eloise.

Maxwell.

Everyone I care about in one small room. Well, almost everyone.

Maxwell, of course, notices me first and gets to me just in time to let me collapse into his warm and welcoming chest.

"You guys are here?" I cry, my unintelligible words muffled into his cotton tee.

Just before I'm mobbed by my well-intentioned, loving group of friends that, somehow, became my family without me noticing, Maxwell touches his lips to my forehead and whispers, "I'll always be here."

And even though I feel like my heart has been broken and scattered all over my dad's hospital room, right here, being held tight and safe in Maxwell's arms, a new piece falls into place.

"JUICE MAN IS here," Maxwell announces as he walks into my dad's hospital room. He holds up the 7-Eleven bag with the grandeur of Rafiki lifting up Simba.

"My man." Dad pushes the button on the side of his bed to raise him into a sitting position. "Did you get a lemon-lime?"

"I got four," Maxwell says, pride evident in his voice as my dad's eyes light up.

Ugh.

Why do they have to be so damn cute together?

The inside of my brain has basically been a disaster since my dad was wheeled back into the room four days ago. Part of this could be because I haven't gotten an actual good night's sleep because the vinyl chair is actually a vinyl pullout. It's so uncomfortable that my entire body is screaming at me. It could also be because I saw my train wreck of a mother, and through her insane rants she made me realize that beyond our looks we are nothing alike. And although it's a huge relief, it's also made me recount my entire adulthood and all the good guys I passed over. I missed out on a lot. I just know that I may not be able to rewind the clock, but I can make sure that, from here on, I invest myself fully into my relationship.

And luckily for me, I get to do it with Maxwell.

On that thought, Maxwell turns to me and holds up a separate bag.

I jump out of the vinyl monstrosity and snatch it from his hands before he can even say what he bought. "Taquitos!" I don't even give him a hug or say thank-you before I pull one out and shove it in my mouth . . . you know, how you eat when you're in a new relationship and keeping things sexy.

To be fair though, I've been living on kale salads and green juice (my body has fully rebelled against this, by the way). The cafeteria here has things like cheese fries, but I didn't want to make this any harder for my dad than it already is. He hates kale. So it's made his liquid diet more appealing.

You really do sacrifice for the ones you love.

"If you think that's good, what are you going to do when you find out there's a Slurpee waiting for you in the car?" Maxwell winks.

"I'll probably ask why it's in your car and not in my hand," I say after I finish chewing. I do have some manners.

"Nope," Dad pipes in after he nearly drains his first glass of Gatorade. "You're not sleeping here tonight. I'm kicking you out."

"What?" I drop the taquitos on the tiny table by my chair. "I'm not leaving you alone."

"You are," he says, and I'm almost a little relieved to hear the full force of his dad voice, even if I'm annoyed by the actual words coming out of his mouth. "It will do us both some good. You won't feel sore in the morning, and I'll get a good night's sleep without your snoring waking me up."

My eyes bulge and my face catches fire. "Dad!" I turn to Maxwell. "I do not snore."

"She does," my dad says from his hospital bed.

Maxwell flashes his white teeth and pulls me into a hug. "You do." He tightens his arms around me when I try to push away. "But it's an adorable snore."

"Jerks." I glare at both of them. "You're both jerks." And I no longer think they're cute together. I consider arguing with my dad a little more about staying overnight again, but the truth is my body is so pissed at me. My neck hurts, my back kills, and I desperately need a shower. "Fine," I say like I'm doing them a favor and not the other way around. "But I'll be back tomorrow and I'm calling right after shift change, so don't ignore my call."

"Yes, ma'am." Dad salutes, a decision I know he regrets when his face screws up in pain from the fast movement.

I guess that's what happens when you want to be a smart-ass.

"Later, Daddy-o." I give him a quick and gentle hug, not wanting to add to his discomfort.

"Yeah, yeah," he says. "Get out of here."

I don't make him say it again. My bed is calling my name and I wouldn't want my Slurpee to melt.

I'VE GONE MUCH longer than a week without going to my condo, so I'm not sure why I feel such a stark relief wash over me as I push open the door and step inside.

It only takes me about two seconds to figure it out.

"What in the world?" I stand cemented to the entryway floor—that's now donning a new rug—as I look around my once bare apartment that's now bursting with personality.

"Vonnie," Maxwell says, like that should explain everything. And it does.

I've never met a person who redecorates their home more frequently, and she's the reason we've changed the barstools at HERS twice in the last seven months.

My white walls are the perfect shade of gray. My couch is overwhelmed with new throw pillows. My old frames are filled with pictures, and new frames are scattered along my walls and on tables. There are placemats on my dining table and brand-new dishes set on top of those. And the icing on the cake is the amazing glamorous, mod chandelier hanging in the middle of my living room.

"Dammit, Brynn. Do not cry again." I close my eyes and try to fan away the tears with my hands and fail miserably. "How do I still even have tears?"

"Don't worry," Maxwell says. "Vonnie'll love this, she was hoping for tears."

I turn to look at him, and he's got his phone aimed directly at me. I throw my hands in front of my face and lunge at him. "What are you doing?" I ask, even though it's obvious that he's recording me.

Since I'm using both hands to conceal my puffy, dark-circle-covered eyes, I use my feet and shoulders as weapons. And I fail miserably again. We both end up sprawled out on my couch, but the only reason Maxwell quits recording is because he's laughing too hard to hold his phone.

I make a mental note to register for another self-defense class soon.

"Sorry, you know I can't say no to Vonnie." He tucks the phone into his sweatshirt pocket. "She scares me."

"Touché." She is terrifying when angry. Which reminds me . . . "I forgot to tell you, but my mom signed the papers!"

"Already?"

"Like you said, Vonnie is scary." I shift into crisscross-applesauce position on the couch. "And Eloise went with her. I imagine both of them together as some kind of high-fashion, crime-fighting superhero duo."

Now that I'm really thinking about it, I might need Aviana to pitch it to the CW.

"Speaking of your mom and Eloise though," Maxwell says, changing the subject, and the hairs on the back of my neck stand up. "I know what happened with your mom in the hospital was hard and I'm sure doing it in front of a crowd was even harder. But I want to let you know how much it meant to me that I could be there for you. Obviously, you are aware that there is a lot of conflict between me and Theo. It's deep and it's ugly and it's something that I've never really talked about before." He laces his fingers with mine and lets out a deep breath. "I want to talk to you about it. Not tonight," he adds in quickly. "I have to check in at the hotel soon and you need a decent night's sleep, but soon . . . if you want."

"No, I mean yes, I do want. I want to talk." I trip over my words, but my dad had a heart attack and I haven't slept in days, so I feel like I have a good excuse.

He leans in, touching his lips to mine. I think we both want more than that, but after the last few days, Maxwell knows that I'm too tired—physically and emotionally—to act on it.

"Wanna try and squeeze in a couple episodes of *Parks and Rec* before I leave?" he asks.

And I hate myself for it, but my eyes well with tears again.

A few days ago, I feared my life was splintering and would never be complete again. But now, sitting on a couch, watching a show, all I can envision is a full and beautiful future with this amazing fucking man by my side through it all.

Thirty-eight

I ALWAYS THOUGHT I KNEW HOW MUCH I LOVED MY JOB, BUT being away from it for a week made me even more aware.

I love my customers. I love my staff. I just love it.

My dad's heart attack has made me realize how freaking short life is and how fast things can change. I feel like a new person. There's this zest for life inside me that was never there before as I serve drinks and greet customers. Having my man looking fine and kicking some serious football ass on the TVs surrounding me doesn't suck either.

Poppy is at the hospital with my dad so I could come into HERS for a while today. Vonnie offered me a ticket for her box, but I've been gone for too long and I knew today was going to be extra crazy with it being a playoff game.

Paisley took amazing care of the place while I was gone, and I know that I need to give her a promotion. She deserves it and I'd actually like the freedom to take more time off with the way things with Maxwell are progressing. She even came up with a playoff cocktail. I tried it when I got in this morning (when it's your job, drinking vodka in the morning isn't a problem, it's dedication) and almost kissed her.

"Two Championship Chuggers." I place the icy mugs in front of the women in their Mustangs jerseys. "Just holler if you need anything else."

I start my walk back to the bar, weaving between huddles of women and a few scattered men, when applause and cheers break out all around me. I look at the closet TV and join in the celebrating when I see Maxwell getting off the ground with the football in his hand. He tosses it to the nearest referee and the camera zooms in on him as he runs to the sideline, his teammates slapping the back of his helmet as he goes . . . his tight ass looking extra freaking fabulous today.

I make it to the back of the bar, but when I do, Abby is chewing on her bottom lip and looks nervous beyond belief.

I feel my forehead wrinkle as my eyebrows scrunch together. "Is everything okay?"

"I—I don't know? A police officer came in. He said he needed to speak to you, it sounded urgent. I had him go wait in your office."

I look over my shoulder and see that my office door that's normally closed and locked is cracked open.

Now, if I were thinking clearly, I'd know that if anything had happened to my dad, Poppy would get in touch with me, and there's really no reason a police officer would come when no crime was committed. But thinking clearly and rationally has never been my strong point, and fear nearly chokes me as I sprint to my office.

I push open the door and see the officer in his uniform standing in front of my picture wall.

"Theo." My shoulders sag in relief. "What the hell? You scared me."

"Sorry about that. Didn't mean to." He tucks his hands into his pockets. I'm not sure if it's a move to highlight the fact that he's armed or if it's an innocent gesture, but either way, there's something not right here.

"Well . . ." I close the door behind me and make a point not to lock the door. Maxwell's warning about Theo echoes in my mind. "What can I help you with?"

"I just wanted to talk to you when I knew Max wasn't going to be around," he says, and a fizzle of unease starts to crawl up my spine. "I know he hasn't been honest with you, and I don't want you to be blindsided when this comes out."

The unease blossoms into full-blown dread. I know I should turn him away and wait for Maxwell to open up, but part of me just needs to get this over with.

"Have a seat." I gesture to the open chairs as I round my desk. My knees are already starting to knock together, and I'm thinking that sitting through this conversation is the best decision.

"I'm sure you've caught on to the fact that there's tension between us?" he asks.

"Ummm, yeah. It's pretty hard to miss." I try to keep the sarcasm out of my voice, but this isn't the kind of conversation I appreciate dragging out.

"Well, it wasn't always like that between us." He leans back in the chair, and the acrylic groans under his weight. "We actually used to be really close."

Now this is harder to believe and does not match up with the little that Maxwell has told me. I stay silent and he picks up the clue and continues on.

"Then he went to college and everything started to change. I'm older than him. I went to college, I know what happens when you're away from the nest for the first time, and honestly, his freshman and sophomore years were fine. He did the normal sleeping around that athletes do . . . sorry," he says when I cringe at the idea of sweet, caring Maxwell being the stereotypical asshole jock. "But his junior and senior years were different. His senior year, things were getting out of hand and our dad reached out to me. He wanted me to go check on him. I had just joined the force in Philly and he thought I could talk some sense into him."

I open my mouth to say something, anything, but it just opens and closes like a fish out of water.

"You know . . ." He stops and looks at me. "Well, actually you might not know. But when you're black and in these predominately white colleges, you already stick out. When you're black and on these campuses and you're slated to go in the first round of the draft, you become royalty. And that can go to your head . . . that *did* go to his head.

"While I was visiting, he wanted to show me around. I went to a couple of his classes with him and then, it was a Friday, that night, we went to a party."

It's like I drank acid and my stomach is eating through itself. I keep teetering between listening to the rest of the story and asking him to leave. I know how I feel about Maxwell, and letting Theo finish seems like a betrayal. But also, if he hadn't kept leaving me in the dark, I wouldn't be in this horrible situation to begin with.

"The girls were all over him. Like I said, he was a rock star on that campus. Yes, all the girls were going to school and getting educations, but apparently that didn't diminish the appeal of becoming a trophy wife."

"Hey now," I interject. None of my friends are simply "trophy wives" and that shit pisses me off. "I know a lot of wives and girlfriends, Theo, and they all have a hell of a lot to offer."

"Which is why their husbands married them. They weeded out the ones who had nothing to offer." He shrugs and I want to disagree, but I don't know if I can, so he continues on. "Anyways, there was one girl he wanted that night, and of course, she was the only one not paying him any attention. He followed her around the entire night and she laughed at his jokes and drank the drinks he brought her . . . and believe me, he brought her a lot of them. She never flat-out blew him off, but it was clear she wasn't interested, and I told him that. But he wouldn't listen."

Holy shit.

As the direction this story is going starts to become clear, nausea begins to rise in my stomach.

I shake my head, willing it not to be true. "He didn't. He *wouldn't*." Not my Maxwell, he would never.

"I was older, too old to hang in a college party, so I left a little early. But, before I left, I told him she was drunk. I told him that when a girl is on the verge of unconsciousness, she cannot give consent. He said he understood and that he wasn't interested in her anymore anyways. So I left the party feeling good.

"I woke up the next morning and he still wasn't home. The party was at his teammate's house, so I didn't think too much about it. I hopped in the shower, grabbed a couple of coffees, and then headed back to the house. It was early, so when I got to the house, everyone was still asleep, and when I finally found Max, he was in bed with the drunk girl from the night before and they were both naked."

No fucking way.

The roiling of my stomach almost causes me to reach for my trash can.

"How?" I wipe away the stray tears that manage to break through the sick shock.

"I'm really sorry that I had to be the one to tell you . . . or that there is something to tell at all, I really am." He leans forward and offers me a tissue, his eyes earnest and full of regret.

I take the tissue and blow my nose, giving in to the feeling of sorrow. "How did he get away with this?"

"I knew he was entering the draft that year and was slotted to go high. I didn't want his career to end before it started. So I woke him up and told him to leave. I hoped she'd be too drunk to remember what happened. Maxwell left and I was looking around the room to make sure he didn't leave anything that would jog her memory, when she woke up. She rightfully started to freak out. She was screaming and crying and when people came to check on her, she pointed the blame at me. And what could I do? Everyone knew I was with Max, and if I denied it, they would piece together the puzzle and he'd be ruined. So I took the fall."

I close my eyes and inhale deeply, trying to fight back the second bout of nausea rolling through. This story gets worse with every piece of information he feeds me. I don't know if I can handle any more. I was planning a life with Maxwell and not only did he assault a woman, but he let someone else pay for his actions. It's fucking disgusting.

"Is that everything?" I ask, ready to shut my door on the Lewis brothers for good.

"Not quite." He cringes and leans forward, resting his elbows on his knees. "The woman didn't want to go through a trial and relive it all. So we settled outside of court."

This doesn't surprise me at all. Who would want to get crucified in court for being a victim and relive your shame and pain for the world to judge? Certainly not I.

"Okay?" I ask. My mind has officially shut down and is no longer capable of guessing what other dark corners this twisted, sordid tale is going to take me to.

"When we settled out of court, Max obviously paid the settlement, and the girl signed an NDA. I thought it was over." He takes a breath so deep that even I brace. "I got a call from a reporter a few months ago. She was looking into cases for a segment she was working on and got a sniff of the case. Somehow she was able to follow the money and link it back to Max. I've been keeping quiet, but she's been reaching out to some of his old teammates, and I heard through the grapevine that's she's almost ready to air the piece."

It's like the floor has been pulled from under me. My thoughts are running rampant and colliding into each other. It's just too much.

I start to laugh—a full-on belly laugh that cause tears to leak down my face.

"I'm sorry," I say to Theo, wiping the tears and trying to regain my composure. "I used to think my friends had drama. But this week my dad had a heart attack, my crazy mom came back and I had to have lawyers serve her divorce papers, and now, my boyfriend is going to be plastered all over the news for sexual assault." My laughter starts to pick up again and a snort slips out. "I can't even blame the Lady Mustangs for this!"

"I know I probably messed things up with you guys, but even though we don't talk, Max really is a good guy. He made a mistake, but I'm sure he learned from it. Just . . . can you tell him to call me? I've been trying to warn him about this, but he never hears me out. Maybe if you tell him, he will. I might have a way around this."

"Why should he get a way around this?" I ask, bitterness creeping into my voice. "Did his victim get a way around it? Serves him right that he finally gets what's coming."

And even though I mean every single word, a piece of my heart shatters. For me. For the woman. Even for Maxwell, even though he doesn't deserve it.

"I understand if you don't." Theo unfolds his long body out of my tiny chair. "But he knows how to find me if you do." He tips his chin and then he's gone.

The door doesn't even close behind him before Paisley is inside my office and locking the door behind her.

"What was that? Is everything okay?"

"No, everything is so far from okay that I don't even know how to get back to okay."

And then I start fucking crying. Again.

Thirty-nine

WHEN I TALKED TO MAXWELL, WE DECIDED THAT HE'D MEET ME AT my newly decorated apartment after the game.

But that was before I knew he was a total fucking scumbag.

"Are you sure everything is okay?" Dad asks for the millionth time.

"Yes! How else do you want me to say it? I. Am. Fine," I snap.

He doesn't flinch. Nope. He starts to laugh. "Very convincing, Brynn. I totally believe you."

"Real supportive, Dad." I roll my eyes and bite back the rude comment on the tip of my tongue.

"Supportive for what?" He reaches for one of the Jell-Os the nurse brought him. "You said you're fine. I'm the one sitting in the hospital bed."

"Now I see where I get my dramatic tendencies from." I walk to his bed and hand him the yellow Gatorade I had stashed in my purse. "You know you're going home tomorrow, right? You won't have nurses bringing you Jell-O all day."

"I know that." He looks down, staring at the Jell-O like the secret to world peace is hidden inside, and color rises up his cheeks and the tips of his ears.

"Dad." I bend over to try and catch his gaze, but he turns his head. "Dad? Is there going to be a nurse bringing you Jell-O?"

"I'm just a nice guy and the nurses like to make sure I'm settled," he says, still not looking at me. "I'm a good patient."

"I'm sure you are, but that doesn't explain why you can't look at me. Wait a minute . . ." I narrow my eyes in his direction. "Are you crushing on your nurses?"

"No!" His head jerks up and he finally makes eye contact with me. But only for a second, then he's back to being shifty again. "I mean, maybe I think Deanna is pretty, but I'm not crushing on her."

"Never mind." I shake my head and try to clear away the images of my dad flirting with nurses.

When I look at my dad again, he's blushing harder than I've ever seen before. Yuck.

Happiness.

Bah humbug.

There's a quick knock on the door before I hear it open. Neither of us says to come in, but not even five seconds later the curtain slides over and Maxwell steps through.

"Finally!" My dad whoops. "Maybe you can get her out of this foul mood she's in."

Doubtful.

"Yeah . . . I'll try." Maxwell looks at me, confusion and hurt written all over his face. I turn away from him before my icy heart tries to thaw. "How are you feeling? Heard tomorrow's the big day."

"I'm great," Dad says. He lifts his cup in the air. "I got my Gatorade and—"

The curtain swings open again and Deanna waltzes in with a bag full of Jell-O cups. Of. Course. "Guess who brought more . . .

oh!" She startles when she sees me and Maxwell. "Sorry about that, I didn't realize you had company. I'll just drop these over here." She walks toward the sink, but she doesn't get far before my dad is kicking me and Maxwell out.

"You can stay," he says. "They were just on their way out."

My eyes threaten to pop out of my head and I shake my head no as obviously, yet discreetly, as possible.

He ignores me.

Deanna talks instead.

"I wish I could, but I have to check on some other patients. Call for me if you need me," she says, but instead of leaving, she lingers for a bit.

"Just wait one second." My dad gestures to Deanna before looking at me. "I'll call you in the morning when I know more about when I'm getting discharged."

He doesn't even wait for me to respond before he's adjusting his bed and talking to his nurse.

What the fuck?

I don't know if I'm irritated at my dad's flirty voice or if I'm just a bitter Betty that my relationship burned to the ground and now my dad's love life is starting to take off.

He deserves it. Don't be a selfish cow.

"Nice seeing you, Deanna." I do my best to swallow back the bitchy undertone. "See you tomorrow, Dad."

"Have a good night." Maxwell nods to them both and links his fingers through mine.

My back goes straight at his touch. I leave my hand in his because I don't want to cause a scene and my dad is in such high spirits. He loves Maxwell. I'm not ready to break his heart, at least not literally this time. But every second with him touching me confuses me that much more. Lust and desire are fighting with disgust and hatred.

As soon as we reach the hallway, I snatch my hand out of his.

"What's going on?" Maxwell runs his hand over his freshly cut hair.

"Not here." I avoid his eyes and speed up my pace.

His long strides catch up to me before I create any kind of distance. "Is everything all right with your dad? Is that why you came here instead of meeting me?"

"I said not here!" I snap, startling the two older ladies walking past us. This is what I didn't want to happen. I close my eyes and inhale and exhale until I know I have my temper back under control. "Listen." I turn to face him. "I found some stuff out while I was at work today. I don't want to talk about it here, and honestly, neither should you. Let's just meet at my place and we can talk about it there, okay?"

"Okay," he agrees, but I can see the change in his posture, and the shutters close off his eyes. He's a smart man. Before I talked to Theo, I might've called him the smartest man I know. So he knows as much as I know that we are over.

SOMEHOW, I MANAGE to beat Maxwell to my place by ten minutes.

I don't know if I was driving like a bat out of hell or he was doing his best Sunday driver routine, but by the time he knocks on my door, I've gone over what's about to happen so many times, I've almost psyched myself out.

I open the door in silence and Maxwell walks in without saying a word. The tension is so thick, I might choke. I take off my sweater because I'm suddenly sweating . . . even though today was a high of fifteen degrees. As soon as Maxwell sits in his usual spot on the couch, I just blurt it out. "Theo came to HERS today."

Even though Maxwell was doing a decent job of looking laid

back and relaxed, as if he didn't have a care in the world, that changes the second he hears his brother's name. He leaps off the couch and starts pacing across my living room, mumbling things I can't quite hear beneath his breath. He comes to a sudden stop, pivoting his feet to stare at me. "Is that all you're going to say, or are you going to tell me how the brother I told you to stay away from somehow got so deep in your head that you're ending us?"

I already knew he was aware of where this was heading, and even though it was my decision to end this—well, I kind of feel like my hand was forced—hearing it out loud causes all the air to leave my lungs.

Once I've regained my composure, I square my shoulders and look him dead in the eyes. "He told me about the person you were in college."

His head flinches back slightly and his eyebrows knit together like he has no idea what I'm talking about. "My behavior in— wait." He puts both hands in front of his chest and looks down to the floor as if everything is starting to click into place. When his head snaps back up, his nostrils are flaring, and throbbing veins are protruding from his neck. "That son of a fuckin' bitch." He digs his fingers into his scalp, and then drags them down his face, leaving scratch marks on his otherwise flawless skin. "He's not allowed to fucking talk about that shit!"

"Really? You're harping on him breaking a rule?" I keep my tone calm and even. "Are you worried he's going to ruin your perfect little image? And really"—I drop my ear toward my shoulder and stick out my bottom lip—"after what you did, do you really think I'd actually care?"

His head snaps as if I've slapped him. "Wait." He tilts his head to the side, staring at me like I'm a stranger to him. "You think that I did it?"

I hold my fingernails in front of my face, examining the polish-less nails with rapt interest. "I know that the overwhelming majority of victims don't lie about sexual assault. I also know that Theo saw you in bed with her after he warned you that she was too drunk to consent, so yeah"—I look into his eyes—"I think you did it."

"Wow." He nods his head, his whole body seeming to roll with the small movement as he steps away from me. "That's how you see me?" His lips curl up in disgust like the mere sight of me turns his stomach.

"Give me a reason not to." I flex my fingers into a fist at my side, ashamed by my overwhelming desire to go and comfort him. That despite everything I know now, my body yearns to touch him.

He shrugs a shoulder and waves a dismissive hand my way. "I thought I already had." He grabs his jacket off the couch and slips it on over his usual sweatshirt. "I guess you aren't who I thought you were either."

The way he looks at me, it's like *I've* betrayed *him*. Like I'm lower than the dirt under his shoe? *God*. My sinuses start to sting but I don't move. I push the faceless girl to the front of my mind and try to focus on her. On the pain she's felt, the injustice of being shoved into the dark while her abuser is in the light, lauded for his charity and kindness. And I say nothing as he takes the painful measure not to so much as brush against me before he's gone, my door slamming shut behind him with so much force that one of the new frames Vonnie hung up falls off the brick wall, splintered glass exploding all across the hardwood floors.

I cross my apartment, not making an effort to avoid the broken glass, and stand by my window. I watch as Maxwell hurries to his car and climbs inside, reversing out of his spot without so much as a glance up.

When his brake lights disappear into the distance as he drives away, I slide to the floor. The feel of broken glass slicing through my leggings and into my skin is the only thing preventing me from becoming completely numb. My tears, as heavy as the blood dripping down the backs of my thighs, start to fall.

I've never had a boyfriend, so I've never had a breakup.

I always rolled my eyes at my friends who moped and cried over them. I didn't understand.

I was an asshole.

Because now, sitting on the floor, I feel like the world has ended. The future I envisioned with Maxwell disappeared with him as he walked out of my door. And picturing my life without him now is impossible. Just a dark and miserable void where I'm alone. Always alone. The tagalong to my friends as they get married and have babies and go to their homes overflowing with love. And I'll just be.

Alone.

In my condo. Bleeding and crying on the floor. Nobody will know and nobody will care.

I wish he had cheated on me. I wish he had ended it with me. Because now, worse than the total and utter darkness that has surrounded me, the loneliness threatening to consume me, is the guilt . . . the doubt that maybe I did the wrong thing.

I push my legs harder against the glass, hoping that the pain can help me conjure an image of a broken girl, just becoming a woman, and Maxwell stealing her trust . . . her innocence. But I can't.

Shame eats away at me as Maxwell's face haunts me. My eyes open or shut, his face haunts me. The protectiveness he showed when I was stranded on the highway. His quiet kindness as he sat holding my hair while I was sick. His reverent touch the first time we made love.

The look of disgust and betrayal as he left.

None of it makes sense.

And as much as I want to hate him for what he did, I can't, because the person I've grown to know . . . to love isn't capable of it.

Then I remember that I never even told him I loved him, and the life I knew we could have together barely started. The tears that stream down my cheeks run hot and angry because we could've been something. We could've lasted. But he hid his past. He kept me in the dark and now I'll never see the light again.

Forty

"HEY, DEANNA," I SAY, REPEATING THE SAME GREETING I'VE MADE for the last five days since my dad got out of the hospital.

"Hi, Brynn." She smiles bright. Her voice, when it isn't on the phone, telling me about my dad's heart attack, is actually a very lovely one, and I almost feel guilty for how I talked to her. Only almost because I've tried to apologize to her multiple times and she waves me off every time, telling me I was actually one of the nicer people she's broken bad news to. So that's lovely, I guess. "Frank is in the kitchen even though I keep telling him he shouldn't be standing for that long yet."

"He's so stubborn." A trait that did not get passed down to me. "I'll force him onto the couch."

"Good luck with that." She slings her leather tote over her scrubs-covered shoulder. "I'll be back tomorrow. See you around?"

"You know it." I was hesitant when she first started coming over, but that changed once I realized that I finally had somebody on my side when it came to scolding my dad. I'm actually really enjoying having her around. "Drive safe, the streets are terrible."

The weather has been awful lately. It's like my mood has altered Colorado's normally sunny nature and turned it into a gray, swirling mess of sadness and uncertainty.

"I thought I was the one who had a heart attack, but I still look better than you," my dad says as I walk into the kitchen.

"Rude." I toss my purse haphazardly onto the table, loose receipts and change spilling everywhere.

"But where's the lie?"

"Dad." My eyes roll to the back of my head. "You have to stop hanging out with Ace. You aren't allowed to use phrases like that."

"Haters are everywhere," he says, purposefully trying to get under my skin.

"Oh my god," I groan. "Why are you so weird?"

"What's going on, Brynn?" He slides into the chair across from me, his worried eyes trained on me. "You've been miserable for days now. Are you finally going to tell me why?"

After everything went down with Maxwell, I kept it from my dad. I mean, he was just getting released from the hospital and I wasn't going to add stress of any kind to his plate. So I plastered on a fake smile and came over every day, thinking those acting classes Naomi gave me years ago were really coming in handy. But I guess I won't be getting that Oscar nomination anytime soon.

"Maxwell and I broke up." I keep my eyes down and trace the scratch I "accidentally" carved into the table when I was in high school and was supposed to be writing a paper.

"I figured that out that day in the hospital, what I don't know is why."

I open my mouth to tell him what Maxwell did, but at the last minute, change my mind.

"Did I ever tell you Maxwell has a brother?"

"He does?" His eyebrows shoot to his hairline.

"Yeah, Maxwell didn't tell me either. I found out when Theo, that's his brother's name, came into HERS one night before I closed."

"That's strange." My dad gets that far-off look he always does before he gives me a good lecture.

"I know, I don't know why he'd hide his family from me."

"No." He shakes his head. "Not that. That his brother would come to you on his own, late at night. That didn't ring alarms for you?"

I shrug my shoulders, thinking back on the uneasy feeling I had being alone with him. "I mean, I guess at the time, because I was alone and he startled me, but he just wanted to get in contact with Maxwell."

"How many times have I told you to listen to your instincts?"

I smile my first genuine smile since Maxwell left my apartment. "Millions?"

In high school, my dad used to record (and not on DVR, but actual VHS tapes, because that's how old I am) every episode of *Oprah* and *20/20*. He would then curate a lineup that had to do with trusting your instincts and how to—hopefully—avoid dangerous situations. I guess he figured Oprah and Barbara Walters were more credible than he was . . . He wasn't wrong.

"So this Theo made you feel uneasy and Maxwell made you feel what?"

Geez. He hasn't grilled me like this since I moved back home after my one year in Texas.

"Happy? I don't know? You know I always liked Maxwell. Even after the bar scenario, it was hard for me to hold a grudge." I throw my hands into the air. "But maybe I shouldn't trust my instincts. What if they're wrong? Theo told me some horrible things about Maxwell . . . things I never thought he was capable of."

"And Maxwell admitted to them?"

"Not exactly." More like looked at me as if I was the scum of the earth for even considering he was guilty of what Theo accused him of . . . not that I tell my dad that.

"So he denied them and instead of you discussing whatever it is with him, you believed a man he isn't close with. The same man who gave you a bad feeling?"

Thankfully, before I'm able to answer, my phone starts to vibrate.

I grab it like the lifeline it is and almost kiss the screen when I see Paisley's name pop up. She only calls me while she's at HERS if it's an emergency.

"Sorry, Dad, work calls." I grab my purse, already walking to the door, and not actually sorry at all. "What's up, Pais?"

"Abby just called in, actually, her mom called in. She has strep and of course a bachelorette party just walked in." As she says it, I hear the now-familiar screeches of women who are ready to let loose. "I need backup."

"I'm already en route." I zip my jacket up as far as it will go and angle my head down to avoid the harsh, freezing wind that's trying to eat my face.

"You're the best, thank you." She doesn't wait for my response before the line goes dead.

I've buried myself in work and my friends since Maxwell left my apartment. My thoughts are not a place I really want to be. However, after talking to my dad, maybe it's where I need to be.

Maxwell has given me no reason to believe he would ever do what Theo is accusing him of doing. In fact, he's given me every reason to think the opposite. Every time I've been around him— sans the bar incident—he's been nothing but respectful. In fact, when I think back on our relationship, consent has never been questionable. Even when I thought my body was going to explode and I was practically begging him to take off his pants, he still insisted on me telling him I was okay.

That is not the behavior of a guy who would do the horrible thing Theo said.

But then does that make me one of those people who doesn't believe the woman? I've built my business on women supporting women. What does it say about me if I'm doubting one who needs support the most? I would never want to cause more pain to the suffering she's inevitably been experiencing for years.

Torn.

I feel like I'm being split down the middle, ripped in two, and I don't know how to stop it. I've never felt so torn before.

Either I believe the man I love or I believe a woman who had no reason to lie.

I want to do both, but I don't know how.

Forty-one

"FOR THE LOVE OF GOD!" VONNIE CHARGES INTO MY OFFICE AND commandeers the mouse to my computer from me, exiting out of my music before I can even blink. "I can't listen to any more of that sad-ass country music! Pull yourself together!"

It's now been two weeks since I last saw Maxwell, and some could say I'm not handling it well.

"Some" being everyone around me.

Not only do I want to call him every second of every day, I also can't stop checking my phone for ESPN alerts telling the world about Maxwell's past. I've scoured the Internet, signing up for every Mustangs fan forum I can find, reading every blog, looking at these sites that Vonnie told me is where all the "groupies" discuss their conquests. And I've found nothing. Zero, zilch, nada.

I thought I had enough questions to occupy me for a lifetime, but every single day, I get more.

In simple terms, I'm a hot-ass mess.

And making it worse? The Mustangs were knocked out of the playoffs on Sunday and I haven't been alone for more than twenty minutes. Without football to distract them, the Lady Mustangs have used all of their free time to harass . . . I mean . . . dutifully support me.

They even invaded my apartment. They pinned me down to my couch and decreed we could only eat food that came in cartons (e.g., Chinese food and ice cream), drink wine, and watch Nicholas Sparks movies. I suspect they created a schedule to make sure I'm too occupied with them to sulk. Even Sadie, Poppy's friend whom she used to work with, has popped by my condo for unannounced sleepovers. She brought a glitter face mask that I'm pretty sure was made for little girls but I enjoyed nonetheless. She also brought two bottles of wine and extra-long straws so we could skip using glasses.

I've been so unalone that I forgot what being alone is even like.

I go to push Play only to realize that Vonnie stole the mouse and unplugged my computer. "Damn! Why can't you let me be great?"

"I don't think any interpretation of 'great' includes memorizing all of the world's saddest songs and being on a first-name basis with Dairy Queen workers," Charli says.

"Well, then you'd be wrong." I nudge my trash can filled with empty Dairy Queen cups farther under my desk.

"Holy crap," Eloise pipes in from the doorway. "You guys should've called me sooner."

"Eloise. You're here. Yay." I bang my head against my desk.

Don't get me wrong. I love my friends and how much they love me, and I've actually come to really like Eloise. But I'm not exactly proud of my behavior recently, and the last thing I need is an extra witness to the depths that I've fallen to.

"Oh, shut that shit up," says Vonnie, who for the most part has been using kid gloves while talking to me . . . or at least her version of kid gloves. "No more moping. We're figuring shit out now. The guys are taking too long and we're smarter anyway."

"I'm not even joking when I say I have no idea what you're talking about." I fall back into my chair, but focus on her since my computer screen is black anyways.

"Do you really, in your heart of hearts, think that Maxwell would ever do something like that?" Charli asks.

My head jerks back at the mention of the "incident."

In a moment of weakness—fine, whatever! As soon as they walked into my apartment—I told them everything that Theo told me. To say they were shocked would be an understatement of epic proportions. I told them that Maxwell didn't deny it . . . even though he didn't exactly admit it either. But after this initial conversation, nobody has mentioned it.

"Most abusers are very personable." I tell them the rationale that's been on repeat in my head since Theo told me. "If they are dicks from the beginning, it'd be really hard to find victims."

What I don't tell them is that I've been asking myself that very question for two weeks straight, and each time, my answer is the same. The Maxwell I know wouldn't do this.

"Yeah, I watch serial killer documentary shows too." Charli rolls her eyes at me. "But Maxwell isn't outgoing and personable. He's shy and quiet and avoids attention wherever he goes."

This is true. This is also why I don't want to have this conversation right now.

"So are you saying the girl lied about what happened?" Guilt starts to gnaw away at my bones for even saying those words out loud.

"No." Eloise slides into the conversation. "We're saying that Theo lied."

My head whips to her and I look at her, really look at her, for the first time since she came inside. She looks tired. There are dark circles underneath her bright blue eyes. Her normally perfect hair is disheveled. Her shirt is wrinkled and she's in flats instead of her usual steep stilettos.

I stand up and round my desk to face her. "Are you okay?"

"Not great." She squeezes my shoulder and cracks a smile. "But I'm thinking still better than you."

An unexpected bubble of laughter falls out of my mouth. It might be the first time I've laughed since Maxwell left, and it makes me remember how good it feels to laugh and smile when it's not forced or fake. Even when it's at my own expense. "That's probably true."

"Please," Vonnie says. "You're both a mess. So let's move this along so you can get back to your normal, wild selves."

"I'm in." I shrug because . . . well . . . things couldn't get much worse for me and because I know that these women would never intentionally lead me to more pain.

"Then load up." Vonnie spins her finger in a circle. "Everyone is waiting for us at Poppy's."

Oh lord. Maybe I should've thought this through a little bit more.

"Maybe we should grab milkshakes before we get there."

Vonnie's face crinkles into a look that says, *What the fuck?* without her having to say a word. Then she starts shaking her head and walking out the door mumbling about crazy friends and being owed an abundance of French martinis when this is over.

WHEN THEY SAID we were meeting at Poppy's, I thought we were just meeting at Poppy's. I didn't realize they had an entire investigation headquarters set up—complete with a giant whiteboard and everything.

"Where did you even get that from?" As soon as I walk in, I

point at the whiteboard that stretches across almost the entire wall.

"TK is very serious about coaching Ace's soccer team. They watch film and then draw up plays at night." Poppy says this like it's a completely normal occurrence.

"Oookay." I still think it's weird, but hey, what do I know? "Why do we need it though?"

"There's always a big board in situations like this," Aviana says.

And if I thought the whiteboard was strange, seeing Aviana with her hair in a tight bun and wearing thick-rimmed glasses that she definitely does *not* need and a fucking turtleneck makes me wonder if I'm hallucinating this entire freaking thing.

I pinch myself . . . a little too hard. "Ouch."

"Why did you do that?" Aviana frowns, looking at the red spot blooming on my arm where I pinched.

"I was making sure I wasn't dreaming this situation up," I say. "So . . . does anyone want to fill me in on what you guys have been up to?"

"Oooh! Me!" Poppy jumps up and down, holding one hand under her cute little—but not that little—belly. "My whiteboard, my presentation!"

"That's not a real rule." Jacqueline pouts.

"Is so." Poppy sticks her tongue out at Jac before turning to the rest of the group. "Now, everyone have a seat so we can fill Brynn in."

Poppy has a ruler in her hand for some reason, and all I can picture are the stories my grandma used to tell me about the nuns slapping her with rulers. So even though I want to run back to my office and hide under my desk, I sit down.

"Brynn"—she looks as me, and I have a sinking feeling that she has practiced this—"while you've been moping and eating ice cream and still not gaining a pound, which we all find to be insanely unfair, we've been busy proving that Maxwell is innocent in this." She yanks the lid off of her marker with impressive theatrics and then points it at the whiteboard because it's not a marker . . . it's a laser.

Then I almost slide all the way off the couch because I'm officially dead.

I cannot with Poppy.

"A laser, seriously?"

"Yes, a laser." She points it in my eyes. "And you'd do well to remember that I know how to use it."

"Geez, sorry!" I rub my eyes, hoping my vision hasn't been permanently damaged.

"As I was saying, we don't believe Maxwell is guilty of what he was accused of. In fact, after a little investigative work of our own, we think he's the victim of a much more sinister plot."

"Girl," Vonnie says from a chair across the room. "This is not a Netflix original. Get to the point."

There are a lot of silent nods of agreement around the room, but everyone is equally afraid of Poppy's pregnancy hormones, so no words are said.

"Fine." She scrunches her nose. "We think Theo is blackmailing Maxwell."

All the air leaves me in one whoosh as memories I've been working hard to suppress come rushing to the forefront of my mind. Warnings he gave me about Theo. The look of concern he wore when I told him Eloise was seeing him. His insistence that I not ever be alone with Theo.

"Holy shit," I whisper, my sinuses on fire as guilt threatens to consume me.

"We were already talking about how something wasn't right when Eloise came into HERS looking for you. It only took a little bit." Poppy's eyes widen and she lifts her hands in front of her chest. "Okay, we basically kidnapped her and demanded that she tell us what she knew. But—wait, Eloise, you tell this part, you're way better at it."

Poppy doesn't wait for Eloise to answer before she plops down onto the couch next to me and sips her sparkling water out of a wineglass.

"Well." Eloise stands slowly and makes her way to a table that I'm only now noticing is covered in papers and manila folders. "Theo had come to me about a month ago and asked if it was possible for me to look into a case. He said he was worried that Maxwell was in trouble and he wanted to make sure his name couldn't be found. I didn't see the big deal, so I said yeah. I like doing that stuff anyways, I'm a little nosy, so this is a perk to my job," she says, and I'm reminded how much we are alike. "But once I looked into the case, a few things stuck out to me. The names were all blacked out. Theo told me that he was the one who took the fall for Maxwell, but in the papers, it mentions the defendant's brother was willing to testify against him. Why would Maxwell do that if Theo was helping him? It didn't make any sense. So I made a few calls."

I'm pretty sure my heart is about to beat out of my chest. The cuts on my legs, even though they are healed now, start to ache behind my jeans.

"By telling me and you about the attack and settlement, Theo broke the NDA, and I was able to get in touch with the lawyer from the case. And while she did confirm that Max paid her client, she insisted that it wasn't to keep the woman quiet *and* that Max paid her attorney's fees. She said that her client hadn't wanted to acknowledge it at all, but once Max got drafted and received his first paycheck, he sought out her client and told her she deserved justice and he'd pay for all of her legal fees if she chose to do so. Then, when she realized what a trial would entail and decided to settle out of court, Max paid the settlement because he knew Theo never would."

"Wait . . ." I put my head in between my knees. This sick sensation of overwhelming relief and gut-wrenching regret makes me feel like I'm suffocating. She's telling me too much, and while everything she's telling me should make me feel better, it does the opposite. I *knew* I should've trusted Maxwell. But even though I thought I was ready for a relationship, I used the very first excuse I could find to run away. And by doing that, I believed the worst about him. I fucking hurt him.

Our first hurdle and I ran in the other direction.

Forty-two

I DON'T KNOW WHAT HAPPENED FOR THE REST OF THE MEETING.

And not because I couldn't focus.

Because as soon as the room stopped spinning, I grabbed Poppy's car keys and took off. I think I heard them whooping and clapping as I ran out the door, but I can't be sure that I'm not creating my own upbeat, romantic-comedy movie ending in my head.

Both are very likely.

It's actually a really good thing that I took Poppy's car because I forgot about the guard protecting Maxwell's gated community from crazies who steal their friends' cars and show up unexpectedly at their exes' front doors. But Poppy's car is on the list of preapproved cars, so the guard lets me in without any issue . . . like calling Maxwell and having the mortifying moment where I'm turned away.

And I continue to push my luck by using the code he gave me and entering his house without knocking. I'm not too sure about the legality of it all, but I'm hoping he won't call the cops and I will never have to know.

"Maxwell!" I shout, running into his house like a fucking maniac. "I'm so sorry! I know Theo lied. But I have to talk to you, you have to know—" I stop screaming and come to a sliding stop when I find him sitting on his couch . . . but he's not alone.

A woman is sitting beside him. Both of their eyes focus on me as I stand in front of them panting and out of breath.

"Um . . ." My eyes shift between them, and I try to talk over the bile rising in my throat. "I used your code, I'm sorry. I shouldn't have . . . I should . . ."

"Why don't I come back later?" his new . . . companion . . . asks.

She stands up, straightening her skintight pencil skirt, and I have the sudden urge for the ground to open up and swallow me whole.

She is stunning. Her skin looks as if she's just made of gold—warm and rich and glowing even in the middle of winter. Her hair is masses of beautiful, black coils. And her body . . . dear god . . . her fucking body. Even being conservatively dressed in a pencil skirt and a blouse buttoned all the way up to her neck doesn't detract from the curves she's been blessed with. Her butt is so round that even I want to cry tears of joy from the opportunity to see such perfection in person. I want to hate her, god do I want to hate her, but I can't. Her smile is too open and her eyes are so kind that, even though I know I'll never have a chance with Maxwell again, I have to just appreciate her . . . and maybe ask her if she also would like to work at HERS.

"Ugh, no. Sorry." I start to step away slowly. "I'll just call Maxwell later, I shouldn't have barged in like this."

I turn around and am taking painful measures not to run,

when Maxwell's hand on my elbow stops me. "Brynn," he says, and just the sound of his voice that I've missed so much over the last two weeks causes tears to brim in my eyes. "I'd like you to meet Monica Laris, my attorney."

And when I say that Maxwell has to tighten his grip around my arms because I almost sag to the ground in relief, I'm not exaggerating.

"Well, one of many." Monica smiles her bright smile at me and reaches out her hand. "Nice to meet you, Maxwell has told me so much about you."

"Oh my god." My eyes bulge out of my face. "He's not going to sue me, is he?"

Monica throws her head back laughing like I just told a joke, but after the last time I talked to Maxwell, I most definitely am not.

"You're right, Max, she is funny." She wipes a finger beneath her lashes that, if she wasn't physically perfect, I'd think were fake, but they're probably hers because the world is so unfair. "Well, it looks like you two have things to catch up on. I'll take these back, draw up some papers, and get back to you later this week. Nice to meet you, Brynn."

"Um, yeah, nice to meet you too," I say to her back as she sashays out of the room.

"So . . . you're here," Maxwell says once we hear the front door close.

"Looks like it." I roll back onto my heels, not knowing where to start. Maybe one day I won't act so rashly, because I'm seriously regretting not forming a better plan.

Maxwell takes my hand in his and brings it to his lips, dropping a soft kiss on my knuckles. "I'm glad."

"You are?" My jaw falls open at the same time the butterflies I thought died a horrid death with Maxwell's departure start fluttering back to life.

"I didn't handle what happened well. I should have tried to explain to you, but there were so many legal details and I didn't want his victim dragged into this mess all over again. I didn't know what to do and I was so fucking angry. At Theo . . ." He drops his gaze to his feet. "At you," he says quietly.

"I was so wrong." I squeeze his hand tighter, afraid to get any closer, but never wanting to let him go. I'm so worried that he'll come to his senses and remember how I betrayed him. "Even if you didn't warn me about Theo, there is no reason I should've believed him without talking to you. I just . . . things were too good between us. Good things don't come to me so easily. I knew something had to be wrong and that you couldn't actually be that perfect. And so when Theo came to me, I latched on to him and his lies. I used it as a reason to push you away before I could fall any deeper for you."

He takes my other hand and pulls me into a hug. He burrows his nose into my hair and I nuzzle into his neck, smelling him, feeling him, remembering everything I almost threw away. Tears leak onto his shirt, but I don't care. I want him to know exactly what I'm feeling. I don't want to hide any part of myself from him.

"There's a lot to sort out there," he says. "We can start with you finally admitting that I'm perfect."

I roll my eyes and let out a very unattractive snort of laughter, but I don't pull away. "I knew you weren't going to miss that."

"I think that you see yourself in a completely different light than probably every other person who comes across you. You are not only the most beautiful woman I've ever had the pleasure to be around, you're also the kindest. I've never met another person who so freely hands out genuine and meaningful compliments, who hands out jobs like they're candy, and is so fiercely protective of her friends. You started a business in an industry where women are not seen or heard, and you are thriving. And not only that, you inspire and encourage other women to follow in your footsteps. Maybe things don't come easy for you, but that's because the people and things you've surrounded yourself with are things worth working for."

It's a good thing I want him to see my tears, because I couldn't hide them now if I tried. "I'm the one who is supposed to be apologizing right now," I say, even though it's barely comprehensible between my sobs.

"I should've told you about Theo," he says without hesitation. "He has been threatening me with this on and off for years, but I never had anything he could hold over my head. I did my job and I came home. He could never plant the seed with anyone. I should've warned you . . . been honest about our past."

"I mean, my mom is insane, but Theo is a sociopath. I can't imagine it's a subject you'd want to broach with anyone." I don't blame him at all. Plus, we were so new, and look how I reacted at the first hint of trouble. I didn't exactly earn his trust. "But we should probably tell each other about any other crazy family members we might have before they come out of hiding. I think I have a third cousin who has been on the receiving end of a couple restraining orders."

He looks at the ceiling like he's thinking really hard. "My great-aunt thinks she can talk to the dead. She's harmless, but she says some wild-ass stuff and then blames it on the 'spirits.'"

I throw my head back laughing. "That's not crazy, that's amazing and I need to meet her."

"Well"—his smile turns serious—"the season is over and my parents have been hounding me about finally meeting the girl who's stolen all my attention these last few months."

"Meeting the parents?" I look up at him, my smile threatening to crack my cheeks. "That sounds pretty serious."

"Very serious." He nods.

"So does that mean we're back together?"

He brings his mouth to mine, stopping just before they touch. "Brynn, it means that I'm never letting you go again."

I don't wait for him to kiss me.

I lean in and kiss him, the only man I ever want to kiss for the rest of forever.

Epilogue

"I CANNOT BELIEVE YOU HAVE ME SITTING IN A BOX FOR THE championship game," Marlee moans. "And with the enemy at that!"

"I can't believe it took a fucking bartender to convince you to sit in a goddamn box!" Donny, my new favorite person—right below Maxwell's great-aunt Glenda—says.

"I own an entire business, Donny," I say for the thousandth time. "How would you like it if I called you a paid groupie?"

He grabs his gin and tonic that he insisted I make and takes a giant gulp. "I'd say that's very fucking accurate."

"Well," Marlee interjects. "I'm still pissed at the bartender."

"We'll have a reception or something one day," I reassure her, even though I've done this every day for the last two months and she still gives me shit. "We got a wild hair, what were we supposed to do?"

"Ummm, I don't know? How about not get married at a freaking courthouse!" she shouts, and then cringes when Posie starts to stir from her nap. "Shoot, sorry, Poppy," she whisper yells, even though Posie is decked out in the bedazzled noise-canceling headphones TK ordered for her. "But if she does wake up, you know who to give her to." She starts pointing to herself.

"You'll have to fight him for her." Poppy nods her head at TK, who's chasing after Bea and Van, Marlee and Gavin's two kids. Bea is running around with her curly pigtails flying and all the crystals on her custom jersey dress shining. She's four and her outfit is honestly better than mine.

"Nah, I brought a stash of Dum Dums to bribe them with. I'll have them sugared up and on TK's hip all day." Marlee winks, but I know she's serious. All she talks about is wanting another baby, so seeing Posie is too much for her to handle.

"Speaking of . . ." Naomi takes the seat next to me. "Any baby news of your own?"

I nearly choke on my own spit. "No. No, no, no. Someday, just not today. Definitely no."

Maxwell and I have talked about kids and they are definitely in the future, we just want time being us before we bring little humans into the world. My dad has been on our backs constantly about it and so has Maxwell's family . . . well, not his brother. After Theo lost his job when all the details came out about what he'd done, he left Colorado and we haven't heard from him again. We're both totally okay with that.

HERS is at the top of its game right now. Every time I'm sure we've peaked and are going to start seeing a decline in sales, things miraculously get even better. I've been working my butt off to keep it new and fresh and not just ride the coattails of *Love the Player*, and it's paying off. And when news that Maxwell and I eloped went public, people flipped out. We had waitlists for two full weeks before it started dying down, but even now it's crazy.

Paisley keeps sending me pictures of the bar today, and each time it makes me want to cry. Women of all different shapes, sizes, and colors sporting their football jerseys, holding their drinks in the air, and having the best time at my bar.

"Brynnnnn!" Eloise calls my name and holds up a bottle of vodka. "Can you please make me something that doesn't burn my throat? Donny said you taught him a recipe, but I think he gave me vodka straight."

"Vodka with a splash of gin, drink of fuckin' champs," Donny yells and I cringe. "Get a little hair on that fucking chest of yours!"

"I'm a woman! I don't want chest hair!" Eloise yells back at him.

"You're not even drinking that!" I throw a cherry at his head and immediately apologize when every parent in the box goes on high alert for the potential food fight I just started.

I mix up something fast for Eloise, and I'm tucking the bottle back into its spot when Marlee yells, "The fog machines are starting up!"

I skip down the few steps to my seat and make it just in time to hear the announcer start to speak. "Football fans!" His voice echoes through the speakers. "Are you ready to meet your champion teams?"

The stadium goes wild. All these fans, the most die-hard of all, willing to fly to another state and spend ludicrous amounts of money to watch a single football game. The floor beneath me starts to rattle, and the energy inside our box is so supercharged that if I started seeing sparks, I wouldn't be surprised.

Then, on the JumboTron in front of us, the Mustangs come into view as they walk from the locker room and onto the biggest stage of their career. The starters' faces pop up in the corner of the screen as they tell everyone watching what position they play and what school they went to. Happiness blooms inside of me as I see my friends' husbands. Then the one I've been waiting for comes on. And maybe it's just me—I do tend to be a tiny bit biased—but the stadium quiets. As if what he says means the most, like they are aware of exactly the kind of man he is and know that any chance to hear him speak should be taken full advantage of.

"Maxwell Lewis, defensive back, Princeton University." Short and sweet and all mine.

I look for the wink he told me he did, that he said was his shout-out to me, and the butterflies that have been flying for over a year straight take off again.

Marlee takes my hand on one side and Poppy takes my hand on the other. I thought this was the life I never wanted. Me in my Mustangs jersey, Marlee in her New York jersey, and Poppy not in one at all stand together and watch as the players take the field. And as I stand, hand in hand with two of my best friends, watching my husband, tears begin to fall because I realize I always wanted this. I just didn't know how to dream this big.

Photo by Kristie Chadwick

Alexa Martin is a writer and stay-at-home mom. She lives in Colorado with her husband—a former NFL player who now coaches at the high school where they met—their four children, and a German shepherd. When she's not telling her kids to put their shoes on . . . again, you can find her catching up with her latest book boyfriend or on Pinterest pinning meals she'll probably never make. The Playbook series is inspired by the eight years she spent as an NFL wife.

CONNECT ONLINE

Ready to find
your next great read?

Let us help.

Visit prh.com/nextread

Penguin
Random
House